The Burning Islands

A Novel of Love, Loss & Redemption
Newfoundland: 1937

by

Patric Ryan

Sarawak Studios Press & M.L. Ryan Publishing

The Burning Islands

A novel of Newfoundland: 1937

Author of *The Fogo's War Trilogy, Surviving Well is the Best Revenge, The Paris Shooter's Union & The Burning Islands*

Sarawak Studios & ML Ryan Publishing
1974 Bruce Rd #9.
Lion's Head, Ontario Canada N0H 1W0

Email: patric@patricryan.com
www.patricryan.com

Cover design: Sophie Ryan & Cover art by Patric Ryan

Canadian Cataloguing in Publication Data
Ryan, Patric D.M.

The Burning Islands
ISBN 978-0-9698003-5-4

1. Ryan, Patric D.M., 2. Newfoundland 1937, 3. The Great Depression, 4. The IRA Rebellion. Drama. Fiction

For my mom, Mary, who lived through the Great Depression and who was married in the spring of the year 1938, at the climax of The Burning Islands. Mary helped make the publication of this and other works possible. The work is fiction but many of the events retold in *The Burning Islands* may be found in our memoir
Closing the Newfoundland Circles

A special thanks to Sophie for her cover creativity and to my patient editors: Sarina, June and Dorie.

The Burning Islands

Part One

'Fogo's a harsh and wonderful island apart. A sentinel in the Atlantic...you know by the sounds and smells when you're near...protecting the Nor'east coast of Fortress Newfoundland. The rocks are hard and the sea is cold. Fire though, and not the Devil's kind, is our comfort and scourge, outside of God Almighty. Anyone who wishes to get a living from land or sea, holds His elements in awe.' Garret Dwyer 1938.

Love: Breeze & Lliam

Béhathook Cove: 1937. She faced the fresh wind and waited.

"Breeze! Bread's ready t'come out, 'fore it's all clinkers!"

"Yes, Mum." The kitchen door was open behind her. Mother O'Keefe called out again but Breeze waited a bit longer, watching her ocean and the ice island on the horizon. Breeze O'Keefe had Beothuk, Irish and Portuguese blood, high cheekbones and broad features, with dark eyes, and a long, curling black mane captured by a blood-red scarf. Could have been a Gypsy slave held prisoner on barren Fogo Island, her heritage and her ocean a wide gulf to be crossed, the old books and the fire pit her only companions.

"Have you lost all reason, child?"

"In a moment, Mother."

Breeze knew the signs: *Mother O'Keefe in mourning is a dark cloud on the horizon, the spiritual storm warnings like hurricane flags.* Breeze gazed at her ocean, tasting the salt air on full lips, the warm September morning sparkling clear and the blue Atlantic rolling in forever from Ireland. An ice giant in the offing, a rare late summer iceberg, riding the Labrador Current to a slow death in the Gulf Stream, made its presence felt as a sweet edge on the sea wind. Breeze worshipped the freedom of the wandering ice, hesitating to go in even though the firewood made her arms ache.

"Do you want me to catch my death, girl?"

"Sorry, Mum." Breeze kicked the door closed, crossed the scrubbed kitchen and eased the splits into the box behind the stove; the aromatic resin of the spruce mingling with the molasses smell of hot bread. Mother O'Keefe, propped up like an invalid in her rocking chair, made a show of tucking the woolen throw around her swollen knees, then let her clawed hands fall into her lap, flapping weakly like a wounded bird.

"You left the door open again."

Mother O'Keefe's in that mood, she whispered to the fire whistling in the stovepipes. "I know, Mum. Thought you might like some air, is all. It's a wonderful warm day." Breeze shucked her rubber boots behind the door and wiped sticky hands on her apron. Amber sap clung to red fingers, pulling away skin. *Damn an' bother,* she whispered.

"I've told you what would happen if I get a chill," Mother O'Keefe scolded, picking at her shawl, drawing it closer, almost breathless, her sharp gasps the harbinger of bad news. "Oh...poor dear, Margaret," Mother O'Keefe sighed, dangling the statement like a cod jig.

Breeze took the bait willingly, wrung out a cotton bag in the wash bucket, relieved that the bad news was about to be shared. "An' what about *poor* Margaret, Mum?"

Mother O'Keefe gulped air in shallow drafts, clutching the shawl to her breast. "Lliam Dwyer's been seen about."

Lliam Dwyer! The name stabbed at Breeze's heart. "Lliam, is it?"

"In St. John's...comin' on like a drunken mummer, so they say."

"So they say?" The question was a sword parry, too late. The cut was deep and painful. Breeze opened the oven door, took out four loaves of golden brown, crusty bread, adding more pans from the warming shelf.

"News come 'round from Fogo this mornin'...but you was too busy wanderin' off some wheres."

"I was over to Aunt Liza's with her broth, an' to gather up Uncle Naaman's wash." Breeze turned the hot loaves out on a flour bag.

"Suppose he's home, finally," sighed Mother O'Keefe, convinced of tragedy.

"Finally?" *The whole Dwyer family put a curse on Lliam's leaving,* she said to the hot bread.

"Another mouth poor Margaret's got to feed."

"It's not *poor* Margaret, Mum." Breeze stirred the steaming pot of fish stew then filled the big iron kettle with water from the bucket. *It's poor Mum an' poor Breeze*, she said under her breath. She opened the fire door. The glowing embers reminded her of the ancient fire pit on the beach: her special place as a child, a refuge to dream as a girl and pray for deliverance as a woman. The pit had been there as long as anyone could remember. A pagan place, they say, shunned by the faithful. Father Hennessy said mass in Coughlin's parlour and seldom set foot further than Sarah Coughlin's kitchen and Jeremy's brandy bottle, other than to administer the Last Rights. They talked about building a Catholic Church across the Cove, the Lord's own place of worship to counter the Evil One...Breeze burned the pit on certain nights when she could get away. Whisperers said she was a pagan fire worshipper. They might have whispered, *Irish Witch*, but there was no proof. Breeze added fresh splits to the fire. "I need to fetch some water, Mum."

"Don't be long...an' shut the door!"

Breeze closed the kitchen door softly, letting the spring latch bind just short of home, walked down to the box well at the foot of the garden and carried up two pails of tannic water, leaving them on the bridge. The door creaked open. "Breeze! The door!"

"Yes, Mum," she called from the entrance to the cold cellar in the hillside above the garden, genuflecting to enter the low portal: a dark grotto of dead smells. Her shrine to the Madonna of Circumstances and Dying Opportunities, was dark and dank as a tomb, curled leaves the bones of dried up saints. The winter cabbage stacked in tiers like skulls in the Paris catacombs, hollow eyes staring back like an engraving in her book. She returned to the kitchen with a basket of potatoes and washed and peeled the last of the old season. The dirt encrusted redskins all eyes, wild sprouts like hair, and wrinkles. 'Grandmothers', they call them. "That's the last of the old ones."

Mother O'Keefe watched her daughter closely as if she might be snatched by malevolent hags and flung back to the Old Country. "New potatoes' ready to dig my girl. You'll see to that the once."

"Yes, Mum." Breeze dumped the soft nubs into the stew pot and carried the thick rinds outside to the rot pit, leaving the door ajar, pausing again to drink in the view of the ocean.

"Breeze! The door!"

"Sorry, Mum," she said when she returned. "I'll take some bread up around to Uncle 'ebert," she announced, carefully wrapping two loaves in the flour bag and placing them in the canvas carrier.

"An' what about your poor mother?"

"I'll make up our tea when I come back."

"An old woman could perish in her own kitchen...an' not a soul would care."

Béhathook Cove. 1630: *Dusk. A damp black fog, with fluky winds, held the Cove in thrall. Newfoundland waits, subdued and patient, all the time in creation. A white-hulled ship moves blindly through the fog, working to the Nor'west, dark eyes on deck and aloft straining for some sign. Waves crash on the rocky shore of Pigeon Island. "Rocks! Port side!" A Portuguese seaman leans over the rail, pointing. The captain scans where the keen-eyed sailor points. Glistening sunkers loom at him like jagged teeth in the mouth of fantastic sea monsters adorning their faulty charts. "Steer more to starboard," orders the captain to the wheelsman. They are close enough to smell the land and the fires and hear the breakers suck and foam around the fractured granite guardians. Now the other danger is revealed. "A fire! There's the devils, Captain!" European sailors fear many things on the cursed foreign coast. Only the fish lure sailors from their warm waters to cross the Atlantic. It's said that Portuguese fishermen never see the summer sun until they retire, crippled, forced out of the game. They fear the fog, the drifting ice, the storms and wayward currents, the sunkers: all the demons known and imagined, and the mysterious, painted savages.*

In the small cove a family rests on the coarse grass at the verge of a

4

rocky peninsula, tending a fire in a stone pit. The hunter, tired from a day of fishing, are lounging near the driftwood fire, drying caribou leggings and talking about the season past, the winter to come and their fear of encountering the white devils. Soon they will retreat to the interior of the island for the winter.

The women prepare mounds of mussels to be steamed in seaweed. Some will be eaten with roasted fish and fresh berries, the rest dried in the smoke. Naked brown children pick partridge berries from low bushes further up the hill and smear the juice on their faces and bodies, a change from the ochre mud adornment. Chubby babies nurse or tumble nearby on the soft heather. The children, from their vantage on the crest of the peninsula, are the first to see the Portuguese ship, like an apparition out of a saga tale. Wild stories are told of the monster-headed longboats from the rising sun, sailed by fierce warriors with red hair and bristling beards, dressed in furs, with bare legs and wind-burned skin. And before them came the valuta men in skin boats, searching for a home. The stories of blue-eyed men are very old, but the black-bearded, black-eyed Portuguese are the new menace. A child shrieks...

"Father! Look! It's one of them!" The men quickly gather up the children and move the family inland. The Europeans may come ashore looking for fresh water and women.

The rust-running fishing vessel from Nazaré works cautiously through the black fog near the place the Portuguese call, Islas des Fuegos: Islands of Fires. The dangerous outlying rocks are too close to port. The weary, sea-hardened men watch and listen for signs of doom, trembling and praying to Santa Maria. Another break in the black fog reveals the glow of the pit fire on the shore near the beach. Seen many times by passing ships, a warning but not a beacon.

"There! Fuegos. Captain! See the fire?" "Good, steer well away to starboard. The red-devils won't get us today."

The Portuguese fishermen seldom land on Isla des Fuegos. They sail by on their way to the fishing grounds in the Strait beyond the French Shore, avoiding the rocks and the natives. It is legend among the fishing fleets that bands of bizarrely painted heathens roam the coasts in search of Christians to torture and eat, but the unfortunate ship is fated to remain in the New Founde Land forever, wrecked that night on Drover's Rock, a mile northeast of Round Head. Most drown, or are crushed by their own ship on the sunkers. The impaled ship broke up the next day and pieces drifted ashore, some into Béhathook Cove. One man, clinging to the wreckage, was saved by the hunters.

Béhathook Cove Night: Breeze O'Keefe tends a fire in the pit and sings..."*Cold mother sea will carry me away...*" begins the hymn. Shimmering light from glowing embers dance across the water to The Watcher in the shadows of an abandoned schooner. Breeze adopted the castoff hull, dreaming a child's fantasy of sailing over the horizon to Ireland, to find Grace O'Malley. The Watcher waits his time, listening to the song. The sweet voice seems to drift out of the fire. "*Cold Mother Sea will carry me away...*" A prayer intended only for the gentle night. *"And the sea shall carry me to shores unknown, an' when the wind makes a turn for home, away shall I tack with the Lord my God at helm...away to Arranmore."*

Breeze stirred the embers, placing more bleached wood from one of the wrecks across the coals, building the fire to a comforting blue and green companion. One night, after Lliam Dwyer had left the village, she'd found an ancient piece of ship timber, an iron spike had blackened the tough Portuguese oak and Breeze imagined it was a spear point, the oak the breastplate of a Crusader and the black stain his blood. "Pierced to the heart but still not dead," she whispered. "Rise up!" *Old wood burns best because it has experience,* she reasoned. "Salt-wood fires do look nice with their green an' blue," she said aloud, wondering which of the many wrecks had fuelled her fire: the little cove was a catchall for errant flotsam. Once she had found a drowned sailor in a sodden life vest, nudging the rocks as if looking for a home, the vest a beaten breastplate and she imagined a fallen king, cut down in youth. She turned the body to see if it was King Richard, didn't believe Richard was a monster murderer, had seen his portrait and knew by the eyes he was falsely accused, as she was herself...With a piece of charcoal she drew an Irish cross on the breastplate...But her

6

drowned sailor had no eyes. The men carried the body to the cemetery and marked the grave with a small white cross. She mourned and celebrated King Richard and her drowned sailor with fires. Since that time she offered her cove to all drifting corpses in exchange for a promise of release from bondage and made fire offerings to the dead sailors with the bones of their derelict ships. How many hulls had she burned over the years, the flankers drifting up like newborn stars, releasing souls to heaven? The spirits were silent, the silence relieved by a gentle surf running above the tidal slime, washing over polished granite stones, *swish-a-wish*, like the rustle of silk...Breeze's only luxury was a beach fire. *"And the cold, cold sea shall carry me to shores unseen...and God commands the helmswoman, Grace O'Malley, my true Queen."* Breeze laughed, but the laugh was bitter. She made a sign over the fire and the flames rose up to touch her fingers. "Grace O'Malley, my Pirate Queen, indeed."

The Watcher in the shadows knew deep down that he was too late; a tale of heartbreak unfolding, and he was a player, perhaps protagonist, not simply voyeur; the evidence as clear as the sky and as overwhelming as the stars. But, if Breeze still sang of Aranmore and Grace O'Malley the Pirate Queen, and still longed for freedom, as she did in their childhood, there was hope. *"Breeze,"* he whispered. *"Breeze, my love. By a fire..."*

It wasn't done in Depression Newfoundland: idle fires on beaches. *Only some foolish notion, my child,* her mother chided, *to sit alone at night, tempting the spirit of Grace O'Malley with a pagan fire.* Breeze loved to watch the stars on a restless ocean, no blinding moon, or wind-ravaged clouds to spoil the effect, nor the fire grand enough to compete with the brilliant points of light. And forever, like the stars that wheel around the Pole Star, the ocean sighs and moves even in restless sleep. Whether her ocean was gently rolling or wild and roaring, Breeze came to stand near the dangerous element that defines her narrow world: her home, family, the small outport in an obscure cove on a barren island in the Western Ocean.

Her mother's bloodline ran deep in Fogo Island lore. Whispers circled the village that Breeze was descended from a Beothuk woman

7

and a Portuguese fisherman. Mother O'Keefe protested but her native ancestors could claim the desolate island before the Europeans arrived. Before St. Brendan and his Irish monks seeking The Promised Land. Long before the desperate Albans, fleeing the brutal Norse. The Norsemen in turn, wind-driven westerly, waded ashore in search of survival. And who else lost to antiquity?

Fogo was also the adopted island of her Celtic ancestors: the indentured West County fishermen who fled Ireland in English ships. They came in the sixteen hundreds to escape the poverty of their rain-drenched island. Then later to escape the famine that killed or drove out half the population. The sunbaked Portuguese came for the fish. The West County Irish and Portuguese, like the Jersey Island fishermen, were recent arrivals, as the centuries go. She wondered why the Irish had chosen this island prison over the other. Fogo had less charm and fewer opportunities, only fish.

They have much in common: Fogo, Jersey and Ireland. Hardscrabble and unforgiving islands at best, when raw beauty is not sufficient. The Western Isles have weather enough to kill the hardiest. Inishmore and Aranmore are just harsh rocks, like her own Fogo. Endless labour barely wiggles a living from poor soil and dangerous water, always one bad season away from starvation, a chance moment from drowning. Death by water is a hard won death, if lucky, when simply drowning is a blessing, painless and clean. The kin at home are left with only memories or a few hand-carved pieces of furniture. One less mouth to feed, but one less provider...Breeze was becoming morbid again. She disliked being morbid, especially when it was peaceful and still beside the fire, but it was the quiet times, between conflict and toil, that her mind sought the darker truths of her existence.

"And the cold, cold sea shall carry me to shores less known...and when the wind makes a turn for my true home, I'll away to Arranmore..." Breeze was trapped between rocks and water. No brothers or sisters to share the work, only Mother O'Keefe brooding in her chair by the fire, feigning death when necessary, dreaming of a past that never existed. *Sean O'Keefe is not the father*, they whispered.

She took it out on Breeze, as if Breeze was responsible for a betrothed lost at sea so that Mother O'Keefe was cheated of the daily worry for her own sailor, watching the clouds for a sign, with only a thin jiggin' line to prove against starvation. But Captain Sean O'Keefe was a well-to-do sailor who promised to marry her mother, then sailed away, *to escape*, they said. Brigid Pearly Moon Ortiz, a spinster-bride, took his name and became the widow Mother O'Keefe in her own mind. Breeze knew in her heart that she was a Fogo bastard.

The Watcher pressed closer. Breeze pushed at the fire with a weathered stick, wondering where the stick had travelled. *Sticks have ancestors,* she said to the flames. *Grand trees on temperate shores, by the look.* The stick didn't originate on Fogo Island, carried to her rocky cove by tide and circumstance. *If I threw myself into the water, where would I fetch up?* The thought had been with her since childhood. She would stand on the verge, in hand-me-down sea boots, watching the tide rise over the cracked toes, until it tempted the holes, bare feet separated from the elements by worn out leather; wondering about the awful world out there, with only cast off boots to protect her. The children fight over the old canvas and rubber boots when a fisherman casts them onto the stage. It meant the expense of new, or time to patch and tar the old pair for one more season. A man wants a good pair of boots to go to the seals. Death or amputation is the fate of the bootless and there is death or dismemberment in every act of an outporter's life. Sealing was the worst of slaughter and hell, not to be missed. The only waking moments free from peril were spent in church, beside his stove, or resting near his family on a rare occasion of illness. Then they watched him as they might watch a dinner guest, to see if the Old Man was still good for it. Or was he home to stay?

The eldest son had to know if it was time to take the dory and row out to the grounds. And the son would need a wife, selected from the dwindling stock in the village or around the headland in the next cove. Maude or Mary or Haddie Rose had blossomed over the winter and was as ready to mate as an egg-glutted salmon. But the leap to manhood is a hard thing for a young man, no longer a game like leaping ice flows in the spring. It's easier to face a sharp Nor'easter

9

with the promise of a bitter day on the grounds and a chance to die quickly in the cold Labrador Current. A fisherman understands the dangers, as he understands the fish, his constant companion. Even ashore, asleep in his bed, the fish are with him. Understands the fish and the birds and the sea more than he understands the gentle woman waiting naked beside him. Life is what happens on the spawning grounds where the Northern Cod mingle, throwing eggs and sperm to an eternal rhythm. King Cod is Lord of all.

Humans have needs more complicated than procreation and there are mysteries beyond the musk and smells to attract a mate. One is beauty. Breeze O'Keefe blossomed early to a handsome young woman. A prize catch, they agreed, but Breeze would be no fisherman's trophy, though she had been selected many times by hopeful suitors sporting about the cove in freshly painted skiffs, throwing a nice bow wave. But she would not be plucked out of her home the way boys pull a lobster out of a trap. And there was Mother O'Keefe to tend like a flock of sheep, a living to be scratched from the thin soil, potatoes and turnips to dig, bread to bake and washing for the bachelors of the village. And there was Lliam Dwyer returned. *Lliam*, she said, *the Prodigal Son, running away to escape the outport way*.

Lliam Dwyer was home, her mother had warned, using his full name as if Breeze wouldn't remember the pain. Breeze shivered. Someone was watching and she felt the presence of a familiar spirit.

Lliam stepped out from the shadows. "Breeze. My beautiful, Breeze."

Her heart raced. "Yes. Who is it?" She knew.

"By a pagan fire, as usual," he said too casually. Lliam negotiated the curving shore with halting steps, unused to slick rocks, blinded by the firelight. Breeze would hardly recognize the tall form filled out to manhood. The rebellious red hair combed back in waves. But the lilting voice was familiar enough, even though six seasons had come and gone since Lliam Dwyer rejected her and their shabby village.

"I've come for you, Breeze darlin', as I said I would."

The voice was familiar, and so were the sensations. She vowed to react differently when they met again, as they must in the tiny outport.

10

He was seen in St. John's making the rounds of the waterfront bars; the news of Lliam's homecoming preceded his landing. News travels quickly along the coasts. Fishermen know Uncle George in a distant outport is starting a new boat the moment the keel is laid. The women know which sister is having a baby as soon as it's conceived, even though they hadn't seen their relative since the wedding; after the long, tormenting night of chivaree, when the sleepless bride took her place in a skiff, her borrowed veil a swirling cloud of lace, all mixed together with the black smoke from the swilin' guns. If less lucky she stepped into the bilge water of her husband's battered dory, rowing out together with her dowry in a crude box and an iron pot, to begin their life in another cove, clinging to the rocks like a pair of limpets. The whole coast would know when the spruce-built house was finished. Who made the homey plaque with the bible verse that hangs in the bright white kitchen. News is a precious commodity and about the only thing outporters can trade at a fair price because the merchants never devised a way to profit from gossip...She listened to his uncertain footsteps coming toward her and feared her future.

"Lliam? Is that you?"

Lliam stepped into the moving circle of light. "Hello, Breeze, me darlin' girl," Lliam said, dropping his cultivated Boston inflections.

Breeze bristled. "Saints preserve us. Lliam Dwyer...An' we thought you'd been carried up to Canada or some other foreign place, an' lost forever."

The handsome face splashed with freckles, opened in a grin of good teeth...A rare sight among adults in an outport. "Sure I've been to Boston this while. I only just landed with the coastal boat an' made my way around from Fogo with Bert O'Halloran. I inquired about you straight away. Bert's woman told me I'd find you here."

"Bert's woman has a name. It's Beatrice." One of the few women who treated Breeze with other than envy or suspicion. "Well, Lliam, Mother said you was on your way, but you took your sweet time."

"Aye, I missed the coastal boat a time or two," he said. "An' what else did Mother O'Keefe have to say?"

"That you're a shockin' lay-about, an' unholy trouble."

11

"I am, to her mind, I suppose." Lliam laughed too easily. Breeze forced her thoughts back into the vaults of memory. The flames leaping between them were more than a barrier.

"Can we talk awhile, Breeze? I've much to tell you, in private, like."

"What's more private than my beach?"

In the kitchen of the Dwyer House, just along the shore beyond the clutter of stages and moored boats, Lliam's grandfather rocked in his chair beside the stove. His window gave a view of the glowing fire and two dark figures on opposite sides, one sitting and one standing.

"What in all Creation makes these youngsters want to be out in this cold night?" He opened the fire door, the glowing embers painted a fallow field of deep lines, grey stubble and wind-burned skin. The once strong, well formed face, became a moving sculpture of twisted beauty, the pale blue eyes in perpetual tears, dimmed by years of keeping the deck of a sailing ship. Thin lips, running spittle, tainted sepia from strong tobacco. Gaps where teeth had been and what teeth remained were like blackened stumps in a burned over forest. Grandfather Dwyer was every sailor who survived a hard, uncompromising life, to come ashore for his reward: to rest and observe, free to comment on life. He spit bitter tobacco juice into the flames. "Idle ones'll come to grief onto Lord's hard rocks. Mark me woman!"

Lliam's casual air was a thin pretense; in truth he was as awkward in her presence as Breeze was aloof, remembering their last time together: the heather a soft, scented mattress, the sun warm and wild hair wilder with the wind, young passion hot but incomplete. How would he approach her now? How to rekindle that fire and consummate the promise? With worldly women like young Molly McCracken of Boston, he had never known the depth of that bittersweet adolescent agony. It was the thing that drove him to return to their outport.

"Were you lonely for me, Breeze?"

"Lonely for you? What a foolish question, Lliam." How could Breeze describe the deep ache, dreams evaporating like the morning mist with every sunrise? "Now why should I be lonely for the likes o' you?"

"What have you got in Béhathook to replace me?"

"My books, my fire, an' my ocean."

"What a fickle lover is a searing flame, an' books are only someone else's pain."

"A nice turn o' phrase, Lliam. Your time away wasn't wasted then, but what of the third element? The ocean, of which I never tire."

"The ocean is salt water, cold and deep, a man's heartbreak, a lover's leap."

"Poetry yes, pretty words, but you've no regard for the things I love."

"You cannot love a fire, girl."

"Fire within is proof of love's desire," she countered.

"You're capable of the lyric as well as a sharp tongue to deliver it, an' well I remember."

"Don't make me remember unless you want the entire story."

"I want you Breeze, the way you want the ocean and your fire."

"I can have them any time I choose."

"They can't satisfy a warm woman like you."

"I answer to no man for my desire."

"But, they're only dumb things, my love, earth's elements that surely don't get along."

"No worse than what you means to me, Mr. Dwyer."

He was stung, but not surprised, well schooled in Breeze's bluntness, a tongue-lashing could be painful and deep. "That's harsh me love. You're your mother's daughter in that way."

"I've no mother's longing on a night like this."

"Wonderful fine night just the same," he offered.

"Suits me enough to get away from her."

"How is your darlin' mother?"

"Mother O'Keefe never changes."

The barrier was still sharp, like fresh ice. He tried a downwind tack.

"Can I sit with you awhile?"

"Why ask for my permission? It's not your family's way."

"My family? And what have they to say about anything I do?" His long rooted suspicions turned to fear.

"'Tis a grand island, Lliam. You could sit wherever you please on Fogo."

"I know, but there's no fairer place in all of Newfoundland than in your warm glow, Breeze...I've told you that."

"You an' your fancy words."

"From me breaking heart, girl."

"It doesn't help when you come around talkin' poetry an' tryin' to break my own heart."

"I've come back for you, my only love."

Unsettling words. Breeze felt the flush and the tightness in her breast. "An' I suppose you've been the whole world over?"

"I've been to Boston, sure. That's world enough." He thought of the beautiful Molly and dark Anna Louise, and the depravity, killer of the soul. He felt guilty but had to say the next line. "Walk the streets of Boston town on foggy nights with your heart aching for your one true love, you'll see the world come and go. But now I'm back."

"Where were you when Sean O'Keefe was lost an' Mum took to her bed? I needed some words then. An' when the boys used me? An' where when your own brothers..." The question began in anger, softened to a plea, "An' where were you when Gerald decided I should be his woman?"

"Gerald? You married my brother?"

"I'm betrothed."

"But why, in God's name?"

"Because he said so. Everyone agrees."

"Anybody but Gerald!"

"It was you I wanted, Lliam, but you was off on some adventure, studyin' the King's English."

Lliam retreated to the water's edge, gazing beyond the harbour to the dark horizon. They had talked endlessly on long winter nights of bridging to that horizon, using books as their vessel. A small wave broke and slopped busily over the stones. Lliam jumped back to save his city shoes. "I wanted a better life, is all, like you. I want nothing to do with the bloody fish. They stink an' they break the backs of every man on this God-lost island!" He turned to look at Breeze. "Come away with me, Breeze, darlin'.'"

"You're too late, Lliam."

"I wanted you then, but you said no, you was too young. Wait awhile, you said. Well, my girl, I'm begging you to come away now."

Escape, the thought that carried her through the bad times. "Stop it, Lliam! I can't leave me mum."

The old woman understood obligations, her own sorrow set like a trap no amount of steel could fashion.

Lliam also knew the power of emotional traps, used the first time he tried to leave his father's house. Now returned, the Prodigal Son, still unclaimed. 'Malich's Pariah' was the term Lliam liked to use in the bars of Boston.

Malich Dwyer raised four sons to drive as free labour, a family's insurance against a harsh life, necessary for survival even if it meant feeding them in bad times. The arguments were strongly put when Lliam tried to leave the first time. Then at age eighteen he ran, without Margaret's tears or Malich's blessing. It was the beginning of the Depression and his prospects were limited. He did what he had to do to survive in Boston, and almost succeeded, but with a career in hand he succumbed to the lust for Molly. Threatened, he ran to the only sanctuary he knew. He was back for one reason, he said. "Breeze, Breeze, my girl...You're some stubborn."

"Then save your fine words."

He changed tacks again, prepared to sail the long way around. "You'd never tell us how you got your name, Breeze o' Wind." He moved to the fire and sat on the rock beside her.

Breeze shifted enough to make the point. "You made fun of me. You an' that crowd of rowdy brothers."

"I'm a big boy now. I won't tease you."

Breeze looked to see if he *was* teasing. "I'll tell you then, if you promise."

15

"I promise, as God is my witness."

"You needn't go that far...It was November month. A harsh November and there was a gale o' wind on the night I was born. A livin' storm with thick snow. A proper gagger', Sean called it. Sean O'Keefe was home from one of his damned voyages. He said there was a fine Irish breeze blowin' up Mother's Portuguese arse, an' I was born in a rush, all standin'. Squallin' an' kickin' like a fores'l tackin' over."

Lliam laughed, trying to summon their childhood. "Some *breeze* indeed! A fresh breeze you've always been to me."

"You promised not to tease!"

"Not a bit of it. 'Tis true. Go on then."

"A demon breeze o' wind from the Voodoo Island bore Sean away one day. Always leavin' again an' never likely to come back, that's a sailor. One time when she was angry, Mother told him I wasn't his child. Sean O'Keefe had flame red hair, all wavy like the ocean, like yours. He left the next day an' we never seen Sean O'Keefe no more."

Not Sean O'Keefe's child? The news of Breeze's bastard birth, in her own words, was an unsettling revelation, but there had always been rumours. The whispers too close to home. He chose not to sail that course. "A sailor's lot for sure, but I'm no sailor, nor fisherman neither."

"That's you as well, Lliam. You'll go away again."

"No, you're right about that, girl. I watched Father an' Mother fight their losing battle with the fish an' the bloody merchants. I swore I'd get clear."

"That's fine for you. I'm happy you cleared away from us so clean."

"An' so can you, Breeze."

The taste of freedom swelled until she almost choked. "I'm condemned here like a whale stranded in a tide pond."

"Yes, my girl an' if you marry Gerald you'll spend the rest of your life waiting to be a widow."

"It's a common life. Why should I be different?"

"With him gone half the year to Labrador, or to the bloody seals, or to who knows where, Gerald'll be home only long enough to leave you with another brat. An' if you're lucky, me darlin' girl, he'll survive to be old. And then he'll sit by the stove like Gran'father, so you can feed him an' clean him up, an' one day dress him proper an' lay his body out in the parlour." Lliam put his arm around her shoulders.

"Lliam, don't..." Breeze moved out of range. "You paint a nice picture you do. An' what, my dear man, am I to say to that? Rescue me? Take me away from my ocean to some Mainland place so I can cook an' do for you, an' have your brats, 'til death do us part?" Breeze let her shoulders drop.

Lliam was behind her like a cat on a fallen bird. He took her by the shoulders, gently. She didn't resist. The firelight painted her dark features more beautiful than Lliam remembered. She turned to him, eyes wide and bright with tears and expectations. *Would he strike her or hold her*? she wondered. He kissed her on the mouth, roughly. Why did they always do that to her? Breeze tried to break away. He held her and kissed her again, tenderly, and she gave up the struggle. He kissed her with the depth of feeling she had only experienced once...Could sink into his ocean...but not with Lliam. She returned the kiss, falling into green water, deep, peaceful, even the promise of escape. She needed that kiss more than the breath of life itself but she suddenly broke away and ran, stumbling in the loose stones along the tide line, splashing, splashing away to hear the sound of her own escape.

"Breeze!" Lliam called. "Breeze! Meet me up on Fortress Hill tomorrow!"

Grandfather Dwyer sucked his pipe, the glowing shards of coarse tobacco lighting his face like a signal beacon, rocking in time, watching the scene near the beach fire through tear-dimmed eyes, the shadow play, as old as emotions. Breeze now running blindly along the path between the harbour and the houses, the dark, slender shape in the long dress, with her shawl afly, skirts held high, heavy boots thumping the hard packed ground. She passed his window on the run. He shook his head. "My son, that's some wonderful strange, the way these young'uns carry on."

Grandmother Dwyer, steadying his chair, said gently, "Time for bed, my dear."

Grandfather hooked claws over the arms of the chair and hauled himself up. Stooping to open the top of the stove, he spit bitter juice into the dying fire and pronounced, "Those children nowadays don't understand a thing about life. Not a blessed thing."

The Dwyer Fishing Station Coast of Labrador: Two hundred miles to the Northwest, in a small anchorage hidden from the Atlantic gales, four men prosecute the fishing trade by firelight, cleaning up the day's catch. By daylight they haul the heavy trap net, praying for the big 'strike in' that would shorten their season, jigging cod on the outer grounds every moment they can steal from the elements. At night they process their fish and keep at it until the job is done. A heavy trap skiff and a dory are hauled up on the beach stones. Nearby, asleep like a gannet on the black water, just visible outside the circle of firelight, the family schooner waits on her tether like a patient beast of burden.

Malich Dwyer, broad and paunchy, with powerful arms too long for his body, hunches over the cutting table, hands glistening with blood and slime. He was once handsome, in a dark, brutish way. The right eye is sewn shut. An accident, they say, playmates angling for Tommy cod from the wharf. The Dwyers and the Sheens. It had been part of a boyhood curse, some whispered.

Malich and three sons, Gerald, Doyle and Garret, work like somnolent trolls by the light of a driftwood fire; their movements thrown into jerky relief against the guardian rocks. The fire crackles with fat and the grey smoke boils into the black sky. Unlovely grey-brown fish appear from a barrel, are deftly beheaded and the bellies sliced open by Gerald, passed on and the offal scooped out by Doyle. Then the lifeless thing is passed on again to Malich; deft slashes and the long comb of a skeleton lifted away as if by a conjurer's trick. He flings the skeleton into the fire. The triangle of white flesh disappears into the dipping tub. Garret, the silent son, plunges an arm into the cold salt water, retrieves the death-white fish and lays it gently into another barrel and spreads coarse salt over the corpse.

The thick cutting tables, hatch covers from the schooner, run rivers of blood, a ritual of the butcher's art. The heavy planks are constantly replenished by a fountainhead of fish. A numbing killing industry, a macabre dance carried out along the coasts like a ritual for four hundred years.

Europeans came to the treacherous coasts even before kings sent mercenaries and missionaries on voyages of plunder to the Southern Oceans. The Basques came first, for the whales in the Straits of Belle Isle. The Portuguese, the Spanish, the Bretons and the French came next for the glut of Northern cod. The English with their boatloads of indentured Irish, then the Norwegians and Germans, followed. They weren't explorers, only simple fishermen who came for the Great Northern flow swarming up the coast in such numbers that the sight could move a merchant's heart. The merchants sent cockleshells into the fog and ice of the Labrador Current. No thought of Southern gold or exotic Eastern spice, only fish, unlovely and cold, yanked from the ocean until the crude dories nearly foundered.

The Basques were fishing the coasts of Newfoundland a hundred years before the upstart navigator from Genoa conned the Spanish throne. Columbus, the cruel opportunist, with eyes only for the Golden Beach, took the safe, down-wind routes deep into blood-warm seas of the Southern Ocean, hungering for the riches of the Orient, careening headlong into tropic islands he hoped were further west, killing off the natives as he found them. The European plunderers found Inca and Aztec gold eventually but it was the lowly Northern cod that filled the coffers of the merchants. Fishermen, not freebooters, were the instruments and the servants of Almighty Cod. It was cod that fed the world when other foods failed. Humble cod drove foreign economies to riches or ruin and countries to war, and reshaped the political face of Europe. And it was King Cod that nurtured and killed more of mankind than gold could ever claim.

Malich Dwyer, bone-weary and mind-numb, one link in an unbroken chain, attacked another fish. Malich never cursed the fish. If there were no cod it would be a hard winter, and there was always another hard winter ahead. He did curse the hours, the cuts, the stone-cold fingers that had to be pried away from the knife; the aching legs, the freezing salt water running into boots, the soggy leather apron, and the salt sweat in his eyes. He stopped only long enough to rekindle a blackened pipe with a brand from the fire. Stab and slice, split open and fling away, reaching for another fish...Not counting the fish, only barrels and quintals matter. When the quintals are counted up by the merchant the rewards are small enough for the labour that produce the dried slabs that resemble sand-encrusted leather and smell like nothing else on earth. But a fisherman becomes immune to the smell. The stench is pervasive: in the house, the bedclothes, the hands of the amazed father holding a newborn son. The baby crawls through fish guts and slime and plays with seal flippers and whalebones and takes the cod liver oil and learns to chew the dry flesh the way Mainland children use candy. The son is born to fish and forage, his future to search the horizon for signs and jerk fish over the side so long as he is able. The mother learns to salt and dry and cook the fish in all forms. And when the fisherman comes ashore for good and is nailed into his rough coffin, the years of accumulated smells are buried with him. Malich prayed that the fish never ran out. If the Northern migration failed it would be a disaster and Newfoundland was deep into the Great Depression.

Malich split the back of a big fish with deft slashes. He remembered jigging that one, after a disappointing lift of the trap net. They had overhauled the trap and reset and then spent the remaining daylight jigging cod before heading in. The ugly fish, a female, was thirty pounds wet. His arms ached from the weight and his rough hands were marked by the strain on the jiggin' line. There were still a few monsters in the deep. The flesh went into the barrel. He flung the skeleton onto the fire. It sizzled and snapped and smelled sweet. The huge head was saved and later Garret would cut out the cheeks and tongue to fry. The heavy livers slid into a separate barrel, to stew in their natural heat and release the precious oil: amber gold, rising to the surface as the rotting flesh dissolves and sinks to the bottom. A miracle of alchemy rivaled only by the ability of rotting grapes to make wine, of curdled milk to make cheese, or yeast to rise dough. If Columbus wanted gold he should have steered his vessels north when the Basques presented him with a map of the New Founde Land. He could have fished like a real man and carried golden cod liver oil back to his masters in Spain.

Hour after hour the fire roared and the fish flew until Malich sagged with fatigue. The necessity of the task drove him to stand at the table long after his body demanded rest. Gerald and Doyle, copies of the father, were dog-tired too, but dared not waver. Gerald, hard like his father, was almost as lazy as Doyle, and had to be driven. Doyle had the soft, slack features of the village drunk, and the manners to match. Only Garret, the red headed mute, thin and tall like Lliam, was allowed to vary his routine. It was Garret's job to bring empty barrels and stack fish and measure salt over the fish as they rose in tiers in the barrels. He went about his tasks with a quiet efficiency.

The last fish hit the table. "That's the ol' bitch we've been lookin' for. She's always on the bottom of the barrel, eh?" Malich chuckled, dispatching the bloody mess and stabbing his knife into the plank. "That's the ol' lady we work for, b'yes." The joke had worn desperately thin. He made the Sign of the Cross. "Lord thank you an' deliver us of our labours, an' may there be fish a plenty in mornin'. Leave off now an' Garret'll make up."

Gerald sniggered and blessed himself. "Bloody courageous long day, even for heathens!" said Gerald, relieved of their cloister silence, spitting tobacco juice at the fire. Malich forbid them to talk as they worked: said it distracted from industry.

"Yes, b'ye, an' pray that tomorrow's even longer," Malich shot back.

"I only just managed this one," said Doyle, the third youngest son, who craved a smoke of a hand rolled cigarette more than he craved a woman, "An' I only accomplished that fuckin' feat by fallin' asleep all standin'."

"You've been asleep most o' your miserable life," chided Gerald.

Doyle made a rude gesture and stripped off his leather apron, flung it on the ground for Garret to wash, and staggered away from the table to warm his hands in the iron kettle. Frequently during the night the boys had to plunge their hands in the kettle, believing the tannic acid of the tea toughened their hands. Malich refused. He knew the hot tea would only make his hands soft and vulnerable. "Mother Garret," Doyle said to his younger brother, "...no need to boil up tongues for supper, my dear. I've had me fill o' stinkin' cod. I'll just eat me left hand when 'tis done." He laughed at his own joke, drying his hands on his underwear, rolling a cigarette with raw fingers.

"You're not careful you'll cut it off one of those times," teased Gerald.

"Then I'd be quit o' this fuckin' racket now, wouldn't I?"

Garret stood with the wooden shovel poised over a barrel, always puzzled by Doyle's lack of respect for their trade. Gerald threw his knife down on the table and wiped his hands with a bloody piece of burlap. "...An' I'll feed the rest o' you to sharks," continued Gerald, spitting at the fire again.

"You'd have a nice job to handle me with no arms...I swear, Gerald, I'm that vexed with this fuckin' place I'd carve you proper for an easy day in Hell."

"Get on with it then...let's have a go!"

They grappled and pushed impotently. Malich knew it was pointless to chide his sons for their lifelong childish games. Garret was an easier target for his moods.

"Garret!" yelled Malich. "Salt your bloody fish!" Garret jumped and dipped the shovel. Malich reloaded his pipe and fired it with a coal held between two sticks. The fire, having consumed the wood and bones, sagged into a mass of glowing coals as if tired also. Malich built the flames with driftwood.

Garret resumed shoveling salt into the barrels. Gerald joined Doyle beside the fire, pouring strong black tea from the kettle, ignoring the blood and slime in the kettle. Gerald *horked* the chewed out wad of tobacco into the fire and took a sip of tea, rinsed his mouth and spat what looked like black blood. They continued to jostle each other like children and drank the foul brew, smoking, cursing and spitting.

Malich stumbled stiff legged over the stones to wash in the cold salt water, drying his red hands on the tail of his shirt. He puffed his pipe to crackling life, the smoke whirling around his head, vanishing like a visiting spirit. He stood looking at his schooner hanging quietly on her anchor chain. The dancing firelight made the little black ship come alive, moving to a restless surge. Although the night was calm, a long, easy swell, *sophed* around the guardian rocks at the entrance to their cove; one of many uncharted in the wall of granite known as the Down North Labrador.

Deep-keeled Grand Banks schooners could not enter the cove. The tiny cleft, known locally as Dwyer's Station, had been the summer home of the Dwyer family for three generations. The take of cod from the trap net around the headland was average in the best of seasons but the protection was perfect. Almost. Even during a gale of wind only a moderate surge reached the vessel, and the wind screaming over the barren islands could not dislodge a good kedge anchor. Proper hurricanes, though infrequent, were another matter.

Malich ordered thick hemp warps run ashore when there was a chance of a blow. The boys grumbled about the extra work, but Malich remembered the October storm of 1885. He was a boy working the coastal fishery when ninety schooners were lost or damaged and seventy fishermen perished. And then there was the July 1908 storm, the year Gerald was born; a southern hurricane of great intensity, sired in the hot winds off the coast of Africa, engorged with moisture, churning like a malevolent reaping machine, scoured the Eastern Seaboard. Done with New England, the cyclone skipped out to sea and slammed the Newfoundland coast with a bestial fury, tearing fishing schooners loose from their anchors before helpless crews could get canvas on and run for open water. Another sixty schooners were wrecked, cast ashore or sunk with cargoes and crews. He couldn't risk losing the schooner. She was only fifty-feet long, and twenty-five tons burthen, small by Grand Banks standards, but typical of hundreds of small coastal schooners: the workhorses of the Atlantic coasts. Family-built, she was their only means of staying even with the merchant who supplied the fittings and the gear to prosecute the fishery. The merchant controlled their lives, their necessities and even the wormy hardtack, the sailor's only friend in bad times.

"Nelson's Birthday Cake for you, my dear," said Gerald as he reached into a wooden box for a chunk of hard bread. He inspected the biscuit in the firelight. "Wonder if there's any worms left for flavour?" He tossed it to Doyle.

Doyle soaked the rock-like biscuit in his tea, slurping at the moistened dough. Dipping again, holding it under. Small white grubs that looked like white coats, wiggled out of the cake. "They floats off an' swims around likes pups off a growler, my son!" exclaimed Doyle in mock surprise. "Look here. Some good." He plunged the cake back into the tea, laughing. The hard bread had to be softened and eaten in layers, like peeling an onion. The indestructible round cakes are meant to be soaked, then boiled with fish. Codfish and hardtack, a repulsive mound of soggy dough and salty flesh, the staple food of coastal Newfoundland called fish'n'brewis. A refined palate might blanch at the steaming mess, running with molasses or sizzling pork fat topped with scrunchions: shriveled bits of pork rind cooked to the consistency of gravel. Fish'n'brewis has fed generations of Newfoundlanders and no fish-dependent people work harder for their survival.

Gerald, too tired to eat, sprawled on a piece of canvas beside Doyle. He cut a slice of leathery tobacco from a plug he kept in his back pocket. Doyle rolled another cigarette and lit it in the fire. They sipped tea, smoked and watched their father gazing at the schooner. Garret worked at the barrels: shoveling salt, washing down the cleaning table with seawater. Doyle tossed the dregs of his tea into the fire and laid back, arms under his head, as if lounging on a southern beach. "Gerald, ol' son...What do you suppose that unfortunate young woman o' yours is doin' on this fine night?"

Gerald had his eyes closed, on the cliff-edge of sleep. "Wha...? Me darlin' Breeze? She's layin' abed in 'er own tight tilt, dreamin' o' me cod piece 'bout that far into'er hold," he said, holding up a blood encrusted arm, fist clenched, measuring to his elbow with a twisted fore finger.

Doyle snorted. "Courageous dreamin's all she'll be doin' 'less I gets aboard of 'er first."

"Oh, aye? An' you'd look some good dryin' on flake, all split an' salted proper, like."

"G'wan with you! I was in there right behind the ol' man, but then he had to wait on Garret didn't he? What took you so long?"

"Listen," he spit a line of black tobacco juice close to Doyle, "You was never with Breeze, but if I got a whiff o' you up her sweet cunny you'd be swingin' by that shockin' little thing you call pecker." He threw a small stone at Doyle's crotch.

"Safe enough, ol' son. There's not a tree on this grand fuckin' coast to bump your head against. But I knows somethin' back on Fogo I could bump away on."

Gerald *horked* another line of black liquid into the fire. "Brother, there's trees enough on that filthy little bummer for the likes o' that Jack pisser." Gerald pointed at the crosstrees near the tops of the schooner's masts. Painted white they stood out like a gallows against the black sky. "I'd hoist you up balls first, then see you dance."

"Not much fear there. Them's like to go over side with rot, put any weight onto'em. That fuckin' foremast's gone shawley as your brain."

Malich had heard enough. "If you two can't speak well of Breeze O'Keefe, at least speak well of the schooner. Your miserable lives depend on her! Now get some sleep. One more day an' we got fish enough. Gales won't wait. I want to be quit o' Labrador soon's we can dry an' load."

"Oh, aye," agreed Gerald, "won't break me heart to leave this fuckin' coast. Sooner I'm home an' speakin' polite words to me darlin' woman, the better."

"Go on with you," scoffed Doyle. "Wouldn't know a polite word for lass no more than boot'er in twizzle."

"I'll twizzle you!" Gerald said, rolling on top of Doyle throwing tired punches.

Malich uttered an oath and shoved the dory into the water. "Ain't fit company. I'm goin' to sleep aboard."

"Night then, ol' man," said Gerald, rolling off Doyle and spitting into the fire. "Give our respects to our darlin' boat." He whispered to Doyle, "Goin' to make love with the poor ol' thing tonight is my guess."

"Yes, my son, better move back up beach a piece. The humpin' an' heavin's like to wash us all away." Doyle laughed and snorted like a pig. Gerald grunted and turned his back, pulling a piece of rotting canvas over his shoulders. Doyle watched Garret mixing flour and sourdough starter for their morning meal of bannock and boiled fish, then slept without dreaming.

It was colder by dawn, with a touch of frost higher up on the berry bushes. Weather clouds hung about on the great plateau inland, but clear skies with a fair wind off the ocean promised a good drying day.

Gerald and Doyle woke stiff and sore. Garret had the fire going, making pan bread in an open skillet, the unleavened dough frying in rancid lard. Thick tea boiled in the kettle, refreshed with a handful of leaves and a few spruce buds thrown into the dregs. The blood and fish slime bubbles percolated away through the spout and hissed in the hot fire. In a black iron pot, suspended on a crane, chunks of white flesh floated up through grey oil, like beluga whales surfacing playfully in a cesspool.

Gerald crawled to the fire to warm his hands. Doyle, lighting his first rumpled cigarette of the day, lay with his feet almost in the flames. "Garret, old son," said Doyle, "just pour breakfast in me boots. I'd rather be warm than eat that fuckin' mess, sure."

Garret was hurt but managed a thin smile. It was just like Doyle.

Gerald, not to be outdone said, "An' Garret, no insult intended, but that lovely bread'd be some good for pecker pokin'."

"Be nice warm piece, at least." Doyle laughed and choked on his cigarette smoke.

"'Bout all you'll ever get."

Malich moved about on the deck of the schooner. The little 'bummer', as Gerald called her, looked less lovely in the revealing light. She was sturdy enough and had seaworthy lines, rough-built in the island way, the result of decades of build-by-eye and refine-by-use. Poorly designed boats fail more often. Malich's little 'Jack', like hundreds of her kind around the Newfoundland coast, was a utilitarian workboat that suffered from hard use, a tool of the trade, an accessory to the business of wrenching fish from the sea. She looked old and tired but her useful lifetime was only half spent. In a few years, if she lived, her hull would be stripped and beached beside Breeze's wreck.

Malich eyed the condition of his tough little schooner. "God willin'," he whispered, she would carry them home and take what the North Atlantic had to offer. He loved his boat, a friend, a confidant, when no one understood his terrors. His good eye saw her pleasing shape as well as her bruises. His rough fingers traced the scarred wood of the cap rail. *The rigging should be renewed,* he said to the wind. She was, *Good for it, a few more years at least, Lord be merciful,* he said to himself, making the oath so as not to queer her chances. The family often discussed installing an engine, but year after year the margins were too thin and the cost would put them further under the weight of the merchant's ledger.

The faithful *Margaret & Maude* was their only hope. He vowed to give her a good refit, if only he could drive his lazy sons to make the effort. He watched his sons on the beach idling over their breakfast. Garret moved from one job to the other without prodding. Breakfast done Garret was at the barrels extracting salted fish, washing them in the dipping tub and piling them on the two-man handbarrow.

"Damn you lazy, b'yes! Get them fish unto flakes!" Malich ordered as he sculled the dory ashore. His own breakfast was a hurried affair of boiled fish with oil-soaked biscuits and scalding tea, standing beside the fire, noting the bank of clouds over the ranks of blue hills. *Not a threat today,* he reasoned, *but tomorrow or the next day.* Another system hovered far out over the Atlantic, moving east. Above was blue sky with a fresh drying wind. The fish had to be laid out quickly. Every minute of sun utilized. It would take two, perhaps three days to finish the drying and load for home. The weather was good. Soon the weather would turn.

Malich surveyed his crude fishing station. Not much to show for a lifetime of effort: a work-littered beach, rusted out stoves and broken anchors, tumbled down cabin with the tarpaper roof sagging like a broken horse, and the spindly drying flakes that required constant rebuilding. Generations of toil a thin legacy. They had given up repairing the old tilt and slept on the shore in good weather. They were between 'Stationers', those who live ashore in tilts, and 'Floaters', sailors who live aboard their boats and follow the fish like nomads, drying on the beach or selling 'green' fish to the collecting agents.

The Stationers, without schooners of their own, were also called 'Freighters.' They took passage with their families and all their gear on one of the big schooners heading down to Labrador in May and June. Another class of Labrador fishermen, called 'Liveyers', occupied desolate coves, surviving in near destitution even in good years, selling what fish they could to the agents who paid in trade goods. God alone knows what kept the Liveyers there, generation after generation, some going a lifetime without seeing a doctor until the Wilfred Grenfell Mission ships appeared in 1892. Visitors and adventurers could barely comprehend the poverty and hardships they found in the poorest Labrador outports. The Dwyers were well off by comparison.

It was a harsh, cruel life, but a possible life and, without the merchant's stranglehold on their trade, independent fishermen prospered or at least had a more dignified existence. There was no lack of fish or a waiting market in good times. It was the merchant's monopoly and debt system that kept the outporters in abject poverty. And yet the system prevailed until the Second World War because many merchants provided the only means by which a family could survive. The merchants prospered and sent their children to England or America to be educated. The poorest of the Newfoundland outporters were lucky to feed their children and raise them to be little better than slaves. Fish were a valuable commodity. Human life was not. Malich knew the rules, had been raised in the system and asked for nothing more than a chance to fish and provide. Their drying flakes and schooner were the keys.

Malich's drying flakes, built by his grandfather fifty years before, were spindly platforms, constructed of spruce poles, 'longers', shipped as deck loads on the schooners. Some poor ground spruce grew close at hand but the stunted trees near the exposed coast are twisted to a tangle of scrub, tormented by gales and frozen by icy winter winds. Spruce forests of any size were three miles away, up the fore shore cliffs and across the insect infested plateau to the protected valleys of the ancient hills; a rocky climb and a muddy march around boggy ponds, through soft, sinking peat or flinty talus.

They repaired the flakes as necessary, and each season, before the first salted fish were laid out, Malich's boys had to cut spruce bows to make an airy mattress to cradle the tender carcasses.

"Pick up your feet, you clumsy sod!" chided Gerald.

"I wasn't ready, was I," Doyle grunted. They hefted the two-man handbarrow piled with wet fish, slipping and stumbling on the loose rocks. They made small piles of salted fish on the flakes. Malich and Garret separated the piles, spreading the fish, skin side down, so that the flat, wedge shaped, yellowing bodies lay head to tail, close for economy but not touching.

When all the 'green' fish were laid out, the four of them capsized the previous day's fish so the flesh would dry evenly. They had chanced leaving them exposed on the flakes over night. Now, already wrinkled and stiff, the slabs of firm flesh, with the salt growing in crystals, were doing fine. Experienced hands could tell by the weight and colour how the drying was progressing. A promising haul, if the fish were properly 'made'. They watched the weather, tended the fish and prayed.

Laying out and turning finished, the Dwyers were preparing to push off from shore in the skiff when Doyle spied a battered dory rounding up into their cove. At the oars sat a ragged, dark little man with a small head and a tangle of grey, spiky hair. One broken oar was held together by a rope splint so that the dory moved unevenly, like a gimp on rough ground.

"There's trouble, Father, if trouble could pull a busted sweep," said Doyle.

"Moses bloody Sheen," commented Gerald, spitting tobacco juice on the rocks.

"Aye, he's trouble." Malich recognized the wind-burned little man in the dirty cotton jacket, a ne'r-do-well Liveyer from the next cove. "'Tis a Sheen all right. Can smell'im from here. Sure Moses ain't stole enough fish at nights, he's got to come beggin' by God's light."

"Marnin', Malich," Moses Sheen called across the cove. The last surviving brother of the Sheen clan was about the same age as Malich. Sheen's older brother Josiah, the boy who hooked out Malich's eye, committed suicide to escape the father's wrath. Their father Seth, of the Change Island Sheens, was a contemporary of Malich's father, and another sad story. "Foin time you'se 'ad o' it," Moses continued, indicating the full flakes with a jerk of his head. The splintered forefoot of the dory ground hard on the beach stones. He dropped the oars and slipped painfully over the side, holding the gunnel of his sinking boat as if supporting a cripple. His old boots leaked and his personal rig needed mending. Man and boat were well matched. He eyed the plug of tobacco in Gerald's hand. "Couldn't spare a nip o' baccy, could ya, son?" Gerald handed over the plug, willing to share his dwindling supply even with the ragged looking Sheen. Sharing was surviving. Sheen didn't acknowledge Gerald directly. "By da looks o'er, you an' dose foin b'yes made a crack season, else you'se charmed dose fish onta fakes wit' magic." He tried to bite off a corner of tobacco with bad teeth.

"No trick to that. We worked hard all summer, is what, Moses Sheen."

"An' bless'd wit' a gang o' strappers. Yis, b'ye. Moi son!" He cut off a chunk of tobacco with a rusty clasp knife and handed the defiled plug back to Gerald without comment. "Now you'se take dat 'ard lot o' mine..."

"No, you take'em, Moses, an' when they've grown some make 'em work, like I do mine."

"Oh, Malich, me dear man, if only 'twere so easy as dat." He shifted the tobacco around in his mouth. "A lazier crowd o' urchins ya niver seen."

"Your oldest can't be more than ten, sure!" said Malich, the anger showing. Moses was working on his second family. The Sheens had a reputation for misusing their children, far worse than the Dwyers. "You can't expect 'em to work like grown men."

"Me oldest one? Let's see...Eleven or twelve, I t'inks 'e was, dead dis year, but so what? Dey's louts an' dat's it. I've a job to feed me crowd dis winter comin'. Bad toims, moi son, bad toims. D'oldest son died on me, lung rot, an' most else is sick wit' chills an' shakes now...an' me ol' woman 'as a pinch an' says she can't bare no more babies. Worse toim's comin'. Now if you'se could jus' take us ab'ard dat little bummer, an' carry we on up to Carmenville...Woman's got a sister..."

"Jack enough room aboard boat for us, Moses, let alone that crowd, an' all your gear. An' I'd have to feed you'se besides. We're not into business of given passage to Freighters. G'wan aroun' to Hamilton Inlet or Cartwright an' catch on with buddy or coastal boat."

"Dey's all gone up by dis toim, an' if a one was dere dey wants fish fer passage. We've nary fish nor 'baccy, an' only some dried bakeapples to eat a few days from starvin'."

"I'm sorry, Moses. I can't take you."

Sheen edged closer to Malich,. "Could ya not at least tow we up across da Straits, as far as Cape Bauld or Quirpon, ol' son? Maybe we'se could make'er to Twillingate from dere, or die tryin'."

Malich held his ground. They were nose to nose and the stench of Moses Sheen turned Malich's hardened stomach. "That ol' thing you call a dory wouldn't make even Cape Charles without drownin' your crowd, an' I won't have your miserable life on my conscience."

"If ya condemns we here we'es bound to perish wit' da frost, if us don't starve first."

"I'll leave the cullage on flake. Pay me back next season. That's about all the good you fish anyways..." Malich tried to turn away.

"Malich!" Sheen barked, grabbing Malich's arm, "I beg ya...us means to quit dis awful place a'fore we'um all gone ab'ard from scurvy. If us could jus' huddle along into your big skiff, tow us on, like. We'd be no trouble t'all."

"No! Moses, me dear man, it's not a thing to risk." Malich shook off Sheen's grip and retreated up the beach.

Moses Sheen spit the wad of tobacco on Malich's tracks. "Den you'se can risk da curse o' da Sheens, Malich Dwyer! An' twice curse dat ugly, lazy crowd wit' ya! May dey burn in Hell an' your fish rot a'fore ya reaches Fogo!"

31

Malich turned and made to go for Sheen but Gerald stepped between them. Moses shoved his dory into deep water and sprang aboard more nimbly than he disembarked. Malich whispered..."Mary, Mother o' God, an' all the Saints, preserve us." The Sheens had a reputation beyond abusing children. "Jesus, Mary an' Joseph...intercede on our behalf."

"You don't believe on that curse, sure?" asked Doyle, as they watched Sheen pulling hard for open water.

"It's just a bunch o' nonsense, Father!" said Gerald, eying the disgusting looking wad of his precious tobacco. He spit tobacco juice where the bow of Sheen's dory left a groove in the beach. "Isn't it?"

Malich put his good eye on each son in turn. "'Twas a Sheen cost me an eye."

"Only accident, Ol' Man," offered Doyle, grinning, his crooked lips arching as if deformed by a stroke.

"Bad luck. Nothin' more." Gerald spit on the beach again and laughed self-consciously, uncomfortable in his father's hard gaze.

Only Garret understood the gravity of the curse but his comment was a twitch at the corner of his mouth. Malich turned away and cursed Moses Sheen under his breath. A raven called in the high distance. Malich eyed the black bird and cursed it also, but blessed himself.

It was mid morning when Malich and his sons headed out in the trap skiff towing the dory. Precious jigging hours were lost and Malich was in a foul humour.

Béhathook Cove Same: Lliam's journal entry that morning: *Breeze promised to meet me up on the Fortress today. Must be on my best behavior if I'm to turn her heart. What could she be thinking to marry Gerald? She'd be stuck here for the rest of her days. I can't get away from this godforsaken place fast enough, and if Breeze will have me I'll find a way, this time.*

Lliam Dwyer climbed the hill above the village, the familiar, hard-packed path meandering around frost-broken stones and clumps of pale green mosses. On either side of the beaten track the low juniper bushes and tufts of dry grass seemed to thrive in the thin soil. Rock outcroppings, covered with Caribou lichen, poked above the bushes. As a boy he would race his brothers to the Fortress to see who would be the king for the day, but six years of idleness had taken their toll. He stopped to catch his breath, surveying the scene of land and sea. To the north and east the ocean foamed over shoals and sunkers. The tumbling white caps looked like pure white sheep skipping across a green field. He had forgotten how beautiful and fresh it could be on their hill. And only as a lonely young man on the dirty cobbled streets of Boston, had he realized that Newfoundland is not barren. Every inch of the place, above or below the water, is crammed with life: giant whales, fish and lowly mussels, haughty caribou and humble lichens. He never thought of his island as beautiful or bountiful. It was just a place where he was raised and longed to leave, hating the damp fogs, the windswept barrens, the piercing cold that drove through clothing, the meager meals when the season failed and stomachs pinched from hunger. The coldest winter always followed a bad season, when the wind howled and snow never settled; paths between the trembling houses impassable with glitter storms. The dwindling spruce splits never seemed to get the big iron cook stove hot enough to defeat the chill on frost-bound nights huddled around the kitchen table in the light of rationed lamp oil, with only a tattered atlas to relieve the monotony.

The nearest school was in Fogo Harbour, too far to travel by land or boat each day and Malich refused to pay for the boys to board out. They were a working family and education was for the merchant's children. The few books available were carried home from foreign ports by sailors like Captain O'Keefe. Breeze shared hers with Lliam and they talked about the adventures of runaways and stowaways, cast by shipwreck on warm South Sea Islands awash in pirates and savages. Breeze wondered why it was only boys in the stories having adventures. Girls were left behind to learn to cook and sew and study manners and insects, waiting for their playmates to return and claim them as brides. Breeze learned early that it wasn't a fair game. She had a wandering heart, like Lliam, like Grace O'Malley, but outport girls

33

seldom escaped and Grace O'Malley was more cutthroat capitalist, born to wealth and privilege, than a legendary pirate queen, still...

Lliam reached his objective, sweating and chilled by the wind. The Fortress Rock was only a patch of weather-blasted granite tumbled to rough crenellations, that a child's imagination easily made into ancient castles, dungeons, moats and thrones. He sat on their throne rock, running memories of a simple childhood, searching the village below for a glimpse of her. He shut his eyes, remembering Breeze as a young seabird, wild and free, flying from heart to heart as if they were branches on a trembling tree: a sudden move and she was gone again.

Breeze parted the lace curtains...Her mother, Brigid, stitched those curtains one long winter, like Penelope, waiting for her sailor to return...Searching the crown of the hill for him. She could see Lliam above the summit and felt the chill. She dropped the curtain slowly. *Why?* she wondered. *Why am I afraid?* She had put Lliam Dwyer out of her mind but not out of her heart and it made her doubt the future. Breeze untied the scarf that imprisoned her black mane, letting it flow around her shoulders, preening in front of the small mirror between sepia photographs of her family: Mother O'Keefe, looking stern even in youth, and Captain Sean O'Keefe in uniform, who looked so dignified but distant, already at sea. She smoothed her apron and entered the kitchen.

"I'm going out now, Mum, for some air."

Mother O'Keefe, in perpetual mourning, rocked beside the stove, legs covered by the woolen blanket, a bowl of bread pudding in her lap, skeletal fingers limply holding a spoon that tapped impatiently on the edge of the bowl. The only resemblance to the once handsome woman and her beautiful daughter was a hint of colour in the high cheeks, the combination of Beothuk, Portuguese and West County Irish. Breeze's black mane was thick and shining; the mother's, once her crowning glory, resembled salt foam and sea wrack. "Out? You're always, goin' out."

"Just for a walk, Mum...You'll be fine."

"Walkin' this time is it? Only idle feet have time to walk about, my girl."

"I've done all the chores an' there's wood enough," she tried.

"The Devil preys onto the idle ones weak of resolve."

Breeze sighed and took up the bowl. She offered a spoonful of mush to her mother's mouth. "You know I'm not idle, Mum. I work every moment of the day."

"You're just fertile ground for bad seed. 'Twas them books," she said, taking the offering, swallowing with exaggerated difficulty.

Breeze spooned another mouthful. "Eat up then an' I'll be off."

"Are you tryin' to gag me an' leave me to die?"

"No, Mum. Had enough?"

Mother O'Keefe nodded. Breeze took away the bowl, wiped Mother O'Keefe's mouth with her apron and patted some loose grey hairs into place. She put the bowl on the pantry counter and rinsed the spoon in the bucket. Mother O'Keefe watched every move. "You treat me like I was just a piece o' furniture an' nothing more."

Breeze took off her apron, hung it on the peg behind the door, smoothed her print dress, the blue and green one she wore for special occasions because it reminded her of the ocean, and began putting on her rubber boots out of habit. She shook them off, selected the pair of prized leather walking shoes Captain O'Keefe had brought from Spain, feeling the rush and tingle of anticipation. Also the guilt: betrothed, spoken for, trapped. She fought the feeling, telling herself that she was just showing Lliam Dwyer that she was a proper woman. A grey shawl that she had knit from wool she spun the winter Lliam left home covered her shoulders. "I won't be long, Mum. Just a bit o' fresh air."

"You took fresh air night last, so you did. But when you come in you was all lathered up like slide pony haulin' load o' wood up hill."

"I need to get out for a spell, is all."

"Puttin' on airs for that no good Dwyer's loafer. Poor Margaret's killick. An' how can I look her in eye, with Gerald away, a proper workin' man. A fisherman's wife has no time to be gallivantin' about the hills. You'll be leavin' me a derelict soon enough when you marry Gerald Dwyer. Dwyers's good, hard workin' folks, aside o' that Lliam Legabout. They don't want a frivolous miss who spends her time moonin' into fire half a night, an' traipesin' about for whatever reason."

"I'm not a fisherman's wife yet! An' I don't intend to leave you a derelict, or any other way."

"You take after Sean O'Keefe, so you do, rest his Black Irish soul. You've never had a solid foot, nor a stable mind. You'll come to grief on a hard place. Mark my words."

Breeze wanted to counter with the rumour about Sean O'Keefe and Margaret Dwyer. "But I'm just goin' for a walk."

"An' wouldn't I love to just go for a walk now. If only I was able."

Breeze took a deep breath and opened the door. "You could step dance a bloody jig, if you'd only put your mind to it." Breeze slammed the door harder than she meant to.

Mother O'Keefe ground her teeth. She could usually stall Breeze's attempts at independence. Guilt made as good a shackle as iron. She hauled herself out of the chair, and, using the table for support, made her way to the window. She picked up Sean O'Keefe's heavy brass telescope.

Lliam opened his eyes when Breeze jumped off the big rock, admiring her pirouette as if she was an actress on a stage, her hybrid colours showing true in the sunlight: her black hair, burnished and blowing about like Irish battle pennants. She jumped back across the gap before Lliam could reach for her, full skirts like a flurry of feathers, the seabird poised, ready to fly. Suddenly she was on the ground, a wildcat circling him. Lliam laughed at her antics and lay back, watching his chance. After some sparing and feinting, Breeze sat down beside him, tossing her hair like a ship's bow tossing aside a wave. The effect was not lost on Lliam, but to reach for her was to reach for a cloud. Breeze could vanish like blown mist.

"Iceberg, way off there, to Nor'east," he said, pointing.

"I know. I've watched'er for days." Breeze shielded her eyes and gazed at the distant ice island. The sun was still to the east of the iceberg and the sculptured rogue could show off its deepest blue-green clefts. It was not uncommon to see such an iceberg in September.

"Probably she got caught up in May month," Breeze reasoned. "She's most likely fetched up on White Island Bank all summer, an' now she's free to drift away an' die."

"Free? As if icebergs could be imprisoned."

"She was once locked up in ice field, an' was born, so to speak, then held against her will. She's blown clear now...free to wander."

"She? Are icebergs feminine?" he asked. *Was Breeze's sense of humour coming back*, he wondered?

"All adrift, alone, but free. Driven away from her home by wind an' current, Lliam. What's a woman to do?"

"Make a journey with me, my girl, worthy of a free spirit." Breeze pretended not to hear. "I said, make the journey to Mainland with me, Breeze, darlin'."

"A lonely journey, Lliam. I don't know you."

"Know me? We've been mates since we could walk."

"Have you ever known icebergs to mate an' travel along together?"

"Ice mates with the vast ocean, its natural home, able to circle the world," he countered.

"True love, once denied, melts away, as ice to water."

"Maybe the subject of ice is not a good analogy."

"Nor are expectations of a young girl grounded in a remote outport."

They were silent, searching for words. Finally he said, "Remember when we were children, Breeze? We used to play up here. This was our castle. I was always just a lowly knight's vassal 'cause Gerald an' Doyle would pull me down whenever I raced them to be king. But when I was alone you were always my Queen. I must've vanquished a thousand dragons," he said sweeping his arm through the air, "an' fought all the rouges in the realm for your fair hand." He took Breeze's hand in both of his but she gently pulled away and stood up, spinning, her skirts flaring out, showing off her long, slim legs. Lliam felt the sensations, remembering those same bare young legs traced by his own hand, helped by hers, both trembling with emotions...

"Oh, yes, remember I do," she whispered. After a few moments she recovered. "Dear Garret was always the poor dumb beast wasn't he?

37

An' your brothers used to beat Garret up when he grew weary of being the dragon."

"Poor Garret indeed!" said Lliam, pretending to be annoyed. "He suffered enough under our cruel hands, I suppose, but I suffered more because you always favoured Gerald."

"I never did! He forced me to be his queen."

"An' now he's won you." He tried to approach Breeze but she skipped away to the other side of the rock. "An' don't forget, Gerald an' Doyle beat on me near every day just to impress you."

Breeze looked far away into the ocean distance. "He's sufferin' some cruel still."

"Who? Garret?"

"Poor Garret. Malich an' your brothers use him like a draft horse."

"The hard work? 'Tis nothing. Father keeps him busy on purpose. When Garret sits idle he tries to think an' it makes him that unhappy because he can't speak."

The wind gusted suddenly, racing up the slope from the chill ocean with an edge of ice. Breeze put her back to it and hugged herself, forcing her firm breasts against the thin fabric of her Sunday dress, the hard nipples pointing at Lliam. "I'm perishin' up here."

"Why did you come, Breeze?"

"You asked me."

"Is that why you're marrying Gerald? Because he asked you?"

She turned away and showed her profile. "He didn't ask. He told me, a dozen times."

"You could have said no."

"I did, a dozen times, an' more. An' still do!" Breeze turned to Lliam. "Catch me!" She suddenly jumped off the rock into Lliam's arms: still slender but no longer a feather.

Lliam staggered to hold her weight then let her slide slowly down his body until her toes touched his shoes. They were eye to eye. "You're a proper grown woman now, an' of your own mind."

"Lliam, I don't want to fight with you."

"I didn't ask you up here for that, girl."

He tried to hold her close but Breeze broke away, laughing. She picked up her leather shoes and ran lightly down the path on tiptoes to a sheltered spot in the sun. She flopped onto the heather and laid back with her hair fanned out, the black waves barely ruffled by the sharp wind searching overhead. Lliam followed and sat down at her side, listening to her rapid breathing, trying to control his own. She was playing with him and he was torn between anger and passion. The silence was more difficult. They both knew why they were there, the sheltered hollow familiar territory. Their names scratched in the rock not completely covered by lichen. "Look, Lliam...there's yours."

"An' yours just below." Awkward, almost shy, they stared ahead and waited.

"Remember Grace O'Malley, the Pirate Queen?"

"Yes, my dear girl," chuckled Lliam. "You'd bore us to tears with her stories."

"When you'd listen! You boys were always so full of yourselves you'd never let me play the Pirate Queen unless I beat one o' you senseless."

"I still have the scars," said Lliam pretending to be hurt. Breeze pouted and turned away. "All right then, what was so bloody important about a pirate who was a wild, unmannered witch?"

"She was no witch! Grace was a real woman!"

"So was Nancy Sims, an' she was born here at least. Why didn't you want to be like her?"

"Not content with Fogo was she. Her mother sold'er to some Duke. She changed her name and became Princess Pamela, whore of Ireland and France, an' they say poor Pamela died in a French convent, alone an' unloved. I was too good for such trifling. But Grace was defiant an' brave."

"So that's it?"

"Grace O'Malley was a woman who stood up for herself an' her people an' wouldn't be bullied by Queen Elizabeth, an' all the English soldiers. She was the first Irish rebel, an' she's preserved on Clare Island an' still speaks to women who would defy their lords an' masters."

"That's nonsense, Breeze! She...only her bones are. I read about your pirate. It's her skull that's preserved an' it has no brain to think, nor lips to speak. Let's talk only of your lips." Lliam kissed her and put his hand on her breast. She pushed it away, gently.

"Wants to play the remember game some more?" she asked.

"It was only childish nonsense."

"Not so childish this time. Besides, you started it." She turned on her side to face Lliam, her hips rounded to pleasing curves. "We were older, before you went away. Remember the day you tried to lay me down right here? I was no more than fourteen. We were still too young but I wanted you some bad. We fumbled around like two kids wrestlin' over old boot, an' neither knowin' what to do first, you were that shy of me."

"I wasn't shy!"

"You were that shy, Lliam. You left off first an' made some excuse, but wouldn't stand up to chase me when I dared you. Why wasn't you able to stand up, Lliam?"

"Breeze, it's a hard thing...to be a young man in love." He chuckled at his own joke, remembering the embarrassment of the erection that wouldn't go away.

She lay on her back, breasts heaving with laughter. "So, it's easy to be a young girl 'cause we've nothing to show off?"

"I wouldn't know about that."

"No, my dear, suppose you wouldn't. A boy never knows nothin'. He just goes about layin' a girl down like she was a helpless baby seal to be sculped."

"That's hardly a fair analogy."

"You use that word too much."

"Analogy? It's a...well, hard to explain, like, comparing things."

"You mean you wouldn't compare me to a white coat? We hear the stories about lonely men on ice, hot after those lovely young things with big brown eyes."

"Breeze!" Lliam was losing his composure. "I wasn't ready, for you."

"I wasn't ready for you neither, at first, but your brothers were."

"My brothers?"

"An' Lliam, my dear, when I was old enough to have you as much as I wanted you, you was away to Mainland fillin' your foolish head with poetry an' such. I was that warm for you, I couldn't wait."

"Gerald? Gerald laid here with you?"

"No, not Gerald."

"Not Doyle? I'd die if you laid with Doyle."

"No, not Doyle neither, though he threatened me often enough. Guess again, me love."

Lliam looked at Breeze, eyes wide; he feared it was Malich but whispered, "Garret?" He waited for a reaction, searching her lovely profile for the answer. She stared at the blue sky sprinkled with wind-driven clouds, a dreamy composure on her flushed face. "Garret?" he repeated, louder. Then he laughed. "My God! Garret. Who would've thought?"

"What's so odd about that? I'd have married Garret if he'd asked, but he never made a sign all the time we was together. He's that shy." The dreamy look returned, further away. She sighed deeply at the pleasant memory. "No, Garret never said nothing, but oh, my dear!"

"Jesus, girl! What could you be thinking of? Lay with Garret an' you'd populate Fogo with half wits."

"You're the half wit, Lliam Dwyer!" she laughed, rolling over on top, pushing him down. They kissed, playfully. The next kiss was more intense, the looks deeper, eyes searching. They began pulling at each other's clothes. Then Breeze recovered. "I can't...I'm sorry, Lliam."

"Breeze..."

"We shouldn't do this. I'm promised. Gerald expects I'm waitin'." She tried to push herself up and away but Lliam held her tight.

"What, Gerald expects a virgin? I guess it's too late for that, my girl."

"If you hold me so close, I can't stop you."

"You're not taken yet, an' I'll not let you go to Gerald without a fight." He brushed her lips tenderly with his lips, her hair, shoulders, the warm place between her full breasts...

Breeze sighed and pressed down with her whole body. She helped him raise her skirts, Lliam gathering the soft folds with tingling fingers, sliding the light summer dress to her shoulders, and away; retracing the journey to the carefully chosen undergarments, her bare skin dazzling white as Greenland ice. A chrysalis shedding her cocoon in the sun. The fresh wind felt achingly good on bare flesh, like silk...She had never experienced silk, except in books...

Dwyer's Fishing Station Same: "Heave, b'yes." The Dwyer men worked the heavy net over the gunnel of the skiff. "Heave, now! Heave, now! Heave, now!" called Malich, grunting with the effort.

There was a jerky rhythm to their movements, grunting with each new effort. The heavy trap net came up from the cold depths a few feet at a time. Easy swells surged and sucked around the glistening rocks close behind them: more fuss and foam than fury. They were used to working only spitting distance from disaster. It would have to be a good spit, down wind, but to a landsman it would seem perilously close.

The Dwyer trap net was a box affair made of tarred twine, set on a shelf of sand near the shore rocks where the bottom was gently sloping. The net, attached to four killicks, had a leader, a fence of mesh, that ran to anchors ashore. Protected from the deep Atlantic waves by a clutch of barren, tide-submerged rocks, the berth was well situated but was not on the main migration route. Their fish, survivors of the traps set from Nain up the coast of Labrador to Hamilton Inlet, were forced outside of Spotted Island, where the migrant flow swept east, then south again. Only the fringe mob skirting the shoreline passed the Dwyer berth inside of Frenchman's Island, but Malich stubbornly refused to move the station further north. Malich's gang fished long days, driving himself and his boys to exhaustion.

They strained as the bottom mesh neared the surface, forcing the fish against the far wall of the box. 'Drying out' they called it. But they weren't straining enough to suit Malich. He could tell by the lazy boil at the surface that it was a poor haul, a few hundred pounds of fish at best, but they had a good load of dry fish already on the flakes. A big final haul would have been a bonus. Luxuries for the coming winter: a supply of tobacco, bottles of rum, bolts of cloth for Mother Dwyer and new boots for all. Instead they had a few more meals to fend off starvation or bribe the spirits.

"We'll wet-salt this pitiful lot an' cut for home. No deck load this time, Lord ain't seen fit," Malich said bitterly, remembering Moses Sheen's curse. "No curse, b'yes, just the Lord's way." He spat over the lee rail and said the words again. He tried to ignore the mocking calls of the ravens wheeling over the dark headland.

"Us could eat this small lot on way home an' still sit down to supper with Gran'father," Gerald said, countering Malich's dark mood.

"What I wouldn't give for haunch o' caribou for me own supper," said Doyle, to counter both of them. "I'm that sick o' Garret's fuckin' boiled fish!"

The bottom of the trap broke the surface. Fish thrashed for freedom but their escape was blocked. The weight increased as the fish were heaved out of their element for the final swim over the gunnel. Garret put an extra effort into the pull and the thrashing fish were capsized into the boat like a small wave. Suddenly relieved of the strain Doyle slipped and went down in the bilge water.

"Curse you, Garret! You bloody idiot!"

"Here, Doyle, get up out o' that mess," laughed Gerald. "No time to be layin' down." Gerald grabbed Doyle by the collar and hauled him to his feet. Doyle came up spluttering and glistening with fish slime. Cod flopped and slithered around his boots. He picked up a big one and flung it at Garret. Garret instinctively ducked and the big fish sailed over his head, missed Malich and landed with a great splash beside the skiff. Malich made a lunge with the dip net but the fish recovered and dove away.

"Damn you, b'ye! 'Tis a curse to waste a good fish. An' that one was your own supper. If you want to eat you best go ashore an' run down that bloody caribou!"

"See'im up there now, on hill, laughin' at you, Brother, said Gerald."

Doyle glared at Gerald and Garret in turn, as if his brothers were the cause of all his worldly trials. Garret seemed to sympathize with

Doyle's discomfort but Doyle's response was to throw another fish, careful not to throw it over the side. The fish skipped on the wet pile around Gerald's feet and slithered up against the pen boards. Gerald grinned back at Doyle, which only made Doyle madder. "You wants to join that other fella, just keep lookin' at me like that."

Gerald kicked the fish back across the pen. "Temper, there, Doyle, ol' son. You'll be throwin' yourself out o' boat next."

"I'll stuff a fish in your ugly face!"

"C'mon then."

"An' while I'm at it, I'll stuff this one up your arse, where your brains's to!"

"Let's have at it then."

"Enough! Both of you," ordered Malich. "Garret an' Doyle...hoist up the bloody killicks an' leader. Me an' Gerald'll take the box."

Doyle kicked at the errant fish and clumped angrily into the dory. Garret followed, untied the painter and shoved off. Doyle sculled to the first float and Garret untied the net. They went to each corner and then released the box from the leader float and when it was freed they climbed back aboard the skiff to help Malich and Gerald haul the rest of the slubby, weed-fouled net over the rail. Silence ruled except for the grunts.

Malich primed the make'n'break engine and spun the flywheel. The one-lunger spluttered to life and got down to business, leaving Doyle and Garret scrambling to get back into the dory. The heavy skiff *chugged* and *chuffed* away around the headland toward the cove; the exhaust noise banging off the cliffs like an accusation.

Doyle and Garret began heaving up the heavy grapnel anchors. Doyle hauled hand over hand in silence, taking the weight to work out his anger. Garret coiled down the slime-grown line and gave Doyle as much room as the small dory allowed, wishing his brother would talk to him or make jokes. They hauled the leader mesh towards the shore, the dory almost awash under the weight of wet net and anchors, in danger of being dashed against the rocks.

"Keep the damned thing steady!" Doyle jumped over the bow of the pitching dory onto the rocks to release the shorelines. For Doyle the thought of drowning was less a concern than not giving an inch to his silent brother. It was a normal day for the Dwyers who had been feuding all their lives.

Aboard the *Margaret & Maude*: Malich, on his knees beside the lazarette hatch just forward of the wheel, appeared to be praying for good weather. He passed another stack of fish into the lazarette, a tight, unhandy area right aft, where gear and cargo could be stored. Gerald was down below forcing slabs of cod into every available space. A pile of dry cod still remained on the deck beside Malich but the little schooner was stuffed. The quintals of fish packed into the main hold strained the lashings on the hatch cover. Doyle and Garret had to dance on the planks so Malich and Gerald could wedge them down.

"About all she'll take, Skipper, side o' clear run to steerin' box," Gerald said, rising as if by levitation out of the hold.

The steering gear box had been leaking all season and would require attention during the voyage and repairs over the winter, Malich calculated. "Right enough. I make it near twelve quintals in lazarette, forty-two quintals in hold. Six barrels in salt an' ten barrels oil. At least we won't starve."

"What about this lot?" Gerald asked, indicating the remaining pile of dry fish.

"Lodge the rest up fore'rd."

"Not in fo'c'sle again!" protested Doyle. "Last time up we had to sit on fuckin' fish to eat our supper, an' sleep with them besides." Doyle and Garret were hoisting barrels of fish aboard using a block and tackle off the end of the fore boom. Garret was doing the hauling while Doyle guided the barrels.

"I'll put this lot handy to Doyle's bunk, then we'd never notice the smell," said Gerald, carrying an armload of slabs. Doyle pushed the barrel toward Gerald. Gerald sidestepped the pendulum's arc and turned his back to Doyle, making a farting sound. "That's for you, you stinkin' little Tommy cod."

"When it comes to that, me darlin' brother," said Doyle, catching the barrel on the back swing and guiding it down to the deck, "we'd never miss you into fog. You wants to keep a cod fish under each arm when you takes Breeze up hill, an' a big one between your legs so she ain't too disappointed." Doyle laughed in snorts until he could barely stand, sprawling over the upended barrel. Gerald had to pass Doyle returning aft and Gerald couldn't resist giving Doyle a push that almost sent him over the side. They wrestled until they were on their knees, hanging over the cap rail, strong hands on throats strangling each other: both would go and neither would let go.

Malich had seen enough. "Leave off the foolishness, now! Time to cut an' run. Get dory aboard an' lash 'er good. Gerald, finish stowin' them bloody fish. Garret, you see skiff's tied astern proper. Last time she come adrift an' we lost half a day fetchin' 'er back."

Gerald and Doyle untangled themselves with a push and a shove. Gerald tossed the rest of the fish into the fo'c'sle. Doyle climbed down to the dory to attach the sling, caught the running block and slipped the hook into the eye of the sling. Before Doyle could regain the deck, Gerald gave the hauling part a hard tug that sent Doyle sprawling over a thwart. Sharp oaths banged back and forth. Malich shook his head and dodged down to the main cabin to record their cargo in the logbook.

Garret untied the painter and led the heavy skiff aft, making hitches around the wooden grump on the starboard side. Heeding Malich's warning he made more hitches back along the painter, and another series of hitches on the port grump.

Malich, returning to the deck wearing his watch cap and sea-jacket, stood at the starboard rail looking east, beyond the guardian rocks. The deep lines of his face and the tight furrows above his eyes were not caused solely by the sun and wind. There was nothing in the blue sea or clear sky to auger badly for the voyage, but Malich seemed to be looking beyond the limits of a mortal world to some spiritual hell: a dark force lurking over the horizon. Irish spells and curses swam in his memory and he tried to discount the Sheen curse. He couldn't delay sailing. A skipper could avoid sailing on a Friday; superstition allowed a variance so as not to tempt fate, but that was a sailor's unwritten law. Otherwise a sailor leaves harbour when the vessel is ready to sail and takes the consequences. "Good Lord, you know we don't need no more trouble. Jesus, Mary an' Joseph, if I don't get this load o' fish home it's the Devil to pay."

Dwyer's Kitchen: Lliam's journal. *I'd cut and run if there was a place to go to get away from this crowd. Why I ever come home is a question I'll never answer, except for Breeze, but I doubt she'll come away with me before it's too late. If I only had the courage I'd challenge Gerald...*

An outport kitchen is a cozy refuge when the whole family gathers and the cook stove sends comforting gouts of steam from boiling kettles. The kitchen is the focus of the home: the meeting place, the working space. For the laundry and for late night courting on the daybed, the social and recuperative center, the hospice and the place where the body of the newly deceased is prepared for the final journey. The parlour is reserved for the wake, prayers and formalities, so that the real wake, the socializing, could go on in the kitchen. The bedrooms above are only used for sleeping, procreation and birth, as well as dying. The kitchen door is the main portal, leading to the bridge, wharf or stage, the fenced yard, the garden and the store: the man's workshop. The kitchen always has at least two windows that look out on the harbour. Other windows have a view of the ocean, well-worn paths, gardens and the neighbour's house, often only a short spit away.

An outport kitchen with part of the family away fishing is still a refuge, but the remaining family members are on edge, waiting for arrivals or news.

Grandfather Dwyer rocked and smoked beside the stove, looking into space, like Malich, bridging the miles. He knew every act in the drama of fishing the Labrador. Had spent half a century at sea or making the yearly run Down North, jerking fish over the gunnel; the endless hours, the cost in health and lives, the slim rewards, the cold, the danger, the disappointments. But there were the splendid sailing days when the sun dazzled the helmsman's eyes and the fresh wind pressed the sails taut as drumheads. Then there were the deadly storms that lashed the coast and drove the sea into a frenzy of foam and a sailor to despair. On the dark nights of cold fog or stinging sleet, he prayed he was in the hands of God, and not the terrible grip of the Iron Coast. Grandfather had lost friends and relatives to the sea, could trace their faces in every wave. He smoked and rocked and missed the times fishing or crossing oceans. Would love to make one more run, always one more time 'down'. "Malich should be near cleaned up an' ready to cut for home," he said, between puffs.

"Dare say," agreed Mother Dwyer, Margaret to her friends. She dumped a bowl of turnips into the big cooking kettle, stirring the pot with a timeworn wooden spoon. Bread pans waited near the oven, dough expanding in the close, steamy heat, rising to glory to feed the family for another few days. The kettle steamed and the dough heaved up, but beyond that the big kitchen was barren. The food supply was nearly gone. Only the sparse, flinty garden stood between them and starvation if the season failed.

"I taught'im that," Grandfather puffed. "Malich, I says, you cut an' run 'fore the equinox. You can't go wrong if you're clear o' Labrador 'fore the fall gales. Betimes you could lay by into October month, an' wait 'til they've had their way, then run on up with the Nor'westers. Clear weather then, my dear, the finest kind; the Hindian Summer we calls it."

"We knows, my dear," said Grandmother, rocking and knitting on the other side of the stove. "You've been tellin' we that very same thing for fifty-odd years. I think us got the story by now."

Grandfather continued as if she wasn't there. "...Now Malich's got to teach them young'uns, an' that other one...what's his name, Mother? The new one from away?"

"Lliam," answered Grandmother.

"Who?"

"Lliam!" shouted Grandmother.

"Lliam Dwyer. Your own Gran'son," sighed Margaret.

"Lliam is it? I knows that, to be sure, a denser crowd o' b'yes I never seen. Shockin', 'tis. Sooner sleep then eat, clear o' Garret."

"Garret's a good boy," agreed Margaret.

"They's all goin' down in the same basket just the same. Mark me!"

The sudden harsh pronouncement cast a chill over the heated kitchen. Margaret counted the loaves. Seven. She made the sign of the cross, saying, "Jesus, Mary an' Joseph, forgive me." She had forgotten Lliam, and what else? Besides her youngest son home, like the Prodigal Returned, there was little food to greet Malich. She had a gnawing fear about their season and there was also Breeze O'Keefe to deal with. The shocking antics of her son and Breeze were already village gossip. She spoke to the loaves of bread, her solace in times of doubt. "I had a terrible dream last night. All of us was into the smoke, thick as any fog I ever seen, an' fire droppin' all around like rain, an' us treadin' on the sparks, only sparks turned to snakes an' drove away."

"No snakes on Fogo, sure!" shouted Grandfather, who was perfectly able to hear when it suited him.

"Bad luck to say a dream in mornin', Margaret dear," cautioned Grandmother. "You've got to wait 'til night falls an' the Devil's asleep or nosin' around for Protestants to torment."

Margaret opened the fire door. A spark jumped out and burned her hand. She turned away from the others in pain but said nothing. Grandmother talked on...

"...Aunt Sadie was the one for interpretin' dreams. Do you mind the time her oldest son was killed in war? 'Twere a good many months later when the news came about that terrible battle. What did they call that ruckus in France, Father?"

"Ruckus? The Regiment died all standin' in Battle of the Some-such-River. July First it was. Cousin Ned was there, sure, an' John Flynn, my sister's eldest...Beaumont somethin'...."

"But Sadie, she fashioned it out from a dream. The day was the very same. An' there was the time when the *Greenland* went down up to Gulf with all hands an' a log load o' sculps? Sadie's brother was onto'er an' she know'd it that very mornin'. We never heard 'bout that awful thing for weeks, my dears. But Sadie knew, an' she never told a soul, feared it might be true. An' 'twas. Poor souls. Sadie knew 'twas true."

Lliam entered the kitchen with a rush of wind and banged the door shut. He looked disheveled and flushed, but pleased with himself. He heard the last of Grandmother's statement. "What's true, old girl? That you're the best looking thing in all Fogo?" He held his hands out over the stove top, rubbing them together. Grandfather stared at Lliam as if he was a stranger. "I'm that starved I could eat..." he looked into the cauldron, "...boiled turnips. Hope there's a bit o' fish in that stew."

"There's fish enough, to give it a taste," said Margaret, avoiding Lliam's eyes.

"And how's Grandfather this fine day?"

"There's to be some bread if ever I get an oven hot enough, but you'll have to work for it. You'll find a nice little stack o' wood your brothers made 'fore they sailed."

"Children nowadays don't understand a thing about work."

"I'd split a tree with my bare teeth for a taste o' fish'n'brewis."

"...Them don't understand a thing."

"Too true old man," Lliam said, chuckling. "And if you think it's a muckery on this island, you should see them over to Mainland. In Boston an' New York there's grown men sliding around the city streets wearing the most gosh awful getups this side o' Mummer's days. Calls themselves Zoot-suiters. They don't do a blessed thing all day except slide around, swinging long chains an' holding up light posts, drinking swill out of cola bottles. Worse than screech, sure."

"Light posts? Why do they hafta hold 'em up? Are they like gaffs, with pitch burnin'?"

"No, no, Gran'father. Light posts are like strouters, stuck into ground with lights on top. Some burn gas and others are electric...bulbs that burn like fire."

"Dare say!" exclaimed Grandfather. "Why'd they want to do that?"

"Light up the streets. Turns the night to day."

"Them Mainlanders feared o' dark?"

"Truth to tell...a man ain't safe to walk dark streets in the city for fear some land pirate puts a knife to your throat an' extracts your loose change, for no other reason than he's thirsty and there's a pub across the alley."

"What's this sorry world comin' to? She's all goin' down in the same basket, if you asks me."

"And that's not all, old man. You should see what the dance hall girls do to themselves: lips coloured and skirts hiked up to here." He showed Grandfather how high. Grandfather grinned at a memory. He'd been around the world on sailing ships and had seen worse in shadier ports, but never told all the tales to the family.

Margaret had heard enough silly man talk. "You were with Breeze O'Keefe up hill just now."

Lliam pulled up sharp with all sails back and sheets flogging. He should have known that not a breath is taken nor an oath uttered, that isn't common knowledge throughout the village, especially if the event is as shocking as cavorting on the hill in plain daylight. Adolescent mating games often take place near the Fortress, in good weather, not worth watching, but the pairing of a betrothed and a Prodigal Son was news. Lliam looked out the window at the harbour, searching for an explanation, or a convenient lie.

"What's this sorry world comin' to?" asked Grandfather, leaning forward for more of the story. "The children's all awash I tell you. My sonny boy, them's got no more sense than dead skate rottin' on wharf!"

"Ah, Breeze and me...we're just friends. Like we was as kids, you know?"

"Don't lie to me, Lliam! Mary came by while I was hangin' out wash. Brigid O'Keefe told Mary she seen you an' Breeze up hill."

"We were just talking."

"You wasn't talkin' neither! Mary said you two was lyin' down."

"We were just talking..."

"Mary seen you! Hardly a stitch between you an' God. Talkin'? Mary said you two was humpin' away like randy sheep."

"Damn this place," he whispered

"An' Breeze betrothed to your own brother. Poor Gerald, away at the fish an' can't answer the hurt."

Grandmother continued knitting. Grandfather sucked his pipe and rocked until he nearly went over backwards with excitement. "Children ain't got the sense o' dead mackerel. Lay out in sun an' get right dried up."

Lliam exploded. "All right then! Since the whole bloody village knows. I love Breeze. Always have, since we were kids. It's not a sin to love someone."

"It's a sin to go away while the ones you leave behind has put lives on a different course, an' then you come back an' turn things upside down!"

"Yis, b'yes! Got the tiller 'ard over now!" interjected Grandfather.

"I only came back to make a life for me an' Breeze."

"An' what do you think you're goin' to do? You don't want to go at the fish. You've neither trade, nor job on Mainland. All you got is some fancy way o' talkin' to make us all out to be foolish. Poor Gerald."

"Breeze never wanted to marry *poor* Gerald. She only said yes because you all said she should. I'll take her away, if she wants to go." He didn't sound convinced.

"An' break your poor brother's heart? Gerald needs that girl. It's time he was startin' a family."

"Is that all you think Breeze is good for? To make a home an' make babies?"

"You don't understand the way of it, Lliam. Gerald has to raise sons to feed us all when we get on. Who's goin' to do it? You? You goin' to send money from Boston to keep us from starvin' when Malich's no good for it?"

"You think of her as a slave. Well she's not! She's a free spirit. She doesn't belong in some god-lost outport making babies in the middle of the bloody Atlantic!"

Grandmother finally spoke up. "Lliam Dwyer, don't talk to your mother in that tone. You're not that old I can't take you over my knee."

"That's the ticket, Mother!" shouted Grandfather. "Take'e down to fish room an' put'e over barrel, like me ol' dad used to do...Likes I used to do with Malich when'e got the wind up."

"The proof's ruined." Margaret turned her back on Lliam, angrily ejecting lumps of dough from the pans, punching them together.

"Perhaps if Malich had done that very thing more often...such foolishness." She addressed the dough as if Lliam wasn't there.

"Foolishness?" Lliam cried, circling the table. "I was a fool to go away, but it's not foolishness. I won't have you bring it down to that, Mother. You people have been shut up on this bloody little island too long!"

Margaret slammed the mound of dough with her fist. "Our people came from a *bloody little island,* an' life was no different there, my son. You work for a livin' just the same, an' suffer for no good reason other than 'tis God's way...an' there's sins an' there's foolish sins."

"Why do you go on about sin? What did we do wrong?"

"What if Gerald an' Breeze O'Keefe was already married?"

The table was between Lliam and the door. "I won't listen to this tirade another moment."

Margaret left off pounding the dough into moist submission. "You'll fetch in wood if you want your supper," she said calmly, glaring at her son.

Lliam was confounded by his mother's logic, stopped cold by the simplicity of her statement. He stood watching the woman he hardly knew, remembered only as the 'house woman'. She had conceived and nursed him, but he had no memories of a warm breast, or soothing hands after a scrap with his brothers. Could not remember softness. There wasn't time. She had always been a handsome but stern-faced outport mother, raising four troublesome boys, spending her days in the kitchen: forever kneading mounds of dough, washing clothes and stirring pots, casting red eyes to the window. Venturing out only to dig in the garden, to turn cod or string squid and attend burials. He remembered little of a childhood beyond the fights, the hunger and the cold. Breeze was his lighthouse in the dark sea, growing up in a marginal outport where winters and summers danced around the seasons and games were preparation for the adult world. And it was only when he was growing into manhood that he saw Breeze as more than a playmate and his Fortress Queen.

Their relationship changed when passion interfered. Lliam did not understand the feeling of love, never having experienced the sensation.

The pain of his physical need to make love to Breeze terrified him. To Lliam it was one more threat, like the pinch of hunger or the searing pain of freezing seawater. Yes, he had run, but he had run from fear. He learned about lust in the beds of Boston. Didn't have what it takes to be a man, a responsible man...even a sexual man, or a hard driving man like his father...If Malich was his father. When Lliam ran from Béhathook Cove he was running from himself as well as Breeze, and perhaps the truth of Breeze.

"God Almighty! I can't believe this! Yes, my darling mother, I'll fetch your bloody wood, if that's all there is to it." Lliam stormed out, slamming the door.

Grandfather jumped. "Now what do you suppose makes these young'uns bang about so? They've no more sense than, that door...my son!"

Grandmother clacked her needles, a soothing sound of industry, and watched the old man relighting his pipe. She remembered the long days when her new husband spent summer days away in the dory, 'gunnin' for turrs,' he assured her, although she had her doubts. Talk about foolishness. The number of sea birds he returned with could have been shot around the headland in an hour's time. Then he was gone away as master on foreign voyages, then home summers, gone again to Change Islands. She heard the rumours. She wasn't fooled, but she knew better than to object.

Grandfather disappeared into a cloud of smoke, also remembering those days as a young man, rowing a dory the fifteen miles to Change Island. 'The Duty' done he'd row home again with a few birds and retell the lie...He could hear the axe *thunking* as Lliam took out his anger on the spruce. He was remembering the creaking rope whiffs on the thole pins and the stroke of the oars, the measured dip and pull, heedless of the waves or the weather. He was strong then. Hot youth and foolishness ruled. But 'The Duty' done...

Margaret slammed the bread dough. "My, oh my...an' what are we goin' to do 'bout poor Gerald?"

Breeze cried softly as she peeled potatoes with the well-worn throating

54

knife, hacking off chunks of rind rather than peeling with her usual deftness. Her thick black hair hung in wisps and tangles, still adorned with bits of moss.

Mother O'Keefe rocked in time to Breeze's sobs, the chair squeaking as if the runners were squeezing out the tears. She looked like the figurehead on a pitching ship, staring down, watching Breeze until a chunk spun away.

"Look what you're about now! Wastin' half those poor things an' we've no pig to feed," she said, as though it were Breeze's fault they were pigless. "An' you can stop that snivelin'. I'm the one what's been harmed. The whole village knows, sure."

"You had to tell Mary O'Hara."

"Could I walk to Dwyer's with news like that? An' what are you goin' to tell Gerald when he comes home?"

"There's nothing to tell."

"I seen you with me own eyes, girl! Rollin' about on ground with that no-good Go Boy, an' him pawin' you, an' you both...well, now what I saw made me ashamed."

"I'm not ashamed. I don't care if the whole world knows!"

"There's a punishment waitin' those who flaunt His rules."

"Lliam begged me to go with him, but I said no. Want to know why? Because I'm bound to look after you 'til the day you die...so I'm bound to look after Gerald Dwyer as well. If it's punishment you're talkin' about, that's punishment enough to last a lifetime."

Mother O'Keefe stopped rocking, hands clenched on the curved arms of the chair, as if poised to spring. "That's right, break me poor heart, just like Sean O'Keefe did when he left me with a young whelp who has no heart an' no love for the one who bore her."

"I was a child when Sean left. How could I be blamed for that?" Breeze wanted to go to her mother. It was a natural inclination, but she, like Lliam, had never known the gentle hand or spiritual nurturing. But unlike Lliam, Breeze's emotional neglect was from indifference rather than the physical necessities of a hard life on the edge. She attacked instead. "Why did Sean O'Keefe leave you?"

A guilty look crossed Brigid Ortiz's face. Breeze interpreted it's meaning: confirmation on the side of the ledger that added up to the truth about her origin. "This'll come to no good end, you mark my words, child..."

The *Margaret & Maude* Coast of Newfoundland: A well-found schooner, racing the waves, is a harmony of elements. There were days, the old timers say, when heading up from Labrador with a log-load of fish and a quartering wind, a fisherman could ask for nothing more in the way of God's blessing; equal to strong sons and a good wife. They speak of sparkling autumn days with fresh westerly winds that make the sheets hum; a thrumming cadence accompanied by the drumming sails and taut connection between the keel and the rigging; boiling seas hissing past a black hull and seasoned wood creaking in time to the roll. A good sailing ship is a singular instrument in a symphony that has been playing out on the oceans of the world for centuries. Without fanfare or applause, with only the blue sea, the high sun and flying clouds as witness, the elements of sound shipbuilding and seamanship render a performance unmatched for lyrical beauty, even if the supporting characters are louts and ruffians, like the Dwyers and the Sheens.

Garret was enjoying a rare idle moment at the bow, mesmerized by the frothing tumble of the bow waves and the sense of speed, and ahead was their island home: a warm kitchen and a comfortable bed. He'd worked hard and earned a moment's peace from the rough labour and taunts of his boorish brothers.

Malich Dwyer at the helm, like his father before him, knew the way home as well as he knew the path from their stage to their kitchen door. The humble schooner, *Margaret and Maude*, laden with salt fish, driven by a smart wind off the North East Peninsula, her patched and prayed-over sails drawing tight, slashed her way south, putting Cape Bauld behind her by noon. The high cliffs were three miles distant but appeared to loom over the tiny vessel as if they would swallow her whole. The real danger though, the low-lying White Rocks, only a half mile away to starboard, seemed ten miles distant; an optical illusion that could cost a mariner his ship even in clear weather. But on a good day the lighthouses, headlands and traditional steering marks are familiar signposts that keep the wary sailor safe enough. At Cape Bauld there had been a bank of fog and a late iceberg trailing the tide southwest along the Strait of Belle Isle, drifting toward Point Amour and the French Coast, but Malich was headed Southeast for Fogo. The familiar coastal passage as safe as being in bed, he assured himself.

Malich, who knew the elements could turn with cold indifference, was steering by dead reckoning, making the best time possible. He respected the ocean and its allies: wind and fog, but he considered the elements as accessories to his main concern: survival. He feared fire and the curses hurled at him by Moses Sheen and it was the Sheen curse occupying his thoughts as his schooner rushed homeward. His heart didn't sing with the rigging, nor did he wax lyrical about the bursts of jeweled spray off her shapely bow. Drum-taut canvas and straining sheets meant miles put astern. He was not steering a winged chariot or Neptune's Car. He was a workingman and his boat was his necessary vehicle, like a farmer's reliable old tractor, nothing more. "Moses Sheen be damned, and all the bloody Sheens I ever knowed," he said, spitting tobacco juice over the lee rail into the frothing wake. "Garret, get below an' make up our tea!"

Doyle and Gerald sat on the lee side of the main hatch with their backs against the combing, feet braced against the cap rail, sharing a rum bottle. They hooted and cursed each time the bow dug deep into the steep face of a swell. The giddy decent into the trough began as the schooner raced over the crest of a wave, then surfed down its backside and dove into the next, throwing green water up and away. The west wind curled the spray over their heads and showered the deck with diamonds. Each drenching was cause for a drink. Malich disapproved of their moronic behaviour but let it pass. He had driven them hard since March on the sealing ice and then down to Labrador. A day of acting the fool and singing ribald songs was little enough reward for their reluctant industry. *Thank God for Garret,* he thought. But he couldn't resist causing them some discomfort.

"Gerald! Doyle! Fores'l wants a tug up. An' ease the jib a touch!"

The brothers, like Tweedle Dumb and Tweedle Dee, grumbled and rolled to their feet. Gerald tucked the rum bottle under a flap of canvas. "Wait there. We're not finished with you."

They sweated up the throat halyard to tighten the luff. Malich knew it would be a hard pull with the wind pressing on the drum-taut canvas and the boat pitching over the steep waves. The big waves from the Southeast running Northwest to exhaust their energy pounding the unyielding shore rocks, were stacked up higher by the shoaling water of White Rock Ledge.

It was a routine adjustment, and could be called upon when necessary to punish his sons. The wet manila halyards, bar tight as they were from saltwater, came in reluctantly. A handybilly tackle was necessary to gain the extra purchase. The blocks protested but the throat of the gaff rose a few inches, drawing the luff tighter. Then the peak halyard was sweated up. Gerald cleated the line and looked aft. Malich cast his gaze shoreward. No acknowledgment or sign.

Gerald gave Doyle a shove aft to tend the jib sheet. Doyle had only to loosen the lee jib sheet and let a few inches run out. The jib bagged nicely. Malich nodded his approval. They would soon be safely past the dangerous White Rocks, with Storm Cape and Griguet Harbour abeam beyond the White Rocks. The next mark would be St. Lunaire Bay opening with St. Lunaire Peak, angling away from the coast with names like Great Brechat Bay, Cremaillere Harbour, Cap Haut et Bas and Notre Dame Island: a legacy of the years the French fishing fleets dominated the Northeast Coast. Then they would have a clear offing to Fogo Island, running free, carried along on the Labrador Current. If the wind held...If luck held, and curses were foiled...

Gerald and Doyle resumed their drinking station, backs to the wind, facing the sun, passing the bottle, hoping the old man wouldn't find another sail adjustment.

"Ol' man's just thinkin' up 'nother job for we, guaranteed," said Doyle, tipping the bottle to his thick, wind-burned lips.

"Right enough, an' if he can't find a job o' work for we today, he's already schemin' to refit this ol' bummer before March month. Seen him given her too close a look 'fore we left Labrador. Sure sign the ol' man's jiggin' up a grand job. An' guess who's the b'yes what got to slog aroun' in muck all winter with oakum for hair and tar running out our noses like snot?"

"Job I hate best is paintin' the bottom o' this fuckin' ol' scow. Corkin' ain't so bad. Least it stays where you puts it to. Fuckin' cheap paint Malich mixes up runs down on we like bilge water."

"Just needs to boil up the cod oil longer. Make'er thick like lassie an' then puttin' 'er on with broom an' run like hell." Gerald laughed, took the bottle and gulped a big draught.

"Here, Gerald! That's got to last a nice while."

"Don't worry, me son, I've another soldier tucked under Garret's bunk. Swore I'd break his leg if'e told ol' man. I'm tempted to fashion out a good big head, then eat whatever mess Garret makes up, an' then sleep 'til Little Fogo Island's abeam."

"Ol' man'll have other ideas, sure."

"*Ahh*, jink the 'ol' man. He's due to find'is heart any day now. You can steer us home while I sleep."

"Right enough, an' what should I do with the body? There's nary room in hold, nor salt enough."

"Prop he up in skiff with one hand on pecker an' other up his bung hole."

Doyle was taking a swig and almost choked. "Ah, Gerald me son, you have a way with words. Then we could paint this ol' boat any colour clear o' black. How about blue? Nice blue, like that water way off there?" Doyle pointed with the bottle to a cloud shadow patch of indigo.

Gerald took the bottle. "You lame brain, blue's bad luck onto boat. Specially dark blue."

"That's just woman's talk, sure."

"No, 'tis true! You heared the story 'bout this schooner built by buddy over to Bonavista? Skipper loans the money from merchant an' builds he a nice little thing, 'bout sixty-ton. Proper boat for Labrador, eh? When time comes to paint'er up, Skipper orders black paint as usual."

"That's it, see. Just like I say. Fuckin' boat's always black. What's the matter with blue for change?"

"Merchant says the same thing, an' he orders blue paint instead. There was *some* ruckus when the merchant shows up with blue paint. Buddy an' Skipper near come to blows. Skipper swears up an' down that he's not puttin' blue paint on his schooner. Merchant reminds Skipper that she's *his* schooner 'cause he put up the money an' if Skipper don't like it he can shove off for Cobb's Arm. Skipper has to give in an' paint that boat blue an' launch'er off."

"So, what's the fuckin' story from that?"

"I'll tell you, Doyle, you moron." Gerald took a drink to emphasis the seriousness of the tale. "Fifteen years to the very day she was launched off, she strikes a growler in night an' sinks with all hands, not five miles from Kate Harbour where she was built."

"Fifteen years? That's a fuckin' miracle lifetime for these beat up ol' boats, sure! Where's the bad luck into'er?"

Gerald took another swallow to draw out the tale. "Well, me son, that merchant by'n'by retires, an' decides to take a little chance down Labrador an' visit his fishin' rooms. Buddy never seen the Labrador or the miserable place his fishermen spend their time toilin' for his fortune, see, an' not only that, but 'twas the only time that merchant set foot on his blue boat, an' she answers by goin' straight-away to bottom."

"An' what's the proof o' that?"

"She waited fifteen years to get'im, see?"

"G'wan, Gerald, 'tis pure foolishness. Your head's load lined. Give us that bottle."

"Then answer me this. It wasn't ol' Skipper at the wheel when she took the hook. Skipper died in his bed years 'fore that. Merchant's own son was skipper now, an' he never wanted to paint'er blue neither. Now, Doyle, you sod, tell me that ain't won'erful strange."

"Strange may be, but 'taint no clue to bad luck. My son, Gerald, you do come up with the queerest ideas. Good thing Garret can't talk."

But Garret could hear. He listened to Gerald's story while peeling the last of their rotting potatoes, adding them to the boiling pot on the Fisherman stove. Garret's stove burned coal and could be fired to red heat. That day the stiff wind on the starboard quarter was blowing down the companion way and at the same time sucking the smoke out the short chimney. Efficient as a forge bellows and only the deck iron kept the metal pipe from charring the planking...Garret had left the slide draft of the firebox wide open to get the damp coal burning, using a cup of thick coal-oil to start the fire. He wanted to hurry the midday meal and get back on deck to enjoy the sun. To stand at the bow feeling the motion of the boat racing the waves, and taste the salt tang. He didn't mind the spray that left his lips tingling and the salt crystals on his skin, like dried up tears. A pleasant relief from having his nose constantly in fish or stew pots...The rancid lard in the big frying pan was reaching smoking heat. The left over pork bits, flies and other unidentified solids collected over the summer in the fat, sizzled and hissed. Garret was frying fresh cod dipped in flour, a change from boiled salt fish.

Garret couldn't talk but he could whistle. As he cut the cod into chunks and dredged them with flower and pepper, he whistled a tune from last year's Christmas celebration. A Celtic reel played in the steaming Dwyer kitchen by Malich and neighbours. They danced and stomped into the wee hours.

Garret had danced as hard as any; danced the hardest with Breeze, who matched him step for step until Gerald ended Garret's delirium of happiness by throwing him out the door into a snow bank. Garret forgot the pain and humiliation and kept the dance alive by humming and whistling the tune whenever he worked. His version was halting and tuneless but it spoke of his mood. He was happy to be sailing home. He was happy to be with his cruel brothers and brutal father on a successful season and he was happy that soon he would gaze on Breeze O'Keefe again. She always had a kind look, which made him shy and withdrawn, but filled him with an inner glow, remembering the exquisite pain of their love making and the amazed look on Breeze's face as her first deep orgasm seized her body with the fire of her desire, the ecstasy like an epiphany. He worshipped Breeze but didn't know how to tell her. And if he showed any sign Gerald would beat him to a bloody pulp or throw him off the nearest stage into the harbour. Garret suffered both love and fear in silence...

The rogue wave rose out of the sea like a malevolent hand to slap the impertinent schooner down. It was an unnecessarily violent act, like striking an exuberant child simply for having fun. The schooner had risen to the first rogue wave, climbing higher and higher. First Malich, then Doyle and Gerald sensed the rogue's vanguard and braced for the inevitable deep dive. An opposing gust of wind blew the crest backward in a burst of curling spray and at the same time drove the little schooner over the edge, careening headlong into the trough, bowing in supplication at the foot of the master. Heavily laden with fish, and obeying the laws of gravity, she smashed into the next on-rushing sea with all her force. The wall of green water enveloped the helpless vessel and the men on deck could only gasp and hold on. The sun was blotted out. Blue sky disappeared, replaced by a luminescent green. The wave collapsed majestically in an explosion of foam and a crushing weight that slammed the crew to the deck and pinned them there breathless.

An agony of time passed before the little ship rose again. Had the giant raked the vessel from stem to stern, instead of collapsing on them, the crew would have been carried overboard. Instead, Malich wrapped himself around the wheel and held his breath. Doyle clung to Gerald. Gerald wrapped one arm around Doyle and the other around the deck pump. Water charged with foaming fury around the deck, spilling solid over the rails, tearing at the dory's lashings. The dory came adrift and was smashed against the main mast, then went over the side in splinters. The spent sea poured over the lee rail and through the scuppers as the schooner staggered to the surface. Doyle narrowly missed being crushed by an errant barrel of cod oil as it rolled over the rail with the last rush of water. The little schooner stalled and sat in irons, fore sails flogging like demented things, then, relieved of the weight, shook herself free like a water dog. Malich was dumbfounded as the schooner wallowed in the trough. Gerald and Doyle, waiting for Malich's orders, rolled back and forth in the chaos of rigging and splintered wood.

Doyle rolled clear of his brother and sat up. "Brother, your arm's all akimbo."

"My son!" Gerald had been so twisted around his right arm was pulled out of the socket, but he never let go of the pump or Doyle. Together they unwrapped the useless arm from the base of the deck pump.

"You're all undone, ol' man."

"My son, that's a queer thing," he said studying the odd angle, the elbow pointing at his nose. "Now how do you suppose I'm going to hold a bottle with this fix up? Better give me a drink now, Doyle, I thinks she's comin' on to pain."

"Doyle! Gerald!!" bawled Malich. "The sheets! Let go the bloody fore sheets!"

"Got to get Gerald a bottle," answered Doyle in shock.

Doyle stumbled forward to the companionway, bracing against the roll of the schooner as she wallowed in the trough of the big waves. She rose to the crest, heeled down by the wind in her rigging, the sheets flogging and the sails snapping like rifle reports.

No one thought of Garret trapped in the fo'c'sle. Garret's first instinct, when he felt the bow rise higher and higher, was to close the companionway doors. He was climbing the ladder as the schooner dove over the first big wave. Flung backwards by the impact, he turned to face the stove, arms outstretched. The frying pan was sliding, tipping, the smoking grease rushing over his hands and the stovetop and into the firebox. The fire roared out of control. Garret capsized the boiling kettle but that only carried the flaming grease onto the deck. Old planks, grease-soaked with years of spilled fat, ignited like tinder. Garret opened his mouth in a silent scream.

Doyle saw the smoke, lurched to the companionway and threw open the doors. The fo'c'sle was a mass of flames. Doyle staggered back in disbelief. "Fire!!...Garret's down there!" Orange flames and black smoke burst out of the companionway. Doyle, almost paralyzed with fear, fell back. Gerald pushed him out of the way with his good arm, turned and backed down the ladder before Doyle could recover. Gerald disappeared into a dark cloud framed in orange, like the Devil descending into Hell with a backward glance and a grin. Doyle recoiled and croaked out..."Pa...Fire!"

In moments the little schooner was transformed from a well-found sailing machine, obeying the laws of nature, to a yawing, thrashing beast out of control. Malich, uncomprehending what Doyle was yelling, cursed the flogging sails, angry with his drunken sons. The schooner was caught broadside in the trough of the waves. The wind screamed in the rigging, green water crashed aboard. The motion was absurd, the rigging tearing at fittings, booms and gear thrashing about, and sails beginning to rip loose from their boltropes.

The galley fire was out of control but still contained in the small fo'c'sle, the smoke torn from the galley port, racing away downwind in shreds. It was not unusual for smoke to be coming from the galley when Garret cooked. Malich allowed Garret to cook only when they were going downwind to avoid the stench of burning coal. He could not see the fire in the fo'c'sle, only the look of terror on Doyle's face.

"What's got into you, Doyle?"

"Gerald's down there!"

"We have to heave to, damn you! Get stays'l freed up...let fores'l go!!"

Doyle, dumbfounded by Malich's orders, didn't move until the schooner threw her starboard rail down. Another barrel broke free and rolled at him. He jumped aside and it smashed into the base of the foremast. A cascade of amber oil flooded the deck, leaving the wet planks shining as if a glitter storm had passed.

Malich cursed Doyle and let the jib sheet fly. The jib went into a paroxysm of slashing and flogging, the sheets jumping about like skipping ropes gone berserk. He released the main sheet to haul the big mainsail taut to force her head. The fore and main were still drawing, forcing her head more to windward, but only far enough to keep the ship in the trough. He wanted to turn into the wind, to 'heave to' until they could sort out the mess, but the foresail had to be eased and the staysail let go.

"Where's Gerald!!?..." Malich screamed over the racket. Doyle hung on, shaking his head. "Where's Gerald!!?...Damn you!" Malich had a vision of Gerald washed over the side. He managed to harden up the main sheet to bring the big sail amidships. The schooner answered and ranged ahead, gathering steerage, but still not enough for Malich to bring her head up to windward, Gerald's only chance if he *was* overboard. He leapt for the wheel. The bow moved only a few degrees "Doyle!! Are you deaf as well as dumb? Let go fores'l!!" The schooner was now sailing hard for the White Rocks, that malevolent patch of sunkers that guard the Southwest approaches to White Island. The 'White Rocks' is a low, jagged ledge that jumps up to the surface from sixty fathoms in less than half a mile. Malich knew it. Doyle knew it. Malich was shouting curses at Doyle. Doyle could hear screams of pain below his feet. He was sailor enough to know that they had to sail downwind, not heave to, or it would be impossible to rescue his brothers from the fire.

"Pa!!...Turn down wind!! They're down there!!" Doyle pointed downwind. Malich saw the gestures but he also saw the White Rocks dead ahead. He would have to tack the schooner across the wind before he could heave to, or head Northeast out to sea, too late to save Gerald, so he believed. Doyle kept motioning to turn to port, downwind. Malich shook his head and pointed to starboard.

"You bloody fool! Have you lost what little brains God give you!!? I said, *let go fore'ard!!*"

Doyle was being flogged senseless by the jib sheets. He shook his head wildly, unable to let go of the mast and risk being sent over the rail. He freed an arm to point again at the companionway.

Malich fought the wheel, trying in vain to make his ship cross the wind. His view of the tragedy was blocked by the masts and he still didn't see the flames, the open companionway or the hairless figure clutching at the sill, trying to pull himself up with raw hands, flesh melting away, sticking to the wood like wet dough. The blackened head emerged slowly, eyes wild, white teeth too stark. Lips pulled back, mouth open in a noiseless scream. The body gave a sudden lurch as if butted from behind. Doyle thought he heard the scream, but couldn't be sure in the rush of terrible events and confusion. Then the hideous thing sprawled on the glittering deck at Doyle's feet and the Devil had his hand on his shoulder.

Malich saw the smoking body roll toward the scuppers. He couldn't place it in the present context. It looked like a seal that had just been clubbed to death on the ice, skinned and still steaming. A boarding sea, frothing and churning, erased the vision, but Malich knew a terrible thing had happened to one of his sons.

The hull rose and fell. The keel struck the ledge and the schooner stopped in her tracks. A shiver went through her and she staggered back as if a living thing had been dealt a mortal blow. Another sound was added to the nightmare: wood grinding against the rocks. The wave that smothered the burning body came over the starboard rail, thrown back by the barrier ledge of the White Rocks Bank. The schooner, still trying to sail forward, staggered again and again as her keel slammed down on the unyielding rocks. Prevented from going forward, she spun on her keel to face the wind. Thick grey smoke boiled toward the stern and Malich knew in one heart breaking moment what Doyle was trying to tell him. "Oh, my sons...They can't live in that!"

Béhathook Cove Two days later: Lliam wrote: *It's a fine day. I'm going to ask Breeze to come for a row in the Rodney. Many were the good times we had in the old boat, when all of us were young, before my brothers became louts and idiots. They were always bullies. Breeze hasn't changed, just more beautiful. Today I'll ask her one last time to go away with me. Don't know what I'll do if she says no. Kill Gerald for sure, is all I can think of...*

Lliam Dwyer found the rhythm of the stroke and sent the Rodney skimming across the ripples of the cove towards the tickle. Rowing hard, back to the warm sun, looking at Breeze O'Keefe sitting in the stern, dress pulled up to avoid the sloshing bilge water. "She'll take up. Always did leak a drop after a layup."

"I hope 'tis soon, or we'll drown before we get to the Head," said Breeze in her lilting, teasing way.

"I'd almost forgot about this old boat."

"You forgot many things."

"I never forgot you."

"I don't believe that for a moment, Lliam Dwyer." She said it with a smile but intended to make him pay the price for his neglect. How long he paid depended on many things. "I, at least, looked after myself the while."

"Old boat lay just where I left'er, but you didn't," he countered.

"No, I was used regular enough, an' had to repair myself, didn't I?"

Lliam dodged the painful subject of her forced infidelity, since it was Lliam that had abandon her to his brothers. "Gran'father built she for me when I was just a lad. I think it was the last boat he ever built. Once, Gerald tried to burn her 'cause he was jealous. See the marks there?" He pointed with a bare toe to a place under the stern sheets where the wood was blackened. Breeze had to lift her skirts higher and spread her legs to bend down to see. When she sat up she stretched her bare legs across the thwart, straddling him, raising her skirt for Lliam to see. "Lliam, you're goin' off course, unless you want to visit Uncle 'ebert's stage."

Uncle Hebert was busy on the stage-head cleaning up some fish. He had a full view of Breeze's white thighs and Sunday-best panties. Lliam looked away in time to avoid the head of Uncle Hebert's wharf, grazing the spruce strouters with the blade of the oar. Breeze shrieked and laughed and showed Uncle Hebert more. Uncle Hebert cast his eyes away, making a strange clucking sound with his tongue. "My sonny boy!" he breathed, blushing. Within hours all the men gathered in stores and on stages around the harbour would be apprised, in detail, of what Uncle Hebert had seen, *'as close as dat!'* Breeze and Lliam, and Gerald, would be discussed at length. Conclusions drawn. The prognosis was not good.

Lliam regained control of the Rodney, if not his own composure, shaping their course for the open water beyond the entrance to the small harbour. Uncle Hebert continued to stare, mouth open. Breeze was amused by how easy it is to disorganize the minds of grown men.

Followed by swooping terns, their course took them around the headland to a deserted sandy beach with green hills on either side, a fresh water stream winding through the sand at one end. Sheep grazed above the stream. A small iceberg, once an ice-giant left behind when it grounded off the North Head, was smashing itself to pieces on the shelf, like the Dwyer's schooner smashed herself on the White Rock Ledge two days before.

Lliam beached the Rodney on the gently shelving sand and jumped over the bow. The tide was making and in two hours the boat would float itself. He offered his hand. She hoisted her skirts and stepped over the gunnel, wading away parallel to the beach. He was forced to wade in the freezing water or relinquish her hand. They walked carefully on the fine sand, feeling the current tug at their legs, avoiding bergy bits tumbling and wallowing drunkenly in the busy little waves.

Breeze picked one up and held it to the sun as an offering. The salt foam was blown away by the wind and the melt water ran down her arm and returned to the sea, carrying away the salt and grains of sand and sea lice. She touched her tongue to the translucent ice. "'Tis fresh now. Taste it."

Lliam reluctantly put his lips to the ice. His feet were already freezing and he didn't relish freezing his tongue as well. "Wonderful..." he said with mock enthusiasm, trying to edge Breeze toward the beach.

"See the birds hoverin' around that little lost ice island? They take the fresh water from the top. I've watched them bath in the pools. I think they adopt a small berg an' follow her south 'til she melts away, an' then they fly north again to find another to satisfy their needs. Much like people."

"That was much too obvious, my girl."

"'Tis only nature, sure. Birds got to look after themselves. What could be safer than iceberg, where mean little boys can't throw rocks?"

"You aren't talking about birds. What made you hate us?" he asked, assuming he knew the reason.

"You might not like the story, so I'll tell another. I once read about the Vikings who came from the place where the ice islands are born. Did you know that this piece of ice is ten thousand years old? It's just snowflakes that's been locked up in a glacier for all that time, only waitin' patiently to be free. Now look..." She threw the chunk of ice back into deeper water. It splashed and dove out of sight and popped up again and headed back to shore. "See, I give her freedom, but she comes right back to die on beach. Why is that, Lliam?"

"Breeze, you don't even want me to answer that riddle. It's just another parable to punish me."

"I'm glad to know it's not wasted."

"No, I'll warrant. They're getting to the mark."

"You know, Lliam...I think the Vikings must have come by way of Fogo. They sailed ever so far, up an' down Europe an' over ocean, makin' a nuisance of themselves. It's only likely that they might have come this way lookin' for somethin' else to burn an' plunder. Not to mention ravishin' any unlucky women they come across."

"Likely they only got blown this way by the god of awful winds that seem to come straight from Ireland about eleven months of the bloody year. An' bring all the cold in hell to boot!"

"Your feet are cold...is that it?"

"Yes, my bloody feet! Look at them. Gone right blue."

"Let's walk on the sand then."

"While I can still walk."

Lliam gladly followed Breeze, but his only regret was that Breeze would lower her skirts. Higher up the beach, above the seaweed line, the sand was soft and warm. They buried their feet and stood looking seaward at the wonderful nothingness and smelled the salt and rotting seaweed and the iodine smell.

"'Tis a long way off," she said.

"What is?...Ireland?"

"Happiness."

"I shouldn't have asked."

"Should you not? Ask me anythin', Lliam. I'll answer, in my fashion. If you'd have guessed happiness, I'd have said Ireland. Neither are that close, so either works as well."

"Happiness is as close as your answer."

"Is it, Lliam? You make it sound so simple. Is your poor feet warm enough, my dear?"

"Yes, they're fine," he answered, wary of her sudden show of tenderness.

"Let's walk then."

They strolled along the high tide line. Breeze grew silent and melancholy. Lliam could feel the distance growing. "What is it, Breeze? Because they could see us rowing out together? Uncle 'ebert's a better gossip than Aunt Til? There's no use to hide now."

"We've not been foolin' anyone. Mother knows what we done. The whole village knows. Only Gerald doesn't know, an' I doubt it matters. But I've hurt so many people, an' I'm about to hurt you as well."

"I know what you're goin' to say, so to hell with Gerald an' all of them. To hell with the future I had planned for us, if that's what you want me to say."

Breeze looked seaward and noticed the boat driving hard for the Cove. Fear swept her face as if she had just seen a vision of the inferno. "Lliam...I want to go back."

"No, my darlin' girl. We've got only a little time. Let's make the most of it, like they was the last hours of this poor old world."

She pointed to the big power dory. Breeze recognized the man at the tiller, a worker from the merchant's premises in Fogo Harbour, who often delivered goods to their cove. But it was Sunday: they never came on a Sunday, and Breeze had a premonition that the boat carried a message about her future.

The other man in the boat, the Messenger, was a Notre Dame Bay man from the Long Rocks light station near Twillingate. The dory didn't slow until a few boat lengths from the village wharf. This show of haste attracted the attention of the children playing around the cove, the women visiting after church and the fishermen idling on their stages. At the last moment a gaff was thrown out to arrest the motion of the dory. The Messenger tied the painter to a strouter. The Merchant's man pointed and said, "That's the Dwyer House." A boy heard and ran ahead. The Messenger strode up the wharf and along the path with resolute steps, head bent to warn all those moving toward the wharf that he was the bearer of bad news. The other children maintained a respectful distance, not acting foolish as they often did when a stranger called.

The word was passed before the Messenger was clear of the wharf and found the path to the Dwyer's residence. "Messenger comin', Missus," the boy had time to say at the open door.

The scene in the Dwyer kitchen was a tableau in a Chekhov play: the characters in their places, motionless, waiting. Grandfather was asleep in his chair. Grandmother, in contemplation of her husband, put her cup on the stove, wondering if she should awaken him. Margaret, at the table darning socks, let her work drop into her lap. The knot in her stomach had been growing by the hour, although she would not have said what it was. She knew women who saw tragedy...The sharp knock on the doorframe, a man's knock, didn't startle her. The sound was the message, not the Messenger, because in Béhathook Cove no one knocked unless there was tragedy about. She pushed the needle through the wool.

Grandfather woke at the knock, reaching for his pipe. Grandmother felt about for her knitting.

Margaret looked to the crucifix above the table, on the East wall, between the two windows that looked out on the cove. "Yes, my dear man, come in then."

The Messenger, a silhouette in the frame, entered slowly, doffing his wool cap; a menacing silhouette, shapeless in working clothes. The children gathered behind him, in bright sunshine: the innocents.

"Mother Dwyer?" the man asked in a low tone.

"Yes, I'm Malich Dwyer's wife."

"May God bless all here, Missus," the Messenger began.

"An' you as well," Margaret, whispered, completed the customary greeting. "You have news..." Margaret said resolutely.

"I come soon's we got the wireless, Mother Dwyer."

"Malich?" she asked softly. Which of her men? All of her men? She was thinking many things, not just about the mourning to come, there would be time for mourning.

"Us don't know which, Mother Dwyer. Message from St. Ant'ony was about the schooner what belongs to this family."

"The *Margaret an' Maude*?"

71

"Yes, Mum...The *Margaret an' Maude's* gone, an' one's dead, an' one's hurt bad."

"What cause?"

"Fire, Missus...she went down on the White Rocks. 'Tis all we know, 'bout the cause."

"Oh, my God." She bent her head and stifled a sob. "Fire. Malich's worst fear."

"What is it, Margaret?" asked Grandfather, striking a match on the stovetop.

"Schooner's gone," she answered flatly. "Fire, this poor man says."

"Fire? I told Malich one day she'd burn. Too much fat into'er, see."

"Yes, Father, we know..."

"Remember the ol' *Diana*? Right soaked up with fat she were, an' them merchants never looked after'er, noways. She got pinched in ice one time...spring o' twenty-two it was, an' all stove in. Only ice holdin' 'er. The b'yes set fire to'er 'cause skipper was fixin' to give their sculps over to 'nother ship an' let she sink. I don't know 'bout that, but in night the ol' *Diana* burned, an' the b'yes went on ice, see? Cousin Albert was into'er that year, an' says she was some fire. *Some fire*, he says! Feared the ice would melt out from under. Only foolishness, about ice burnin'..."

"I think that's enough story for now," chastised Grandmother gently.

"Is there anything else?" Margaret asked, turning to the Messenger.

"Only 'bout the one burned. They had'im up to Grenfell Hospital at St. Ant'ony. They left in boat this mornin', burned one's along with'em. Don't know more'an that, Missus."

"Ask that man to sit a spell," said Grandfather.

"Will you have some tea?"

"Thanks all the same, Missus, an' you good people. I'm expected back to Twillingate the once."

They had come to the end of the beach where the stream cut through the shifting sand. The water was tannin-coloured, but the water was good, filtered through peat. Some sheep that had come down to drink shied away, moving back up the slope to their rocky meadow. Breeze waded into the warm stream and let her feet sink in the soft sand. Then she stepped up to a rock, and on to another, widening the gap. Breeze watched the stream struggle to the sea and spread over the saltwater like a brown stain, running out to meet the chunks of ice. "If you didn't know the difference, Lliam, which water would you drink? The dark, or the clear?"

"Breeze, please answer my question without posing me another riddle."

"You see, Lliam, I don't know about your Boston anymore than a stranger would know that the dark water was pure and the beautiful clear water could kill you."

"Boston's a wonderful place, sure. You'd feel right at home, in your own place like...flats they call them. They're small but comfy enough, just right."

"Comfy? What does that mean?"

"Comfortable, you know, just big enough."

"Is one big enough to swing a cat?"

Lliam laughed. "A small cat, to be sure, some...but they come in all sizes."

"I have a house. An' Gerald said he'd build a bigger one if I wanted. I said I neither needed nor wanted another house."

"Imagine a gas fire you put a match to, an' running water as near as..."

"I have runnin' water right here. The finest kind."

"You carry heavy pails up the hill."

"It's me own hill."

"An' there's a loo right there in the flat, some have. No need to walk out on stage in snowstorm."

"There's no starfish to see in bottom of a Boston loo, sure."

Lliam sighed and pressed on. "There's ever so many folk from Newfoundland, an' from old country, mostly Irish. The Gaelic flies about like flocks o' sea birds. There's automobiles, an' buses, an' trucks, all darting about at some business...busy as anything. Why, if you want to go across town, you just get onto bus and they take you miles and miles."

"I can walk anywhere on Fogo I want to go."

Lliam was intent on getting out the litany of miracles he had rehearsed. "And the shops, Breeze, you wouldn't believe what you can buy, just for walking a few steps from your door. There's merchant's on every corner, shops filled to the roof with goods. And the huge department stores...let me tell you about those wonderful places at Christmas time."

"Sure an' the merchant's premise over to Fogo's full to the roof with goods from all over the world, but that don't mean we have the means to buy without sellin' our souls to the Devil."

"But in Boston you can take a job. They pay you real money that you can spend on whatever you wish."

"What kind of job?"

Lliam stepped into the stream and sank quickly, wetting the bottom of his rolled up pants. He jumped for the rock Breeze was standing on. She helped him get his balance. "Oh, you know, a lass can get work in factories making clothes or shoes. Some like to do chores for rich families...housekeepers, nannies and such like...look after their children."

"I can do that right here, for Mother an' Gerald, an' have babies of me own, besides."

"You can have babies in Boston."

"I don't want babies in Boston. An' besides, Mum says there's a Depression on in America too, an' everybody's out of work an' near starvin'."

"I admit there's some hard times. But a man can find work if he's willing. And I've almost got my certificate for teaching. I can tutor for the rich folks meantime." He did not want to pursue that line of the story. "Another year or so an' I can name my price...Well, once I get a position."

"An' what do you jig for survival in meantime?"

"Well, truth is, I've give that some thought." Lliam slipped off the rock. He was looking up at Breeze. "You know there's a little commotion getting up over in Europe. They say there's to be a war and

England's likely to be in. Just a skirmish, mind you. They need to settle old accounts, on account of they never really settled the last war...anyway, can't last too long."

Breeze jumped to another rock and then to the sand on the far side of the stream. Lliam waded after her, heedless of his city pants. "We hear scattered rumours about some German Chancellor," she said and shrugged off the Germans.

"Adolf Hitler? He's in all the papers. Threats mostly. The Germans want some land back and the French object. England has to back up her Allies, France mostly, to protect herself, being an island and all...like us."

"You mean to go then?"

"I plan to join up, if it comes to war, after we settle in Boston. I can save up my army pay, an' send it back to you." Lliam circled in front of Breeze who was headed for the grass meadow. "I'll take my certificate by correspondence and when I come home we'll be right as rain." Breeze outflanked Lliam and climbed up the rocks to a flat place where short green grass made a fine carpet. "Meantime you can get a job and save money, and we'll buy a little house...and you can have a dog or pet bird, and I'll go teaching school. There, simple," he said, almost out of breath. Breeze sat down on the grass. "How's that sound? Breeze...?"

She was crying softly. Lliam sat down beside her, awkwardly, and tried to hold her. She resisted. Then he laid her down so that the sun filled her face and made her tears sparkle.

"Diamonds. The finest kind," he said, tenderly touching a tear. "Say yes, Breeze." He traced the line of tears, following the soft contours of her cheek to her neck, untying the bows at her shoulders. Searching for her rounded breasts, kneading the nipples to hardness. Breeze felt like bread dough under his cool hands, but didn't resist, thankful that at least Lliam's hands, although cold, were soft and gentle, unlike his father's rough hands.

He put his hand under her skirt and stripped off her panties. Clumsily he removed his own wet trousers, cursing the long johns that had to stay on or Breeze might flee up the hill. He undid the lower buttons with trembling fingers, shielding the hard penis from her sight, guiding it into her dry vagina without foreplay. She ignored the pain; pain is to be ignored, if not avoided. *Like father, like sons,* she thought.

They made love in the sunshine with the brown stream flowing against the incoming tide, the iceberg beating itself to pieces against the headland, the bergy bits flinging themselves at the sand like suicidal squid, rolling helplessly in and out with the waves, and the sheep on the rocky ledge looking down, chewing, dull-eyed. Lliam made love desperately, grunting and panting, disappointed that Breeze did not respond the way Molly and Anna responded during their afternoon trysts. Breeze lay shivering with her dress pulled up to her shoulders, legs apart and her eyes open, head to one side looking back at the sheep, until Lliam was finished.

When Lliam finally moaned and rolled away Breeze dabbed at the cold semen with her panties, pulled her dress down and had a clear view of the sky and the building cloud structure. *Weather in the offing, an end to sunshine,* she wanted to say. She preferred Garret's silent, tender lovemaking.

"Will you come away then, Breeze?"

"I might, when you do it right."

"What? Are you teasing me?"

Breeze almost laughed, vowing that she would never experience an orgasm again unless it was Garret who touched her. She thought about the last time she was with Garret. Breeze contrived the few occasions but he was away more than at home, and kept busy with work, always preparing to leave. An outport runs on seasons. City dwellers, at least those with jobs, didn't realize how lucky they were to have the luxury of organizing their days into uncomplicated routines.

"Breeze, darlin'...answer my simple question."

"Simple?"

"All you have to say is, *yes.* Say it!"

"*Yes*, then."

"Yes, you'll come to Boston with me?"

"No."

"You just said, *yes.*"

"I said *yes* because you said I should. It's the same reason I agreed to marry Gerald. It's the same reason I say yes every time Mother demands another moment of my time. I say yes, and might mean, no."

"This is very confusing."

"You said it was simple."

"Simple if you mean what you say," Lliam said, buttoning his long johns, embarrassed, as if he had been stripped naked in a crowd on Boston Common. The last drip of semen felt cold and useless running down his thigh. Too late to take it back. He danced about on one leg pulling on his wet trousers. He knew he looked ridiculous and wanted to lash out. She, sitting there on the grass holding her soiled panties, looked self possessed, and maddeningly beautiful. The background sheep, like dumb judges in their gallery, accusing him. "Breeze, how can you do this to me?"

"What have I done? You went away an' came back. I spread my legs for you. I said 'yes' when you demanded."

"Stop this, god-damnit!"

"You needn't lay curses on too. Doyle's the boy for cursin'."

Lliam felt a stab of pain. He pulled back his arm as if to strike. Breeze didn't flinch. Her cool dark eyes bore into his, not with reproach, but with something more devastating. Confronted by Breeze's stoic acceptance of his male stupidity, Lliam suffered a crushing defeat. Heart racing, head pounding, Lliam turned away and splashed through the stream, stumbling, falling and marching on like a pouting child. The Rodney floated sideways to the incoming tide.

The somber group on the wharf stood frozen, like a diorama in a museum. The colours of the village matched the mood. The sun had fled and the tones were grey with smudges of yellow and deep reds in the hills. Dirty scraps of clouds sailed over the hills, racing out to sea to meet them. The high cumulus had already stolen the grand light from the day. Seldom colourful in dress for any occasion, except Mummer's Days, Newfoundlanders present a picture of dour, hardworking, sturdy folk, perpetually ready for a funeral.

The families and friends waiting for them on the wharf were already in mourning. Margaret Dwyer was at the center of the tableau, flanked by Grandmother Dwyer and Grandfather Dwyer. Brigid O'Keefe crowded Margaret as close as her crude crutches would allow. Behind them ranged the rest of the village, save for those too infirm to make the journey.

Breeze saw them first. Lliam, rowing with his back to the wharf, didn't bother to turn. "So, they're all waiting on the wharf for us this fine afternoon."

Breeze straightened her dress and brushed back her hair with both hands. "Aye. The whole village, by the look."

"God! This bloody place! Old 'ebert gets a look at your knickers an' the Philistines gather. Have they got stones and staves ready? Burning pitch?"

"Lliam, I don't think it's just for us."

"Of course it bloody is! They've nothing better to do on a Sunday than condemn us for going off together. They probably have scarlet letters ready. Is your mother with them?"

"Yes, but Margaret's foremost. Something's wrong."

Lliam sighed deeply. The silent journey home, after the clumsy attempt to claim Breeze, was more than an embarrassment. He believed it was the end of a dream that had been doomed from the start. He knew it would be difficult, the homecoming at least, and he was prepared to do battle with the old country prejudices. But the outport morality was something else. He was certain his own father, if Malich was indeed his father, had used Breeze, and that his brothers had abused her more than once. By her own admission she had been with Garret, and probably Gerald. He wasn't sure about Doyle. How many others? What could he say? He had abandoned her in a village where life is lived on the margins of survival. Morality was relative. Necessity was a much stronger guide. And who was he to judge? Boston was a vibrant city of many temptations and he had fallen prey to most of them: a young Molly left behind with his baby, and the guilt followed him home. He felt in his heart he should have done the right thing but the problem was his enduring image of Breeze as the beautiful innocent who, in his dreams, was supposed to wait

78

unblemished.

Breeze was the most beautiful creature on the island, but her beauty was the problem, and she was a puzzle not to be solved apparently. He rowed harder, his anger rising with each stroke and had only to take the reciprocal bearing in Breeze's eyes to guide their approach. Lliam gripped the oars tighter and vowed to not give them the chance to strike. He might even announce he was leaving that very night, rowing the skiff in the darkness and the rising storm, perhaps to perish in a welter of foam. What was there to life but a painful transition, and what rewards were there for being young and foolish? He'd show them who Lliam Dwyer really was.

The Rodney bumped the wharf. Lliam seized a strouter, tied off and helped Breeze step from the dipping gunnel to the wharf deck. Breeze's skirts and bare feet rose from view. Only then did he climb up to face his accusers.

They were staring, yes, but he saw sorrow and pity directed toward Breeze. Mother O'Keefe looked hard at him then looked away. The others just stared, their assessment of him difficult to read.

"What are you all staring at? Breeze and me were just out for a row, like civilized folks. And you all traipse down here to stare at us like we're the worst kind of criminals! 'Tis none of your business what two grown people do." He wasn't sure of his ground but he pressed on, intent on getting it said before announcing that he was leaving Béhathook Cove. "That's the trouble with these bloody minded places. You judge others..."

Margaret took a step toward her son. "The schooner's lost," she said simply. "There's one dead. We don't know who's been taken by the Good Lord."

Lliam was stunned. The words went crashing through his brain like a storm wave on a granite shore. One dead! It didn't matter to Lliam which one; his future was sealed and delivered as surely as the message carried by the Notre Dame Bay man.

"There's one burned bad. Fire's all we know. You've to decide, soon."

He looked at Breeze standing apart like a small ice island floating in a sea of villagers, her eyes fixed on a spot beyond Lliam. The gap was widening.

The curious remained at a respectful distance. *Who to console,* they wondered? Breeze as the bereaved fiancé? Margaret surely, but as widow or mother? They grieved for the old ones. Only Lliam was left out. The villagers made no connection between the Prodigal Son and his dwindling family. Uncle Hebert and the other men had pronounced a bad end to Lliam's return. Now they accepted that Lliam was among them to stay, but in what capacity? Breeze wondered the same thing as she looked back at Lliam, the stranger she knew only in memories of a lovesick adolescence. There were many decisions, all were important, but only one would be right.

Lliam made no response to Margaret. For the moment the scene on the wharf was static, the players waiting for their cue.

Grandfather was gagged by the sight of Lliam alive; delivered to the wharf from the sea. But the boy was of little value to an old man who gauged a thing's place in the hierarchy of survival by it's intrinsic worth: something edible or something that can be used to do work. Lliam was not fixed in the old man's mind, and worse, there was no sea connection to place a value on, like an engine part hung on a dusty piece of fishing twine. The greasy spare part was a promise for the future, like money in a bank and Lliam could not be dried and hung for future use.

Grandfather shook his head slowly, took Grandmother's arm and hobbled up the stage toward the path. The mob opened and filled in behind, moving at the elder's pace, a lumbering, swaying object with several legs. The bodies faded into their separate houses like wraiths returning to their lairs, ruminating on the scanty details, the murmur of speculation low, carried away from Lliam's hearing by the rising wind. Whispers and more pronouncements would be shared around stoves and dinner tables. Spirits invoked to protect the living and speed the dead to heaven.

Left on the wharf to face the wind and ponder his own future, Lliam shivered with the cold reality. The women must be cold too. Should he offer his coat to Margaret, to Mother O'Keefe or to Breeze? His duty was to Margaret but she would reject the offer. In terms of seniority he could offer it to Brigid, but her cold assessment forestalled the gesture. If he offered it to Breeze it would be a slight to the older women. But a rejection from Breeze would symbolically end the quest. He pretended to watch a flock of black sea ducks whistle across the Cove and glide into the pond beyond the village to search for their dinner. *What a simple life,* Lliam thought.

"I'll put on a tea the once," Margaret said. She turned and walked ahead, skirts hoisted to clear the uneven planks of the wharf. Brigid followed, shawl flapping in the wind like a loose jib, crutches thumping planks. Breeze pulled her shawl over her head like a monk and drew her arms tight to her breasts, erasing her femininity, *to shut him out,* he imagined. She appeared to be mourning, but there was more.

Brigid and Breeze followed Margaret home. There was more to the grieving procession than was spoken of, though most of the villagers watching from their windows knew why Brigid and Breeze gravitated to the house of mourning. It was a family affair.

Lliam found himself sitting at the head of the table opposite Mother O'Keefe, with Breeze at his right. He looked out the window to the O'Halloran's house. Small faces peered back at him through narrow gaps in the lace curtains. The curtains were drawn together by large hands. Lliam preferred the children's curiosity.

Margaret rattled about getting plates and cups, cutting bread. "Oh, my...there's not much to serve you. Bread an' jam is about all."

"Tea's fine, Margaret," said Brigid.

"I've some butter by, saved for Malich."

"Small tea's enough, Margaret, my dear," assured Grandmother.

Grandmother and Grandfather Dwyer rocked beside the stove, holding empty cups. Margaret moved about her kitchen, seeding the pot with loose tea from the metal canister, tipping the heavy kettle, spilling some; the drops hissing and sputtering, steam rising in clouds like bomb bursts across a battlefield. Otherwise there was silence during the brew.

Margaret scrubbed potatoes in a bucket, thinking thoughts she would never reveal. "Tea should be brewed by now." She poured for Brigid. Breeze next. Then Grandmother and Grandfather. Lliam last. "You've taken Malich's place at table," she commented dryly.

"Should I move?" he asked.

"No, my son, it may be your place." Margaret put the teapot back on the stove and covered it with a flour bag. Bread and jam were served, set close to Brigid so she wouldn't have to reach. Margaret opened her last can of milk, poured half into a glass pitcher and added a little water. She carried the thinned milk and the sugar bowl and placed them close to Brigid. Brigid selected a spoon from a bouquet of silver spoons in a chipped mug, putting two heaping measures into her tea, adding a generous dollop of milk. Margaret and Grandmother Dwyer watched closely. The cup would hardly be touched.

"Milk an' sugar, Breeze?" Margaret asked, tempering the cold edge to her voice; the correctness of the ceremony had to be maintained.

"Only a little milk, thank you, Mother Dwyer."

Breeze watched the dollop of milk sink and rise, spreading out like the rotation of a hurricane. She had observed that milk, untouched, always swirled in the same direction. Small globs of oil moved about on the currents, bumping and merging. *Ice pans, whelping pans,* Breeze thought. She imagined baby white coats abandoned by their mothers at the approach of the hunters. Felt the blows of the gaffs...the hot sting of bullets, and not understanding why.

Lliam watched Brigid trowel red current jam on a thick slice of bread. Lliam saw blood spreading over a white shirt. He had witnessed a stabbing in a Boston bar, the man dying slowly in the sawdust and broken glass. No one moved to help. Breeze imagined it to be the blood of the baby seal pumping over the white fur and white snow a perfect canvas for the rich colour. Margaret calculated only the amount of jam wasted. Brigid carefully parted the slice, nibbling a corner. Grandfather would eat the bread later.

The stockpot steamed lazily at the back of the stove. Margaret moved it to the hot spot, adjusted the damper and opened the firebox door, adding spruce splits to the bed of orange coals. On the pantry counter a clutch of scrubbed potatoes and one small turnip waited. She counted the potatoes. Seven. This time the count was right, not for the assembly, but for the remaining family. She picked up the turnip and began carving a face.

Margaret made turnip dolls for the children of the village at Christmas time. Each fall she would set aside the smallest turnips. The faces were plump at first, but when placed behind the stove they dried to wizened elders. Breeze thought they looked too much like the shrunken heads in the illustrated book Sean O'Keefe brought from Britain. The steel plate engravings were works of art, but to a child's mind the grotesque features of dead savages from far off lands, like Borneo and Sumatra, New Guinea and Africa, were scenes from Hell that caused the children nightmares.

Breeze watched Margaret carving the eyes, wiping away tears. Lliam watched Breeze, his own emotions rattling between desire for her and revulsion at the scene that, moment by moment, was drawing him down into the Maëlstrom. The tension in the room was growing.

Breeze bolted first. Her sudden rush to the door startled everyone except Lliam who had seen escape in her eyes. Grandfather Dwyer jerked awake and opened his mouth to speak. Grandmother stopped knitting. Margaret sliced the nose off the turnip face. Brigid O'Keefe just stared at her daughter. Breeze opened the door and fled down the path to the Dwyer's stage. The big iceberg had moved on.

"Now, what do you suppose that was about? These children's always racketing about. My son!"

The Northeast Peninsula: Ninety-eight nautical miles to the north the Dwyer trap skiff makes heavy going in a tide lop. The waves are steep and close together, the motion of the skiff uncomfortable as it rises and falls, lurching drunkenly over the sharp crests, riding the south going Labrador Current.

Malich and his son Doyle sit side by side on the middle thwart, straining at the long sweeps; the rusted engine had given up, as if in concert with the forces that destroyed their schooner. They rowed to St. Anthony, spent a dismal night at the Grenfell Hospital and Malich was determined to row home. The doctors did what they could for the burns and protested when Malich announced that they were leaving. They had been rowing since dawn, making thirty nautical miles, praying for the wind to let up or go to the Northwest. The constant jerking motion and stomach-wrenching plunges into the troughs had taken their toll but they were nearing Rouge Isle, between the Grey Islands and Conche Harbour.

Doyle, hands numb and bleeding, was ready to give it up. "Pa, I'm all done in. Can't us run into Conche an' stay a day or two?"

"I want to make Rocky Bay."

"Rocky Bay's another twenty miles! I'll never make it, sure."

Rocky Bay, a small, desperately poor outport on the south shore of the Grey Islands, is a rude harbour, a mass of rocks and shoals, fit only for small boats. Malich had a cousin who eked out a living for his family, as marginal as the Labrador Liveyers.

"Only fifteen miles, an' you'll make it or join'im in the bilge!"

The body was wrapped in cotton and sterile pads with only an old army trench coat, donated by a veteran at St. Anthony, for a cover. Watery blood and yellow liquid seeped through the bandages. Arms flopped about with the motion of the skiff. Fifteen more miles to Rocky Bay meant little to the unconscious one.

"You'll kill us all, Ol' Man."

"You don't hear us complainin', do we, sonny boy?" he asked the body. "Thank the Good Lord you're alive, Doyle. Thank the Lord." It would be dark and perishing cold before the skiff found its way into Rocky Bay. But that was nothing to Malich. He had lost his schooner, a son, probably two, and the season. "Us can only pray that he doesn't suffer over long," he said, looking at the body. "But I'd like to bury'im ashore. 'Tis only thing a Dwyer can hope for in this muckery of a life."

The Dwyer Kitchen Same: Margaret closed the door on the framed picture of Breeze standing on the shore looking seaward. Lliam felt the separation keenly. He had no compatriots in the over heated kitchen, only sets of eyes watching him for signs. Margaret approached the table and took the chair Breeze had vacated. Lliam wanted to flee also, to carry out his vow to leave the outport, run across the bogs, anything to avoid the inevitable.

"Lliam, son," began Margaret, "whoever is dead, you've got to make up your mind." Her eyes burned into his. Lliam gripped the chair arms. His hands were soft. How could those hands be of any use to the family? Malich's hands were gnarled and horny with hard work, his heart and will steeled by years of practice at the art of survival on the narrow margin between land and sea. Lliam felt small and inadequate, a sick feeling creeping from his stomach to his throat. He looked away and there was Brigid O'Keefe. In Brigid's eyes he was everything in life she loathed, especially men. His Grandparent's eyes were softer, but they knew the score better than anyone.

"Yes, Lliam, you've to decide," said Grandmother Dwyer.

"You're needed now," continued Margaret.

"'Tis your duty, my dear," added Grandmother.

"My duty?"

"Children don't know duty from dead swile's dick!" croaked Grandfather.

"If 'tis Malich injured and Gerald dead, you got to take whoever's place at this table, so rest your mind on that truth, my son," said Margaret bitterly.

"What about Doyle? He's the older."

"Doyle? My poor Doyle ain't got the sense to put on his boots, less Malich tells him to."

"My sonny boy, that child ain't got the sense o' bottom fish!" Grandfather rocked faster, fumbling with his tobacco pouch. A match flared and the puffing ritual commenced in time to the rocking.

Margaret leaned closer to Lliam, taking a small bible from her apron pocket. She held the bible in Lliam's face. "We can only pray it ain't Malich. I don't know what we'd do if Malich's gone. God rest his soul." She made the sign of the cross and kissed the bible.

"Then pray you don't need to depend on me."

Brigid's concerns were more personal. "An' if it's Gerald dead, what's poor Breeze goin' to do with neither husband? An' Lord knows we need a man in our house. You've got three more men besides,

85

Margaret dear."

"We need four good hands to fish," countered Margaret.

"With only one dead you've still got three, four if Lliam stays, an' other one ain't hurt too bad. One for Breeze can still turn a hand."

Lliam looked from Brigid to Margaret, hardly able to believe he was hearing the words.

"Four without Malich to guide every step is no blessin'."

"We've neither schooner, guard o' whose dead," interjected Grandmother Dwyer. It was a cold reality that momentarily stopped the debate. "Schooner's gone," she reminded the assembly.

Margaret recovered. "Then we build anew, Mother! Like we always did."

Grandmother Dwyer rested her knitting in her lap. "How in all that's Holy could we build a boat, my dear? You know we still in debt to merchant for the *Margaret an' Maude*, an' she's gone. She was cursed an' we ain't likely to get clear o' that no matter who's dead. 'Tis foolish to think on it."

Grandmother's logic was strong and the weight of the impossible task settled into each consciousness in a different way. Grandfather suffered a pang of uselessness. In his youth he would have thought nothing of picking up his tools and driving his boys into the forest to build what they needed: a house, a schooner...coffins. Grandmother wished she hadn't stated the obvious but there it was. Brigid cursed boats of any kind and hoped that Gerald would find a job in the mines or on the railroad, anything, even if he were away most of the year.

Margaret sighed and got up to clear the table. The brief burst of spiritual energy quickly faded as if a fog had just rolled over the harbour absorbing the outlines of houses, stages, boats and people. "We got to do something, love. We can't all lay down an' die."

"Then pray it's only Garret or Doyle dead," said Grandmother coldly.

"'Twould be best, I suppose."

Lliam exploded. "How in the name of God can you pray for Doyle or Garret to be dead?"

Margaret paused in the act of removing his plate, the simple function of serving and clearing was such a normal thing even the pall of tragedy could not interrupt the routine. She put the plate down and stood looking at her son, weighing the words. "You've never been one of us, Lliam. You don't understand the cost of life on this island. I don't know what they do on Mainland, but here you struggle for every mouthful of food, an' you survive or die. It's as simple as that."

"I know. I've witnessed your life for enough years."

"You seen some of it, my poor son. You seen what you wanted to see an' then you run away."

"You make it sound as though it's my fault...just because I wanted a life."

"If Malich's dead I'm a widow an' we'll suffer cruel for his loss, but I got to go on an' finish my job o' work. If a man dies buildin' his family a boat, the family got to keep on buildin'. If it's Gerald dead, Malich's lost his right hand. Then there's only Doyle an' Garret. They're both morons in their own way when it comes to that, only Garret's not lazy like Doyle. Who do we depend on, you?"

"Me?" Lliam was nailed to his chair as surely as if wooden pegs were driven into his hands, the way boat builders fasten planks to frames. Lliam looked away to the crucifix...*The way they nailed His hands and feet to the cross*...He was Christ, sinking into the loose pebbles of the beach, carrying the heavy boat timbers on his weak shoulders, the rough wood chaffing the skin to the bone. Hands outstretched, fingers curled unevenly, like the plaster figure on the cross, feet overlapping. *Why? Did they not have enough nails?* Treenails are free. 'Trunnels is free for the effort', Malich used to say. *Free for the takin' an' makin'*...

When Lliam was a boy of seven, the *Margaret an' Maude* was a skeleton on the ways in the meadow behind the house. Malich made the boys carve juniper trunnels on winter nights when the gales drove ice pellets through the cracks and stirred the pages of his book. Breeze brought him the anthropology book and hung about in the kitchen to be near Lliam, pretending to watch Margaret make duff pudding. It was just before Christmas...He had carved one special trunnel for Malich, for Christmas, a rude, misshapen thing that was crooked and flattened on one side but he presented it to his father proudly. Malich cuffed his ear and told him to try harder, tossing the wasted juniper piece into the fire.

Grandfather, not crippled with the arthritis then, whittled trunnels so fast Garret was kept busy sweeping away the shavings. Shavings are dangerous. A spark from the stove could send the family fleeing into the freezing night. Malich threatened the boys, telling a chilling story of a family burned alive because a desperate father poured kerosene into the stove to get wet wood burning. The kerosene ran out the bottom of the stove spreading flames across the painted canvas floor. The kitchen, brightened by layers of white paint, was an incendiary bomb. The man fled in panic. The old spruce frame house burned like a pitch torch, his family, incinerated in their beds, only ashes in the morning. When the wind got up again it dispersed the family as if it had never existed. The man went to sea in his dory and froze to death for his sin. The image of flames and freezing stayed with Lliam. He was terrified by fire and ice. "I'm useless beyond my books," he admitted.

Grandfather was quick to say, "Yes, my dears. They's all useless as tits on fish, come to that. 'Cept Malich. I brought Malich up by hand."

Brigid O'Keefe drove in. "Don't forget, if Gerald's dead, Breeze's lost her man at sea, like I did mine, if you'll recall, an' I'm that in need of a man myself. I'm all fed up with that girl. Some days she's no more use than..." She looked around for something useless in an outport kitchen. There was nothing frivolous or unnecessary, except Lliam and Grandfather Dwyer. It was taboo to attack the elders so she settled for Lliam. "...Than that no good Go Boy, son of yours. A pair of'ems not so useful as one Gerald. But I'd even take Garret," she said, continuing the negotiations. "A dumb workin' body's better than no body, in the balance."

"You'll have Garret if Gerald's gone. But I'm warning you, he's a moron an' I'd not want to be responsible for what he might do out from under."

"It's a thing I'd have to risk, I suppose."

Lliam could not remain silent a moment longer. "Garret's not a moron and he's the hardest worker of the lot. Look how father uses him!"

"Yes, an' tells him every blessed thing to do. Without you tell Garret, he's apt to stand in corner like broom."

"Doyle then," said Brigid. "I'll make do with Doyle. He might be almost a moron, like Garret, but he can talk an' got a strong back."

Lliam turned on Brigid. "How can you choose for Breeze? This family isn't a bloody general store where you go in and pick out a tool, or a bloody hat!"

"Lliam, hush! Brigid's our guest. This got to be talked through."

"There's nothing wrong with Doyle," interjected Grandmother.

"Who's Doyle?" Grandfather Dwyer asked. The strain of following the debate tired him. He was losing the fabric of the conversation, but Malich was his son, he knew. The others drifted in and out of his memory like faded pieces of a puzzle, like the grey, wind-blown clouds with undefined edges.

Margaret picked up Lliam's plate. "No, my son, if we got to have one dead then we better pray it be the right one, or this family's in a hard chance." She carried the plate to the counter. "Prayin' to God now is all we can do."

"I can't bloody believe this!" Lliam stood up too quickly, knocking over the heavy chair. The sudden noise startled everyone. Grandfather's pipe dropped out of his open mouth. Grandmother dropped a stitch. Mother O'Keefe gasped and clutched her breast. Margaret turned on Lliam but he was already at the door.

"When you get down on your knees tonight who will you pray is really dead, me?" Lliam went out slamming the door, the noise a companion to the fallen chair.

Margaret picked up grandfather's pipe, crushing the glowing shards of tobacco with her foot. She placed the pipe in his limp hand. Then she straightened the chair and swept the ashes into a dory scoop and *clanged* them into the stove. The cleanup done, she approached Brigid with the teapot. "Garret was such a sweet baby. Always Malich's favourite," she said, selling Brigid O'Keefe on the virtues of her most expendable son. Brigid waved off the teapot with the dying-bird hand.

"Malich was some heartbroken when he found out Garret was dumb."
She continued to speak of Garret in the past tense, gone from the
family in Margaret's mind. "That poor boy just never become a real
man, clear of he was a good soul, an' could work like two men." She
avoided mentioning that he could eat like three. If Breeze had been
present she might have defended Garret's manhood. "Still, he was an
idiot for all that."

"Yes, my son! They's all idiots," declared Grandfather. "'Tis a
shame, b'ye, but that's it."

Breeze was sitting on an overturned dory, facing the open sea, heart
and soul skipping over the waves: her dream of sailing away on the old
schooner just a child's fantasy. She turned her head to look at the
derelict, half submerged at high tide; slime covered and rotting from
loneliness. Even the name boards had been taken from her. Breeze
knew it wasn't loneliness or any human emotion that condemned the
old schooner to a slow burn, abandoned to the elements, to slip away in
anonymity because she was no longer of any value. Breeze was useful.
Because she was useful she had duties and obligations, and she was
trapped, grounded like her ice islands on a rocky ledge because her
worth, like an iceberg, went too deep: not content to play the part of
the outport wife and mother, but not able to escape the inevitability.
Lliam *was* useless, she decided, adrift and free because he had no skills
to bind him to the life. No roots, nor keel, nor bulk of ice below the
surface.

Seagulls, feeding on a shoal of small fish at the harbour entrance,
screamed for territory. Breeze didn't hear Lliam call.

"Breeze?" he called again.

Breeze picked up a sea urchin. A rare one not punctured by gulls or
crabs. She had once tasted the contents of a sea urchin to see if the
mossy-green, grainy slime was edible. She had heard it was a delicacy
in England where they spread it on dry toast. She gagged and spit it
out. Sea urchins sometimes washed up intact, with the spines still on.
They were called pincushions, because there was no place to touch
them except the mouth where the belly should be. A young suitor, who

knew of wartime things, called them marine mines and pretended to sink model ships, but a real war was coming, they said, and their desolate little island would be visited again by sailors in strange boats. The first time had been centuries ago: traders and crofters from England by way of Iceland and Labrador. Then from Norway by way of Greenland, drifting south, timidly investigating the hard coast. Breeze had a passing knowledge of such things, but the concept of floating mines to blow men out of the water was beyond her understanding. She refused to see the ocean depths as deadly. On the surface there was the possibility of escape. Below the surface another type of escape: a silent peace if only she had the courage to go where the sea urchins live...

"Breeze, my love." Lliam was beside her, panting with anger, suspended between Breeze's silent indifference and the deafening screech of gulls.

Breeze turned and offered the sea urchin. He stared at it, repulsed by creatures that came out of the sea, and Breeze could not have explained the offering in words. It might have been a king's ransom in jewels. If she had been holding a wave-washed stone or a piece of driftwood she would have done the same, for the same reason, so there was nothing symbolic about the spiny creature.

"Breeze...do you know what they're doing in there? Your mother an' my mother?"

"Yes, I know, but you're bound to tell me just the same."

"They're discussing who of us should have died, like, like bloody magistrates!"

"It had to come to that, Lliam."

"How can they?"

"An' who did you choose, my dear?"

"You think I...?"

"We all chose, Lliam. Like you chose to leave us..."

"Don't make me tell you why."

"It's only natural."

"It's immoral."

"An' you've got to choose as well."

"I won't!"

"You already have."

"I couldn't."

"You chose to leave us. You chose to come back. You choose to risk being killed for some British war. You want me to choose between you an' Gerald. Between my ocean home an' some tiny flat in Boston. You've done some choosing before, an' now you've another choice."

"An' what would that be?"

"Did Mother Dwyer say you had to stay?"

Lliam looked at the house where their families were discussing the living and the dead. "Yes, an' Grandmother spoke of, *my duty!*"

"An' did she tell you the reasons why she chose poor dumb Garret to be dead."

"Not in so many words."

"An' isn't it Gerald *you* hope is dead?"

Lliam wasn't good at lying. When he turned to answer his voice was almost a whisper on the wind. "No, as the Lord is witness to my sinful heart, I did not...purposely...wish that. Only now, seeing you..."

Breeze weighed the sea urchin, turned it over and dropped it into the water. The fragile shell made only a little splash and floated, dipping in the wavelets, working away from the shore with the ebbing tide. A seagull broke from the flock, swooped low to investigate the hollow offering and screeched away, disappointed. "I know in my heart 'tis Gerald. But Lliam, mine is the greater sin because I prayed for that very thing, even as Gerald sailed for the Labrador."

"Breeze, don't say it. You couldn't wish that about anyone. If Gerald's gone, I promise, I'll look after you."

"An' how do you propose to do that?"

"I'll stay here," he said quickly, "an' never give another thought to leaving. I swear."

"Swearing again? Only words. If you're heart's bound for leavin', Lliam, you should have never returned. Now you're bound here, an' it's my fault. It's the curse, see, an' you'll regret the day you ever come back, but you'll curse this moment for sayin' you'll stay. It's an oath you've made, my dear. An oath contrary to a curse an' that makes

92

the spirits work ever so hard."

"What curse?"

She got up and turned away. "I've got chores."

"Wait, I need to know."

Breeze was running along the shore toward her home. Lliam watched her go, as he had so many times. Each time she moved away the distance was greater: the spiritual distance, the emotional gulf. Breeze was an island, and Lliam was unable to cross over because he was ignorant of the bridge to Breeze's soul.

Tense days passed waiting for the arrival of the survivors. Malich would find a way home, if he lived. Béhathook Cove moved to a subtle rhythm. Lamps came on in kitchens before dawn as usual. Stoves were fired and smoke stood up, moving to and fro in the shifting air. Dark forms in sou'westers and canvas coats appeared out of fishing rooms, loaded gear into dories and motored out of the harbour; dissolving into low-lying mist, to reappear hours later, accompanied by a cloud of seagulls. On fine days the children played along the shore or jigged for Tommy cod from the wharf or stoned flat fish, pursuing their prey in the shallow water from stage to stage, their cries and laughter muted by a strange heaviness.

The fourth day of waiting was heralded by a blood-red sky. A somber mood held the outport in a close embrace; the sun suspended in mid arc behind a thin veil, the morning wind failed and the children were silent, watchful. Fishermen delayed going out to the grounds, using the excuse that the red sky was a warning, a weather breeder. Women paused to watch the sea while hanging out laundry. The chatter, greetings and gossip diminished as the morning wore on.

Noon: They could feel it coming, eyes straying to the horizon. Lliam climbed the hill to The Fortress Rock. He could see Breeze moving from house to house on her errands: delivering bread, gathering laundry. They had avoided each other since the debate. There was nothing more to be said until the survivors returned. She knew the answer and had no curiosity. Lliam never stopped asking himself what he should do.

Breeze was crossing the garden to the root cellar in the side of the hill when the cry came from the wharf.

"The skiff. There 'tis! Dwyers' home!"

In the Dwyer kitchen Margaret added splits to the stove and returned to kneading a mound of dough. Grandfather was splayed out on the daybed as in death. Grandmother dozed with her knitting in her lap, waiting for tea. Margaret heard the cry but didn't change the rhythm of her kneading, working the dough as if the future could be compressed and shaped, creating life and forestalling death.

She also heard fast footsteps on the path. Of course they would send the fleetest of the children. The door was flung open. "They's at the wharf, Missus."

The elders awoke in confusion. Margaret turned to face the boy. "Who?"

"Your men, into trap!"

She knew that fact, she meant, "Who? Who's in boat?"

"Skipper Dwyer, an' Doyle, I thinks."

Her heart thumped and her voice almost failed. "Who besides?"

"Don't know, Missus. Couldn't see nary else."

She whispered, "Malich, at least...Thank God."

Voices drifted up from the harbour..."Look! It's Malich, an' Doyle for certain."

"An' there's 'nother, besides."

"Wonder who 'tis?"

"Don't know, b'ye. Body maybe. One's all done up..."

Margaret made her way to the wharf alone. She knew that Malich would not land at the Dwyer stage because it would be difficult to negotiate a body up to the rickety deck, and through the cluttered fish room. And she was certain there was at least one body to be brought ashore, living or dead. There was no need for haste. She could see the heavy skiff approaching sedately, and two exhausted rowers. Most of the villagers had already assembled along the foreshore, leaving the wharf-head for the Dwyers. Elders straggled toward the scene, supporting each other. Children darted among the grownups, playing a subdued version of tag, unable to resist the occasion after days of tension. Dogs scuttled back and forth with the children, excited by the commotion.

Breeze accompanied Mother O'Keefe. They met Margaret at the apron of the wharf and became a trio with Brigid in the center. The crowd opened for them and Brigid took her place at the head of the wharf, beside Margaret who cast the O'Keefe women a sidelong glance that said much. She resented Brigid's selfish grief. Either Gerald or Garret was dead so it meant either Gerald or Garret was hurt badly. Either way, Gerald, or his body, did not yet belong to Breeze O'Keefe, or her mother. *Breeze had no reason to grieve,* she thought. The girl had made no attempt to hide her objection to marrying Gerald, and worse, had thrown herself to the ground at the approach of the Prodigal Son. *Did the fool girl think Lliam was her saviour?* She could now plainly see the broad backs of the two exhausted rowers, the sweeps arching, dripping diamonds, but agonizingly slow. The watchers breathed in an out in time to the rowing cadence, and moaned when a sweep skipped over a wave.

Malich looked back to line up the bow with the wharf. He could see the crowd and he could make out Margaret and the other women at the head of the wharf. The skiff seemed to move by inches, pulled back by some force. Of course, the tide was ebbing. *Where is Lliam?* Margaret wondered. Breeze wondered also.

Lliam Dwyer had a broad view of the sad homecoming. He was the first to see the dark speck of a boat hugging the shore to the Northwest, after turning Round Head, working slowly past Henning's Island at a snail's pace; a trap skiff being rowed is a clumsy, cranky vessel. The skiff was abeam Pigeon Island before the children saw it, almost at the entrance to Béhathook Cove.

The wharf was filling up with people, as in the old days waiting for overdo fishermen or the coastal steamer...The steamer stopped calling the year after Lliam left Béhathook Cove, the third year of the Great Depression...And there was Breeze escorting her mother to the wharf.

Even at that distance Lliam knew Malich Dwyer lived. Lliam waited for his conscience to register, somewhat disappointed by his lack of emotion. He knew the other rower was not Garret. Garret, like Lliam, was tall and spare. The rower beside Malich was either Gerald or Doyle. Intuition told him it was not Gerald, something in the gestures, head angle, like a newel post top about to fall off. The bundle of rags in the bilge was too long for his oldest brother's stout body. He asked the question Breeze had put to him...*Did he wish Gerald dead?*

He started reluctantly down the hill, every step a descent into a suffocating dungeon, a self inflicted incarceration. He was free to flee but could not. Each step pounded in his brain as each pull of the sweeps brought the skiff closer to the wharf. If Gerald is dead will Breeze be free? Or is Breeze condemned for life? Is he bound by his oath to stay? Is he bound to stay, oath or not? What is the curse Breeze alluded to?

When he was a child he heard the whispers about the Dwyers and the Sheens. About shared families: the Sheens and his own, that weren't families, and children that were bastards. Old man Dwyer, his grandfather, was a sailor, a wanderer and a philanderer. Tales of mysterious peregrinations to other islands, and deeds of murder committed by insane Sheens and desperate Sheens, haunted Lliam's dreams as the rumours persisted.

When he was older he learned the story, had seen the evidence, but kept his silence...One day, before Lliam left for Boston, Grandfather had offered him a bundle of loose papers, his sea journal he called them, asking Lliam if he would copy the journal pages into a book, but must keep silent about the history. Lliam read the story, incredulous and sickened by the knowledge. Page after page of revelations about an oath, a pact Grandfather made with Seth Sheen, to father boys for him. Sheen's 'wife' was Sheen's own sister, and one of them was unable to make babies. The blood pact, written and signed on a night of drunken oaths, stated that Grandfather would arrive at Change Islands, on a certain moon in summer, bed Sheen's sister and wait. The woman became pregnant and Sheen held Grandfather to his pledge. It was called 'The Duty' and Sheen vowed a curse if Grandfather failed to arrive each season. In a decade 'The Duty' produced five boys and two girls that lived. Four of the boys died under the cruel hand of Seth Sheen. The fifth son, Moses, escaped to the coast of Labrador, started his own family, and lived in abject poverty. The curse of the Sheens travelled far. Lliam refused to honour his Grandfather's wish and another curse was spoken. Grandfather never forgave Lliam.

Curses freely given are dearly paid for, they say. Step by step Lliam was descending into his own sordid heritage. He fled from Fogo to be free of the whispers, running from his own father to escape the truth. And there was his fear of Breeze. There were many reasons to go and one reason to return...His concentration was broken by a small avalanche of loose rock when he slipped and sat down heavily.

His mother and Breeze and Brigid O'Keefe, were sculptures awaiting the ferry to eternity on the end of the wharf: false widows, expectant brides and cheated mothers. Unmarried widows and fortunate wives. The husband returned, to live to tempt the fates. The odds are in favour of fate. The fisherman's chances of dying peacefully in bed diminish with each fish over the rail and each wave under the keel. Every rock and island abeam...The Rodney waited on its tether beyond the head of Dwyer's stage. He could be out of the harbour before he was missed, to perish in the attempt to make Fogo Harbour as darkness closed in, to die of shame...Lliam got up and continued down the hill...Breeze was a puzzle he could not solve. He rejoiced that Garret had survived...He had always hated Gerald, even more than the disgusting Doyle. Gerald was a bully. Gerald was brave. Gerald was a ruffian and a bastard. Gerald didn't deserve Breeze. How could she marry Gerald? Imagined Gerald naked, lying on top of Breeze, rutting away. Gerald's gross body, a version of his simian father, casting long shadows over Breeze...He had suspicions about Breeze and his father. There was nothing of Malich in himself, he was certain...He felt sick to his stomach as he approached the harbour, knowing he would not run.

The heavy trap skiff glided to the wharf and the rowers slumped over their sweeps. No one moved as the skiff drifted away from the barnacle-encrusted timbers. Lliam climbed down the ladder, grabbed the painter and tugged the skiff back to the wharf. Malich turned to look at his son without recognition, a stranger insinuating himself into the affairs of the family. The crowd on the wharf pressed closer, curious to witness the reunion of father and son. Lliam climbed back up the ladder and stood with the painter in hand, unsure what to do. Bert O'Halloran took the painter from Lliam.

Malich nudged the semiconscious Doyle, eased the heavy sweep inboard and tried to stand up. So cramped from sitting on the narrow thwart for days on end, his legs gave out and he staggered, rocking the skiff, throwing the body in the bilge against the frames. The trench coat fell away revealing the muslin wrapped form soaked in seawater, oozing blood and body fluids. The stink, the sweet-putrid smell of dissolving flesh, overpowered even the long dead fish. The watchers gasped. Doyle knelt in the bilge water beside his brother's body sobbing over his own wounds: his ruined hands and curled fingers.

"Doyle! You useless baby...hand up stern line, an' stop snivelin'. You'd think it were you layin' there."

"Who is it...?" someone asked.

Breeze knew who was stinking up the harbour by his long form. Gerald was short, and brutish. Broad, like Malich. "Garret," she whispered. "Oh, poor Garret."

Not since Malich ordered them away from St. Anthony, had Garret had more than a few sips of water. At Rocky Harbour his cousin's wife could do little for the boy. He lay in the skiff all night with a tarp cast over him, no better than the way drying cod are protected from the dew. And the boat was never still, lying on a tether in the exposed harbour with a restless chop rattling about the rocks and shoals of the shallow bay. Every time the boat rocked, the body rolled against the lashings, burned flesh sloughing off...What could the poor woman do but touch a spoon of water to blackened lips and listen to the moans? It made her weep. Malich and her husband got drunk in the over heated kitchen and Doyle gorged himself on thin fish stew and slept on his arms at the table.

The next morning Malich drove Doyle into the boat and refused the tarp to cover the body. It would be an obligation to return the piece of canvas and he had nothing to give his cousin in return. Even the old trench coat weighed on his conscience. He regarded the filthy army coat as an interloper in his affairs, and cursed the generous veteran of the Somme. Even the drugs pressed on his son by the nurses at the Grenfell Hospital were an obligation. He accepted only a rum bottle filled with pond water, from his cousin's woman. There was nothing free in Newfoundland, according to Malich Dwyer's way of thinking.

Strong hands reached down to help Doyle. Once on the deck of the wharf he stood swaying, legs trembling, feet unfamiliar with a solid surface. His dark, deep-set eyes glazed with exhaustion. He didn't look at friends when they spoke to him. He was allowed to fade into the crowd to make his own way to the house.

Malich remained in the skiff. Several fishermen climbed down to stand about self consciously discussing how to move the body. No place on the boy was free of bandages. "Use buddy's coat," suggested someone.

"Right enough..."

"No, b'ye, 'tis not big enough to hand Garret up proper," said Bert O'Halloran, who recognized the form at his feet.

"Aye, that's a fact," agreed Uncle Hebert.

"Need squid net," said Bert. "Billy, get net from me store."

"That coat now, 'e needs a one under'im."

As two boys raced away, the fishermen lifted the body, easing the trench coat under. The cargo net appeared and was passed down. The wharf had a crane above the landing spot. The crane's derrick was swung over the skiff and the ratchet handle unshipped. Greasy wire cable bumped down in jerks and the pulley wheel creaked. The spectators gazed in fascination as if it was a serious entertainment to be retold later over tea. Hands worked the cargo net under the body and gathered the four loops and fed them over the hook.

"Take'e up, easy now," said Bert.

The crank handle turned and the net swallowed up the body. The bilge water and blood drained away from the limp cargo on its slow arc to waiting hands on the wharf. It could have been a white whale or a tattered shark's carcass. They cut out shark's livers to sell to the co-op in Fogo.

Garret's poor body wouldn't fetch much at co-op, thought Breeze. She knew the value of the leaking thing, running its life away. Not much left of Garret but he wasn't a gift for their amusement. "Poor Garret," she whispered. A woman beside Breeze heard the name.

"The O'Keefe girl says 'tis Garret's survived," she said to her neighbour.

"Garret, so 'tis."

"Then Gerald Dwyer's dead," someone realized.

The revelation of Garret's survival and Gerald's demise circled the waiting mob.

"Yes, 'tis Garret, damn you!" said Breeze angrily. "An' you can stop gawkin' at him like he was some freak from the sea!"

The watchers looked dully at Breeze, innocent of the reproach, unused to being spoken to in such a manner. Curious, yes, but moved by pity for the Dwyer family. "Poor Garret." The name circulated through the crowd in whispers. "Gerald's gone then, b'ye." Those who had guessed right just nodded and began moving away. A few stayed to help the family with their burdens. Malich could not climb the wharf ladder unaided so Lliam proffered his hand. Malich regarded the son's offer with unveiled contempt and reached for Bert O'Halloran.

The squid net settled on the rough planks of the wharf, the loops freed from the cable hook by Uncle Hebert. A small circle of men shuffled closer, ready to take up the body. When the coastal freighter stopped at their cove all available hands shoulder the goods to various houses and so it was with Garret's body. They only waited for the signal, shuffling their rubber boots awkwardly, looking about the harbour for answers to their ancient dilemma.

Breeze remembered the steel engraving in her anthropology book: a London street scene from the Herald showing the delivery of a mummified body to the British Museum from the Barton digs in Egypt. A crowd of workers stood about the Museum entrance in frozen curiosity as the muslin wrapped thing in a crude canvas bag, was displayed for the press. The only difference in the tableaus was that

Garret was breathing.

The chest bandages heaved in spasms of pain and the air whistled in and out, fluttering the wrappings around blackened lips. Garret's eyes, so much like Lliam's blue-grey eyes, blinked back at Breeze. The smell was the early stages of gangrene. Breeze knew the signs, had tended the lonely elders of the outport, administering salves and ointments to ulcerous skin; sulphur powder in refined seal fat, or a salt and cod oil paste to stop infections. The outporters only heard rumours of the new antibiotics: miracle drugs, like penicillin. In Breeze's collection of books there was a crumbling, leather bound volume on Native Medicines and Black Healers, by Sir George Henry Bondhead...A collection of the ancient healing arts of Caribbean witch doctors, a combination of African and Voodoo mysticism...Bondhead travelled the world in search of herbs and spells, as well as the dark powers of the Devil, blaming the Devil for most of human failings, other than drowning. For drowning, or the attendant hypothermia, called gelée d'oise, he advised dark rum heated in a large boiler. The victim was immersed until only the nostrils showed above the spirits, and they were to be plugged with cotton soaked in camphor. Newfoundlanders preferred their powerful spirits on the inside and their Devils had to keep out of the way.

Garret appeared to be beyond spells and spirits. "'Tis all right, my dear. I'll look after you," whispered Breeze.

Brigid O'Keefe's hopes dwindled further at the sight of Garret. She feared her daughter had traded away a coarse but steady provider for a useless bit of charred flesh.

"Take him up to the House," commanded Margaret, as if Breeze or Brigid might steal him. Malich, leaning on Margaret's arm, watched as Bert O'Halloran untied the lines of the skiff to move it to the Dwyer stage. It was then that Malich spied Lliam's old Rodney.

"So, you've come home to claim your boat, eh, *b'ye*?" The *b'ye* was a rough reproach.

"More than that," replied Lliam stiffly. He looked at Breeze. Breeze made no sign that she heard.

"Oh, aye? An' what might that be? A place at our poor table?

We've little enough to share out ourselves. Less of course you've come home with treasure, like they do in them books."

"No treasure, Father. Nothing to show for six years in Boston, if that's what you mean."

"'Tis that exact thing. Struck the mark, eh, lad? You're bright enough. Are you bright enough to figure on what we do now? Schooner's gone. Garret's a wreck, an' likely won't live."

"No, Malich...I don't have the answers."

The men arranged around the cargo net rolled up the edges and prepared to lift. They waited for a signal from Malich.

"An' what's Rodney doin' on me tether? Are you goin' out to fish for your supper, *b'ye*?"

"I'm no fisherman, you know that," he said softly, looking at Breeze.

"Then what in creation did you come back for?" Malich asked as Breeze turned away. "So that's it? Breeze O'Keefe," he said. "She's not yours for takin' so rest your mind."

"Gerald's not going to claim her."

"Nor will you!" Malich spoke to the men. "Take'im up, b'yes. Garret's goin' to die in his own bed at least."

Garret's body sagged in the net and he moaned softly. Breeze followed the net litter, leaving Margaret to support Malich. Brigid O'Keefe thumped her crutches in an effort to keep up to Grandmother Dwyer. Grandfather Dwyer, confused by the events not fully explained, fell in behind the procession mumbling. Lliam remained on the wharf. The barrier heightened, the gulf widened, his sense of being the bastard orphan intensified. It was time to decide: get into the Rodney or force his way back into the family?

The Dwyer Kitchen: Malich took his place at the table and poured rum into a mug. Margaret busied herself preparing a tea, waiting for the iron kettle to boil while the family sat around the table in strained silence. Malich began the story of the family disaster. "Aye, 'twas Moses Sheen's curse..." Malich said, in answer to Grandfather's rough comment.

Lliam sat on his right. Doyle opposite, face down on his arms, snoring in fits. Brigid O'Keefe sat uneasily beside Doyle as Margaret served out tea; a mound of sliced bread sat untouched on the cutting board.

"...But 'twas Garret's fire did the Devil's work."

Garret was installed on the daybed. Breeze sat beside him, unwrapping the bandages, revealing yellow and red flesh and thin pink fluids: a limited palate of colours on a barren island of flesh. The wrappings looked like a sea of bloody foam as the soiled muslin accumulated around the body. Garret was lucky. His heavy fishing clothes had saved him from the deep burns that end life. Breeze believed his back, which was less damaged, had been shielded from the worst of the flames, but Breeze could find no words in her experience to describe the distorted contours, the colours or the odours. Grandmother watched Breeze pour warm cod oil over the bare patches and then apply strips of boiled linen. It seemed a waste of precious linen sheets.

"She burned like the witches' torch, b'yes."

Margaret moved the steaming kettle from cup to cup but when she reached Malich's he waved her off, reaching for the rum bottle. Margaret poured for the elders and took her place at the opposite end of the table. Malich drank off his mug of rum and sat back, glassy eyed with exhaustion.

Malich continued the story..."An' my dears, there was not a thing in this world we could do to save 'em." Malich refilled his mug, holding it up high as if toasting the victims. "By some miracle, Garret pulls 'imself up that ladder, hands was that bad." He drank a toast to Garret. If Doyle had been awake he might have added that it appeared as if Garret was pushed out of the companionway. "An' then Garret rolls out on deck, all smokin' like sculped seal on ice. But the black smoke come on that thick an' the flames so roarin' hot us could not get down to save poor Gerald in'is last agony." Malich drank with the vision fixed, but seeing Lliam's face in place of Gerald's. "I 'eard Gerald cry out. Maybe it was a sea bird, but I swear I 'eard 'im. Would break your heart...I'll never forget that sound so long as I live."

Lliam blinked and looked away, watching Breeze tend to Garret.

"Then she's onto the White Rocks Ledge. Oh my dears, how she cried out, like'er heart was broke, an' 'er keel smashin' down again an' again. She finally comes into the wind an' makes we fear for our own lives. The fire see, smoke comin' onto us, as thick as any fog I ever seen, Garret an' Doyle disappearin' an' our poor boat beatin' 'erself to pieces on that ledge." He paused, eyes fixed in space. He drank a toast to their lost schooner. "Waves boardin' 'er now an' barrels rollin' an' smashin', an' all that oil washin' about. Me an' Doyle slidin' this way an' that, an' Garret most washed over side. We only just had time to get a hold an' drag'im aft." Malich paused to drink, looking each of his audience in the eye.

"By this time dory's smashed to splinters, so we go for skiff." Here Malich took another drink and almost chuckled at the memory. "'Tis passin' strange, b'ye. Jus' before us hove up anchor an' leaves Labrador I says to Garret, tie that bloody skiff good so she won't come adrift agin'. My son, 'e tied'er on some good! Us covered in cod oil an' slidin' about jus' like in a glitter storm. My hands were that slubby I couldn't untie skiff, see. By this time flames's got'er sails, burnin' like a Jazuz torch, an' flankers flyin' by like turrs in a fright, an' then that fire's workin' along deck, even the waves is burning, with cod oil, see, an' in the hold, under the deck, comin' for us like the Devil. You could smell cod fryin' in seal fat. We was all goin' to burn in that conflagration."

"I told you she was too soaked up with fat!" shouted Grandfather, as if the story was an entertainment.

"Yes, Father, you told we often enough. An' what was us to do about it? An' now she's gone, an' Gerald with'er, an' you can remind me 'til the day you dies!"

"That's what got ol' *Diana*..."

"Yes, b'ye, an' the same thing's awaitin' us all in Hell!"

Malich downed his rum and held up the mug. Margaret moved to fetch the teakettle but he waved her off. She replaced the kettle and sat down in silence. No one touched the mound of fresh bread. The white slices with the crisp brown crust looked too much like human flesh.

Breeze continued pulling away dirty bandages, the visible affirmation of Malich's tale. Malich sighed and resumed.

"By some Holy luck a knife's washin' about in scuppers, see. Like a sign from Our Lord that it ain't time to die, eh? So, I grabs the knife an' cuts the line. Us had a job to get skiff alongside and keep'er from gettin' smashed up." Malich is running down like an old phonograph player. "By'n'by we gets Garret into skiff...By this time the Jazuz fire's got into'er lazerette. Hatch blows clean off an' then she's all aflame, with black smoke, an' nothing to see but the tops of 'er masts for flames." He took a drink to punctuate the scene. "My son, don't she roar an' crackle. We pulls away then, an' the sticks fall near to us. First the forem'st burns away. Saw a conflagration in forest one time. Those old spruce trees went up like torches. Never thought I'd see me own masts go like that. But there 'tis." He waited, processing a vision. "By'n'by the mainm'st goes over an' she settles down to burnin' herself out, breakin' apart on White Rock Ledge. It was a battle, see, whether fire'd get the job done or rocks'd rip'er open an' sink'er. We drifted away an' in a little while she's burnin' down to water line. The rocks couldn't kill'er see. She was too tough...But fire, my sonny boy, never a poor boat was built that could live through that." Malich raised his mug in a toast to tough old boats. "Then, by'n'by she's gone, all hissin' an' sputterin' an' boilin' up...an' all I can think of is...at least the flames get to Gerald before the crabs. 'Tis a bad bargain into it..." He drank to Gerald, seizing the bottle. He slammed the bottle on the table. The listeners gasped. "Then I remember what Moses Sheen said day before we leaved Labrador. He said, *may you'se burn in Hell an' your fish rot before you'se reaches Fogo*. My son, he was right enough on that!"

Breeze whispered to Garret, "The Sheens again." Garret made a sign. "Garret, I'm going to teach you to read and write. I want you to write down what you know. We'll start first thing tomorrow."

Breeze had a plan. She knew where Lliam kept his journal. She would teach Garret by copying the journal, but that was only part of the plan. She also wanted to know what Lliam wrote about her. She knew it was wrong, but only a little indiscretion, considering that

105

Lliam never once wrote to her while away in Boston. She resented that as much as she loathed Malich Dwyer and his dead son.

Lliam's family was cursed, he realized. He was part of the curse and there was no escape in Béhathook Cove, St. John's or Boston Town, so where did he belong?

Margaret retreated to her stove. Malich drifted down into the depths with the wreckage of his schooner, heavy eyes half closed, peering at Lliam as if seeing him for the first time. "So you've come home again, eh? My sonny boy, they try you." Malich was torn also, wanting to reach out for that shred of family, but he was too far into the bottle, with too many hurts, swimming for the bottom. "Mainland women can't please you neither, I suppose?" he said, maliciously.

Lliam was watching Breeze. He envied Garret, would take Garret's place for the chance, but doubted he could take the pain. Garret was raised in pain. Lliam was a dodger. "I just came home," he answered Malich. "I came home...to be home, I suppose."

"Did you bring a pocket full o' Yankee dollars to buy us through the winter?"

Lliam shook his head. He had spent his last dollars on a punishing crawl through the pubs of St. John's. Malich was slipping into exhaustion. Lliam reached out in turn. "How did you get the boat home, Father?"

Malich was on the White Rocks, waiting for the resurrection of his favourite son. "Wha? Home? To Fogo?"

"Did you actually row all the way?"

"Yes, b'ye! Best way we knows when Lord takes engine as well."

"Just the two of you?"

"I said that, didn't I? Took Garret to St. Anthony. They did what they could an' we come on."

"But that's at least a hundred miles."

"Hundred an' twenty nautical miles from where Gerald lays, Lliam. One hundred an' twenty...but that's nothin'."

It was nothing, and there was nothing else to say.

Dawn: After an early breakfast of thin fish stew with fried bread, he followed Malich and Doyle into the fenced garden. The soil was as cursed with rock shards as he remembered, and it reminded him of the blasted tailings he shoveled in a Pennsylvania coal pit. It had taken only a day of digging and slipping in the loose rock to prove that there were jobs worse than jigging cod. Back home, Lliam was digging potatoes but he had only to push in the fork, lift the plants, shake free the loose dirt, pick off the potatoes and poke about with the fork. He picked and sorted, inspecting them for blight and put them into boxes: late keepers and the early eaters. Two rows of probing and pulling left Lliam sweating, hands blistered from the rough shaft of the fork.

The Dwyer garden gave a view of the O'Keefe garden. Breeze was also digging potatoes, working quickly and surely. She separated and sorted, stopping only to carry a basket to the root cellar. If she noticed Lliam she made no sign. Malich mounded turnips nearby. The turnips were covered with dirt borrowed from the potato plot. Doyle covered the new mounds with straw cut along the fences. Mounding the turnips for the winter saved space in the root cellar, although the harvest seemed inadequate to feed the family.

"Jus' tell me how, sonny?" asked Malich.

"How what, Father?" Lliam asked reluctantly.

"How do I feed you lot come March month with the season gone an' not a cask o' train oil to burn lamps?"

"I don't know, I'm sure."

"Thought you was the thinker in this family. Ain't that what you run to Mainland for, to get a livin' without you have to work for it?"

"There are more ways to work than breaking your back. They pay people to be clerks and accountants. Even teachers get paid. It's no shame to work in your brain, Malich."

"You think we don't use our brains in this God forsaken Paradise? My son, the cod don't swim onto the flakes, an' the trees don't fall into our stoves."

"That's not what I meant."

"You meant to say that we're a crowd o' ignorant slaves, what God provides for only out o' His mercy."

There was no use arguing with Malich. Verbal beatings were harder to endure than the cuffs and kicks. He wondered what the Sheen home on Change Island must have been like. He had seen the results of abusive fathers and heard rumours of the distant Sheens. They were rough, violent and dishonest...so the rumours say, and he had seen the written evidence in an old journal kept by Grandfather.

Lliam returned to digging. *It isn't such a bad job,* he told himself. At least there would be food on the table at the end of the day. How many days? He thought of Boston and the Irish market. Lliam had only to select what he needed, and pay if he had the money. There was no credit on the mean streets of a big city, unlike that extended by the merchant in Fogo. Money was the universal problem for city dwellers and credit was the attendant curse for the outports. In Boston he had been offered 'easy money' by a bar owner who ran a business from the back room of his pub. The business thrived on gambling and women. The man needed an accountant who could keep the records and keep his mouth shut. Lliam's natural sense of trouble warned him to keep clear. He told the man his reasons. For his insight and honesty the man threatened to have him dumped into Boston Harbour, laughing about a Tea Party. Lliam knew the story of the famous incident that sparked the American War of Independence but could see no parallel, nor the humour. He moved from Bunker Avenue to a more anonymous address in the East Docks area. The cobbled lanes were narrower, the flats smaller and cheaper. He made his money tutoring merchant's children...He stopped digging to reflect on the relative safety of his rude Boston flat, and the comfort of his books, and Molly...

"Get on with it! You're as lazy as Doyle."

The workday ended when the rare fall sun suddenly dove into an ominous bank of black clouds and cold rain with cutting sleet slashed in off the ocean.

By dawn the following morning Malich had the skiff's engine repaired and sent Doyle and Lliam along the coast to cut wood. The rugged Southeast corner of Fogo has no sheltered harbours, therefore remaining wild and abundant, shared by anyone willing to travel among the seabirds and berries bushes. Trees of a size were further inland where a skittish heard of caribou roamed, being hunted, like the Béothic Indians, to extinction.

They motored to a shallow cove, little more than a depression in the rocks with a sloping gravel beach, mooring the skiff in deeper water on a falling tide. By the time they finished cutting and hauling the skiff would be near the beach stones. They waded ashore and Doyle led the way over the rocks, around boggy ponds and across open ground to the stand of stunted spruce a mile beyond the beach.

Lliam tried his best but his best wasn't good enough for Doyle who worked on him every chance. They felled the small spruce with a cross cut saw that slipped out of Lliam's grasp too often to suit Doyle. They limbed with hatchets, Lliam flailing away dangerously. Doyle scoffed. Lliam bore the abuse in silence because there was no point arguing with Doyle either. Doyle was dull witted, but Doyle worked harder than usual to intimidate Lliam. In six punishing hours they had enough small logs to fill the skiff.

On the voyage back to the Cove, Lliam sat in the bow with the lengths of sweet smelling spruce between them. He preferred the tang of spray and the resinous aroma to Doyle's company and the exhaust of the rattling make'n'break. Over the sound of the engine, Doyle yelled what passed for good-natured abuse. Lliam ignored the taunts and watched the rocks and the black and white sea birds. He never tired of the stark beauty of his island, harsh and unforgiving as it is. Mainlanders might be repulsed by the bleakness of the Newfoundland coast but there is an attraction that Lliam could never fathom.

Close to their port side the surf rolled and foamed around dark rocks. To starboard the grey-green seas marched at them in endless rows. The ocean is never still and death just a slip away. It is dangerous but the sea birds and fish seem to endure...*So do men like my father*, Lliam mused. If they worked with the dangers and survived, they were allowed to thrive, in good years. Could he make himself into a fisherman like his father, without having to be hard and cynical and abusive? Lliam wondered if the granite exterior and the rough talk of the man was just a façade? And what of the story Malich told of the long row home with the charred body of his mute son? How could a mortal man face such terror and go on with life unless he had an iron will or utter contempt for death? Then Lliam remembered Malich's eyes as he told the story, the need to reach so often for the rum bottle...*It's all Malich has ever known for a life.* For a fleeting moment Lliam fancied himself to be the stronger man for having the courage to run...The skiff lurched and rolled in a swell as Doyle altered course for the harbour.

They staggered through the fish room with lengths of spruce.

"You'll not eat," bawled Malich, "'til it's all stacked proper!"

Malich didn't look up from repairing an old cast net. Most of their fishing gear had gone down with the *Margaret and Maude.* Gear had to be resurrected, and they would need fish to bait the rusty hooks. The old tubs of trawl lines were last used when Grandfather Dwyer still fished close to shore, between voyages. To keep a hand in, he'd say.

"...An' muck out that mess in skiff."

That evening, while Breeze tended Garret's burns, Mother O'Keefe, in a black mood, watched her daughter administering to a dead man. Lliam watched as Margaret cooked and served those at her table. Brigid O'Keefe complained of pains. After a meager dinner, Grandmother knitted, Grandfather smoked and dozed while Malich and Doyle retreated to the store to repair nets. Lliam was left behind to brood and scribble notes. Another day of tension ended in Béhathook Cove.

Malich left before dawn. Lliam lay in bed listening to the hesitant *put-put-putta-put*, mutter of the make'n'break engine as Malich headed out of the harbour and rounded the Turning Rock for the Southeast. Malich had torn the engine down and did what he could but it still miss-fired, and seemed ready to quit at any moment. But he had to go. The capelin were gone for the season. The main cod body was off the near-shore jigging grounds but stragglers remained. He heard from Uncle Billy that there were scattered herring hanging about the offer rocks. Some mackerel might be in a bay further along. The morning was cold but clear and later the sun would be warm with a land breeze.

Lliam and Doyle had tea and fried bread with oatmeal porridge and went out to cut the logs they had harvested the previous day. They bucked up the spruce logs into stove length pieces, laying the logs out on a box-like jig, moving along the sectioned box, getting five pieces out of each log. The sun was half way up the horizon when they finished cutting and Margaret brought them out a mug of tea. They could see Malich in the skiff, a mile to the Southeast, casting his net near the rocks. They could see other fishermen trying their luck also.

"Time to split'n'stack, Brother. I'd better be on the end of axe or one of us can join ol' John Kenny playin' checkers." Doyle swung the axe, neatly parting two halves of a spruce section. They joined a growing pile around the splitting stump. Lliam stacked the splits in a circle, creating a silo half as high as a man. The rest would be tossed inside to dry. They could also see Breeze in her backyard using cutting a big pile of spruce logs that she had traded bachelor Morgan O'Dell for a year's worth of bread and laundry. If she noticed Lliam she didn't let on.

"She can work, that one," said Doyle. "Not like some fellas."

"Why does Breeze cut logs? That's not women's work."

"Just'er way, I suppose. Ol' lady's got some money aside but won't spend none of it as long as Breeze's able to do a man's job. Breeze does most everything besides, 'cept fish down Labrador. An' I believe she'd do that too, but good lookin' girls 'board boat's just trouble, if you ask me."

"Breeze's a grown woman."

"Ol' lady O'Keefe won't let'er outta her sight. Man marries alongside o' Breeze get's more than a wife, sure."

"Was Gerald willing to take on the Old Lady too?"

"Don't be daft, Lliam. Gerald never looked past gettin' up Breeze's skirt as often as possible."

"Were they, you know...?"

Doyle snorted. "Oh my, Breeze's a one to tease, my son! Gerald had to chase'er down like rabbit. An' no one runs them rocks like Breeze, I knows that."

"But, Breeze said she never laid with Gerald."

"Where's your head to, Brother? What kind o' fuckin' saint do you think she is? So far as I know, Gran'father's the only one o' this family what ain't had their way with Breeze. An' I ain't that sure o' Gran'father. Then there's Morgan O'Dell an' Harnet, an'..."

"Shut up, Doyle!" Lliam wanted to seize the axe and cleave Doyle's stupid face...The gap toothed gargoyle who defiled Breeze just by talking about her...The thick blood running down the hill and Doyle's two half heads stacked into the pile to dry: to burn like kindling on a cold night...One swing of the heavy axe...He tossed the armload of splits at Doyle's feet. "Stack it yourself!"

Lliam went out the gate and along the path to the O'Keefe house, not certain what he was doing or why. He had no claim on Breeze. He pushed through the gate, almost forcing it off its hinges.

Breeze was startled. "Lliam...?"

"I've come to help you cut wood."

"I'm used to workin' alone."

He took hold of the bow saw. "I'd like to."

"Saw's right for one."

"Then I'll do it myself."

"As you wish." She watched Lliam handle the cranky saw, jerking it through the bark and into the fresh wood. It kicked and stuck. He tugged and cursed. The saw blade skipped out and nicked his hand. He found the kerf again and jerked too hard. The log lurched at him, almost capsizing the cutting box. "Lliam, you don't have to do this. You're not..."

"Curse the thing! What a stupid instrument!"

"Here, let me. I don't mind, really." Lliam surrendered the handle. She drew the blade deftly and easily, a shower of sawdust falling around her boots. "There, Lliam, see? It's easy when you have practice. It's like you when you write a poem, I suppose, though I don't recall you sendin' me any."

Again, the deep cut. The jibe. The nick on his hand began to throb with pain. Breeze was right. He had never written to her. He had written about her. "I'll chop for you then."

112

"If you wish. I do lack the strength sometimes. Mother says I just don't try hard enough. Sometimes the men will stop by and split wood." She continued cutting.

In exchange for what else? he wondered. Lliam wrenched the axe out of the splitting block and set a chunk. "Careful you don't cut off a foot, now. I've enough invalids to care for." She meant it as a joke. Lliam seethed. He swung the axe and the head glanced off the narrow piece, landing dangerously close to Breeze's foot. "Maybe you should start out some slower, my dear, 'til you get the hang of it, otherwise one of us is apt to finish up like Uncle George when he come back from the Great War." Again Breeze was joking. She had experience dealing with the Dwyer men who, except for Garret, were short tempered and subject to violence.

Lliam picked up the axe, fingers close to Breeze's boot. The wind blew her skirts around. Sawdust whirled. White, smooth skin showed above her rubber boots. He wanted his hand on her legs, to run his hand up her thighs. *Gerald's only desire was to get up Breeze's skirt,* said Doyle. And who else? Everyone it seemed. She was looking down at him, smiling. She looked odd from that angle. Dark, like an Irish witch. Taunting him. Casting a spell. *No better than a whore in a witch's disguise.* The whores of Boston did not wear rubber boots. Molly McCracken wore soft yellow dresses that swished when she moved but she did not wear rubber boots. Not even the whores of St. John's on a rainy day. Lliam dragged the axe back to the splitting block.

"Lliam, my love? Are you all right? Maybe you should start with..."

He swung the axe again and found the center. The split was clean. The two halves leapt away and the axe blade drove deep into the splitting block. He pulled at the handle. The block toppled. He set the block upright and pulled harder. Then he put his foot on the block and wrenched the axe out and stumbled backward. Breathing hard in frustration he put another piece of wood on the block. He swung and the wood flew away. He had the mark now. He swung and chopped and swung again, grunting with the effort. Breeze backed away, out of range of the axe and the flying wood. She picked up a basket of potatoes and headed for the root cellar. Lliam threw the axe down.

The root cellar was dark and dank, with a low ceiling and shelves, barrels and bins for vegetables. Most were still empty. Breeze had her back to the door. His shadow fell over her. She turned. "Lliam, don't..."

He was on her in one step, forcing her against a shelf. The shelf gave way and potatoes rolled across the dirt floor. Dust boiled up like smoke. He threw her against a barrel. She didn't resist.

"Lliam, dear...you don't have to do it like this."

He thrust his hand under her skirts. She gasped, eyes wide. He clutched at her underwear, pulling them down to her knees. But when he touched her pubic hair his attack softened as he probed into her, then he was rough again. "Is that the way Father did it?" He kissed her mouth hard. Then he was tender again, rubbing gently. Breeze began to relax, her breathing becoming one with the movement of Lliam's fingers. When Lliam realized her desire rising he changed again and the attack became an attempt to humiliate her. He pulled at her heavy skirt but it would not give way.

"Lliam, don't...not like them."

"Who?"

"Your brothers...your damned father."

"Malich an' Gerald? Here, Breeze? Over potato barrel? You said Gerald never did you up on hill, like Garret did. Where was it, Breeze, my darlin'? In skiff? Did you go fishin' with Gerald? You'd like to fish with the men, Doyle said. Was it on a mound of nets in fish rooms with Doyle?" His voice rose with every accusation. "On stage for everyone to see? Was it around the Head on a Sunday with Malich?"

"Stop it!" she cried, pulling away. "You said yourself, 'tis nobody's business what grown people do."

He wanted her to deny every rumour, but Breeze could not lie. "You're nothing but the village whore!" He turned away, striding into the sunlight.

"You don't know what it's like for a woman in this place, Lliam Dwyer. You're no different than the rest o' them!"

Lliam spent a sleepless night tossing about in Gerald's bed, as if his dead brother's ghost prodded him, jolting him into consciousness so the guilt and the rage could battle it out. By the black hour before dawn he'd vowed to forget Breeze, then exhausted, slept only moments it seemed, before Doyle kicked him awake. "You're wanted to breakfast, Brother, dear."

The low ceilinged bedroom was cold and damp. Grey walls almost invisible. He could have been staring at the bleak horizon. He dressed in Gerald's long Johns and work clothes and made his way in darkness down the narrow stairs.

Garret was asleep on the daybed, avoided by the family like a sick dog dying in a corner. Breeze came everyday to change his bandages and feed him. Margaret changed his rag diapers and emptied the bedpan when necessary. The smell of pus and putrid flesh dominated even the smell of fresh bread. Margaret had been up for two hours baking bread and scrubbing clothes before she woke Malich. Grandmother and Grandfather still slept in the bed set up in the parlour with the good furniture.

When Lliam entered the kitchen, Malich and Doyle were at the table bolting down porridge, hot bread with jam and scalding tea. Without a word spoken Margaret put a bowl of porridge and a mug of tea on the table. The big iron kettle steamed on the stove. Doyle made slurping, chewing sounds, as if a machine was at work. Lliam washed his face with cold water in the china bowl on the sideboard, dried himself with a flour bag and took Gerald's place at the table. He added molasses to the porridge and toyed with the mess that resembled deck tar, sipping at the strong black tea. He ate some bread with bitter jam. The supply of sugar was rationed and there was no butter or even lard to spare.

"B'yes," said Malich, holding his cup out for Margaret to refill, "best eat a good breakfast. We'll be gone the day."

Margaret dried her red hands on her apron, crossed to the stove and filled Malich's cup. Lliam was about to comment that his father could have reached the kettle himself, but thought better. "Oh? An' where might we be going?"

"'Round to see merchant Mulroney."

"Why do I have to go?"

"Because..." Malich's reason for taking his sons was to play on the merchant's sympathy. He'd have taken Garret also but the trip would kill him. He thought of loading the elders into the skiff as well. "Because, sonny, you need to know what it's like to deal with that man. Heartless, greedy, but Ashcroft in Twillingate's worse even. They own us, lock, stock an' barrel." Malich gulped his tea, scraped his chair as a signal that it was time, and took his coat from the peg behind the door. Lliam continued eating. Doyle departed behind his father, bread in hand.

Garret opened his eyes and looked around the room. He focused on Lliam. "It's me, Garret...Lliam." Garret nodded and closed his eyes. Lliam was seized by a vision of the world closing in, choking the life out of him. "Goodbye, Mother," Lliam said, taking Gerald's old coat off the peg. He wanted to kiss her, to hold her red, swollen hands.

"Goodbye, then...Lliam. Do be careful."

He met Breeze on the path. She was on a mission, carrying a pot of broth. "Morning, Breeze."

She looked pale in the grey light of dawn. "Mornin', Lliam. How's Garret?"

"Fine, I suppose. He's awake just now."

"Oh, I've brought some broth. He's had trouble with the fish."

"I see. You'd better..."

"Better go in before it cools."

"Yes. Breeze, are you all right? I mean, you look, tired." He meant sick, and it was his fault.

"I'm not damaged, if that's what you mean?"

"No, I was only thinking, that..."

"I was sick to my stomach this mornin' Lliam. I puked on the floor while makin' Mum's tea."

Lliam didn't make the connection. Breeze stepped aside, rubber boots slipping on the wet stones. It had rained in the night: a brief, slashing fall gale that left the morning air washed and fresh. He reached out to steady her. "I'm sorry to hear that. I hope you're better, Breeze."

"I'll live."

He watched her open the gate, tread the boardwalk to the porch and enter the kitchen. Shutting him out. Always going away.

The sea gives. The sea consumes. The sea is a constant force in the lives of the outporters. They came across the sea for the fish, clutching at the rocks like barnacles. They dwelt on the land but needed the sea. Communities grew up in the best harbours close to the fishing grounds. They fished and ventured inland to augment their meager living. They went after the seals by boat and travelled from cove to cove, island to island, to renew the species and share the news. Goods and news travelled by water, in all kinds of weather. If an outporter waited for good weather nothing would be accomplished. Malich and his boys pushed off at dawn in the skiff with only a brief look at the morning sky.

"Dirty weather, comin', b'yes," Malich shouted over the *thumping* engine.

Dirty weather could mean a brief squall with ice pellets that as quickly turn to splashes of sunshine, or slashing gales in a grey day of rain and fog. Squalls come down quickly and the fishermen in their small boats endure. It's the dangerous weather breeders from the Southern Ocean that the fishermen fear most. But hurricanes take their time, brooding over the horizon as the massive low-pressure system pulls the elements into its coil: announcing its presence as a dark smudge on the horizon at dawn, the Eastern sky going from grey to black, then purple or green as the wall moves relentlessly northward. By mid afternoon the sun wears a halo of high frontal clouds, like the veil that hides the face of a mysterious woman. The fair winds drop off and the atmosphere becomes heavy. The dreaded calm, the waiting time..."She's likely to be a big one, my sons, jus' waitin' to catch us out, eh?" Malich said, taunting his sons...The slow approach, throbbing and deadly. Hurricanes have no need to be shy or in a hurry. They announce their coming and strike at the soul of the mariner who has pulled his boat well clear and tied his home to the rocks. Hurricanes can whip forests into a twisting frenzy, and leave them flat like prairie wheat after a summer cyclone. "A broodin' bitch, Lliam, them hurricanes. Mean an' cruel."

It's just foolishness to personify hurricanes, thought Lliam. He had often heard his father talk of the weather as if it was a malevolent enemy.

Malich, standing in the stern sheets, gnarled hands on tiller, studying the high-flying clouds, said, "Nothing to harm us this mornin'. Cup o' wind maybe."

Lliam, sitting at the bow, could barely hear his father's dismissive pronouncement over the persistent *thump* of the engine. He had his doubts about the weather, and the engine. The engine sounded inconsistent, irregular, as if it couldn't decide whether to run or stop. Black smoke exploded from the base of the engine. Malich explained that it had something to do with bad petrol and a weak battery or corroded igniter points, or all three. Lliam never understood the temperamental gas engines that East Coast fishermen trust with their lives. He eyed the rocks on their port side as they turned North into the chop set up across the long swell. The sea looked grey and cold. The fresh wind gusted up and salt spray blew over the rail to chill him. The bigger seas from a distant storm alternately worried at the slime covered rocks or crashed in with power, sucking and frothing around the ancient brown feet of the cliffs.

Lliam summoned the scanty sea-lore he had learned as a child: how to spot the rock dangers by reading the colours. Blue or green meant deep water. Tumbling foam meant rocks just below the surface. Light green to yellow water meant a boat was too close to shore. And there were the sounds. He remembered trips to Fogo Harbour or fishing near the Change Islands. Always wet and cold, even on summer days when the ocean was on its best behaviour. But the Indian Fishing Islands were the worst. Exposed to the open ocean and the send of Hamilton Sound, they were a nasty place to be caught out in any direction of wind. The children, who seldom had good boots or warm coats, were always on the pang edge of hunger, allowed only a crust of bread with lard, and cold tea. Malich tried to harden the boys. Gerald took to it naturally enough. Doyle protested but had no choice. Garret never made a sign, as resigned to his harsh working life as he was to his silence. Lliam suffered and dreamed of the Mainland. He and Breeze read books together and planned their escape. Breeze wanted to resurrect the derelict schooner awash on her beach but Lliam insisted the key was the coastal boat to St. John's.

The coastal boat called at Fogo twice a month. Everyone left Newfoundland by way of St. John's or Lewisporte, unless they made the journey by train from Alexander Bay Station or Notre Dame Junction to Port aux Basques and escaped on the ferry to North Sidney. To a child, who knew the outside world only in books with exaggerated illustrations and fairytale monsters, it might as well have been Hong Kong or Singapore. Some escaped as sailors in foreign ships.

Lliam did not want to be a sailor. Breeze wanted to be a sailor, but that was out of the question for a girl. They had heard about famous air pilots who stopped at the new airfield at Harbour Grace before flying across the ocean to Europe. Some disappeared. Flying didn't appeal to Lliam either, and all the flights seemed to be going the wrong way. But Breeze knew about Amelia Earhart who landed at Harbour Grace the same spring Lliam left home. Amelia replaced Grace O'Malley, the Pirate Queen, as her hero. She longed to see icebergs from the air, but Newfoundland girls didn't fly airplanes either. When Lliam did leave it was by skiff to Twillingate Island and a southbound schooner from Twillingate to St. John's, then a working passage on a tramp coaster to Portland, Maine and on to Boston by train. His experience on the rusting freighter only reinforced his distaste for the seagoing life.

Ahead and to port the coast was a serrated mass of dangerous rock outcroppings, alternating with shallow coves and rocky beaches. Sea birds wheeled from the cliffs and called warnings at the intruders. The annoying exhaust explosions bounced among the rocks like accusations. The engine coughed, hesitated and picked up. Malich cursed. Waves crashed on the rocks and flung spray into the air. The sun broke through the clouds and caught a broken wave at its height and showered diamonds and rainbows. A restless, dangerous beauty held Lliam in a trance, suspended between fear and wonder.

Fogo Harbour: Doyle displaced Lliam from the bow. Lliam retreated amidships, not trusted with the simple act of tying up the skiff, and sat taking in the sights of Fogo Harbour. He knew the history of the place too well: fish and fishing.

Fogo Harbour is bounded by rocky hills, grassy meadows and fish flakes, and more rocks topped with frame buildings. When all the building sites were taken, newcomers simply moved on down the coast to another refuge like Shoal Bay, Joe Batts Arm or Rocky Cove. For three centuries after its discovery as the cod capitol of the world, there was no plan to make Newfoundland into anything other than a summer work stage for European fishermen. But desperate men wanted freedom, jumping ship and running from servitude. The outports grew up with a random appeal determined by the location of enough ground for the simple, flat roofed frame houses, meadows, and gardens. The island rewarded the tenacious settlers with an abundance of water, trees and fish. It was a paradise for anyone satisfied taking a living from the land and sea but the price was hard work. And it would have remained a paradise of abundance had it not been for human nature. Greed and neglect turned The New Founde Land into a scrambling colony of merchant pillagers and absentee landlords controlling the fishing families. The fishermen became no more than slaves to the merchant class. *Merchant families like the Mulroney clan*, thought Lliam, as he looked about the familiar landscape.

The Mulroney Premises dominated the waterfront with its sprawl of buff-painted, burgundy-trimmed frame buildings, stores and warehouses, a palatial setting beside the fisherman's weathered buildings, with their smatterings of red and yellow ochre, all blended together in a lump like bread pudding. The good harbour was surrounded and protected by hills. The hills were bare of trees but not barren. Everywhere there was colour and growth hugging the rocks as if an artist had loaded his palette with earth tones, heavy on the berry bush reds, oranges and yellows, with some olive green left in the juniper mat. Frost eroded rocks, the fragments scaling down the slopes, were greys, browns and buffs, with rust bleeding from iron oxide deposits.

It was tranquil in the harbour after the tumult of the coast: the water flat and reflective until the wake rolling away from the skiff sent it tumbling and breaking up on the rocks. Malich slowed the engine, its irregular muffled explosions announcing their arrival. But a trap skiff chugging toward the Mulroney Premises was hardly an occasion. A few eyes noted the Dwyers; the story was well known, but unremarkable: tragedy and loss a common enough event. The speculation among the watchers was how Malich and his brood would survive under the thumb of the Merchant Mulroney.

A. J. Mulroney and Sons: The sign over the door, in raised, red lettering on a gold leaf background, would not look out of place in the commercial district of London or Boston. A style imported from Olde England. Mulroney shipped most of his goods on his own schooners, cutting out the middleman but not offering the savings to his serfs. The 'Sons' were in England to get an education, the oldest expected to return and continue the dynasty while the other pursued business interests, extending their reach to the Continent. A. J. Mulroney stayed in Fogo because he could live like an emperor and be close to his roots. He was a simple man, more comfortable with sailors and fishermen than with the upper crust, only now recovering from the Depression and again spending money in Europe. But there was a war on the horizon and profits to be made for those well set up. There was gold in international trade and the world had not yet been divided into warring camps. Lessons from the Great War had been learned and the Barons of industry, at least, would not be caught napping by the Nazis. But for the present, A. J. Mulroney was concerned with indebted fishermen who failed to make their seasons.

Malich hesitated at the big mullioned glass doors, doffing his worn peak cap as if entering a church or a courthouse. The Mulroney Premises was both to poor fishermen. He pushed open the heavy door, motioning for his sons to follow.

The boys entered reluctantly, idling behind Malich, gazing at the groaning shelves piled with luxuries like Hamburg boots, swanskin mitts and fine clothing. Brass table lamps, cut glass and painted china flanked a gleaming silver tea service. A copper bathtub stood in a corner looking odd behind the coils of hemp rope and barrels of flour. A bathtub was an expensive conceit, not for the likes of Malich Dwyer's crew. Simple dry goods and the necessities of life were the goal. They gazed at counters loaded with bolts of broadcloth in dazzling colours and patterns that their mother longed to sew into garments for her clan. Margaret hadn't been to Mulroney's since her wedding year, nor had she been further from Béhathook Cove than the hills to pick berries, except for the one trip home when her father died, but she remembered the fabulous colours that would make Sunday dresses. She also had dreams, but the realities ran more to salt and bulk tea than to silks and tea services.

Malich ran his fingers over a pair of Hamburg boots, the polished black leather almost reflecting his haggard face. He strayed to a pile of soft peak caps, fingered the fine wool and looked at his own tattered cap. "My son!"

Lliam did a survey of the price tags. "Would you look at the bloody cost of this stuff!" said Lliam. "You wouldn't pay half that much in Boston, sure."

Mulroney slipped into the store from the backroom. "Boston's a long ways from Fogo, young man," he said, his flat tone as condescending as a father speaking to a child.

"Lliam, take off yer hat. It's Mr. Mulroney himself."

"Good day, Malich Dwyer...and to you, Doyle."

"Mornin', Mr. Mulroney," answered Malich. "Fine day."

"Aye, fine enough. An' who's this lean an' hungry hawthorn?" Mulroney asked, nodding at Lliam. "He doesn't look like a Dwyer." Mulroney was the antithesis of Lliam: fleshy faced with the typical jowls of the overeater, large head and thick neck, which seemed to be one with the squat body and bandy legs. But the arms were powerful even hidden by the shopkeeper's shirt and waistcoat. Thinning hair close cropped, wiry with flecks of grey. The wild eyebrows met above a pince-nez and matched a perpetual frown.

The Mulroney clan had sprung from peasant stock, as did the Dwyers. The dark complexion showing middle European, Southwest England, Bristol to Bournemouth, but his traceable ancestors came from the West Counties of Ireland, as were the Dwyers of Donegal. The Dark Irish. They could have been related in misty times, an errant branch of the long vanished Armoricans, driven from Brittany, across the Channel to England and Scotland. Perhaps some managed to infiltrate Ireland, defying the ruthless Celts. Before that they may have been driven out of Rumania, Turkey or Northern Italy to settle briefly in Southern France before being sent into exile and lost to civilization. The unlucky tribes of history happened to be enemies of the Celts and in the path of the Roman Legions pacifying Northwestern Europe. How they got to the West Counties of Ireland to darken the Celtic line is a puzzle, as the Dark Irish are a puzzle even to themselves. *Perhaps Roma Gypsies spawned them,* Lliam speculated. Breeze insisted there was Portuguese blood in Ireland...

"That's just Lliam, me youngest. Back from Mainland."

"Visiting the family is he?"

"Maybe not, sir. He's bound to help 'is family in our time of sorrow an' need. Truth is, sir..."

"Doesn't look much like a fisherman either, more like a fish out of water, but I suppose he could be 'made'." Mulroney laughed at his own joke. Doyle laughed because Mulroney laughed. Malich tried on a grin that was more a grimace. He was not getting through to Mulroney. "Here to help out your father, are you?" Without waiting for a reply Mulroney excused himself and went back to his office, leaving the Dwyers standing about awkwardly, surveying the emporium. Doyle needed a new coat. His threadbare fishing rig could no longer hold the tar. Malich coveted the Hamburg boots. They were no good for fishing, without generous applications of tar or oil, but they would be spectacular for step dancing during the Mummer's Days.

Lliam thought of Breeze and his own mother, Margaret. He imagined dresses made of the bright broadcloths, remembering both of them dressed in Sunday best for occasions when they could go about without coats or long wool shawls: and all the woman and girls lining the paths, glowing like spring flowers. Lliam resented the girls' ability to wear colourful things, the men confined to dark clothing, but the occasions for colour were rare and there were too many solemn processions to the cemetery when the dresses had to be hidden...

"We heard about the unfortunate incident, Malich," Mulroney intoned on his return, carrying the heavy black ledger. It could have been the Bank of England's Accounts, or the Book of Kells. The first entry had been made by Mulroney's father in 1883 and the first outport debtor was a Dwyer from Tilting. He put it down ceremoniously on the high writing table. "We are sorry for your losses."

"Thank you, sir. It's what we come to discuss."

"I expected you would," he said dryly, as he turned the pages to the Dwyer Family of Béhathook Cove. There were long columns of figures in Mulroney's precise script. The items and dates entered in black ink. Beside them the cost figures in red ink. The amounts paid back over the years in black on the right, the balance always brought down in red. The ink resembled dried blood. "But I'll tell you straight out, Malich, I can't give you more credit, without collateral. You an' your family are deep into me books as 'tis."

"Aye, sir, we knows that. You see, sir, with the times..." He trailed off, intimidated by the amount of the debt. Malich and Doyle could not read the written words, but the last figure in red was plain enough.

Lliam tried to get a look at the items listed and match them with the prices but many of the items he did not recognize. The items he did understand seemed very expensive. He could only guess what a simple one-cylinder engine, imported from Lunenburg, could have cost Mulroney & Sons when it was new. The engine was twenty years old, failing and still not paid for. But with credit charges, batteries, petrol and spare parts, it seemed the engine debt was higher than the original cost. Was there no end? The other thing Lliam noticed was that the price of cod paid to the fishermen: a quintal of dried fish returned less each year, declining as the Depression deepened and catches increased. The cost of trap nets and trawl lines escalated coincident with the catch tonnage, so it seemed that the harder the fisherman worked the less he received, and the more the merchant pocketed for his generous credit.

"As to what you calls, collateral, sir...we got nothin' left to put up, 'cept Gran'father's house, what his own father built with bare hands."

"I'm sure it's a fine house, and worth something in its day, but I've enough rotting old houses on the books now to accommodate half the bloody island."

"Me family's like to starve this winter, sir."

"Aye, an' mine the winter after if I gave all my failed fishermen credit. We're into hard times, Malich." It was a familiar argument repeated by merchants around the coast of Newfoundland in the depths of the Great Depression.

"I've three grown sons, sir, a wife, as well as the elders."

"A man of my good nature can do just so much, then I put my own family at risk," countered Mulroney.

Lliam almost laughed. He could imagine the risks Mulroney's sons were taking in London and Paris. The risk of missing a reservation for dinner, or the opera, because Malich Dwyer needs boots, and his wife needs flour to feed the family.

Malich had one more option. It was a hard thing for a proud man to consider, a ship owner himself, even though that ship was cradled in deep water off White Rocks Ledge. "I'll skipper one o' your schooners next season."

"Malich, my son, I've got captains working as deckhands now."

Malich knew that as a fact of life. Seven years of Depression meant most owners had been forced to lay up ships for lack of cargoes, and put experienced seamen ashore. Desperate captains used their seniority to bump junior officers out of their berths. The independent fishermen with their own boats were the lucky few, even if they were robbed of their profits by the feudal system. It was a delicate balance that worked in good times. In bad times the merchant might suffer also, but if he could hold out long enough the good times always returned and he still had his surviving fishermen ready and able to go at the game. Malich was in a silent rage.

"Do you hear me, Malich?"

Malich eyed a wicked looking flensing knife. "Aye, sir, I know nothing else to offer you, 'cept me own blood."

Mulroney sensed Malich's mood. *What desperate measures was this Black Irishman capable of?* he wondered. The bloody histories of the Dwyers and the Sheens were well known.

"Malich, my good man, desperate ones before you have shed blood, an' it's done nothing but hurt their families. You remember Shamus O'Farrell from Wild Cove? Gutted himself like a fish on our wharf, before our eyes, and three of his own sons as witness. We said it was an accident to protect his family, but you know his oldest boy went mad and the story eventually had to come out. The desperate mother took the family to Labrador. The next winter that poor lad slaughtered and salted his own mother and brother because they could not make it as Liveyers, with no adult man to guide them. The other son, the youngest, went to war and was never heard of again. That poor family was destroyed, Malich, because Shamus ruined more than himself."

"Aye, some days I'm that close myself, Mr. Mulroney."

Mulroney walked to the window and looked out over his empire. "You have a fine trap skiff and two hands. You can still fish."

"She's got cranky engine an' wants overhaul. That means parts from Lunenburg or what I can beg from buddy. An' besides, we lost all our gear when schooner burnt. We can't fish with rusty trawl 'cept to get a meal or two...certainly not enough to provide a winter. We got to eat more than fish, sure."

"You have a garden, no doubt, like the others."

"A poor crop o' turnips at best, an' some blighty potatoes. Got scabbies."

"There might be work in the mines this winter. I hear the markets are opening up with this war promised in Europe. Wouldn't surprise me if the price of fish went up too, eventually," he said wistfully, counting potential profits to make up for the Depression years.

"Family'd perish 'fore we got home with pay come spring."

"There's seals in March month."

"Same thing with seals, sir. There's no time."

Mulroney returned to his ledger, retreating into the comfortable logic of the numbers. He turned pages slowly, comparing profits and losses. Stalling for time, a plan forming behind his mask of indifference. "I don't know, Malich..."

"We'll not make it, sir, without I get credit. There's the old ones. Father still eats like slide horse. Then there's Garret sick an' needs things beside a meal now an' then. 'Sides else now we got to feed Breeze O'Keefe, when she tends Garret, an' more often'er mother comes along, an' she eats enough for two. Then there's these strappin' lads what eat twice what they're worth. An' I got to have a bite now an' then myself."

Lliam realized Malich had not mentioned Margaret. "What does Mother eat?" asked Lliam. "Is Mother a saint, expected to fast for her sins?"

"Mother? 'Course she eats, you daft lame brain!"

Doyle whispered, "Lliam lame brains."

"Shut up, Doyle...That's right. She not only eats, she prepares your meals an' washes your clothes," continued Lliam, ignoring Doyle who was skipping around him with a woman's bonnet perched on his head, the price tag an appendage of his nose.

"What's the 'count o' that? Course she does! It's just'er duty."

"You never really thought about it did you? Did you ever once consider Mother as part of the crew?"

"What's got into you, sonny? You stay out o' this. 'Tis none of your affair."

"Shut up, Lliam lame brains," Doyle whispered.

"You brought me here so I could see first hand how you deal with Mr. Mulroney and now I watch you practically beg an' grovel."

Mulroney had heard enough. A family feud in his Premises was not business. "Well, Malich, looks like you got yourself up to a hard place." He tapped the ledger with a pencil as if conjuring some magic solution. "I'm a compassionate man an' won't see a family starve for want of enterprise. You an' your father, an' his father before, as my own dear father testified, were always hard workers."

"Yes, sir. I can vouch for that. The record shows..."

"An' I hope your sons carry on that tradition."

"You can mark it down, sir." Malich shot a look at Lliam that dared him to contradict. He could sense a ray of hope but misjudged Mulroney's direction. "Truth is, sir, I got me oldest son dead. He was the one to make things go, even if he was a bit lazy given half a chance, an' I got Doyle here. He's willin' but not that smart, an' likely to follow Gerald into lazy ways. I got me idiot, me best worker burned bad, sure, an' likely to die on me. An' I got Mr. Soft Hands from Boston. Don't seem much but he may come to bait."

"Dare say, it's not encouraging. But here's my proposition. You've heard of the *Black Fenian*, built by Seth Sheen, over to Change Island?"

"Aye. Everyone knows about the Sheens."

"A Jack schooner, twenty-five tons, 'bout the same size as your own."

"Yes, sir, I knows of'er." The sad story and rumours of the *Black Fenian* were well known. Malich wondered what Mulroney was getting at.

"She was almost finished. A shame. She's in a little cove on East side of Change Island. The Sheen homestead. Some call it Sheen's Cove but most know it as Desperation Bay, Cutthroat Cove, an' other names."

"We know some of the story, sir."

"Yes, I'm aware you do." There was sarcasm in his voice. The rumours were not confined to Béhathook Cove. "I took the *Black Fenian* against the Sheen debt. As far as I know she's still good, new built as she was, but by now she'd want some work."

"An' you wants we to do the work?"

"I'll supply the rigging, line an' canvas, but you got to do her up an' provide whatever she needs else. Probably just wants a good overhaul an' new sails to make her fit. What do you say, Malich?"

"Dare say she'd want more than sails an' overhaul, sure."

"That may be, but that's my best offer. You do up my little schooner for next season, an' I'll see you through this winter."

"An' strike the Dwyer's debt besides?" ventured Malich.

"The entire debt?"

"Mr. Mulroney, with all due respects, sir, that little schooner's apt

128

to be stripped bare an' some rotted to boot. My guess is she'll want spars, an' more than a little gear, an' we'll have to work winter an' spring through just to make'er right. For that we need the family debt struck, sir."

Mulroney was momentarily set back by Malich's boldness. Only desperation could make a bondsman stand up to his master. "That's a hard bargain, Malich Dwyer."

"We walk away free an' clear?"

"Yes, I suppose...If you do up the schooner like she was your own. That's the letter of the agreement."

They carried a ton of goods to the wharf: barrels of flour and tubs of salt beef and pork, kegs of molasses and salt herring. Bales of dried cod, a case of tea, another of sugar and boxes of canned milk. A case of rum was disguised as trawl twine. Tobacco in bulk: the coarse shards preferred by Grandfather. Skeins of wool for Grandmother and, at Lliam's suggestion, a bolt of colourful broadcloth for Margaret. There were new coats and boots for Doyle and Lliam. A wool cap for Malich. Lamp oil. Parts for the engine and barrels of petrol. The supplies Mulroney allowed for the schooner included three rolls of sailcloth and balls of twine, plus a myriad of rigging wire, spools of rope and dozens of blocks for the tackle. The skiff settled deeper as their debt load increased, but Malich could see a way out. All they had to do was rebuild a schooner, a task he at least understood.

Malich was happier than he had been since the *Margaret & Maude* was launched fifteen years ago. He even slapped his sons on the back when the cargo was stowed. He didn't curse the engine when it refused to start, instead he dug out the new parts, tore down the igniter and changed the worn out points. With a fresh battery and petrol the engine responded to a spin of the flywheel. Malich broke out a bottle of rum and drank and sang the old songs as the skiff *chugged* resolutely across the harbour, leaving Fogo Head to port, setting a course for Brooks Point Light.

It was getting dark as they passed the entrance to Shoal Bay. The sea was unusually calm with a long, lazy swell running underneath the oily surface from the Southeast. The bottle was empty, tongue thick with drink and singing, and the mood had changed. Lliam didn't like the feel of the heavy atmosphere. The only happy note was the steady, resolute *chug-chugging* of the engine. But Lliam distrusted the rusted relic even more in its deceptive industry. Worse, there was a low mist building over the water, blanking out the shore and the light at Brooks Point: unusual conditions on their coast in September. A tropical depression lurked beyond the horizon about to collide with the cold Labrador Current.

Somewhere ahead was Drover's Rock, the dangerous granite pinnacle rising sharply from thirty-eight fathoms with only it's top awash. Over the centuries the Rock had wrecked many ships. The first a Portuguese fishing vessel three centuries before. A spirit presence hovered in the stillness, ghosts of dead sailors swimming in the mists above the black water. Lliam wished the engine would sputter and Malich curse the thing. Something real. They passed Drover's Rock by the sound, without a sighting.

Malich was preoccupied with the echo of the engine off the rocks to starboard, judging the distance to Brooks Point, and straining to see Storehouse Island Light and Little Fogo Light to port: the twin towers separated by three miles of sunkers and small islands; some of the nastiest sailing grounds on the coast of Newfoundland. First, Storehouse...there, just above the grey mist, almost abeam, and Little Fogo Light should be on the port bow and they could turn South by Southeast and run straight to Béhathook Cove with nothing in the way save Pigeon Island. *But Pigeon Island's like being in me own bed*, thought Malich, and he could smell his way in from there. He said as much to Doyle when his son shouted... "Where we to, Ol' Man?"

"Can you not hear Drover's astern, off to port there?"

"Not over fuckin' engine!"

"Right, then..." Malich flipped a switch on the side of the engine house and the heavy flywheel slowed down, kicked back a revolution and then, silence. Heavy fog muffled the restless ocean. Sea birds cried out for territory, but their plaintive calls only intensified the isolation.

"There, can you hear Drover's now?"

"Jasus, Ol' Man. What if she don't start?"

"Then you an' Lliam can row an' we'll smell our way in, jus' the way I find your mother in bed." He snorted and belched.

"Ol' Man, what if we makes up with rocks, an' all goes over?" asked Doyle.

"Then I'm over too, with a bottle in each 'and for ballast!" He laughed again, louder. His raspy, boozy voice mingled with the sudden crash of breakers on the rocks of Round Head, close to their starboard side, and then Drover's Rock further away on their port stern. Rogue waves rose suddenly in the shallows. The long, languorous swells had travelled many miles from the storm far to the South and East. The unsettling noises seemed to be all around them.

How could anyone tell one sound from another? Lliam wondered.

"Now can you hear it? *Awh*, both o' you'se useless as tits on turr!" He laughed louder. "Tits on turr...jus' tits on turr, with no fur!"

Lliam realized his father was roaring drunk. "Father, this isn't funny. We've got a winter's worth of goods. You have a responsibility to get us home safely."

"Responsibility? What kind o' big Boston word is that? I'll tell you 'bout responsibility, you flamin' lay about! It's not runnin' away from home an' leavin' yer family short. An' then comin' back with not a blessed thing to show, an' no sense o' what we do for work. That's what, Lliam-lay-about-lame-bones!"

"Lliam-lame-bones. Lliam-flamin'-lame-bones!" shouted Doyle.

"Shut up, Doyle! I won't argue the point, Father. It's as you say, but right now we seem lost, and you're drunk."

"Well, Mr. Boston-lay-about-soft hands, I knows precisely where we're to. Like that word? Precisely? I been on this god-damned fuckin' coast long enough I could get around stone blind. That's Little Fogo Light, right there!" He pointed at the wavering pinprick of light to his left, barely visible in the drifting fog. An' you can plainly hear Drover's right there, off our stern, an' if we go that way we run smack into Nor'west end o' Pigeon, an' from there see the light in our own fuckin' kitchen window! We could beach skiff in Sandy Cove an' walk home!"

Malich closed the switch, stumbled forward and gave the heavy flywheel a sharp pull. The wheel kicked back breaking two of Malich's fingers, but the hot engine responded instantly, taking only three revolutions to settle into it's rhythmic *put-put-putta-put-put*. Malich stood in the stern sheets cursing his injury. He opened another bottle of rum and gulped mouthful after mouthful to kill the pain then began singing a song about a wench named Jenny who disguised herself as a boy and went to sea. As the captain's 'cabin boy' Jenny saw more than the sea in verse after verse. Doyle joined in, taunting Lliam with altered lyrics, shouting *Breeze* instead of Jenny. Lliam slumped in the bow thinking of killing Doyle, not caring where the boat was pointed. The darkness of the black fog was complete. He was in the hands of fate, guided by rum-soaked lunatics.

Sunday Dwyer's Kitchen: The atmosphere in the Dwyer kitchen had undergone a sea change by Sunday evening. Two more kerosene lamps enhanced the brightness of the light glinting off the stout ceiling beams. The table, covered by white linen, was set with a feast: new potatoes, turnips, salt pork and cod. Chicken and gravy bubbled on the stove beside boiled peas pudding with a bread and raisin duff reinforced with rum.

Malich, at the head of the table, glowed with his own inner fire. He poured a dollop of rum into a water tumbler and passed the bottle to Doyle. Doyle splashed in a measure of the amber fire and filled Lliam's glass. He passed the bottle to Lliam who offered to fill a glass for Breeze. Breeze declined but took the bottle and poured an ounce for Brigid O'Keefe, who sat opposite. Breeze also poured for Grandfather and Grandmother Dwyer. Margaret declined and set the breadboard on the table and took her own place at the far end. It would have been more expedient for Margaret to occupy the chair nearest the stove, but that was Malich's spot, even though he touched nothing on the stove. That was Margaret's duty. Malich arched an eyebrow at Margaret's refusal to share a drink. He held up his own glass as if to make a toast, the broken fingers swollen and twisted. The injury was nothing. An inconvenience. "Won't drink a drop with us, Mother?"

Margaret cut the bread and passed a slice to Grandfather and then sent the breadboard on to Grandmother who passed it to Breeze without taking a piece herself. The breadboard made its way along the table to Malich. Malich took his slice then the board was passed back to Margaret. Breeze broke her bread and turned to look at Garret. Breeze held up the slice of bread, making a buttering motion. Garret shook his head and closed his eyes. Doyle began eating in his usual graceless manner. Malich slapped Doyle's hand with a knife.

"We got to thank the Lord, an' drink to Mr. Mulroney, you ignoramus!" He looked at Lliam to see how his learned son would react.

Doyle sang tunelessly, "Ignoramus, pigneramus, with feet an' hands, pick-yer-amus, Lliamus!" Doyle snorted like a pig.

Lliam cast his eyes down then flicked them up at Breeze who was looking steadily into his own. He couldn't read the look. He looked away to survey his family. Garret was asleep in his cloth shell and cloister. His mother was preoccupied with serving her family. Grandparents seemed unconcerned, but Brigid, starring back at him, was annoyed by his presence. Doyle ignored Lliam and vacantly mocked Malich, who was again sullen and contemptuous.

With no allies in the room, Lliam felt sick to his stomach and sweat rolled down his sides. He stunk of ammonia but he doubted it would be noticed in the hot kitchen, ripe with heady odours of fish and humanity. He wanted to run, but where? Retreating to his room was childish. Leaving home again was a painful option. Nor did he relish the idea of crossing the six miles of rocks and bogs to Fogo Harbour, the trails running off in a dozen directions. And he had had enough of boating in the dark. Besides, the calm of the approaching tropical depression foretold certain destruction for even experienced sailors caught out in small boats. The challenge was to stay and see it through.

The outside air was ominously still, but long swells breaking on the beach of the narrow peninsula shook the house. Following a thunderous crash, Malich stood up, grinding his chair, startling the assembly. Garret flicked opened his eyes. Grandfather almost choked on a piece of bread. "Never thought I'd see the day I'd bless A. J. Mulroney," began Malich, weaving with the strong rum. The booming of tons of water collapsing on the pebbles punctuated Malich's speech. "But here's to Mr. Mulroney. May God bless'is cold heart!" He drank two fingers of rum and wiped his chin, the back of his rough hand rasping across grey flecked stubble. He looked serious, dark and dangerous: the power of liquid fire glinting in his Dark Irish eyes.

Another breaker rolled in and collapsed on the beach stones. Soup bowls rattled in the sideboard and the crucifix over the washstand went out of plum. Malich looked at Doyle and then Lliam to gauge their reactions. He saw fear, as he expected. The inevitable winds to come would be destructive. He wondered about the old roof, and the foundation. Their home rested tenuously on the bare rocks. His father had driven steel rods through the foundation timbers into the rocks and threaded the rods. Malich noticed the old timbers going shawely, and bolts bleeding rust down the rocks and the moorings questionable. Some outporters anchored their homes with salvaged ship's rigging, crossing the roof like a web, ratlines and all, and leading to anchors in distant rocks, but Malich didn't have the room for proper guy wires, hemmed in as they were by neighbours. After the last hurricane he drove a series of anchors where he could into the cracks in the rocks along both sides of the house. "By'n'by we'll put some lines over house, I suppose."

"By'n'by might be too late," commented Margaret, dryly.

"You get that big hawse outta store an' heave'er down good," advised Grandfather, shifting to his rocker beside the stove.

"There's precious little to get purchase onto, but I suppose I could *drive* these two worthless pegs into ground an' tie hawse 'round their necks," he chuckled, indicating Lliam and Doyle. He meant it as a joke. No one laughed. "Well, b'yes, then here's to the *Black Fenian*. All we got to do is do'er up an' we're free as the bloody birds! Here's to Squire Mulroney, an' the *Black* fuckin' *Fenian*!"

No one drank. A breaker shook the house. They could feel the power through their feet now. And still no keening wind to explain the fury of foam and the noise like thunder on the outer beach. Grandfather stared straight ahead with jaw set: watery eyes looking at a vision a long way into the past, remembering days of fury as a deep-water sailor.

"What is it, Ol' Man? You can't drink neither to a little work, an' a chance to get out from under? What in Hell's fires wrong with you all?"

Grandfather Dwyer focused on his son. "Malich...do you know the story of the *Black Fenian*?"

"'Course I do! Everybody knows 'bout *Black Fenian*. Seen'er myself, after buddy built'er."

"I mean the true story, son?"

"Ol' Man, there's only one story, sure..."

"An' you don't want to see'er again, 'cept in flames. Put bloody torch to that one, first thing! There's a curse on the *Black Fenian*. A black curse."

"There's no curse, Father!"

"That little bummer's a killer, Malich, mark me now."

"G'wan, Ol' Man. She's just a boat," Malich said strongly, to convince himself. He had heard the rumours. Stories with tragic endings are common currency, traded among outporters by way of news and entertainment. Stories pass from cove to cove by the oldest means of communication. Even if a story changed before it made its way around the coastline of Newfoundland, there remained a thread of the original tragedy, the dark deeds, the undercurrent of superstition.

"'Twas a new boat Sheen built, then abandoned'er. Why would a man do that? Because she'd a curse into'er an' no one could figure how to get her clear." Grandfather sighed, looking beyond the confines of the kitchen to a darker time, locating his own place in the story.

Malich took a drink of rum. All eyes around the table were on him, waiting for the clan chief to speak. They needed to be reassured because the *Black Fenian* was their only shred of hope.

Breeze and her mother were not exempt. Their own fortunes were tied to the Dwyers since the loss of Gerald with the *Margaret & Maude*. There were supplies enough for the winter, but what of the next, and the next after that? They had been plunged deeper into the

135

merchant's books and the way out was a rotting hull shrouded in myth and mystery. It was survival against superstition.

"I say there's no curse, Father," declared Malich.

"She's cursed, b'ye!"

"She was just give up to Mulroney for debts!"

It was Grandfather Dwyer's turn to drink. Bony hands held the ceremonial glass as if it were a chalice. He raised the glass slowly, lamplight playing off the facets, casting rainbow sparks around the room. A collapsing breaker shook the house. The beach wash *sophed* among the pebbles like a deep sigh, the foaming water tumbling to the base of the rocks and then rushing back to sea. It was low tide, the least dangerous time. But the tide was turning.

Grandfather spoke like a prophet...*"Black Fenian* were built by the Sheen crowd, right where she's layin' to. I knowed Seth Sheen. He was husband to his own sister, from Weslyville, she were. Poor woman. A harder drinkin' man never was, an' drove his sons with a whip. The b'yes all worked some hard but never got nowhere 'cause Seth could never get clear o' bottle, see. They built that boat in one cruel winter. Tore her out o' forest with bare hands. Worked like all the demons in Hell was standin' over." Grandfather Dwyer took another drink. He had his audience. His distant memory was clear and the cold fire of the rum masked the pains of reaching back into another time. "Then the curse commenced...my son! That very winter one boy lost his feet to frost, an' he died a slow an' awful death from the black rot, with nary a doctor nor potion to ease him along. Sheen wouldn't stop buildin' to take boy to Twillingate Island or even ten miles to Fogo. You mark me? What kind o' man could watch his son die an' never lift a finger?" Something caught in the old man's throat. He cleared and spit into the wood box behind the stove. The corner of his eye showed a hint of a tear. Grandfather Dwyer raised his glass in a salute to the first dead son.

Lliam turned to look at Malich. Malich glared back at him.

The old man continued..."'Nother son died that same winter cuttin' masts, when big tree squat'im in forest. Least he died quick like, all standin'." Another sip of rum set him right.

"Seth's got three sons leaved then, an' he drove them b'yes to finish boat. An' they did! Ready to lunch'er off in spring." He drank another toast to the sons, and held his glass out. Malich poured the measure himself. "Demons must be some boat builders 'cause a finer little bummer was never made on these shores, sonny, but that only goes to prove she's cursed. Ship like that never would get done by a Sheen without Devil himself as foreman, an' a crowd o' Black Angles on the mauls!"

"Father, go easy now," cautioned Grandmother Dwyer. "You'll find your heart."

"I'm that close, Mother, a little talk 'ain't goin' to do me sooner."

The listeners were spellbound. Another huge sea crashed ashore to remind them of the fierce element the little ships were built to endure. The hurricane bar, the ugly black smear on the Eastern horizon, was already blanking out the moon and the night air was heavy with moisture.

Garret strained to hear what the old man would say next. Breeze brought him a drink of water and sat on the floor beside the daybed. She could feel the force of the ocean through her body and had no fear because she would only cross wild water in dreams. "Garret, me love, when this little storm blows over an' you're some better, we'll go pickin' bakeapples up in the hills."

"By'n'by they trim'er up, get gear from Mulroney...that's ol' man Mulroney, A. J.'s father...an' ready to launch off an' run down to Labrador. Before they can put'er off Seth loses another son. A Jazus big storm o' wind washes'im off the beach tryin' to save the bummer. A gale o' wind like that one brewin'." He pointed with an arthritic finger. "I can feel that storm comin'." He flexed his fingers and shifted his legs. The rocker squeaked and groaned like the rigging of a ship. "Mark me, she's a gagger...Where was I to?"

"Seth Sheen lost another son," said Lliam.

"Who are you?" he asked, squinting at Lliam. "Never mind...An' Seth lost another son, an' all his gear, when the ship goes over on'er side, see. The curse was onto'er an' Seth both. The Lord was out to punish that man for his evil ways."

"Then why would the boat still be cursed if Seth Sheen's been punished?" asked Lliam, wondering if the Lord used curses to punish his errant children.

"Curses don't go away that easy! Boat's got to be burnt or blessed, to drive out evil, an' I don't think God give you the call to blessin'."

Lliam was intrigued by the story, fantasy or not. "What happened to Seth Sheen after that?"

"Seth's a fisherman, so by'n'by he's got to launch off an' find a berth down Labrador, hear me? But he needs a crew. He takes buddy's big skiff, goes on up Carbineer an' hunts up a crowd o' Stationers. A hard lot, them. Bad crowd from Irish Town, up Carbineer way. Screech swillers an' Protestants. Not all them's bad up Carbineer. I got sister there, Bessie. Well, by'n'by Seth's eldest son come down with a fever an' dies. Only one son leaved now, an' that's Moses, the youngest." Grandfather Dwyer toasted the son, tears welling up again, speech thickening so that he had to clear his throat and spit. The listeners waited as Grandfather wiped his eyes. "He makes a deal for a crew, promises them this an' that. Well, they get to drinkin' and gamblin'. One o' the Carbineer crowd catches Seth cheatin', which I no doubt he was, an' they get to fightin'. *That's it*, says Seth. Seth leaves his crowd behind an' comes on home, them puttin' more curses onto'im, but they was just mad with Seth, an' the curses wasn't more then rude talk. But Seth comes on an' don't he get into a storm an' the skiff's drove off shore half ways to Portugal. Seth an' his son Moses, pumpin' all the Jazuz day an' night. When Seth makes Fogo two weeks later'e pleads with Mulroney's son, A. J. Mulroney, for more gear. Mulroney's that mad! Seth Sheen said that Mulroney could have bummer. Boat's ashore in Sheen Cove so Mulroney can't get'er, see, an' there she stays. An' that's how Mulroney gets to own *Black Fenian*, see?"

"Yes, Father, we know that part. An' now she's waitin' for us to do'er up an' get clear," asserted Malich.

"You damn fool! Got cod tongues for brains? Boat's cursed!"

"You can't blame a bad chance on boat, sure. We know Sheen's were a bad crowd. They don't need no curses."

"Now you wait, sonny..." Grandfather was wracked by a coughing fit. He *horked* up something green and spit it into the wood box, then took a long drink to make things right. "By'n'by, A. J. Mulroney gets English judge to make up some paper nonsense an' orders Seth to launch boat off an' deliver her to Fogo. Seth figures jigs up an' says he will. When they tried to stand'er up, again she goes over on 'er skids. Moses, his last son, escaped in time, an' runs off to Labrador. Seth went right mad after that an' shut hisself into house, an' never come out no more. Murdered ol' woman, daughters too, they say. Some say he's dead...hung hisself with *Black Fenian's* anchor line. But I say Seth's still in there...'bout my age." The old man sunk back into his chair, a dark shroud drawn over his face.

Malich took stock of his own sons: Garret, Doyle and Lliam. He had a vision of Gerald dissolving off the White Rocks Ledge. "If 'tis a curse, as you say, 'tis Seth Sheen's curse, Ol' Man. We got our own curse an' 'tis called Merchant Mulroney...an' only way to get clear is to do up that bloody schooner!" He gulped down his rum and refilled the glass, getting drunk quickly. He needed the rum now, more than hollow words. "An' by the Lord Jazus, we're gonna do it! We'll go March month after seals, soon's ice's cleared off. Then we go to Change Island."

The first searching fingers of the new wind regime crept around the eves of the old frame houses: a fitful sighing, as if spirits were looking for a weak place in the frames, or a tormented man's resolve. Brigid had dozed off. Grandmother Dwyer started knitting when Margaret got up to tend the fire. She opened the firebox and a draught of air rushed over the dying coals stirring the ashes. A gust whistled past the flue damper, sucked out by the low pressure. The barometer was falling rapidly as the ragged leading edge of the Northwest quadrant crossed the Funk Island Bank.

"Malich, better see to house or us could be blown to Change Island by mornin'," said Margaret.

Malich slammed down his glass. "Damn the woman for worry! Man can't find a spell without bein' nagged at."

"I feel the wind is on us."

Malich could not deny the atmosphere. "C'mon you two lazy louts!"

Doyle and Lliam reluctantly followed Malich into the blackest of nights.

They stumbled down the path to the fishing store, feeling their way in the darkness. "Never in me life have I seen it so fuckin' dark," said Malich in awe of the shroud closing over the village.

Lliam kept his thoughts to himself. They made their way using lights in windows as navigation beacons, and crossed the almost invisible main path to the Dwyer stage. Malich and Doyle knew every plank of the stage by heart but Lliam got down on hands and knees to gain the store and groped his way inside. Malich lit a lamp, the yellow flame casting grotesque shadows on the rough beams of the fish room. The old stage trembled and swayed to the tide surge gushing around the cribs. Lliam felt sick to his stomach. There were gaps in the planking and they could feel the rising wind puffing its way in.

"She may not be here in mornin' after this bloody storm blows out," Malich said.

"Queer, ain't it," observed Doyle. "Wind's almost warm."

"Too fuckin' warm for September, sonny," said Malich. "Get hold o' this now." Six hundred feet of manila hawser, salvaged from a wrecked Banks schooner, was coiled under rotting tarps in one corner.

It took them two hours to haul the three cable lengths of hawser up to the house and pass the lines back and forth over the roof. In the utter darkness Lliam was of little use other than to throw some weight on the line to pull it tight. But the heavy hawser refused to tighten. Malich sent his sons to find poles to make a Spanish windless. "She'll set some tighter when line gets wet," said Malich.

"Can this stand a hurricane?" asked Lliam.

"Might do to hold a few pieces from going into harbour," Malich laughed: a morbid, mirthless laugh that betrayed his anxiety, his fear, unnerved by the talk of curses.

The rain came in big warm drops at first.

By the time the job of casting the hawsers and winding them tight was finished, they could barely stand against the gale, stung by rain driven horizontally, mixed with salt spume. The hurricane wall had arrived with malevolent furry.

An Atlantic hurricane is a fearsome beast: a complex, powerful engine, sired by desert winds from Africa, sucking up more heat and moisture over the tropical ocean, then set spinning around its deceptively calm eye. At first it's just a proper tropical depression, building slowly to storm strength, then hurricane force, ponderously slow and unpredictable in it's forward progress, the internal cyclonic winds screaming at velocities humans can barely comprehend.

Malich and Grandfather Dwyer had experienced storms at sea that tear at a seaman's senses, but the hurricane that spun off the warm Gulf Stream and churned over Fogo Island that night, even weakened as it was by its journey across the cold Labrador Current, surpassed all storms in local memory. It was, as Grandfather predicted, *a real gagger*. The air and sea had no definition. The wind did not just shriek, it was a living, breathing monster and Béhathook Cove was chewed on and digested piece by piece. The slowly collapsing eye wall stayed at sea, well East of the Funk Islands, so Béhathook Cove twisted this way and that with no respite as the Northwest quadrant passed over and the cyclone winds backed from Northeast to Northwest and then to the Southwest, to die as a mere Atlantic gale by dawn. But the monster seas would continue to slam into Blow Me Down Peninsula like bombs. The rain was torrential and the black clouds *thick enough to jig cod in*, joked Grandfather Dwyer, but he worried about his friend John Kenney out on Blow Me Down Point.

Dawn would be delayed.

During the long night of torment, Malich remained in his chair, one hand on the bottle, the other gripping the edge of the table, eyes drifting to the ceiling as if he expected the roof to vanish with every moaning, shrieking gust. The house shifted on the foundations but the hawsers held. Doyle got drunk and sang tuneless vulgarity. Lliam, exhausted by the efforts and the tension, slept on his arms at the table, rousing every time Malich slammed the bottle down in defiance. Grandmother knitted and dozed. Grandfather stared at memory visions of better days, alternating with demons and spirits.

Breeze lay on the daybed beside Garret protecting him with her arms, sensing his every breath, moving if he moved, using her strength to keep him alive. She cooed encouragement and didn't let the awful stench of rotting flesh discourage her. At the worst of the storm she changed his bandages and applied oil and thought there was some improvement. Brigid O'Keefe, anesthetized by rum, snored through, with a woolen throw pulled over her head in case the roof collapsed. Margaret had nothing to do but worry. It was colder by the early hours but no fire would stay in the stove. No one was hungry. She paced and prayed each time the house jumped and seemed about to come off its moorings, and worried more, as if her men were out in the storm instead of imprisoned in their own kitchen. And so the long night and the vicious hurricane passed into history.

Morning: The rising sun found a clearing sky with puffy, fair-weather clouds. The winds, fresh and fitful from the Southeast, replaced the tropical depression whirling itself to impotence off Labrador and the cruel sun mocked the scene of desolation.

Béhathook Cove had changed. Miraculously most of the two-story, flat-roofed houses survived, some skewed on their moorings, but nothing else seemed to be in its right place. Outbuildings and tilts were scattered about like fallen leaves. Uncle John Kenny's green and white cottage, exposed at the end of the path on Blow Me Down Peninsula, had been swept away. Uncle John had been warned many times by Grandfather Dwyer, but he liked the ocean in his back yard. He could watch the whales and the boats come and go. Uncle John was stubborn, a widower and cared nothing about himself. He vanished with his cottage, first carried into the harbour by breaking waves sweeping over Blow Me Down, and washed out to sea when the flood tide flushed the harbour. Uncle Hebert, who lived directly across the harbour from John Kenny, joked that he saw John's cottage go and that Uncle John was sitting at his kitchen window, a lamp still burning.

"Probably havin' tea an' boiled herring."

The village wharf was battered and would need costly repairs. The village would come together. Their own fish store was gone as Malich predicted, only threads of the frame holding the remains to the sagging stage. Many stores were reduced to rags of wood and tarpaper hanging off sagging stages or floating in the water like limp laundry. The harbour was cleared of boats. Of the skiffs and dories that were tethered to ride out bad weather, not a single boat floated where its owner had left it. Some were lucky and just sank on their moorings, but more were blown ashore. Precise Muldoon's Boat Yard would be building at capacity for some time to come.

From the remnants of the Dwyer stage, Malich could make out their own skiff in a windrow of white hulls on the far side of the harbour, piled up in Terence O'Hara and Shamus O'Dell's front yards. Shamus' own stage and dory resided in his back yard, or parts of them did. "Must go over an' fetch our skiff by'n'by," said Malich.

Lliam surveyed the devastation and wondered why these people lived in such a place, or why they stayed. No one mentioned leaving.

That morning a meeting of the unofficial town council was held in Uncle Hebert's store because it suffered the least from the flood tide. Terence O'Hara was the headman of the village and Precise Muldoon was the unofficial deputy. Their sons, Thomas and Carly would inherit the roles in their turn. Fishermen gave reports of the damage and resources available. There was no help from a distant government in St. John's, nor was government aid expected. The villagers assessed the situation and a plan of recovery was debated. The main wharf would be dealt with once the families were secured.

Malich attended the meeting but only listened politely to the debate and returned to his own family silent and moody. He had concerns beyond the village. They salvaged what they could of their own store and helped neighbours sort through the debris or searched for livestock hiding out in the hills. Uncle John's son, his wife and kids, came for tea because their own kitchen had been swept by a wave overtopping the beach. They took a hot lunch on the Dwyer's porch, surveying the activity and when high tide returned, Malich, Doyle and Lliam made their way back around the harbour and helped other fishermen sort through the chaos of battered and splintered hulls. The lucky ones found seaworthy boats. The Dwyer's skiff escaped with only bruised paint and splintered gunnels. Easily repaired. "There's a blessing at least," said Malich. "Morgan ain't so lucky, sure."

The news of Morgan O'Dell's great personal loss came earlier that day, shared by the dour crew of a dory scouring the coastline for the body of a young Tilting Harbour girl. Morgan, Shamus' oldest son, wept as he cast aside pieces of his shattered skiff, which, like his wife-to-be, was counted in the toll of the hurricane. The absurdly clean ends of broken planks, like open wounds, looked odd in the tangle of wreckage. He had spent the winter rebuilding the boat, and putting in a new engine. Morgan was to marry the Tilting Harbour girl in December, the marrying month, and make a life in Tilting where an uncle had died and left him a house, stage and fishing gear. It was the most devastating news, as the stories of the hurricane spread from settlement to settlement. His fiancé perished without a trace trying to rescue her chickens: flushed out of their Tilting coop with the flood tide, just as Uncle John had sailed out of Béhathook Cove. "John's eatin' chicken an' dumplings out by Funks, I suppose," joked Hebert when the story made the rounds in the days following the blow, but the joke was thin, though well meant, tempered by the loss of Morgan's bride-to-be.

November Béhathook Cove: September and October were spent cleaning up and rebuilding Béhathook Cove. The losses were tallied and then buried with the dead as the outporters got on with life. Uncle John was the only fatality in Béhathook, but many had hurts. The injuries were acceptable. Nothing permanent. The material losses affected each family according to what they could afford to loose. Things were discovered in strange places as the children were sent on scavenging forays to get them out of the way, returning only if they found something of value. Uncle Hebert's carved cane hung up in a stunted spruce tree. Mother Deary's white enameled bedpan was found

144

far inland, by the water pond. Aunt Till's wedding bonnet was discovered in a meadow, a circle of sheep gazing down at it as if the bonnet was a sign from Heaven. Two sheep were missing. The ram was spotted at the bottom of the water pond and this caused some unhappy days and much waste of firewood boiling drinking water. The missing ewe was accused of being in the pond also, but she returned home in the spring, dragging a broken leg.

Malich wondered about the condition of the *Black Fenian*. If the hurricane had taken the ship then their loss was more serious than a store blown into the harbour. He brooded for days on the possibility but finally convinced himself that the East side of Change Island was protected from the seas by the bulk of larger Fogo Island.

By late in November the weather had turned cold and blustery with frost in the air. In Newfoundland frost could mean just cold nights with a crust of ice around the shore, or full-blown winter with deep snow, and a buildup of sea ice. No two winters were the same. Some seasons stayed relatively civil and the boats returned late from Labrador. The near shore fisherman of the Northeast Coast could ply their trade well into December or January. It could be March before the pack ice arrived to clog the harbours. The odd year the pack ice sailed around Fogo completely, but more often winter and spring saw the ice fields jammed to the horizon and the ice stay until May or June. It all depended on the winds. But nothing of nature's vagaries is without some reward. When the ice hove in shore during March and April, the Fogo Island 'swilers', like those of Twillingate Island and Notre Dame Bay and up the coast to St. Anthony, could walk out and take sculps within sight of their own headlands. Other years they would be out in small boats pushing through slob ice searching for the leads to the whelping pans. The risks were high but acceptable, and the only problems were drifting ice, fog, snow squalls or the wind changing suddenly. March days on the dazzling ice can be clear and fine with long daylight and a warming sun. Or they could be a misery of sudden snow squalls and deep frost, worse than November at the other end. But on this November day there was plenty of sunshine after the broken clouds of an overnight gale had blown away.

The Dwyers were working at the skidway using the rare good weather to prepare for winter.

"Are us still goin' to swiles March month?" inquired Doyle, who liked to know what labour awaited so he could brood on his future discomfort.

"No, sonny, we're goin' to New York to buy us all fur coats."

"Us are? Why?"

"You damned fool! 'Course we go after swiles, like always. Then to Change Island."

"Oh."

Lliam snorted at Doyle, unable to resist a chance to get some back. "It's not a fur coat you need, Doyle, it's a new brain. Seals have brains. Maybe you can get one of your own."

Doyle made a rude sound and pointed along the shore. "There's a nice bitch swile walkin' up on hinder legs."

"Seals don't have legs like that," Lliam said to himself, flushing with heat and shame, recalling the vision of Breeze's smooth, cream-white thighs, the dark patch of promise...

"Doyle, heave that line 'stead of watching tail," snapped Malich.

Breeze O'Keefe, bundled in Sean O'Keefe's greatcoat, walked the shoreline, holding herself tight, withdrawing into the over-sized coat. She was pale and drawn, long dark hair blowing across her face. A rare sojourn away from her many chores, or tending Garret and her mother who seemed to fail as Garret improved. Breeze walked slowly, throwing her black hair back each time the wind whirled it around her head. The move was made with feminine grace but at the same time wild and natural. Lliam ached to talk to her. Be near. Feel her soft hair brush his face.

"Heave the god-damn line would you!"

Malich and his sons were hauling the heavy skiff up the log skidway. The communal skidway was a series of spruce logs placed across runners beyond the water's edge. At the upper end was the Samson post, a deadhead for attaching a block and tackle. Some

146

communities had a windlass, a sophisticated winch with gears and steel cables, salvaged from a schooner or a steamship. Béhathook Cove made due with a tackle that used to be the foresail sheet out of the same wrecked schooner that supplied the anchors and hawsers for the Dwyer house. Malich's father and his crew had chanced upon the wreck coming home from Labrador after the season of the Big Storm in July 1908. They had been fishing a bad year below Nain, the northern limit of the Labrador fishery, and not many boats had passed the cul de sac where the unfortunate schooner met her end. No one knew the fate of the crew because the ship had been reported missing near Hopedale, miles to the South. The Dwyer's knew where she was lying, but didn't say until they had salvaged what they needed. The main mast and bowsprit of the *Margaret & Maude* was fashioned out of clear Douglas fir, a rare prize towed home with great effort, and many valuable fittings found their way into the Dwyer's new boat. Had the *Margaret & Maude* gone ashore she would have been stripped in turn by others, for the same reasons. A necessary economy on the hard coast. At least the practice of luring ships to their doom was no longer an industry in Newfoundland. After the Great War, lighthouses and navigation buoys, radios and proper charts killed the wrecker's enterprise. Naturally occurring wrecks were another matter.

"Heave the bloody line, damn you!"

Doyle and Lliam put a strain on the hauling part and the skiff came out of the water and heeled over to run on her bilge over the slime-slick logs: the slime as good as grease. The sheaves in the blocks squealed like a banshee. Inch by inch the heavy hull crept up the skidway. Lliam hauled hand over hand but never took his eyes off Breeze. When the two blocks came together it was necessary to move the skiff aside so others could haul out. They accomplished this with another tackle. The skiff edged sideways until it joined the line of boats already up for repairs. There were fewer boats on the skidway that winter and many of those needed a great deal of work. Lliam dropped the hauling line and walked down the shore to intercept Breeze.

"Watch this, Ol' Man," snorted Doyle. "Should be some good.

Breeze's like to scratch his eyes out."

"I don't have time to waste on the young pups!"

"Is that only reason, Ol' Man?"

Malich grunted and walked away. "Time for me tea."

Lliam called out, "Breeze..." She turned away, retracing her steps. Lliam slipped on the loose shore stones trying to catch up. "Breeze! I want to talk...to apologize."

She faced him with her jaw set. "Why should you? An' why should I listen?" she asked sharply, fire dancing in her dark eyes, or was it the sun catching the first tears?

"I'm that sorry..."

"Why, Lliam? Malich an' Gerald never apologized for the way they handle me. Are you any different?" She turned and walked a few paces, testing the sinking pebbles with her boots, giving Lliam time to answer.

"You know I am."

She stopped, staring beyond the harbour entrance. "The only thing different about you is that you aren't part of your family. You hate this place. For all I know, you hate me too."

"I don't, I swear. Just tell me the truth."

Breeze took a deep breath, shoulders heaving as if a sob had escaped. "I finally had to promise to marry Gerald to get him to stop chasin' me down, rutting away like I was some animal in the forest."

"But Doyle said Gerald never did, until you said, yes, an' teased him to boot."

She turned. "An' you believe anything Doyle says? I don't suppose he told you he threatened to gut me like a fish if I wouldn't go up the hill with him."

"Doyle did that? Damn his soul!"

"He wouldn't do it of course. Doyle's too dumb, but he did threaten to tell Malich about what Gerald was doin', 'til I told him Malich was doin' it too."

The truth boiling out was like a blow of the fist to the gut. Lliam was breathing hard, controlling the rage. "Doyle said he already

148

knew."

"He only wanted to believe that so he'd have an excuse to come for me. Doyle's a coward! I could put him off. Your father threatened to choke me senseless if I told a soul he did me. An' I believe Malich would do it."

"Jezus!...Breeze, you got to get away from here."

"Why? Because you're likely to keep up the family tradition?" She looked hard at Lliam who was unable to form words, an excuse, even a lie. "You disappointed me is all. That's done with now."

"I can protect you...if you come away with me."

"You already saved me from them, an' don't even know it." She looked him in the eyes, a hard look with no pity.

"I don't understand."

"You will...in good time."

Breeze pulled the greatcoat closer and turned away, walking with a determined gate over slime-covered rock. A walk that said, do not follow.

"Why do you nurse Garret?"

Breeze didn't answer.

"He's our responsibility. Garret's our family, not yours!"

Another November Day The Fortress Rocks: The rest of November was a fog for Lliam. He went up to the Fortress most civil mornings to brood. By day the weather was sparkling clear: windy and sunny, and the wind held steady from the Southwest, allowing the outporters to continue their preparations for winter. The children played hard outdoors, getting in all the sun possible. Fishermen repaired storm-damaged boats, put them off and went jigging around the island as a hedge against the hard winter. Malich and Doyle took the skiff and fished different days in a ten-mile radius, from Ice Ledge around to Wadham Islands. They had their best days off Bishops Island while staying close enough to their own harbour in case the weather changed. But on the ocean major weather changes announce themselves well in advance, if one can read the sky. Malich was tempted to go right around Fogo Island to visit the site of the *Black Fenian,* but Grandfather Dwyer's warnings played on his dark fears; the superstition he could deny, but he couldn't put aside the curse. The vision of his own schooner's end, brought down by the curse of Moses Sheen, was still strong. He reasoned it was more prudent to fish and provide than to go gadding about the island on a holiday cruise. He said as much to Doyle when his son broached the subject...

"Are we goin' 'round to Change then?"

"We'll not go to Change Island, Doyle."

"Just a day or so, Ol' Man, no harm."

Doyle was for the cruise because it would mean a break from jigging and drying salt fish from dawn to dusk. He wasn't concerned about running into bad weather. Around Fogo, or out and back on the same track, was only six miles different, more or less. It could be done in one day, if nothing went wrong. If wind, tide or engine trouble delayed the voyage it could take two days, with a stop over on Change Island or on one of the Indian Islands, a prospect Malich feared. And if they chose the wrong side of Fogo for the trip they could be beat up, storm stayed or wrecked. Malich kept close to home, fished and wondered.

Most mornings Lliam forced himself out of bed before dawn light to breakfast with the family, then, from Fortress Hill, watched the skiff head out to the grounds. It was another form of punishment. Malich said if he was up and eating their food, he could hold a jigging line, but Lliam took stubborn satisfaction in refusing to go fishing. He said he had to think.

Doyle always had a comment as they left, but Malich tried to ignore him. Margaret was coolly civil. Lliam would leave the house before Breeze arrived to tend to Garret and then spend his days watching her every move about the village, when he wasn't scanning the ocean as if waiting for a rescue ship.

This day he was studying a speck on the horizon to see if it was a steamship or a late iceberg. Breeze came out of her house with a basket of laundry. He watched her deftly hang the clothes: men's work clothes and long johns, with half a dozen white sheets. The sheets flogged like a tacking jib and she controlled them by letting the wind do the work. But Breeze seemed to move slower and bend with some difficulty. *Her back's given out from work,* Lliam thought. He pitied her having to work so hard. If only she would go away with him...

A man entered the backyard between the closely spaced houses. He recognized Morgan O'Dell and the anger rose to his throat until he almost chocked. Morgan and Breeze talked for a few minutes. Breeze put her arms around him, kissed him on the cheek and then walked to the root cellar in the hillside. Morgan followed and entered behind her. Lliam felt the heat of anger rush to his temples, taking his heart with it. He raced down the hill, and in his rush to judgment, envisioned Morgan on Breeze, arched over the barrel, rutting away, like...like he had tried to do. Only he had the right to Breeze. She was his! Why did she have to take on all the men of the village?

Lliam bounded over the fence, sending a rotting section crashing in splinters. He scrambled up, and fighting his way through the laundry, came face to face with Morgan who had just bowed out of the cellar carrying a wicker basket of potatoes. Breeze was behind him.

Morgan was polite. "Good day, Lliam. Come to buy some o' Breeze's potatoes? Best on island, sure." Lliam was blocking the footpath between garden plots.

"No, Morgan, I...good day to you."

Morgan sensed the tension between Breeze and Lliam. "Better days ahead, sure. Well, best be goin', I suppose." Morgan waited for him to move.

"Oh, sorry..." Lliam stepped into the garden to let Morgan pass. He watched Morgan go out between the houses to the gate. Heard the gate open and close, and still he could not face Breeze.

"I sell or trade what we can spare. Morgan's goin' to bring me fish for the potatoes. I do his laundry for firewood." She went to the house and closed the door softly.

Lliam was left standing in the O'Keefe garden as if stranded on a foreign shore, or a homeless orphan in a desolate town, a supplicant with nothing in the offing but cold indifference.

December Béhathook Cove: The fine days of November turned to a colder December with low flying grey clouds and ugly squalls with sleet and gales of wind, but there were some fine days thrown in. Malich and Doyle began rebuilding the fish store. Lliam helped to avoid Breeze. After a few days Lliam found that he didn't mind the work. The salvaged timbers became a skeleton and the skeleton was roofed and planked. He had some sense of accomplishment. Discovered he liked working the wood, using his hands, smelling the resin scent in the sharp air. Building was not fishing. As they worked he imagined building his own home on the hill overlooking Béhathook Cove. Not on the water of course. He had no need for a stage or a store. Fantasized that he and Breeze could make a family. He would be a carpenter and work for Precise Muldoon building boats, for other fishermen.

Breeze arrived every day to tend Garret, waiting until Lliam went out to work with Malich and Doyle. It was not easy to maintain distance in a small outport village, but it was easier than facing Lliam. He watched from a distance, pretending not to watch her walking on the path, crossing the bridge, entering the kitchen where she would sooth Garret and touch him with loving hands.

Garret improved under Breeze's ministrations. It had as much to do with the gentle attention as the simple medicine. Antibiotics she had none, other than lye soap made with seal blubber and ashes, boiled-salt compresses and sterile bandages torn from old linen sheets. Breeze traded things for the sheets. As areas healed and scabbed she kept the scabs soft with purified cod oil. She traded vegetables for cod oil and boiled the oil and skimmed and poured off the clear amber liquid. Kept the oil sealed in a blue jar that once held a nice smelling cream that Sean O'Keefe brought from England. The smell of the cream still lingered and the cream smell didn't disagree with the purified cod oil. She dripped the warm oil on Garret's scabs with a warmed spoon. It was slow, tedious work to drip the oil and not let it run to areas still trying to heal. She liked doing his face most of all because she could look into Garret's blue-grey eyes. Garret told her things by his eyes and set of his mouth, even about his fears during the worst of the storm when Breeze talked about her own fears. But she hadn't been afraid of the storm. Breeze said she hoped the old house would sail away and her with it so she wouldn't have to decide. Garret showed that he thought it was selfish of her. Breeze thought so too. But when she said she wished they could go together, Garret agreed.

Garret was a mute who had known only hardship in his short life, but he was as sensitive as an artist and intuitive about the life around him. His family was his foundation but Breeze O'Keefe was his only real joy. He worshipped her as if she were an Angel of God: an angel that allowed him his joy of manhood, in stolen times, when the family was preoccupied or asleep. He studied everyone from the vantage point of one who knew much but was relieved of the duty to speak. He also knew everything about Breeze and the baby. His one fear was that the baby would see him as the monster.

Garret's face was a taught mass of grey and red scar tissue, a hideous thing: a monster out of storybooks. But she held her lips close to his ears so the family could not hear and she told Garret her feelings about Lliam. When Garret recovered the use of his hands he waved his fingers at her, or touched hers as she passed bandages over his body and dripped the oil. And at certain times she would let Garret hold her breasts and run his hand down her belly and massage her swollen clitoris. The act of being gentle was an agony for Breeze. Not the act itself, but being restrained and contained when she wanted to explode with love and be made love to passionately. She had to make do with the stolen moments and fantasies.

The hardest part of the daily ritual was turning Garret to relieve the pressure. Bedsores were indistinguishable from burn tissue. Margaret did what she could, but she allowed Breeze to feed and nurture. Breeze could see the changes. His back and legs were the least burned. He could not tell Breeze how this was possible, since he had had his back to the fire the longest, if Doyle's account were true. He wanted to tell Breeze that it was Gerald who shielded him from the flames and pushed him up the ladder when his hands would not hold the grips. It was Gerald using the last of his own strength, sacrificing his body to save his mute brother. It was Gerald's last gesture on earth. Redemption. Erasing all sins in Garret's book, but Garret could not tell Breeze. Only his eyes and his fingers protested when she whispered about the bully Gerald had been, and the forced marriage promise, and the assaults. When she realized Garret was admonishing her she stopped and began telling him about life outside the Dwyer family kitchen: the repair work, the new store and the changes in the weather. Garret recovered faster.

On a rare fine day in mid December, Breeze was delayed in leaving the Dwyer home because Garret insisted on trying to get up. He had been improving steadily and was becoming agitated with inactivity. Breeze tried to explain that moving could cause bleeding. Garret insisted.

"All right, my love, but just for a bit."

With Margaret's help they swung his legs off the daybed, slowly pulling him to a sitting position, banking him with pillows. The pain registered, eyes watered, mouth twisted. Breeze felt sick to see Garret's stoic agony.

"There, Garret darlin', you've done enough for one day. Want to lay down again?"

Garret's eyes flashed. He wanted to stand up. His fingers flailed. He even moved his right arm, causing scabs to pull. Blood seeped through bandages.

"No, Garret, my dear, you can't...not yet. Please be easy."

He wasn't easy, and when Breeze came close to lay him down he grabbed her arms and tried to pull himself up. Margaret held on to Breeze to ballast her against Garret's weight.

"The b'ye wants up!" said Grandfather. "Let the poor b'ye up!"

"He can't do it," replied Breeze.

"Can to. Look there, he's gonna pull you both down with'im."

"I'll help," said Grandmother.

"Damn these children for a nuisance! Man can't rest." Grandfather pulled himself out of his chair, dropping his pipe on the floor, sending burning tobacco across the painted canvas.

"Now who's the nuisance?" scolded Margaret.

Together they supported Garret, easing him up. Ever so carefully they prodded his legs, asking if it hurt. Garret moved his head 'no'. Breeze knew. The pain was excruciating, but Garret came up until he was standing, knees bent and arms akimbo, as if his body had been reassembled with borrowed parts. He looked like the aftermath of a shipwreck, the survivor of a battle, with bloody bandages afly like ragged pennants, but he was standing.

Breeze cried. Garret cried. What to do with him now? He tried to walk. One step. Disaster was imminent. The five pillars shuffling close together, arms bridging the space like armatures of an unfinished sculpture or the flying buttresses of a cathedral: a ten-legged creature with five separate brains. The work of art began to sway as Garret's strength ebbed. Grandfather and Grandmother wavered. Margaret and Breeze shifted to take the weight. Garret was on the verge of collapse. He staggered, attempting to establish his own balance, slumping, keeling over. Capsizing...

The kitchen door banged open. Lliam entered with an armload of firewood, followed by Doyle. "Oh, my Lord!" Lliam crossed to the wood box, dumping his load with a crash that startled Garret and added to the crisis.

"Jazuz, b'yes!" said Grandfather, letting go of Garret. "Can't you do anythin' without makin' a racket?"

Lliam took Grandfather's place at Garret's side, as Doyle rushed in and took Grandmother's. They stabilized Garret but he was still in danger of falling. Breeze felt him going. "Oh, my Sweet Jesus, get him down, quick," she whispered.

Malich was at the door but did not offer to help. He judged rightly that there was not enough room on Garret for another set of hands. He did take control, like the captain of a ship who happens on a floundering wreck.

"Put him on chair first."

Lliam swung a chair with one hand into position behind Garret and they eased him down, slowly.

"Now what do we do?" Breeze dreaded having to move Garret back to the daybed. Garret pointed to the table. "What? You want to sit at table?"

Garret nodded, making the motion with his fingers.

"No, no, Garret, my dear..."

"If he wants to sit at table, then let'im," ordered Malich. "Pick up chair an' put'im at his place."

"He can't sit up for long!" protested Breeze.

"'Twon't hurt him anymore than layin' down."

They picked up the chair as Malich ordered and placed Garret at the table. He gripped the edge and held himself up by strength of will. Breeze sat on one side and Lliam on the other to make sure he wouldn't topple over, but they couldn't stop the blood and fluid seeping through the sagging bandages. Breeze's heart was breaking to see what the strain was doing to Garret.

"Any chance workin' men gettin' a bit o' food in this bloody infirmary?" Malich took his place at the table. Margaret poured his tea. "Now then, that's more like it. You stop bein' a nuisance, Garret me lad. Time you was back to work. Even this lay-about's doin' a day's work." He shook his head at Lliam. "Never thought I'd see the day."

Breeze was committed to stay even though it meant Brigid was at home with a cooling stove and no supper on the table. She felt guilty, but as she was rehearsing the proper sequence of excuses, Brigid let herself in and took her place at the table without a word. The elders took their places and Margaret served out the meal.

Breeze fed Garret and avoided Lliam's eyes. The meal was accomplished in near silence, only the necessary requests and responses offered as the assembly dealt with Garret's accomplishment. Malich had expected him to die from the moment he saw his smoking body rolling across the deck of the doomed schooner. The others had prayed to God for deliverance, one way or the other. It was done: Garret was a part of the family again.

After the meal, Malich directed the return of Garret to his daybed. He watched Breeze and Margaret make him comfortable then requested everyone sit down. "I've something to say. Mother, fetch me bottle."

Margaret went to the pantry and returned with a bottle of rum.

Malich poured a good dollop into his cup and passed the bottle. All members of the committee, including Garret, accepted a measure.

"Time we was gettin' started," Malich announced. "Come April month or sooner, we have to be on Change Island to do up that little boat. Rum don't come cheap, an' Devil wants 'is due. She'll need plankin' so we need trunnels made. You b'yes'll do that after dinners. My guess is we'll need a 'tousand at least. More's likely. We'll need oakum pulled an' oiled. Father, you can do that, can't you?"

"I can, sonny, on me good days." Grandfather flexed his stiff joints, grinning a rare gap-toothed grin.

"Margaret, you got a job o' work to keep this house up an' family fed. I won't ask you to do more'n that."

She nodded.

"Me an' Doyle got to do up riggin' and' fittin's. An' Lliam you can tag about an' learn something useful."

"I'd like to work wood."

"Would you now? Well, you seem handy enough. I guarantee you there's no wheel left on that boat. First thing they steal. Make one."

"A ship's wheel? I've only seen one in a book."

"Then get bloody book!"

"All right...I will."

"Good. One thing else. Breeze, you're part of this family now. I don't know which part but don't matter. Thing is we got to have sails. Mother used to make sails for our boats but she's no good for it."

Breeze protested. "I'm that busy with my own Mother, an' with Garret...I don't know how to make sails."

"As to that, Mother Dwyer can show you how 'tis done. Can't you, Mother?" Grandmother Dwyer nodded, needles flying. "See, nothing to it, when you know how. All you got to do is learn."

"But, who will look after my chores, an'...Garret?"

"Leave off Garret! Time he started to look after 'imself, else he's apt to lay there for next ten years."

Breeze turned to look at Garret who grinned and flashed a signal to Breeze that said he could look after himself. And so it was agreed. Malich drank rum to seal the covenant.

There was a problem, more than one problem. The marine gear and canvas Malich had hauled home from A. J. Mulroney & Sons had been stored in the fish room on the Dwyer stage. Some of the metal pieces, like the box of galvanized boat spikes and rigging screws, they located at low tide and fished out, but the rolls of canvas vanished, flushed out of the harbour with John Kenney. Uncle Hebert joked that, 'Uncle John probably 'made up sails with the Dwyer's canvas an' he an' chickens is sailin' Hell bent for Ireland'.

"We'll go 'round to Fogo, by'n'by."

Lliam needed a picture of a ship's wheel. He approached Breeze as she readied Brigid for the walk home.

"Breeze...?"

"Yes, Lliam?"

"Breeze, I remember a book your father had, about things to do with boats."

"Yes, it was his Seaman's Manual, from the navy."

"It had a picture of a big wheel. I thought it fascinating, the shape of the handles and the spokes. Didn't look like it fit on old fishing boats."

"Sean loved the wooden wheels. Works of art he called the things that makes spiritual contact with a good sailin' ship."

"Do you still have the book?"

"I do. But Sean had a shipwright's book as well. I believe there's a part about ship's wheels, with pictures."

"That would be wonderful."

"I'll bring it tomorrow."

"Fine. Tomorrow then." He wished it was more than a book he was looking forward to receiving from Breeze, but it was a start.

Dwyer's Stage The Next Morning: Doyle cast off the dock lines. Lliam hung back, determined not to go.

"You comin' or not, sonny?" asked Malich.

"No, sir."

"No stomach for the run?"

"I'd like to study up on ship's wheels. Got book from Breeze."

"Books is it? Boats ain't built from fuckin' books."

"I know that, Malich..." said Lliam, surprised to hear himself call Malich by name, "...but you said yourself to get the books."

"Right, then, get on with it."

"Malich?..." The skiff was drifting away from the stage. Malich flipped the battery switch, opened the gas line spigot and adjusted the carburetor, preparing to fill the primer cup. Lliam emboldened by the growing distance. "I need some proper wood."

"You're not so dumb as you seem."

"Could you ask Mr. Mulroney?"

"Now what kind o' fine wood should I beg from His Honour?"

"I don't know. Whatever they're made of."

"Teak, mostly, sonny. Fancy stuff, from other side o' fuckin' world."

"Maybe he has something else. Oak is good."

"An' what do you expect that Devil will extract from me soul for proper Mainland oak?"

"Just explain that it's for his own boat. I doubt there's proper wood around here for making wheels."

"I'll guarantee there is, sonny."

"But ship's wheels are round. There's no round wood hereabouts."

"There's no round wood anywhere, you moron!" Malich was shouting. "It's curved pieces used to make 'round.'" He made a circle with his hands.

"A hole? I don't understand..."

"The whole thing, you lame brain! See that condemned schooner?" He pointed to Breeze's wreck near Blow Me Down. Uncle John's cottage had passed right over the hull during the hurricane. The old ship, too waterlogged to be carried away, merely shifted her stern and took more damage to her rails. "She's no good above stove crunnicks now, but that ol' hull's got curved timbers what 'makes' bilge, see, an' her tuck frames to garboards. Best is knees at deck beams."

"Garboard frames? Knees?"

"Timbers!"

Lliam looked blank. "Timbers?" He was imagining a forest.

"The sawn frames, like your bones!" shouted Malich, as if Lliam was standing on Blow Me Down. Lliam shrugged. "Frames' shaped out o' crooks o' trees...moors. Knees. The shores. The goddamned tree roots!" Malich was becoming red in the face from shouting across the growing gap.

Lliam looked more awash in the parlance of ship construction. "What are roots? Like tree roots?"

"Aye, roots, the anchors what holds'em up, like shrouds an' partners. Never mind. Just go an' cut out pieces what ain't straight an' use them to make up the curves like...for big circle!"

"Oh...Where would I find those?"

"Best kind's right aft, unde'er counter, see, but then you'd want to be flatfish to get handy, even at low tide."

"Then I don't want those, am I right?"

"You blamed idiot! Course not! Be soaked up with salt water. Take ten years to dry, then they likely go shawley from torpedo worms." He meant the teredo worms.

"Oh. Where else do I look?"

"Fore'ard! The knees are juniper, good as oak any day!"

"Knees, as in...?"

"Lodgin' knees, Hangin' knees. Knees! They's crooked as seal finger." Malich held up his right hand and showed Lliam his broken middle fingers. They were bent in a curve as well as broken. "Infection gettin' in cuts...sculpin' swiles."

"Where are these knees?"

"Under decks. 'Tween beams!" He waited for Lliam to register. "Like those beams in kitchen ceiling!"

"Oh..."

"My son! You be the duncest one." Malich, holding up a cut glass perfume bottle, poured a dollop of gas into the primer cup and spun the big wheel. There was a muffled explosion in the crankcase, black smoke belched out the exhaust and the engine chugged to life. Water boiled up from the propeller. Malich adjusted the throttle, stepped to the tiller and steered the big skiff toward the harbour entrance, the exhaust banging off houses and rocks, mocking Lliam's shortcomings.

Mid Morning Low Tide. Lliam approached the wreck cautiously. Unsure of what tools he needed, he carried Malich's heavy wooden workbox. It had been in the family before Malich was born.

The wreck lay half out of the water, on her starboard bilge so that the deck planking was canted and slippery with algae. The underwater paint was mostly gone, only patches of black hull or green decks showing, and what had neither paint nor vegetation was a pleasant silver grey. It is said that a salt-pickled hull, built with trunnels and never painted, could last for a hundred years, if it wasn't for the teredo worms, or 'torpedoes' as Malich called them. In a way, the marine worms could be as deadly as torpedoes, just slower. Lliam wasn't concerned about worms or rot, wondering how to find the curved pieces Malich described.

The 'bilge', Malich had said. The bilge was in the bottom of the boat, he knew that much. He studied the curved cap rail running to the stem. Not curved enough, according to the pictures in Sean O'Keefe's manual. He had better heed Malich's advice. Look for the 'knees'. *Inside, somewhere, I suppose,* he said to a seagull perched on the cap rail. He felt as though he was about to go inside a beached whale, a carcass of bones and he was the bone picker. But he had to get inside to pick the bones. The slime covered hull was repulsive and gave off odours, the strongest being iodine and decay, like a dead whale. The slanting deck looked treacherous and he wished he had stayed in Boston.

Lliam waded into the water and hefted the toolbox aboard, nesting it carefully in the scuppers. He pulled himself up and over the rail at a place where the deck planking was dry. The main hold seemed to be the easiest way into the interior but that meant crossing the slippery deck and climbing down into the hold that was half full of water, even at low tide. The alternative was the forward gangway just ahead of the hole in the deck where the fore mast had once stood. *The hole looks like a midden, and the smell matches,* thought Lliam. He dragged the toolbox to the gangway, a small hatch opening just large enough for a man to climb into the fo'c'sle.

It was in the fo'c'sle of the *Margaret & Maude* that Gerald had burned to death and Garret nearly died. Lliam peered into the darkness...he had a vision of flames and smoke. The sweet smell of burning flesh and the awful smell of burning hair, he imagined the scene and the screams...As Malich had described again in detail. Grandfather had topped Malich with tales of a burning sealing ship, when fat dripping seal carcasses burned and snapped like Hellfire, and men fried 'likes scrunchions', he said, and the survivors roasting and then freezing on the ice, hearing their mates crying out for help. Why did men go to the ice, or even to sea? He also wondered what he was doing climbing down a rotting ladder into a stinking black fo'c'sle of a dead schooner to find wood to make a wheel for a cursed ship he had never seen, nor cared to see.

He left the toolbox on deck: an excuse to return to daylight and fresh air. Lliam backed down the canted ladder carefully, testing each tread. On reaching the bottom of the gangway ladder he put his foot down into gravel and other things, soft, wet and smelly, some moving: crabs disturbed in their foraging, mussels clinging with thread-like filaments to the gravel. The fo'c'sle was algae-grown and wet right up to the lower ends of the deck beams. When the tide returned the fo'c'sle would be half under water. He felt a moment of panic, as if the ocean would rush in and drown him. "Don't be foolish," he said out loud, to hear his own voice. Without letting go of the ladder he looked around, eyes adjusting to the darkness. There wasn't much to see, at least nothing from the working days. Everything of value that could be removed from the derelict was taken. Not a cast iron stove, not a bench or cupboard or cup remained. Not a single piece of old clothing, or the narrow bunks or an artifact of fishing days. Even the wooden ceiling planks that made up the floor and sides of the inner hull, had been salvaged. Only the maddeningly concentric, curvaceous frames, like a fish's skeleton, the full length of the vessel, remained. The bilge stringer, the oversized timber that also ran the length of the hull and stood out from the frames, was through-bolted from the outside of the hull and the bolts were rusted. But the bulkheads, the walls that separated the fo'c'sle from the cargo hold and the lazarette, had been removed so that Lliam could follow the length of the long bilge stringer through to her stern, beyond the shimmering squares of sunlight pouring through open hatches. To Lliam it was no more inviting than the mining tunnel he had experienced during his brief stint in the coalfields of Pennsylvania, discovering that he could not be in small, dark spaces without good reason.

Children played in the fo'c'sle after the hurricane, so there were things that didn't belong to ships: a broken rocking chair, a hand scythe stashed by small ones to avoid work. A dead cat hung by its tail near the bow. Gutted and salted, but not properly dried, according to the odour.

"Knees...between the beams, says Malich." Beams hold up ceilings, in houses at least, the sturdy pine beams, about two feet apart, like the house. He followed a beam with his hand to where it approached the hull, stepping very gingerly on the gravel, boots slipping on the slick wood. As a diversion he noted the pleasing symmetry of ship construction, the artistry of forms brought together by craftsmen for a utilitarian purpose. He felt along a champhered beam to a curved structure that crossed between the two beams. It proved to be two 'L' shaped pieces of wood fitted together like opposing brackets. "Knees!" he said with relief. He tested one by grabbing and pulling. The knees were bolted with drifts of iron to the deck beams and to a large plank under the deck called a clamp. The clamp ran the length of the ship as did the bilge stringers, but to Lliam it was just a very big, complicated piece of wood. He had no tools in his box to deal with drifts, nor was there a way to get at the knees with a saw. Malich had also mentioned hanging knees. "There, hangers!" Similar knees, single brackets this time, hung at right angles below every other beam. They were also bolted into the beam through a frame but at least there was a way to get at them with a saw.

When he returned from the 'surface' with tools, he found a position on the side of the hull from which he could manipulate the handsaw. With the boat heeled on her starboard bilge, the knee's lower arm was a down cut. The first cut took Lliam half an hour. He was sweating and filthy and exhausted by the time the lower arm was cut through. The upper arm of the hardwood knee meant an over-head cut. This was excruciatingly painful. Worse, the light was failing. He had to stop frequently to rest and clear his eyes of sweat and sawdust. But the more his own arms ached the more determined he became. The thing had to come out.

While Lliam struggled to finish the cut, the tide rose and the sun fell. He waded through the hip deep water to the ladder, climbed to the hatch combing, throwing the hanging knee and the saw ahead of him, he immediately realized his mistake. He heard the saw sliding down the deck. "Oh, Jesus Lord!" The saw was one of Malich's most prized tools. He scrambled out and skidded after the precious saw, watching it slip quietly under the water, where it lay glinting in the scuppers. The hard-won knee escaped over the side. He made a lunge for the knee and missed, sending it further out. The only way was to swim for it. Instinct for survival brought Lliam and the knee back aboard with a great show of floundering and waving of arms. He was chilled through as he collected the toolbox and the dripping saw and headed for home.

On the path, Lliam passed two fishermen working on their boats. The fishermen grinned, having witnessed Lliam floundering around in the harbour. One of the men, Ned Kenney, said..."Don't often see grown man swimmin' this time o' year. That poor saw wants a gub o' grease, Lliam. Oil at least."

"Yes, thank you, Ned." Where would he get grease or oil? Breeze had oil, for Garret, purified and special. He couldn't ask her. Margaret used lard, for cooking. Rendered scrunchions gave up oil. Lamps have oil but would his mother sacrifice precious train oil for his foolishness? He didn't want to approach Margaret either.

Fishermen have drums of oil percolating on stages: the oil a product of rotting cod livers. Most lost their oil drums in the storm but Malich had something he called tallow. Used it to grease the bearings on the engine. But the boat was away, fortunately, so Doyle could not torment him for ending his day in the harbour. Then he remembered...Malich had used a 'gub o' tallow' as he called it, on his woodworking tools and he had seen him draw fishing line through the same substance. Why he didn't know, but Malich was stitching a canvas cover for the engine. The canvas was sailcloth, protected by another oil mixture

164

called 'cutch'. *Must have something to do with preserving the cord also,* he reasoned.

After changing out of his wet clothes, Lliam dug into the tool tray and located a chunk of something that looked like mouldy beeswax. He went to the well behind the house and drew out a pan of fresh water, rinsed the saw and carefully dried it with the tail of his shirt. That done, he rubbed the steel blade all over with the tallow, smoothing it with his hands: the heat causing the tallow to melt and spread. The job was done, another small victory, at least a recovery. Despite being seen by the village floundering in the water, trudging home soaked and shivering, Lliam felt proud of his effort and wanted to show off the hanging knee.

Breeze had left and Garret was asleep. Malich and Doyle had not yet returned from Fogo Harbour. Margaret and the grandparents were occupied with evening rituals of cooking, eating, knitting and smoking. He ate a cold supper alone and the sodden knee languished unappreciated in the wood box.

After his solitary meal Lliam sat in Malich's chair by the stove, watching Grandfather fill and light a pipe. He decided he would try smoking. He wrote his decision in his journal and took stock of his life. He had been in Béhathook Cove only four months. The time had flown and the family tragedies were dealt with: the schooner and Gerald buried, in their minds. Garret improved daily, able to get up with help. The winter had been secured with some hope for the future and he admitted that he was beginning to adjust to the life, the woodworking part at least. There was still the problem of the growing distance from Breeze, but he told himself that with time, he and Breeze could mend their affair.

Margaret gazed often out the window into the growing darkness, pausing to listen for the distinctive sound of the engine. Lamps burned in windows around the black harbour, their reflections undulating like ghosts in the surge. Two fishermen came in just before dark, chased off the fishing grounds by some nasty weather slanting in from the Nor'east. Rain speckled the glass and ran down in tiny silver rivers. The rain turned to sleet with gusts of wind rattling the windows so

Margaret didn't hear Malich's boat approach the stage, but she sensed their coming and moved the simmering stew pot to the hot part of the stove before her men slammed their way into the kitchen, shaking ice off sodden coats.

"Damn me, that's a dirty ol' night!" said Malich puffing and blowing on his frozen hands. It was the only information about what must have been a hard run from Fogo Harbour into the teeth of the gale. He never said what transpired between he and Mulroney as he begged for more supplies to replace what was lost to the hurricane, and what further burden of debt was added to the ledger. Doyle was cold and bleary eyed from staring into the sleet for shore marks. Malich and Doyle stood by the stove, eating out of the pot with wooden spoons. "Uncle 'ebert said he seen the best comedy ever was," said Malich, finally, belching his compliment to Margaret for the fine stew.

Hebert had circled the harbour to meet them at the stage with the news, and told them in great detail about Lliam's water adventure. Before the hurricane took him out to sea Uncle John Kenney would have seen everything from Blow Me Down and been first to the stage with his version of the story. 'If Uncle John hadn't gone for little swim hisself,' as Uncle Hebert put it. News could hardly travel faster.

"Went for dip, did you, Lliam lame brains?" taunted Doyle as he shoveled in hot fish stew.

"You *would* know about that."

"Uncle 'ebert met us."

Malich had to add, "Fetchin' bits o' firewood like fuckin' waterdog, 'ebert said." His laugh was rough and cruel. Malich was feeling the effects of bootleg whiskey consumed with cronies on the waterfront before they left Fogo Harbour.

"I worked all day inside that damned boat to cut out one of these." Lliam reached behind the stove for the blackened chunk of hardwood.

"Well, sonny, 'tis a start. You only needs 'bout two-dozen more."

The weather worsened over night: slating rain turned to ice pellets, then quickly to wet snow, smothering the outport by the weak morning light. Women crept from house to house to visit and share news while the men retreated to stores to idle over repairs. Lliam and Doyle sat near the stove carving trunnels from a stack of juniper branches. Breeze arrived early for a lesson, going to school on Grandmother Dwyer's knowledge of the ancient art of sail making.

"Years ago we used to lay out sails on ice," answered Grandmother, when Breeze asked where they would find enough room to roll out the canvas. "Prayed that harbour'd ice up at right time. That's why we always done up sails in winter. If ice don't come this year, my dear, then I guess we go up meadow, carry it all up. Then truck the lot back home an' stitch all together, then haul the works up again."

Breeze eyed the heavy rolls of canvas, picturing Grandmother Dwyer trudging through the deep snow. Breeze was used to hard work but had her doubts. "Did you work alone?"

"Odd time. But most often there was two of us women at the sails. Scattered times we needed children to help."

"Didn't the men offer to carry something at least?"

"Oh, no, 'tis some bother to have menfolk around. They stand about smokin' an' waitin' to be told everything. Easier to do a job our own selves."

Mother Dwyer recited the order of things. The ceremony of the sails meant that narrow panels of canvas were laid out on the ice, marked and rolled up, taken back inside and stitched together. Then the whole sail had to be hauled to the ice again, stretched out and marked off to the final measurements. Then the corner patches and the tabling cloth, had to be cut and laid on. Then the sail was carried inside again and the corner patches and tabling stitched on. A third time each sail had to be carried out, stretched flat and marked for reef points, and measured for the bolt roping, the strong manila line that was sewn around the edges.

"But that's the most of it, 'cept for few cringles an' such like." Grandmother made the task sound routine. A schooner carried five working sails, including the bothersome fisherman staysail, or seven if she flew topsails on both masts in good weather, but the coastal workboats seldom did.

Breeze looked out the window at the heaving water, the white caps rolling across the harbour through the snow squalls. "The ice won't make up with this wind," she said.

"Looks like meadow for we unfortunate folks, my dear."

To finish off the sails, rows of reef points are stitched and cringles added where sheets land on patches and where hoops and hanks hold the sails to masts and stays. Handwork that requires skill and patience, as well as the strength to pull the thousands of stitches with doubled and tripled waxed linen thread. Breeze had the strength. Grandmother Dwyer supplied the skill. "'Tis a dirty job to do up sails in meadow. You're never clear o' small bits of stuff gettin' into seams. No, the ice is some better. Can't depend on it just the same."

To Breeze, the rolls of heavy canvas leaning against the wall behind the stove looked a long way from becoming billowing white sails on a trim schooner, slashing down to Labrador through sun-dazzled waves.

"What do we do first?"

"The first thing is, my dear, we got to 'cut ducks'."

"Ducks?"

"Canvas cloth is called ducks, my dear. Could as well been called geese, I suppose, or turrs. Don't ask me why, 'tis not a thing we have to know. Only for we to cut an' sew." She chuckled at her own poetry.

Breeze had envisioned sewing large panels of canvas together as it came off the rolls. The dusty rolls were almost as long as Breeze was tall. "How do we know how long to cut them?"

"No, my dear girl. We don't cut them off, yet." She began clearing the table, sending Lliam and Doyle packing with their tea and trunnels to the extreme fringes of the kitchen. "You put one o' them bolts on table an' roll it out. Margaret, where's that measuring stick to?"

"Behind parlour door, me love, where it's been for these fifteen years."

"Just so." Grandmother hobbled into the parlour and returned with a long batten that had marks carved into it every eighteen inches. Breeze hefted one of the rolls onto the table. "There, my dear. You just lay this stick across like so, an' mark 'em at every nick. Do that every foot or so an' then cut away."

"You mean cut the cloth long ways?"

"Yes, my dear. We got to make the panels first."

168

"But...?" Breeze was perplexed. She could see that stitching the rolls together was job enough, but cutting the rolls into smaller panels seemed a foolish way to get a sail made.

"I know...'tis just the way of it. You got to cut they up into pieces then sew'em all back together again."

"That seems like a lot of extra work."

"Oh 'tis, grand lot o' business, an' triple stitches besides. Scattered times I was tempted to throw the whole lot in harbour, but that's the way. If all them little pieces get put back in jus' such a way, that sail's got shape. Sail without shape is no better than a rag on that measurin' stick. Now come on, my dear, you mark an' I'll cut, an' then we'll change about."

Grandmother took up the big shears, which, along with the special three sided sail needle and sewing palm, are the most important tools in a sail maker's kit, and began the slow process of cutting as Breeze measured and marked with a child's red crayon. Breeze had to take over the scissors at the end of the first cut, then repeated the manoeuvre twice more before they could return the roll to the end of the table and roll it out again. The table was eight feet long. A roll of canvas is sixty feet long. There were four rolls.

Lliam watched the painfully slow process. "What you need is a kind of jig that holds the roll of canvas and three pencils, then you'd only have to unroll an' cut as you go."

"True 'nough, Lliam, but by the time we got that rig-up made, me an' Breeze could have done cuttin'."

"Fine...it just seems to me that it would be much faster."

"Sure, an' it would to, if we was in business o' makin' sails, but we only got this little job come 'round every fifteen years or so. I won't see 'nother suit made."

Then the panels had to be stitched together with overlapping seams, three rows of stitching on each seam, then the corner patches, tabling, bolt roping, and grommets pulled into a tight unit with the waxed sail twine.

Breeze measured and marked and cut as Grandmother Dwyer explained the tricks of lapping and broadening seams. She explained bias cuts and stretch ratios. How the sail had to be made slightly smaller than it would be when stretched by the wind so that it would fit the spars of the *Black Fenian*. Malich and Grandmother could only guess at the dimensions of each sail according to what they remembered. In their old store there had been a box with lengths of condemned heaving line marked with bits of coloured thread. Each colour stood for a different measurement of the *Margaret & Maude's* sail plan. The box of measuring lines had gone into the harbour with the other treasures. Malich and Grandmother only had their memory. It would have to do.

In a long morning of labour the rolls where cut and the panels rerolled, like large bandages, and returned to their place behind the stove. Breeze and Grandmother Dwyer resumed practicing sewing seams, and stitching cringles while they waited for the harbour to freeze over.

That season winter was undecided and the ice was slow to make up, and even then it was only the peculiar saltwater slob ice: too thin to walk on but too thick for the boats. And the good ice would not 'make up' until near the end of February, just in time for the tabling and the bolt roping to be added to the new sails. Breeze and Grandmother Dwyer would make the many trips back and forth to the meadow below the hill with armloads of canvas and tools. Lliam and Doyle offered to help but Grandmother politely refused. Instead, available neighbour children were pressed into service, more than willing to escape books or chores.

In the meantime Lliam was back in the bowels of the wrecked schooner. A day's work between tides yielded two more juniper knees, but one of them was too rotted to be of any use. Lliam flung it angrily into the harbour. Uncle Hebert said later that it looked as though Lliam was training himself to fetch sticks. Day after day he groped in the gloom and sawed and chiseled at the knees, working further from the light of the hatch, starting later as the tide cycle shifted. He exhausted the supply of hanging knees on the low side of the fo'c'sle and was forced to make a scaffolding to work on the high side. As the challenges increased so did Lliam's ingenuity. It became a game. He averaged two good knees a day, learning to avoid the rotten ones, so that by the end of a week he had a dozen sound knees, with one spare. He brought them home in triumph each evening to dry behind the stove but the old wood stunk worse than Garret's bandages and Margaret finally ordered the knees out of the house.

Then there was the problem of where to do the actual work on the wheel. The kitchen was out of the question, being filled with family, sails and trunnels, and Garret's needs.

"Should I ask Mr. Muldoon?" Lliam inquired.

"Don't bother that poor man. Go on 'round to 'ebert's with those things," Malich said. "Uncle 'ebert's got nice little shop, an' all the tools in creation. Never uses'em, see, 'cause of his hands. Fingers gone sealy like." He meant the seal finger infection. "I tried to get tools from 'ebert, but he won't part with a one."

Lliam finished breakfast, said goodbye to Garret and left to make the trek around the harbour. He had a piece of wood under his arm when he knocked on the door of Hebert's workshop. There was no response, but Uncle Hebert was in the store, according to the black smoke pouring from the off-kilter chimney. And there was movement seen through the dirty window. He knocked again.

"Lord Jazus! If you got time to knock you don't want in that bad!"

"Uncle Hebert?"

"Damnation! If you want in, come in then!"

Lliam lifted the carved wooden latch. "Uncle Hebert?" A wave of heat flowed over him. He stood in the doorway squinting until his eyes adjusted to the light from a grimy, salt-streaked window over the workbench, and the orange glow from the open door of the rusting pot bellied stove. Uncle Hebert was obscured by the bulk of the stove, but Lliam could hear him mumbling, tossing pieces of condemned nets into the fire. The tar flamed and crackled. "Close the blamed door less you wants we to freeze solid!"

Lliam closed the door. "Uncle Hebert, I was wondering...?"

Hebert slammed the iron door, getting slowly to his feet. "You was

171

wonderin' if you can dull up all me tools."

"I have a job to do. Malich said..."

"I knows that, else you wouldn't be here. Malich sent you, 'cause 'e ain't got tools enough for job. I got tools. Got me every blamed tool man could want, 'cept I been blessed with hands like these!" He held up his claws for Lliam to inspect. In his right hand he gripped a smouldering pipe by the biggest bowl Lliam had ever seen and it fit so well into the curve of Hebert's fingers that he seldom let go. Hebert's trade mark was the stiff-armed movement of the stem to his mouth, three puffs on the pipe, then down, up, three puffs and down, in rapid succession so that he looked like a clock-work mannequin.

Uncle Hebert was awash in smoke that swirled around his head as if beckoning Lliam into a cloud. Lliam thought of Boston at Christmas Season: the lights, the colours, the steamy sweet and sour smells from street vendor's carts and people breathing out clouds as they crowded to the department store windows. Lliam liked to watch the mechanical Santa Claus wave and slow down and come to a jerky halt as the clock spring ran out. There would be a suspenseful few minutes until a harried clerk noticed Santa had stopped waving and the elves had stopped spinning, and rushed to rewind the display. But Boston was getting further away and Uncle Hebert and his pipe were more amusing.

"Malich asked me to make a ship's wheel."

"Ship's wheel is it? For the cursed *Black Fenian*, I suppose, 'less Malich wants a chandelier for Christmas. Seen one once. Wasted good ship's wheel."

"Yes, it's for the boat."

"My poor, sonny." He puffed away. "Day you put that wheel 'board Seth Sheen's boat's the day someone dies."

Lliam felt a chill. He didn't believe in curses. "I only have to make a wheel. I'm not going to be involved."

"Mark me now, Malich means to drive you to Change Island an' work you to death, jus' like Seth Sheen did his own boys...well, they wasn't his own, but jus' the same."

Lliam realized that Hebert also knew some of the story. "Can I use

172

your tools then?"

"'Course you can. Never needed to ask in first place. What I got to say 'bout who uses me tools?"

"Well, they are yours, and..."

"Mine? Not a bit of it. Tools only belongs to man what can use'em. But, sonny, they don't go out that door, unless over my dead body!"

"Fine, I'll make the wheel here, if that's all right with you?"

"A'right!? Jasuz Lord, man, how else can you work with 'em?"

"Thank you..."

"Don't thank me, just get on with it!"

"Where?" Lliam scanned the immense quantity of things in the store: hand tools in holders around the walls, fishing gear, old nets, barrels, oars, coils of line, piles of rusty anchor chain, killicks and patent anchors, ship's lanterns. Beyond the usual fishing gear there were garden tools, trunks, discarded clothing, engine parts hanging from the rafters, even the remains of a rowing skiff, a mate to his own Rodney, piled in a corner. And more things that Lliam could not define in the bad light. Along one wall, supported by sawhorses, was a large object under a rotting tarp that Lliam assumed was a small rowing punt. He could see the outline of oars, a bow and a stern.

"Needs the workbench, I suppose!" shouted Hebert as if Lliam were deaf as well as dumb. The workbench resided somewhere under an amorphous mass of objects that could only be described as 'things' covered with a unifying layer of brown fuzz. The fuzz was sawdust, dirt and oil, webs and some organic growth.

"Ah, Uncle Hebert, where should I put this stuff?"

"Where else? Pitch it!"

"Ah, where should I pitch it?"

"Pitch it in harbour!"

"But...?"

"The most is just some ol' bother." Lliam didn't move so Hebert stirred himself. "Stand aside, sonny. Move that puncheon." He indicated a wooden cask used for a stool. Lliam rolled the heavy cask aside. It was filled with liquid. "That's oil, swiles, or maybe cod's liver. Can't remember. Was Father's, or Grandfather's. Must be plenty good by now." He chuckled. "See that latch?"

Lliam was standing on a trap door. "This?"

"What am I pointing to, the moon? Heave'er up! Heave'er up, b'ye!"

Lliam took hold of the recessed lifting ring and pulled. A large section of the floor swung up. Below was dark, moving water. Uncle Hebert's store was on the part of the stage that crossed like a bridge to a big rock, leaving five feet of water under the store at low tide. Hebert swept his arm across the workbench sending a cascade of 'things' splashing into the water. A brown stain spread out on the surface like blood. "There, now, you jus' finish up with coaxin' all that truck into harbour an' you can have a nice clear deck to work from."

"This doesn't look like junk."

"Oh, pay no mind to that. All this worthless truck belongs to me brother. He jus' leaved it here to annoy me."

"But there's good tools..."

"Never mind, sonny. All me own tools is gallowsed proper. I never leave good stuff layin' about. Remember that, now. Use'er, you put'er back up where you found'er to. I warned Gaston often 'nough that one day I'd pitch this lot into ocean." He swept another batch of 'junk' into the hole. "Go on, pitch it!"

Lliam couldn't bring himself to imitate Hebert. "Could I buy the tools at least?"

"Got any money?"

"No, but I could work, or trade."

"An' I could die in me sleep waitin' to be King o' France! Pitch that ol' truck!"

"I can't do it."

"*Ahh,* you're some bother! Stand away!" Lliam watched helplessly as Hebert pushed the remaining treasures off the bench into the harbour. Chisels and wood planers slipped over the edge with boxes of copper nails, nuts and bolts and engine parts. A wooden jewelry box with an inlaid ivory top spilled open when it hit the water. Rings, gaudy broaches and pendants sunk to the bottom, glittering like reef fish. Lliam hoped it was only costume jewelry. The deed was almost done. But for good measure Hebert grabbed some clothes off a peg and tossed in a 'Sunday Best' long coat. A pair of leather Hamburg boots, that looked almost new, followed the coat. The coat and boots seemed to swim away.

"Your brother's boots?"

"Just some worthless ol' stuff Gassy left when'e was carried up to Mainland."

"And the jewelry box?"

"Belonged to his wife, Ethel. She's livin' over to Toulengay with our brother Clode. Reason Gassy left we for Mainland. Broken man! Poor soul. Ain't never comin' back." Hebert stood staring into the hole as if it was his brother's grave. Tears filled his eyes. "Close'e up now!" he sniffed.

Lliam lowered the trap door and rolled the puncheon back into place.

"There, now we can work away. You bring rest o' them knees an' patterns 'long tomorrow."

"Patterns? What are patterns?"

"Patterns. The shapes. Need three at least. The outsides, the insides 'tween spindles, an' the spindles too. The hub we can decide on later. Got ol' brass plug some wheres."

Lliam trudged back around the harbour shaking his head in wonder, lamenting the loss of the precious tools. He could have filled his own tool chest. But Hebert had an eye-filling collection, and all he had to do was make patterns for the wheel.

Lliam sat at the sideboard with a mug of tea, a bowl of fish stew and bread, studying a page in the Shipwright's Manuel, an exploded illustration of a ship's wheel with labels and dimensions. The wheel was made up of several curved sections, just as Malich had said. The problem was to decide on the dimensions.

It was lunchtime. Malich and Doyle trooped in and sat on Garret's daybed to eat because the table overflowed with creamy canvas. Breeze had left off cutting canvas to go home and make tea for her mother. The canvas panels spilled across the floor, kicked out of the way to create a passage to the stove. The last long roll of canvas duck dominated one end of the table. The cut rolls were stacked everywhere or loose canvas gathered in untidy bundles waiting to be rolled. The kitchen looked as though a blizzard had swept through.

Garret, draped with a sheet and a blanket, was sitting in Malich's chair near the stove, staring into a mug of tea that he couldn't raise so Lliam held his brother's hand and guided the mug to his lips. Tentative sips and down again. It was too hot. Margaret would feed him his meal and clean up his toilet mess. It was a thing the family had become used to and there was no luxury of privacy except for bedpans at night or a trip to the fish store hanging over the harbour, but Garret couldn't make the trip on his own.

Grandmother Dwyer had a cup of tea with bread and returned to bed, tired from the morning session with Breeze. Grandfather rocked in his chair, mug of tea and a crust of bread close at hand. He seldom ate much at lunchtime. Rock, smoke and watch the others, or doze and dreamed. Lliam wondered what the old man was thinking during those idle hours. Wondered what he himself would be like at that age? Grandfather, like his friend Hebert, was in his eighties: long-lived for an outporter who had suffered the hardships of a deep-sea sailor and fisherman. The dangers, the hours, the bad food, were only part of the toll the sea inflicts on the body. The new trade union rules only applied to merchant sailors and offshore fishermen on company draggers. The olden day's sailors before-the-mast were exploited like slaves, and although the outport fishermen regulated their own working conditions, they were harsh and the rewards inconsistent. And even in good times they were slaves to the merchant's unbalanced ledger. But few outport fishermen would trade their independence for union dues, if they had the choice.

"Father, what size wheel do you want for the *Black Fenian?*"

"Size? 'Bout that round," answered Malich, holding his arms up to describe a circle three feet in diameter.

"Is that the wheel itself or...what do they call them...?" He put his finger to the illustration. "Spokes?"

"That's it. The outsidest size is end o' spokes. Spokes got to be long enough to get both hands onto'em betimes." He held two fists together the way a baseball player would hold a bat.

Lliam had been to a Boston Red Sox game. *A waste of an afternoon and a precious dollar*, he remembered. The hometown team lost to the hated Yankees and he consumed a sausage with greasy fried onions on a soggy roll that gave him indigestion. But the sport reminded him of a game the outport children play with broken oars and balls of fishing twine. Called it 'whackers'. Their game was closer to English cricket because they didn't have enough room in the narrow, rocky meadow to run around bases. He slipped into a pleasant childhood memory of warm sunny days in late summer, after the meadow grass had been harvested. Carefree in the sunshine, shucking clumsy rubber boots, swinging away, running barefoot and yelling: the rules loosely applied. It was all so different from the rules of life, fishing and surviving. They wouldn't let Breeze and the other girls join their game, but Breeze insisted on playing and once beat Gerald up for being a lout. It may have been the day Lliam fell in love with her.

"So make wheel 'bout like that," Malich made a smaller circle with his arms and hands, fingers overlapping. "Lliam?"

"What? Oh, sorry...about two feet."

The next day a mid-December gale with snow, brought another taste of winter. Lliam was up before a dawn that would not arrive at all. The sun had no chance. The clouds driving in low off the ocean were so clogged with snow there was no telling one from the other. He dressed quickly in the dark bedroom and escaped to the warm kitchen and ate his breakfast with Garret and Margaret, feeling the house shake with the gusts, watching the snow clumps gather like grease on the window panes, and the fat flakes illuminated briefly by the lamps, driving past the windows like moths in a hurry. Tongues of cold air licked in under doors and around sashes. He remembered too well his childhood winters huddled around the stove, the cold beds, freezing floors, damp bedrooms with the frost creeping down the walls. Four boys all clinging together under threadbare quilts, making a game of it, playing explorers or encamped warriors, laughing and punching until one farted and they had to abandon the warm tent, rolling about thumping the floor and Malich yelling, threatening to throw the lot out in the snow. They feared he might actually do it so they blamed Garret.

Garret took the blame for everything. "How are you this morning, old son?" Lliam asked when he took his place at the table. Garret nodded and tried to grin, the grin a grimace of pain, indicating that all was wonderful with his world except for the fact that he could not feed himself or smile properly, and every movement was an agony. But he was up, wearing a long nightshirt instead of a blanket and he was holding a mug of tea, even though he could still not bend his arm far enough to drink without help. He wanted to tell Lliam that he had been able to delay his morning bowel movement long enough so that Margaret could get the bed pan under him; a proud moment because Margaret didn't have to clean up a mess. "You look much better this morning. Before you know, you'll be out rolling in the snow, the way we did as youngsters, eh? Remember the time we slid off the Fortress in buddy's old dory an' went right through Old Ned Kenney's fence?" This brought on another effort by Garret, causing more pain and cracked skin. Garret's body shook, a laugh burbling up in his throat, so that Lliam thought he was about to blow bubbles. "Better not get you going, b'ye, you're apt to burst a seam." This caused Garret more emotion. Tears of joy welled up and spilled over. More burbling sounds from deep in his throat. Spasms seized his body. He dropped the mug and almost tumbled sideways off his chair. "Whoa there, my son!"

"Leave off, Lliam! Boy can't be upset like that!"

"He's all right, Mother. Just excited."

Garret wanted to tell Margaret that it was all right. It meant he was still alive, months after he wished he was dead and could tell no one of his inner pain. Not for his own hurts but because he could not convey the wonder of Gerald's actions. It was Gerald who should have lived. Ached for Breeze who nursed him when it appeared he would never be more than a burden, like a rotting old boat that won't sink away decently but needs constant attention and is no use to a fishing family.

A noise from above was Malich pushing Doyle out of bed with his boot, Doyle's protests and then Malich's curses. The last noise was Malich kicking Doyle for cursing him back. Then it was quiet. A few moments later Malich entered the kitchen, looking like he was washed ashore. Garret was in Malich's chair by the stove.

"Takin' over yer ol' man's place have you, b'ye? You an' Lliam's a pair." He pulled another chair to the table and sat in Doyle's place. Margaret poured his tea. "That'll want some o' that canned milk, Mother." Margaret fetched a can of condensed milk from the pantry and opened it with an impinger, a Christmas gift from Malich, then set the can down beside Malich's mug. "What's this? Can't pour a drop for hard workin' man?" Margaret poured the thick yellow milk and returned to making bread.

Doyle shuffled into the kitchen yawning and blinking, pulling on a rough shirt over his long Johns. No one spoke to him so he poured his tea into a cracked china mug and retreated to the daybed. Malich looked at Doyle with disgust but spoke to Garret. "Dare say, Garret ol' son, you're more fit to go at it than that one." Doyle grunted. Garret tried to laugh, the burbling sound again. Lliam was ready in case he tumbled over. "Soon as you can hold a maul get out there an' break up ice on stage."

Garret tried to laugh again. "He gets the joke, Father," said Lliam.

"Joke is it? Not so much joke as you think, sonny. Cold in here, Mother! I'm like to perish."

Margaret left off her bread making to fetch an armload of splits from the box behind the stove, knocking down a stack of canvas rolls. One narrow panel unrolled itself under the stove, an edge hiding in shadow behind one ornate foot. Margaret opened the fire door to stoke the embers, pulling out a glowing coal that landed on the canvas and hid itself in a fold.

Grandmother Dwyer was up and dressed for the day. Breeze was coming and they were going to begin marking panels up in the meadow, if the wind and snow let up. She took her place beside the stove and waited for someone to tip the teapot for her. She sniffed the air. "I smells something queer." No one noticed so she let it pass.

Margaret served Grandmother and returned to her mound of dough.

Grandfather came next, shuffling along like Doyle in loose slippers. He eased himself down to his chair and began the ritual of lighting his pipe: stuffing, filling and spilling, the coarse shards like falling leaves in autumn. He struck a match on the stove and held it to the tobacco. Clouds of yellow smoke rose up, Grandfather disappearing in the cloud, bowl glowing red like the port running light of a ship in the fog. The pungent odour of the coarse tobacco masked the smouldering canvas. Malich gulped his tea and lit his own pipe.

"I would like to smoke a pipe," announced Lliam.

"Would you now, youngster?" asked Grandfather. "Be you old enough?"

"Gran'pa, I'm twenty-six."

"Oh, age got jack all to do with it. Are you old enough to put this rotten ol' thing in your mouth an' puff away, spit'n all, an' the black 'baccy juice suckin' up 'til your tongue burns like you bit into Island Cherry? Then when you get through gaggin' an' heavin' your lungs out, then you're ready to smoke anything, even condemned nets, when you get desperate. Can't beat the tar for taste." Grandfather slapped his knee and laughed.

"It can't be that bad." He thought of the stench from Hebert's burning nets. "I'd like to try."

"Well, if there's no holdin' you back, there's a good pipe in me sea chest, give to me by Seth Sheen the once. That was before. Never wanted to use'er after." Remembering the incident caused visions to flicker across his grey eyes like aging photographs.

"Suppose there's a curse on pipe too?" interjected Malich.

"Maybe. I never wanted to know." Grandfather drifted further into a reverie.

"Ah, Gran'pa...?"

"He's gone for a spell, Lliam. Pipe's in his sea chest," said Grandmother. "You fetch that old thing if you wants it."

Lliam wondered why everything had to have a curse attached? It was only an old pipe. Whoever owned it, or whatever its history, a pipe is just an object, like a fork or a spoon, used by many people over its lifetime. Imagining the forks he used in public houses during his travels, inserted into hundreds of mouths, returned to tables with small bits of food or saliva dried between the tines. Grandfather's fluids were in the family at least.

Lliam slipped into the parlour and opened his Grandfather's sea chest, shivering with expectation, feeling a draft as if someone had walked by, wondering how the old ones slept in the room as damp as it was, with only the spillover heat from the kitchen. There was a nickel trimmed parlour stove in one corner but it was used only on special occasions.

The curtains shifted in the wind. The windows rattled in protest. *No way to live,* he thought. He rummaged in the chest, hoping to find the pipe quickly and get back to the kitchen. He moved aside thick wool socks, often darned, course underwear, and wool shirts, all smelling of mothballs: mementos of other days. A dried up sail maker's palm. Sheath knife. A musty smelling black-bound discharge book with stamps of ships with masters' signatures, customs agents and port authority entry stamps that told of cruises to exotic places: Singapore, Sidney, London, and Lisbon. He imagined that some of the voyages were hard and dangerous. He wasn't interested in Grandfather's sea faring days.

He found the pipe in the bottom of the chest and under it was the mouldy leather folder holding the loose pages of Grandfather's journal. Against his will he flipped it open, smelling the must of history, a consequence of travel and the necessity of learning to read and write to fill out log books and pass long hours at sea. The writing style was poetic, the entries random, but the meaning was there. Lliam felt guilty reading passages written in confidence, between a man and his thoughts. He skimmed until Seth Sheen's name leapt from page after page, along with Seth Sheen's sister's name and 'The Duty', and coastal voyages in a small boat. There were dates, weather and sea conditions. Storm stayed nights on Hare Island waiting to cross to Change Island, but nothing to do with fishing. Then Seth Sheen's boys were named, and the dates and years of their birth: the hard evidence.

He vowed to burn the thing.

"Lliam?" his Grandmother called. "Find that ol' pipe yet?"

"Yes, ah, just putting things a'right."

He poked shards of tobacco into the bowl, tamping it down with the silver tool, striking a match, drawing, and working up smoke. The burning canvas smouldered under the stove adding to the mélange of smells. The kitchen was rapidly filling up with smoke, above the heads of those seated around the table. When Breeze and her mother entered they could barely see across the room.

"What are you burning in here?" Breeze asked, closing the door against the wind.

"Oh, my Lord, the place's afire!" Brigid said.

"Lliam's fit to smoke hisself to death," said Doyle, puffing a cigarette.

"Look at poor Garret!" shouted Breeze.

Garret, eyes wide like an owl at midnight, clutching the table with one hand and his throat with the other, was turning crimson.

"Open the door!" exclaimed Breeze. She turned to do it herself but Brigid stood fixed in place. Breeze clung to Garret to keep him from falling. "Get him down..." Lliam helped Breeze lower Garret to the floor. Margaret opened the door, Doyle a window, cold air rushed in and the smouldering canvas burst into flames, orange tongues licking up around the stove. Garret was lying close to the stove, reliving the vision of Dante's Inferno aboard the *Margaret & Maude*. He flung his hands up to protect his face and tried to roll away, chocking out a garbled, hacking noise, the only sound he could utter other than his burbling laugh.

Breeze and Lliam tried to drag him away from the flames. Garret winced with pain and they didn't know where to grasp him. Brigid opened the door and disappeared into the storm. The rushing wind fanned the flames higher and threatened to spread to the other rolls of canvas. Grandmother fled to the parlour. Grandfather was near the pile of canvas and the flames were spreading along the roll toward his chair. He stared at the scene, the flames, the burning canvas, the choking smoke, as if viewing another incident from his past. Malich grabbed the old man's rocking chair and dragged it clear. Over the commotion Malich yelled... "Throw the bloody bucket, Doyle!"

"Bucket's empty." Doyle grabbed the stew pot and splashed the contents under the stove. Hissing sounds with gouts of acrid grey smoke boiled up.

Malich tossed the smoking roll of canvas out the door after Brigid and opened windows.

When the smoke cleared they gently carried Garret to the daybed and covered him with blankets. He had suffered much and bled in many places. His pain was great, but the psychological injury was worse. Garret turned his face to the wall and drew himself up, rocking his body; and there he would stay for two days despite Breeze's efforts to console him.

"Where's Brigid?" asked Margaret. Breeze left Garret to look for her mother. In the meantime Margaret, Doyle and Lliam put the kitchen back to rights. By the time Breeze returned, with Brigid in tow, the room was a semblance of a normal outport kitchen. The stove was crackling, the kettle was on and the survivors huddled around getting warm. Breeze guided her mother to a chair near the stove and went to Garret to assess the damage. Brigid accepted a tumbler of hot rum to calm her nerves. Finally the door and windows could be closed.

"That'll do for pipes, I hope," said Margaret as she prepared a tea. She had bread in the oven and there was jam. Lunch had gone out the door with the blackened canvas and the neighbour's dogs were finding interesting bits in the snow. Nothing is wasted.

Rum and tea made the rounds, and when the bread came out of the oven all brown and crusty and smelling wonderful, the fire ordeal was almost forgotten. Grandfather, his chair restored to its location beside the stove, defied Margaret's pronouncement about pipes. Lliam watched his Grandfather, wondering about the diary entries. There was more to do with Sheen's sons than cursed schooners; their families were bound together in a web of intrigue and deceit. Grandmother retreated to her knitting. Brigid, sitting too close to the fire, was sweating in the heat...Breeze had found her on the main path, tacking back and forth against the wind coming over Blow Me Down, and by the time they returned to Dwyer's kitchen she required much bundling up with blankets and a large tot, the heat and the rum taking her from paralysis to ebullience.

"Oh my, this heat reminds me of a story me late husband, Sean O'Keefe, told of a voyage home from the Rum Islands. He was captain onto one o' them wooden steamers the Water Street crowd kept for going to seals...*an' never kept them all that well,* said Sean often enough."

"Would you like some tea," inquired Margaret, hoping to divert Brigid from the long story she would tell of her imaginary husband at least once a year.

"Thank you. She was called the *Windward Queen. Wayward Queen,* Sean called her... *'cause she never wanted to go the way the course was to,* he said. An' she was so soaked up with fat from years at The Front, an' coal dust from trips to North Sidney, that he feared the slightest spark would light'er up like a torch. He used to keep the ice explosives under his bed. Said he'd rather be blown up proper, than just get tossed in ocean an' drown. Them was Sean's words. This time the *Windward Queen* were loaded with rum..." Brigid paused to sample her tot of rum, thinking about something lost. "...The engineers was that fond of drink they cut a hole in bulkhead to get at cargo. Well, they took on a cargo of rum right enough, an' one stoker...'smokers' Sean called'em...got a notion to throw a bottle o' rum into fire to see if he could keep steam up that way. 'Twas easier than shovellin' coal, he said. It worked so well they all went at throwin' in bottles, an' pretty soon whole cases, gettin' roaring drunk into the bargain. Well, Sean said it wasn't long before the fire couldn't burn all the rum, an' it started to pour out fire box into bilge, all flamin' like Hell wouldn't have it. An' in an instant up she went so fast only one engineer got to ladder. That fire spread into that old fat an' what-have-you, an' she was done for. Worst fire Sean ever see, he said. Only Sean, the First Mate, an' engineer, an' man at wheel, escaped. Rest was all drowned or burned up to crisp."

"Like scrunchions, eh?" Grandfather added, puffing happily. He had stories to equal that one, and more.

"Yis, my dear, likes scrunchions!" Brigid giggled like a schoolgirl.

"I got a one better then that!"

Breeze looked at Garret. She could tell by his increased rocking motion that the demons were rampant and the stories set them flying around his daybed. There was nothing she could do except hold his hand and glare at her mother. Malich made a sign to his father, daring him to continue. The others just stared into their mugs. The atmosphere in the kitchen was tense, in concert with the storm, the house resounding to the booms of surf on the outer beach. The sky only a degree lighter to announce late morning as heavy, wet, snow drove by the windows. Grandfather remained silent.

"C'mon, Doyle, best get back to work, I suppose," said Malich, heaving himself up, anxious to get clear of the gathering.

Doyle swallowed his tea, took a slice of bread and followed Malich to the door. Neither had taken off their coats or hats. The open door let in a blast of cold air. Those left behind listened to the wind and the snow splatting against the east windows. Lliam and Breeze made brief eye contact but Lliam couldn't read the meaning. They were as trapped in their separate thoughts as they were imprisoned by life on the island.

"I'm going around to Uncle Hebert's," Lliam said.

Uncle Hebert presided over a meeting of his cronies, the unofficial town council, huddled close to the stove. Outport men seldom spend time in their kitchens, even on the worst of days, preferring the company of other men and the pot bellied stoves that did little more than take off the chill on the bad days. The men, as alike in dress and countenance as veterans of an army bivouacked in a bunker, wore peak caps instead of berets, woolen shirts over long Johns and canvas jackets. Their black rubber boots had red soles to match the colour of their weather-creased faces, all of a kind, regardless of size: rugged, broad or narrow, and all with watery eyes and the gap-toothed grins. And they grinned often with the stories, even tragic stories, drinking strong black tea or moonshine from tin mugs, leaning forward conspiratorially, elbows on knees: smoking, always smoking. Chins, teeth and fingers stained like tanned sails. They were comfortable in familiar closeness: sharing their narrow existence.

One or two men acknowledged Lliam with a nod and continued their conversation about uncivil weather, bloody seasons and poor fishing. Lliam idled by the workbench shaping a small Irish cross for Breeze. There was no room for him near the stove and no one offered to include him in the circle. It wasn't a rude gesture. Lliam wasn't a fisherman, or a builder or even an acquaintance. If a fisherman from another cove wandered into the outport he would be seated near the stove to warm up and be plied with strong drink for a story. Lliam was treated as a come-from-away with no standing in the community. His exploits with Breeze on the hill and around the headland, and the comical swim in the harbour, didn't count as accomplishments in their eyes, nor did they count against him. Until he proved himself he was allowed on the fringes of their society, like a child getting his education at the elder's knee.

He had come to find answers to the mystery of his heritage, building since his first encounter with Breeze on the beach, the night of his return to Béhathook Cove. He listened to their gossipy talk but there was nothing to add to his knowledge of his own family. His family puzzled him, but so did Breeze. Somehow the Sheens figured large and Hebert knew the whole story.

Uncle Hebert was not connected by nationality to the community. His family had French, Basque and Native bloodlines...Many inhabitants of Béhathook Cove, as well as other settlements on Fogo, could trace their origins to Ireland's West Counties: fishing towns like Dingle, Kilrush and Kilkee...Hebert's was a fishing heritage well enough, but it was the whale oil that lured the Basques to the Western Ocean, following the harvest to Greenland and Labrador, bypassing Newfoundland for the French colonies. Basque whalers roamed the North Shore of the Strait of Belle Isle west to the Saguenay Fjord and settled in coves only long enough to render the oil so prized in Europe. Newfoundland was a more recent treasure house of codfish and many nations voyaged into the New Founde Land in search of the precious commodities ahead of the legendary Norse marauders.

The migrations and peregrinations of the tribes of Europe and North America are a veiled study in human progress, but Hebert's claim to the land was as strong as the English, M'kmaw, Béothuck, or Inuit migrants. How his ancestors came to Fogo Island is open to speculation. The French fished the Northeast Coast for a hundred years but seldom settled. It is known that fishermen often jumped ship and dwelt among the natives or huddled in coves, eking out a living to escape bondage. Perhaps a French ship returning from the Strait was wrecked and his progenitor cast ashore, as was Brigid O'Keefe's Portuguese ancestor, the first European ship wrecked on Drover's Rock. How they arrived was no longer important. Hebert was a Fogo Island fisherman, retired with standing.

Toward midday the men began to leave separately for their own homes, but one man remained behind, shy and embarrassed. "Say, 'ebert, ol' son, could you spare some 'baccy?" Lliam felt uncomfortable, witnessing a painful ritual that the outport man would have to endure for the entire winter. Hebert put a small handful of coarse tobacco into the man's cloth pouch without a word. The shy supplicant bid Lliam good day with only a nod.

"You didn't come just to use me tools," Hebert said to Lliam as the man closed the workshop door.

Lliam moved to the stove to warm his hands. "Hebert, you've been around Béhathook for some time."

"Born, raised an' died here, sonny."

"Not dead yet, I hope."

"Oh, 'tis only a small matter of the time. My people's mostly gone, an' my poor self soon enough. Got'er all plotted out." He pulled the dusty tarp off the shape Lliam thought was a punt. It was shaped like a boat, and there was a set of oars in brass oarlocks, but it had a hinged lid.

"It's...beautiful. But, I thought, the shape...?"

"Made'er so I don't be wonderin' what they do with me skin an' bones when I go over. I know where me soul's goin' to. Some warm then, my son," he chuckled. The coffin was made of teak and rosewood, inlaid with African iroco, richly carved with fish figures that looked like gargoyles. The hand-rubbed wood glowed in the lamplight. "Double ender, sonny. The bestest kind o' sea boat for the long voyage, eh? Found that wood on beaches all over the world. Got some leaved over, b'ye. We'll use it to make spindles for Malich's wheel. Maybe with enough good into'er we can shake off the curse, but I have my doubts."

"The curse, yes, I wanted to ask you..."

"'Course, Malich's apt to heap on his own curses. That man's a trial scattered times. What think you o' this?" Hebert pointed to the relief bust, like a ship's figurehead.

"A man's portrait."

"Me own self, when I was 'bout your age. First thing I done, see."

"My age?"

"Yes, I believe I was 'bout your age when I started this box." The carved bust was very finely crafted and when Lliam looked close he could see the resemblance. Hebert was one of those spare old men who change very little with time. "I took she along with me on ships an' carved away while me mates was fiddlin' with models an' ol' whale's teeth. I told me mates she was just me personal lifeboat!" Hebert chuckled.

Lliam thought of the story of the White Whale and wondered if Hebert knew Melville's classic. "You were twenty, and you thought of making a coffin?"

"Why not, sonny? A man never knows when 'e needs his coffin, see? Good Lord never guaranteed me I'd be 'round this long. An' I'm gettin' mighty tired o' waitin'."

"It's too nice to put in the ground."

"S'pose 'tis. Maybe they should jus' gut an' salt me ol' carcass an' leave me up on Fortress to dry, likes Hindians do." Hebert laughed and coughed and staggered around the crowded shop bumping into things. "But...I'll tell you what, sonny...I ain't goin' into ground to rot so people got to kneel down to talk to me. No sir, when I set out on next voyage I'm goin' out the tickle after Uncle John Kenney, an' tie off to his bridge...an' we'll jig cod, an' drink tea 'til Hell freezes over!" With that Hebert laughed and coughed until he was on his knees spitting into the fire. "Nearly found me 'eart that time. My son!" Another deep coughing fit produced a large phlegm ball. In the honest glow of the stove Hebert looked his age. He held his stomach, retching silently.

"You've known my grandfather since you were boys."

"All me life...the ol' bugger."

"Did you know Seth Sheen too, before the tragedies?"

Hebert was silent for a few moments, staring into the fire. "I knowed that man! He had brothers lived here too, but Seth Sheen never lasted in Béhathook. He was drove out and landed over on Change Islands. Why'd you ask?"

"Yesterday you mentioned Seth Sheen's sons..."

Hebert slammed the iron door and shot Lliam a look that was both wild and fearful. "Look here, sonny, if you wants to work away in me shop you never mention 'bout those poor b'yes, hear me?"

Christmas Eve was observed with a subdued dinner followed by bible readings. Malich had planned to give Margaret the bright broadcloth purchased from Mulroney's, as a surprise, but the cloth had been hidden in the store with the rolls of canvas. His gift was to say the grace before dinner, thanking Margaret for being a good and steady wife. They shared the special potato and oatcakes on the Eve, and a hot rum drink spiced with cinnamon.

Christmas Day dawned grey and cold and the elders spent the morning in quiet contemplation. Doyle carved trunnels, smoked and fidgeted. Lliam wrote in his journal. Breeze and Brigid arrived after lunch with a gift of new potatoes. Breeze helped Margaret prepare the meal while Brigid complained to Malich about her aches and pains, predicting a troubled future with Gerald gone: the tone accusing as if Malich was responsible. Malich tolerated her, uncharacteristically silent and docile, like a beast resting after a bruising battle. He was plotting the assault on the Sheen schooner.

Christmas dinner was more elaborate: boiled potatoes and salt beef with gravy, a salad of cod chunks with pickled turnips and steamed mussels, peas pudding and crusty rolls, and a raisin duff sprinkled with sugar. Malich offered a toast to Mulroney, the schooner and a better year ahead, and gave thanks for God's bounty, even though the largess was grudgingly provided by Merchant Mulroney. Finally he asked for a silent prayer for Gerald and other lost family members whose tortured souls may be lurking about. It was carried off with rare dignity.

After the meal it was time for gifts. Breeze presented Garret with a wool hat with large flaps to protect his deformed ears. Lliam gave Breeze the Irish cross, fashioned out of wood from her wrecked schooner. She joked that perhaps she should wear it upside down. He mutely registered the inference. Malich recounted the items he had purchased from Mulroney's and said he was sorry the hurricane had taken away his gifts. The family allowed it was just God's way. Grandfather read another passage from the bible, the Old Testament version of Noah's voyage because Noah was a sailor, then reminded the assembly that the Lord promised next time He would destroy the earth with fire. This cheered everyone greatly. Then he told a story about a family Christmas when he and Grandmother were seven years into their marriage with five children born, three who survived, including Malich. It was about the antics of the young male children, one he called Triny. He got the name wrong and the strained silence drew an end to the evening as if the lid of Hebert's coffin had suddenly slammed shut.

Grandmother ushered her confused husband to bed. Malich and Doyle retreated upstairs, leaving Margaret to deal with the kitchen, remembering a happier Christmas when she was a girl. Her father was home from fishing and the cold cellar filled for the winter. Her many brothers and sisters made for a boisterous family that liked to sing hymns. So long ago, fading in memory, with lace edges. And the morning mist vision of her outport home as she sat shivering in Malich's power dory, heading through the Main Tickle for Fogo Island. The family gone now from the homestead in Chance Harbour, spread along the coast, or dead. She remembered brothers lost at sea. Sisters lost to life. Her own mother was still living with a sister on the far side of New World Island but Margaret hadn't seen her since her father died of lung cancer in the cottage hospital in Morton's Harbour. Malich agreed to make the trip only because he had business with the merchant in Twillingate. She was his chattel, no thought of her spiritual needs. Malich believed that a pretty piece of broadcloth was sufficient. News of deaths, births and weddings arrived, and news was sent, and that was all.

Lliam saw Breeze and Brigid home, supporting the bulk of her mother over the invisible glitter ice on the path. Little was said until they arrived at the gate. Brigid went ahead leaving Breeze and Lliam in the utter darkness.

"It was a wonderful Christmas, Breeze."

"Thank you for the cross, I'll wear it right way round." She laughed self-consciously.

"I'd be pleased if you would..." He wanted to say more.

"Well, Good Christmas Night then, Lliam."

"Good Christmas to you, both."

Breeze turned away to the disapprovingly glare of Brigid waiting impatiently for her daughter to open the door.

Lliam returned to his own kitchen and spent an hour beside the stove thinking about many things, including the mistaken name that ended the evening. The name was 'Triny'. Seth Sheen had a son named Trinity.

December 26 1937: By Christmas Week winter had settled heavily on Béhathook Cove. The damp air had a fresh nip and the snow squalls stayed longer and lay against any obstacle that slowed the wind. The meadow, protected as it was by rocks and hills, collected enough snow to make a crust with only a few spikes of grass stalks sticking through, waving little flags defiantly at the elements. Grandmother Dwyer had been waiting for the chance to get the canvas rolls carried to the meadow for the first lay out of the mainsail. But this morning the activities in the Dwyer kitchen were not to do with sails and schooners.

Through a brief break in the clouds the morning sun spilled in, illuminating Garret on his daybed. Garret was sitting up, had pulled himself up in preparation. Breeze vowed that she would remove the last bandages by Christmas time, unwrapping Garret like a present. Not the body, but his life. It was as much a miracle performed as a gift bestowed. She unwrapped his bandages carefully, easing away those places where seeping fluids had dried, but Garret sat perfectly quiet, unashamed of his nakedness.

Breeze had carried Garret through the worst of times when she felt him slipping away, his will to survive weakening with every drop of fluid lost. She filled up the voids with her own defiant spirit; her energy entering his melting muscles, as if her own blood flowed in his veins, now so close to the surface they could see them throb. Hands only deformed claws that, with time, would function. Legs and back, burn damaged moonscape, but healing so he could work. But Garret was a monster, hideous to regard, even for the outporters hardened to life, and would never improve beyond what they saw revealed; like the resurrection of Christ, in the harsh light of morning with the shroud stripped away. Face oddly coloured, his skin stretched like kneaded bread over the bones, the nose a blackened lump of cartilage, the air wheezing in and out, and mucous draining from sinuses unchecked. His cracked lips barely covered bad teeth. Head, set off by the comic ears and the spiky tufts of grey hair, like rafts of wild vegetation adrift on a crimson sea. The smell had subsided, or, perhaps, they were used to it.

Margaret fought back tears of relief and guilt. She had been living with the wreckage of Garret's body for long four months, and now that the crisis was past, she faced the reality of their collective lives: the family and the community would have to deal with Garret as a monster man.

Margaret wished that Breeze would wrap him up again and send him to a hospital for treatment, or incarceration. He was just a piece of meat, like a skinned moose hanging in a corner to cure. At least the flesh of the moose could be eaten and the bones tossed for the dogs, to be fought over until someone kicked the dirt encrusted remains into the harbour.

The children play games identifying bones of seals and moose on the bottom that looked human, and moved with the ripples, scaring themselves with stories of sacrifices on dark nights around fires. Stories came north with the rum boats from the Islands about hideously disfigured Haitian priests, called Zombies. Zombies, they said, rose from the dead and walked in blood dripping rags, like Garret. Some whispered that Breeze was going to sacrifice Garret and was just keeping him alive until the right moment. There was a furtive vigil kept by small eyes, tracing her movements. Secret signals passed in the gathering twilight from behind rocks and fences until called to supper and the safety of their own bright kitchens to listen to the speculation of the adults...Breeze O'Keefe was associated with strange occurrences. Besides the suspicious beach fires, there was the burning of Dwyer's schooner and the incident of the smoking canvas on a stormy morning...A few, like her only friend Thelma, and Uncle Hebert, praised Breeze O'Keefe for the miracle of Garret's survival, while others suspected she used dark powers to prevent God from taking the boy out of his misery to inflict him on their tiny community, to punish them, to make them witness.

Only the men in need of potatoes, bread or washing visited the O'Keefe home, and only the bachelors escaped the silent ridicule of the superstitious, God-fearing women. Breeze and witches were often mentioned in the same breath, and there were stories told about malevolent fairies, faith healers, fables and legends from the old country. And there was the legend of Grace O'Malley as proof, even though none but Breeze and Lliam knew the real story of the Pirate Queen. Even a hint that Breeze herself was the incarnation of the Irish hellion: rebellious, assertive, nightwalker, fire worshipper...

"There you go, my dear...good as new!" Breeze exclaimed falsely as she drew off the last bandages. He tried to flex his fingers, to banish the claws they had become. Breeze held his hands. "Don't try too hard, Garret my love, or you'll pull the skin open. In time you'll use them."

"'Tis a blessing you're still alive, Garret my dear," said Margaret.

When the deed was done and Garret was oiled and draped in a clean nightgown, the family turned to the business of preparing for Christmas Week.

Mummery, or Jannery, the ritual of dressing up in outlandish costumes and marauding about the village, making a racket, knocking on doors and playing tricks, can be traced to the times before Christians organized feast days to celebrate their evolving version of theism. Mummery is a pagan practice from antiquity that has undergone many incarnations. Costuming, to disguise the prankster, is common to most societies and the intent is to hide one's identity from gods or demons, or those who are victimized by the mummers. In the Newfoundland outports the tradition had more to do with fun than demon pranksters.

The festival of Christmas, Christ's birthday and gift giving, is a recent invention of Christianity, but mummery celebrates the ending of the work season, a break from the toil and drudgery of a hard life and the welcoming of a new year with promise for better times. Always better times. And if the times were not to improve at least the mummer's foolishness provided a needed respite from reality.

Even before the Great Depression struck, blunting spirits and robbing the common people of simple pleasures, mummering in Newfoundland was declining in the larger towns like St. John's, where laws forbidding the ritual tried to put a damper on the enthusiasm of riotous mobs rooming the streets. But in isolated communities like Béhathook Cove, the people decided their own course. Mummer's days continued undiminished, and, while mummering was once the right of only male fools, called John Jacks, in Béhathook Cove, as in many other outports, everyone was free to join in the fun. Those who chose not to dress up and invade homes with music and dance acted as hosts, willing or not, to the throngs careening along the paths in any kind of weather.

Malich was sweating from the heat, the layers of clothing and the spirits consumed during the evening in preparation for the first sally around the harbour.

"Malich, try not to tear up your dress this year, m'dear," admonished Margaret.

"Awe, Mother, you've no idea how hard 'tis to keep buddy from steppin' on the blessed thing!"

The 'thing' in question was the well-travelled white satin dress Margaret had worn on her wedding day, passed down from her mother, who did not attend the wedding at the small Catholic Church in Fogo Harbour. The reception was held in the Salvation Army Hall and the dress suffered its first indignity when a drunken brawl broke out between the Dwyers and the Fogo Sheens. Thirty years later Malich was wearing the much-altered dress over long Johns and leather boots. He was holding a concertina, squeaking out notes, limbering up, standing and swaying uncomfortably in the middle of the kitchen as Margaret stitched patches over patches. The lower part of the dress would never come clean but that mattered not at all. Most of the costumes to be seen about Béhathook Cove for the next several days would be mouldy cast offs dredged up out of old trunks, patched and let out, to suffer the abuse of step dancing, spills and bad weather, and stumbling fights when spirits soared too high.

Doyle held up an old party dress with a large bodice and crinolines. "What think of this? I could be like them women who dance on toes. Breeze showed me in book the once."

"You'd look some good, Doyle," said Malich. "You can barely stand on two feet!"

Doyle then tried on a hat with a long, moth-eaten veil. The ensemble made him look like a tarted-up beekeeper. It was anybody's guess where the dress had come from. It wasn't something seen on the paths of Béhathook Cove, except at mummer's times.

Lliam, bemused, watched the preparations, on the edge of boredom. He returned to the Shipwright's Manual, delving deeper into the mysteries of ship construction. The other reading choice was the Bible and Grandfather was peering at its pages through a pall of tobacco smoke, chuckling to himself over something in Lamentations. "They don't know nothin' 'bout misery, those Jews. They wants to come away from Jerusalem an' live on Fogo for a spell. They can study on misery all they like."

"Father, you daren't say down on Bible," chided Margaret softly.

"What in Creation those fellas know 'bout misery? There's nary fisherman among'em!"

195

"There was fishermen into the Lord's crew, sure," countered Malich. "Says so in The Book. Peter's the b'ye."

"Oh, may be sonny, but that was later. This here was afore God sent fishermen an' boat builders to earth."

"Where're you to, ol' man? Noah was first boat builder sure. Built he a big one!"

"Never could a done it without the Lord had to tell him every blessed thing, an' then he never allowed for a jiggin' well, an' nary a stick to hang a bit o' canvas on. What kind a blamed seaman was that?"

"Noah never needed to fish. Could call up all the food he wanted an' was only at sea scattered days with bunch o' animals," argued Malich.

"That's it! The queer ol' fella was just the mate onto floatin' barn! Mark me now, the Lord never called Noah, skipper!"

"You're right there, ol' man! An' he only had pigeon for pilot!" Malich laughed a coarse, howling belly explosion.

"Hold still, less you want this patch sewn to your boot!" scolded Margaret.

"Leave off, woman! Where's me hat? Don't want Shamus to beat me to 'ebert's.'"

The mummers traditionally gathered in Uncle Hebert's kitchen on the far side of the harbour to warm up, and worked their way around to John Kenney's cottage on Blow Me Down, but that was before the hurricane...Hebert always had a supply of hot rum punch, or bootleg whiskey, and neighbours brought cakes and cookies. After step dancing in the heat of the big kitchen, the mummers would begin the halting, rolling march back around Béhathook Cove. There was a memorial cairn of loose stone built on John Kenney's beach but his family wondered what degradations the memorial would suffer when the swell of heated mummers reached the sight of Uncle John's cottage.

It was also traditional that the first night of the mummer's time finished with a bonfire. Since few of the fishermen could swim it was an anxious time for the women who stayed home and prayed. The first night's fire that year was to be a big one, including broken dories and debris from the hurricane.

Margaret stuffed the bosom of Malich's dress with old clothing until he puffed out like a blowfish. She found the wide brimmed hat with the black veil and jammed it on his head. "There, now you look the proper fool." The veil hung all around and covered head, chest and back. In the dark the disguise might fool a stranger, but after so many years everyone in the community recognized a mummer by the costume, but the ritual of 'invade and guess' was continued.

"I'm ready!" Malich played a tune and did a little jig, bowing clumsily to Lliam and Garret. Lliam laughed despite his sombre mood. Garret tried to laugh but produced only a bubble of air and a hiccup. "Easy, Garret..." said Lliam, "It's not that funny. In Boston a grown man in a woman's dress would force the police to arrest the perpetrator."

"What's that? Poor potater?" asked Doyle. "Is that Boston talk for bad pratie ground?"

"Doyle your ignorance is legendary."

"I'll show you ignorance..."

Breeze, with a charcoaled beard sketched on, entered on a gust of wind, dressed as a fisherman, wearing rubber boots and big overalls, a duffel coat and a Sou'wester. The dramatic entrance forestalled Doyle's attempt to deepen his intellectual abyss. "That you could Doyle, without too much effort," she laughed for the first time since the return of the survivors. Breeze was in good humour and ready for the mummer foolishness. "There's already mummers about. Come on, Garret, my dear. I'm goin' to take you out too."

Garret could only blink at her in surprise. He looked from Margaret to Malich as if seeking permission. "Garret's in no fit condition to go traipsin' about harbour like Janney!" said Margaret.

"'Course he is." Breeze held up a dress. "Just what Garret needs, some air an' a bit o' fun. I'll look after him, an' no one would guess so he won't have to take off the veil."

She split the back of the dress to the hem. Garret stood up and held his arms out like a sleepwalker. The dress slipped on and she fastened the back with a few deft stitches. Malich played a lively jig and thumped around the kitchen. Doyle thumped even harder. Grandfather and Grandmother kept time, Grandfather pounding the arm of his chair with the palm of one hand.

Margaret shook her head in resignation. "'Tis just foolishness!"

"It is an' that's just what we all need!" shouted Breeze. Malich and Doyle left off the dancing to watch Breeze. She produced a pair of leather Hamburg boots from the bundle and cut them open. "Sean O'Keefe's Sunday best, but he won't be needin' boots." Garret shuffled into them with some help. She stitched them closed with a sail needle. He was ready, except for the hat and veil. The hat was a silly maroon pillbox affair with some seabird feathers stuck on so that Garret looked like a West Coast Indian dressed for a potlatch. A double veil eliminated the need for make-up. "There!...Oh my! I forgot about your hands."

Garret looked at his twisted fingers, the scar tissue pulled tight over the knuckles, palms a contour map of a barren landscape. Even in an outport where injuries and deformities, missing digits and halting gates, are common currency, Garret's hands could not pass even distant inspection.

"I've a pair o' lovely white gloves," spoke up Grandmother Dwyer. "My weddin' gloves."

"You can't...Mother," said Margaret.

"What in All-That's-Holy can I wear them for now?"

"You saved them for your funeral."

"So I did, an' so I shall. But that's a day or two off," she made the Sign of the Cross quickly. "An' I don't need them tonight, my dear. Where's them gloves to?"

"I'll get your gloves," sighed Margaret.

"How about you?" asked Breeze, turning to Lliam. "Would you like to come with us?"

"No thank you...what I want is a cup of coffee and some answers." He had been thinking of Boston and a corner café near his street, and about certain inconsistencies in the family story.

"Air might do you good. Lord knows you could stand a bit o' fun."

198

"Just a Pagan practice. An attempt to fool Old Nick, who's gamboling about these little enclaves looking for liars."

"Lliam, that's unfair! We're not liars!"

"Oh, there's enough to go around this pathetic little island. An' there's mysteries enough without the good folks hiding their true selves behind Janney masks..."

"That's enough o' that talk, sonny!" said Grandfather strongly. "You've no idea where you're comin' to!" Grandfather disappeared into a cloud of tobacco smoke. Grandmother knitted, pretending she hadn't heard the exchange.

Margaret returned to a kitchen that had become strangely quiet. She searched the faces for the reason but eyes darted away. There was a new tension in the air and she didn't like being left out. She handed Breeze the gloves with a gesture that said, *fine, if you won't tell me now, you will at some time.*

Breeze tried to pull a glove over Garret's hand. He straightened his fingers as best he could. "Oh, my dear, they're too small."

"Give me those scissors," said Grandmother.

"You can't cut those lovely gloves."

"I can to!" Grandmother took the scissors from Breeze and opened the gloves from cuff to palm. "There. When I die you can stitch them on me."

Breeze worked the gloves over Garret's hands and stitched them tight. They would do. "Well, you comin' with us or not?" she asked Lliam again.

"Thanks all the same, but as Mother says, it's just a lot of foolishness."

"Suit yourself. Come on, Garret, my dear. We'll dance, somehow. You come along too, Doyle. You can help me with Garret. There's black ice on the paths."

Doyle, dressed in the hideous purple dress, pulled on a stocking cap...the leg cut from a pair of trousers with the top sewn shut and eye holes roughly cut out...looking sinister and threatening, like an executioner. "There, no one knows me!"

"You wore the same disguise last year, an' the year before that," commented Breeze, opening the door. "Garret, take me arm. Doyle you go first an' help us down the steps, an' don't trip on that ridiculous dress."

Malich played them to the door but instead of following he closed the door and jigged back to the table. "Too late. Crowd's headed this way. Jus' to limber up me ol' fingers." His seal finger curling around the glass, the tiny concertina held aloft, wheezing as if breathing its last. Malich downed the measure and began playing. High-pitched voices carried over the wind, like a bestial wail from the moors, but the voices were greetings, shouts and *whoops* of revelers. Heavy, stumbling footsteps and a startlingly loud rap on the door announced their arrival. Malich flung open the door and a half dozen mummers wearing hats, veils and dresses, spilled in, tramping in snow and mud. The lead mummer, a very large man in a bulging dress, falsetto voice almost breaking, said, "Is any Mummers 'lowed in this place?" It was Bert O'Halloran.

"Any Janneys 'lowed in tonight?" asked another in a squeaky Soprano. It was Uncle Hebert.

"'Tis welcome you are, my sons! Come in, but only if you got fiddle aboard!"

"We got one ol' lady likes to fiddle some."

Bursts of laughter rolled around the room. "I know that one, sure! Black Bessie! The ugliest ol' bitch in all Newfoundland!" shouted Malich.

Black Bessie, the one with the fiddle, stepped forward and held out a gloved hand for a glass and drank a toast to the assembly, shook off his gloves that were attached with fishing line, like a child's mitts in winter, and began a reel. Malich joined in and instantly the other mummers began a wild, stumbling step dance that shook the house. Margaret tried to ignore the damage being done to her canvas floor and clapped along, knowing that soon the mob would leave to plague another household. She would stay behind to make biscuits and tea, thinking there are eleven more nights of the foolishness to endure. Lliam escaped to his bedroom to brood.

It was after midnight when the revelers crashed back into the Dwyer kitchen, dragging two bodies, hooting and stomping, dripping wet after pulling Tim Squires out of the ocean before he floated away like a bloated whale. Jeremy Coughlin had climbed Uncle John's new cairn, fell off and was still unconscious. They dumped the limp bodies on the floor. "Probably just a drink too many," said someone. More laughter. A splash of cold water brought Jeremy back to life. Jeremy was propped in the corner with a drink in his hand. Since Tim was already wet they concluded water wasn't going to revive him. The music and dancing went on for another hour. Lliam listened to the tumult below, noting that he hadn't heard Breeze's voice in the crowd. He drifted off to sleep trying to fathom his family and the thin attraction of Béhathook Cove.

Morning: Lliam roused himself at dawn and descended to the kitchen to get warm, the only resident of Béhathook who had a decent night's sleep. Margaret had been up for an hour, stoking the fire and making tea. Fresh rolls were rising in the warming oven. She began the task of cleaning up, wiping tears away as she went about her duty.

Lliam stopped at the foot of the stairs to survey the wreckage, which resembled the harbour after the hurricane. The folded sails were in disarray because Malich insisted on showing them off. Clouds of canvas kicked into untidy heaps around the room by the dancers. Rum bottles scattered about like dead soldiers after the battle. A chair knocked over. A body on the daybed that wasn't Garret or Jeremy Coughlin or Tim Squires.

"Who's that?" Lliam asked Margaret.

"Dermot O'Dell, come over from Tilton to be with Morgan, I suppose," answered Margaret, voice tired and resigned.

"Then why is he here?"

"Morgan left'im with me."

"An' where's Garret?"

"I don't know what's become of Garret, sure," she sighed, brushing back her hair and wiping away fresh tears.

Malich slept at the table, head on arms, hat and veil askew, looking like a debauched bride who'd been ravished by all the groom's relatives. The concertina dangled by its leather strap from his left arm. Doyle was passed out on the floor behind the stove, head resting on a roll of canvas. Grandfather slumped in his rocking chair as if asleep.

Lliam wandered about the kitchen checking bodies. He nudged Doyle with his foot. "Doyle...Doyle! Where's Garret?" Doyle moaned. "Doyle, you idiot! Where's Garret?"

"Wha?...Garret? Breeze's place. Too drunk to make it'ome, I suppose." Doyle rolled over and went back to sleep.

Lliam skirted Malich's chair and edged closer to his grandfather. The old man looked too rigid, pipe held at an odd angle, in mid puff. Mouth open, the spittle dried in the stubble on his chin. He touched the thin wrist resting on the arm of the chair. Cool. Dry and cool. "Grandfather?" He shook his shoulder gently. The pipe jarred loose and slid slowly down to the old man's narrow lap, spilling ashes like dirty snow over his wool shirt. "Grandfather? Old man...?" Lliam stepped back in shock. He, unlike his family, had never experienced the death of a relative. "Mother, Grandfather's dead."

"I know," she said.

Grandfather Dwyer's death ended the mummer's festival. The preparations for the wake required several days and no one felt like foolishness after it was done. Young Father Hennessy was brought from Seldom Come By Chance in Bert O'Halloran's motorboat. Grandfather was dressed in his dark Sunday suit and laid out on the bed in the parlour with two white candles burning day and night by his head. The melted wax splattering into his iron-grey hair, sticking like bloated lice. His feet were bare and the toes tied together with heavy fishing twine so the fairies couldn't spirit his body away.

Father Hennessy arrived chilled and grumpy, so the small requiem service was a solemn, awkward affair and even the meal after the service lacked the usual festive story telling. There was an argument about burning the bed to drive out the bad spirits, but it was decided that, spirits or not, they couldn't afford to sacrifice a good mattress. Lliam said it was just more secular nonsense. Malich roared insistence and threatened bodily injury. Margaret compromised and agreed to burn the feather pillow. The priest left in a rising snowstorm for the trip to around to Fogo Harbour without blessing the death house. He would say a mass at Fogo and travel overland back to Seldom. It would be a miserable day. The wake and the funeral service was a failure by Béhathook Cove standards.

The burial, such as it was, took place in the afternoon of New Years Eve. It was blustery, bitingly cold, with stinging snow squalls driving off the ocean. Flashes of sunlight between demented clouds teased the freezing mourners. The few who attended in the tiny cemetery stood with hats and bonnets pulled low, backs to the wind, coats and dresses and shawls flapping like Monday laundry: the women like shaggy moor ponies, the men like tundra musk oxen in a defensive circle.

The simple spruce box rested on a bier of stones, trembling in the gusts as if Grandpa Dwyer shivered with the cold. Lliam and Doyle made the coffin in the store with wood Morgan O'Dell had cut for a new skiff. When the mourners filed away the coffin was weighed down with rocks and remained like a ship caught in the ice, with snow drifting around the lee. Grandmother Dwyer and Margaret were the last to leave the hill. Grandmother placed a framed picture of her husband in uniform as a young sailor at the head of the rough casket. When she turned to go the wind blew it over and flakes of snow covered the face. Grandmother never liked the picture because the Old Man would hold it up and go on about his exploits with painted women in foreign ports.

Friends and family members filed down the hill to assemble in the Dwyer kitchen for the last ritual, the burial memorial dinner, to make sure the spirit had left the house.

Lliam was first through the door. The kitchen was empty and silent, except for a soft murmur from the stove; the first time Lliam had seen his home without a parent or elder in residence, even in his youth. He remembered it was one of the difficulties of leaving home: the comforting thread of sameness that tied the family together.

The old man's pipe was on the cushion of his rocking chair. The chair moved. It might have been the wind howling through cracks and around sashes, and blowing the curtains in a jerky dance. The house creaked in sympathy. Iron pots simmered on the stove as if an invisible cook hovered near, the steam rising from bubbles that popped and plopped lazily in peas pudding and thick gravy. He should stir something or move pots, but that was Margaret's domain and she understood what the stove could do left on it's own. He waited for the others, noticing the sailcloth panels had been rerolled and stacked neatly behind the stove. The long table already set for a meal had twelve places. He wondered if one was for Gran', or the Twelfth Apostle, or the Twelve Bloody Furies, and if the family would stand behind the chairs and watch the spirits consume the feast and go on their way back to the suspicion pits of the Old Country. He wished he were Polish or Swiss, doubting there were as many myths and superstitions to bother the pragmatic Swiss, but there was a presence. Lliam shivered with the house.

He went reluctantly to the stove and held his hands over a pot, sniffing the good food smell, looking forward to the simple fare. He opened his topcoat to the heat. The coat had been stylish in New England, but too light for Newfoundland winds in cemeteries, with a gale blowing from Ireland to freeze the souls of traitors. He was a double traitor, not content with his birthplace, as his ancestors weren't content with theirs, but the Irish didn't come from Ireland, originally. They came from Eastern Europe, and beyond, as did all the inhabitants of the New World. He imagined humanity in an endless flow around the earth, stopping only long enough to ravage the land, procreate, kill and move on, always westerly. Béhathook Cove was only a way-station, like a tram stop, and someday the inhabitants would leave or be driven from the pathetic little hamlet. Wondered about Breeze wanting to fly away over the ocean in the opposite direction, and would she keep going east until she landed back in Béhathook? There was no point in leaving her, or leaving without her...

Malich was next in the door, puffing and blowing like a surfacing whale. "Damn me, that's not a civil day for livin' nor the dead!" He went straight to the pantry for the rum bottle. His glass was full of rum

204

before he sat down, without taking off his coat. He didn't offer Lliam a drink so Lliam helped himself to the bottle and sat at the table to Malich's right, across from Grandfather's place.

Doyle came in with Garret in tow. Garret was moving much better since the mummer's night escapade. The booze and the dancing loosening him up perhaps, or he had just willed his tormented body to overlook the pain and deteriorated muscles. He looked almost normal bundled up to his nose in a long coat with Breeze's knitted cap covering his ears so that only his eyes were showing, darting around with life as if he had entered a new home. Lliam thought it was the best thing he had seen in months and he knew Breeze was responsible. He got up to help Garret with his coat.

Uncle Hebert and Jake Kenney followed Garret. They sat quietly on the daybed, waiting to be invited to the table. "Get yourselves a mug," said Malich, "an' we'll drink a drop to the Ol' Man." They took mugs from the shelf and shyly joined the table group. Malich poured their measures and they held their mugs and drank silently.

Breeze entered next supporting Mother O'Keefe, and close behind them came Mildred O'Hara, a slender, mousy girl with big teeth, and wandering eyes that watered easily. She drooled when concentrating on any task, and her nose ran constantly so that her unconscious motion was to her mouth, nose and eyes, followed by a snuffle and a smacking sound behind her teeth. In a Mainland city she might be isolated behind the walls of an institution. In Béhathook Cove she was just another person with a life to live as best she could. Mildred had hopes and dreams, as well as hormones, and she and Doyle exchanged glances. Mildred helped Brigid with her coat, then took off her own, hung them neatly on pegs and found a place for Mother O'Keefe at the end of the table. While Mildred tended to Mother O'Keefe, Breeze poured tea with natural grace, and no self-conscious pretensions about being in another woman's domain. Lliam thought Malich looked too closely at Breeze; moving his large, dark hand under the table as she turned to pour for Lliam, but Breeze sensed the move and shifted away as his fingers grazed her thigh. Malich poured himself another rum as if nothing had happened.

Lliam experienced a deeper rush of hatred for his brute of a father, wanting to kill him too...*I've come home to kill my entire family,* he said to himself. *It's not for Breeze at all...* And now...

Malich was well into his second rum when Margaret and Grandmother returned from the hill, eyes red and cheeks raw and chapped from the wind. They were done with it and it was time to feed the living. Margaret helped Grandmother out of her coat and. Breeze took the coat and gave way and took her place at the table.

Margaret banished the last of the dark spirits. "There now, that's done. Must be famished." She noted that the fire was built up and the pots coming back to a boil. Breeze was a proper outport woman, and she had a momentary ache for loss of Gerald. "This'll have to do for dinner. Father always looked forward to New Years an' a new beginnin'. He always said, 'nothing could be worse than year before'. I don't know about that but we'll give thanks for his long life an' for Garret's life spared, an' pray it's so long as Father's." She said this while carrying pots to the table.

Not to be outdone Malich roared, "To Ol' Man! He's up there on hill looking down at us, so we'd better do him proud," he said grandly, as if he was providing the simple feast. "...an' spill a drop or two for ol' bugger, speed 'im on 'is way."

"Aye," agreed Uncle Hebert. "Angus'd like that, sure."

"May he stay put on hill 'til he's ready to go," said Jake Kenney

"Yes, by Jasus, stay put Ol' Man!"

"You're going to just leave Grandfather out there in the snow?" asked Lliam.

"You thinks us should invite ol' b'ye in for dinner?"

"No...I mean, aren't you going to bury him?"

"He's all right, sure."

"The wind..."

"We'll ballast ol' bugger down with more rocks so wind don't blow he out to sea, an' then, when spring comes we'll get he in ground proper. A'fore we leaves for Change Island."

"What about animals?"

"Should I gut'im an' salt'im proper?"

"No, it's just..."

"Leave off b'ye! He's frozen solid. Let's have a drink to Father." Malich poured measures for those with mugs or glasses. Garret held a glass in both hands, studied the amber liquor and remembered the consequences of mummer's night with mixed emotions: the double ache. One pain, one pleasure. Breeze knew what to do with the only part of his body that escaped damage, what Lliam suspected that Breeze was doing for Garret in stolen moments, and harboured his own confused emotions. He was jealous but didn't begrudge Garret.

"Here's to the Ol' Man..." continued Malich. "Liked a time as well as any. Glad we are that the ol' bugger went out dancin'. 'Tis better than dyin' in bed, or drownin' in the freezin' fuckin' ocean. 'Course, I'd rather that then burnin' for me sins, when my time comes, though I suppose I don't have much to say 'bout that score..." Malich made a Sign of the Cross with his glass. Doyle, Jake Kenney and Uncle Hebert laughed at the black sentiment.

"Oh, I allow as you'll burn, Malich Dwyer," said Hebert, a little drunk and loose in the tongue. "Didn't Moses Sheen say that?"

"Moses Sheen can kiss my rosy Irish arse! To my father....the best ol' gran'father, husband, fisherman, an' friend!"

"Aye...Don't come any better on this Island," intoned Hebert to make amends.

"Don't come better on whole goddamn fuckin' Newfoundland!" roared Malich.

"Needn't blaspheme," protested Margaret.

"Nary blaspheme, the ol' bastard! 'Tis the fuckin' truth of it!"

"You're just drunk," she said.

"Course I am! Not every Newfoundland son gets to bury his father. Most drown at sea. Now drink, god-damnit!"

The mood deepened. Lliam doubted it could be worse but the assembly of mourners was shocked even by Malich's outburst. *Who are these rude peasants?* Lliam wondered. Not his kin surely. There must be some mistake.

"Drink to a fisherman, sonny!" Malich was challenging him. Holding his glass close to Lliam's face, waiting for Lliam to drink.

"Am I right, sonny b'ye?"

"You're right, Father."

"You know I goddamned am!"

"I said, you're right. Grandfather was a good man."

"Best fuckin' fisherman an' sailor on this goddamned fuckin' mean coast!"

"Best fisherman."

"Best sailor!"

"Sailor, yes...They say he was a good sailor."

"I say he's the best!"

"Fine, I don't doubt..."

"You don't doubt? Don't know nothing, is you, Lliam, b'ye. Useless as tits on turr, as Father would say." Malich leaned in closer. " He would say."

Lliam flinched. "He would, yes..."

Doyle sniggered at Lliam's discomfort. The others squirmed and diverted their eyes. Who would come to Lliam's defense? Not Doyle. He enjoyed watching Lliam stripped to the bone. Not Margaret. She had more invested in Malich than in her Prodigal Son. And she had to live with Malich, like it or not. Outport women seldom ran. They might kill an abusive husband in desperation, but there was nowhere to run. Not Garret. He would if he could. Not Grandmother. Perhaps later, out of her grieving time. Not Malich's friends. Hebert and Jake shared the life. They had no stake in Lliam either, until he proved himself. If Malich killed Lliam on the spot it would not jeopardize the community in any material way. Morally? There could be arguments made in Malich's favour. The boy had run away and returned with nothing to help his family. Brigid Ortiz? She saw Lliam as a threat to steal her daughter. Whether he ran again or Malich bludgeoned him with a swiling gaff was only a benefit. Her only concession was a silent prayer that Malich not do it in her presence.

"Why don't you say something then, Lliam lame-brain? Come back to take your ol' man's place have you? Down on wharf, we'll see who's best now, Mr. Soft Hands." He looked at Hebert and Jake. They nodded.

Fight his own father? Maybe, if forced to fight for his life. Couldn't imagine defending his father the way Malich talked about Grandfather, bragging about his prowess as a fisherman and father, on the day of his internment. Imagined he could leave Malich in the snow, with his brains bashed in. A sealing gaff would do, or a slick. Hebert had a giant chisel called a slick, a wicked looking tool with a long handle that could slice through even Malich's bull neck, the head rolling away down the hill, spewing blood in arabesques, pin wheeling across the snow, coming to rest against a rock...bashing it to pieces with the rock to make sure...What point if it was severed? Couldn't be reattached. Couldn't rebuild a body like building a boat: that only happens in stories. Wanted to lash out at the thick lips pushing close to his own face, sneering at him, spewing spittle, breath a poisonous gas...There are gas lights in Boston. Turn a valve and a poisonous gas comes out. Strike a match and have light, heat, or suicide. He had considered it, talked about it with his literary friends, in the booze. Talked each other into it and out of it...just a game. This wasn't a game. He knew his father meant to push him into a corner and have an excuse to beat him senseless. Lliam was breathing hard. A kitchen knife. A broken bottle twisted into the leering face, grab Breeze and flee. Save her from abuse. They were all at her, even himself...no wonder she despised him...

"I said outside an' fight, sonny!"

"Malich," said Breeze in a controlled voice. "Lliam doesn't deserve to be tormented."

He turned on Breeze. "No? An' what did he do to his poor mother? Or you? You mooned about so after the b'ye left, like ol' harp with her pup's head smashed, an' only the steamin' carcass left behind...'Twas pitiful to see. Don't deny it!"

Breeze wanted to strike back, but he could hurt her in so many ways. "I'm just saying, that Lliam came back on his own, an' needs a chance..."

"Comes back with nice city ways to lay about an' eat our food." He turned on Lliam again, leaning closer, forcing Lliam back in his chair, breathing the hot, boozy stink in his face. "Well, sonny?"

"You drink too much," was all Lliam could say.

"You know nothing about the life, but you come back an' tell us we can't do this, we shouldn't do that..."

"Seth Sheen's real curse was the bottle and you're going down the same road."

"Well, sonny, if you don't like our ways, you can always go on back up the fuckin' road *you* come down on."

"You're afraid of something, Father." He said it with sarcasm, pushing the limits, a self-destructive urge to be annihilated rather than flee.

"Afraid? Yes, b'ye, I'm afraid I've raised up a son what ain't fit to be neither fisherman nor landsman. You got soft hands an' fine ways, an' no soul for this life. I'm afraid I got to make do with son likely to cut an' run. If you're plannin' to cut an' run, sonny, you best do it now. I'd as soon Breeze O'Keefe along side we. My son, she can out work the likes o' you ten times!"

"Is that really all you want Breeze for?"

Malich's eyes narrowed and heavy brow darkened. "An' where might you be anglin' to, sonny?"

Lliam pressed harder into the truth. "You want your filthy way with her, isn't that it?"

"What's that?"

"It's called incest, Father..." He was almost guilty himself. Lliam knew he had dug his own grave with both Malich and Breeze.

Breeze was angry with Lliam for stealing her only weapon against Malich. "It's not your business. I can look out for myself."

"Really?" He plunged on, prepared to take the consequences. "A slip of a girl against an ugly, whoring ape like that?"

"Lliam!" said Margaret suddenly. "That's not a thing to say to your father!"

"Why, Mother?" He was determined to get it said, since the damage was done. "Because it's wrong, or because it's the truth?"

"Lliam, take it back!"

"No, Mother, I meant every word." Lliam glared at Malich, hoping the man would lash out and destroy him.

Malich wavered, rum heavy and tired. "*Ach,* yer not worth the trouble."

"You're hiding something!" shouted Lliam. He stormed out, leaving he knew not what shambles behind.

He fled to the Fortress Hill and brooded for the rest of the day, watching the sea in tatters with chunks of pan ice driving back toward the land, and watching the aberrantly clean yellow coffin on the cemetery hill, slowly drifting over with snow. He could not see himself ending up like his grandfather: old and dying day by day in Béhathook Cove, nor could he see an out, without Breeze.

Later that night, when Breeze left and the family shuffled or staggered off to bed, Lliam ate dry bread and drank tepid black tea sitting at the table with pencil and rough paper, drawing patterns for the steering wheel in Sean O'Keefe's book, cutting out the patterns with Grandmother's shears. Doing it carefully to prove something...for himself or for his father? *Which father?* he kept asking himself. *Sean O'Keefe had wavy red hair, like yours,* Breeze had said. Lliam overlaid the patterns on a knee...Sean O'Keefe could be his father...then Breeze was his half sister. But Breeze was not Sean O'Keefe's daughter. He was not Malich's son. Neither was Garret the son of Malich Dwyer. Then whose son was he? Sean O'Keefe's? He felt a chill run through him. The spirits of the ancestors were disturbed. The beasts of denial and deceit loosed upon his head, the house, the Cove.

The winter passed in neutral tension. Lliam worked on his ship's wheel. Breeze made sails and didn't try to conceal the baby growing in her womb. No one mentioned the baby, or openly speculated about its father. The gossips? The women had plenty to say in their circles. The job was to survive and prepare for spring, and the Change Islands.

Part Two

Loss: Change Islands

During the long wet passage from Béhathook Cove to Change Islands, Lliam sat in the bow of the trap skiff, back against the hard timbers, separated from Doyle and Malich by a mound of supplies and a gulf of simmering animosity. Garret sat opposite Lliam, reclining on the gear to ease his limbs.

It had been a difficult winter. The family coexisted under a cloud of denial, speaking infrequently, getting the job of survival done. Grandfather was buried proper before they left for Change Islands. Breeze dwelt within the family in a cocoon of silence. Garret no longer needed her constant attention but Breeze came to the house daily to help Grandmother finish the sails, doing most of the difficult sewing. Doyle and Lliam did the heavy work of hauling the canvas as the rolls grew into full sized sails and the job became too much for the children, but it required a minimum of direction.

Each night Grandmother retreated further into a lonely vigil by the stove, watching Breeze work, offering suggestions only when necessary. Breeze had a natural capacity for learning and the busy work allowed her to relax in the nest of the enemy. There was some silent bond between Breeze and Garret, and that bond was strengthened by their glances and smiles, as if they shared an understanding. The rest of the family was outside the small circle.

Doyle had little curiosity about family affairs, preferring to pursue Mildred O'Hara when his physical needs arose. Malich brooded like a caged bear waiting for spring. Hibernation would have been a blessing for the family but Malich was never one for sentiment or thoughtfulness so his moods were open, his needs satisfied on demand and his special brand of sarcasm spread about freely. Margaret bore the brunt of his demands. Lliam bore the sarcasm and kept his own distance. Garret simply waited for Breeze's visits and continued to improve until he was able to tend the fire and even journey outside to carry firewood. It was not a pleasant winter but no one starved.

In March month, Malich prodded the boys into the skiff to go after seals. It was a bad season. Because the ice didn't compact in broad fields or stay solid, they were forced to chase drifting pans by boat, often out of sight of the Island. The work was dangerous in the loose ice, and the rewards small: shooting from the skiff, they killed a few white coats and their mothers to provide fat and meat, but three adults sank away before they could reach them. At least nothing went seriously wrong in Béhathook, although tragedy was never far away. Two Tilting Cove men with large families were lost when their skiff failed to return from a trip to the ice.

The old trap skiff lurched over a wave and Lliam clutched the gunnels. Despite the Northwest wind driving broken slob ice into Hamilton Sound, Malich had chosen the northern route around the Island because he wanted to stop at Fogo Harbour to stock up. Rum was his main concern.

Mulroney was reticent and grumpy, not wanting to extend more credit to Malich, especially the rum requisition. It was a dangerous commodity and Mulroney was satisfied that the largess provided the previous fall was more than sufficient to get the job done, but he wanted the schooner. A case of rum was placed into the trap skiff, as well as staples like salt beef and flour, sugar and tea, and a keg of galvanized boat nails, an innovation for boatbuilding. Mulroney had plans for the schooner. Long life or resale value meant the same: profits.

Lliam eyed the mound of goods under the tarp. The sails had turned out beautifully: creamy white and soft, with few wrinkles to offend the eye. Bolt roping stitched by Breeze to Grandmother's satisfaction. Even Malich had a good word for Breeze's work. There were burlap bags filled with trunnels. Lliam wondered how they would use up thousands of wooden pegs. The many handmade pulley blocks with their tangle of lines and iron fittings were still a puzzle.

The skiff lifted high and smashed down into a trough of the short steep waves. The wind had hauled further west and was heading them directly, as if to say, *all right, if you insist on going to Change Islands I'm going to make it difficult.* Garret caught Lliam's eye as the spray broke over them, grinning like a boy, enjoying being alive. His skin cracked when the bumping of the heavily laden skiff sent shock waves through damaged cartilage and worn joints, but he savoured the hurts as if affirming life. Held his face up to the cutting April wind. Salt water ran down his cheeks, painting the scar tissue glossy red...*Shining him up for the kill*, thought Lliam...The cold drops felt like ice pellets. The wind piped higher, aided by the forward motion of the skiff. Waves churned and crashed aboard: nature in chaos was conspiring against them in their attempt to make Change Islands before dark.

Lliam was terrified of being caught out on the open ocean, with a rising wind and pack ice coming on like runaway horses. To the north and east the heaving sea went on forever into the Western Ocean and beyond to Ireland. Fogo Island and the dangerous indent of Shoal Bay was cold comfort to leeward, the Change Islands still a dark streak on the spray-slashed horizon with the new breakers heaping up higher than the distant tree line.

Their progress to the west was painfully slow. The heavy skiff shuddered with the impact of each wave, pausing, gathering strength to move again. Lliam wondered if they were going forward or being driven back. Malich, unconcerned, had a bottle of rum in one hand and the tiller in the other. He might have been singing, but no words reached Lliam over the noise of the engine and the shriek of the wind, crash of waves, foam of rollers, crying gulls. The crossing waves competed to toss the skiff off course. Malich fought to keep the skiff pointed in the right direction, adjusting their course to pass the dangerous ice pans, too close for Lliam's comfort. Ugly, grey-black clouds scudded overhead, charging along in a different direction than the surface winds. His two brothers and his drunken father seemed perfectly at home in the maëlstrom of the North Atlantic. *How*, Lliam wondered often, *could sane men live such a life?* Lliam had resigned himself to a cold death long before Fogo Island was left behind and Change Islands seemed within reach.

Sheen's Cove, a narrow, rock-strewn beach with larger, shattered rocks above and the black forest beyond, was shrouded in a dark twilight. The water, as black as the trees, gave no hint of what lurked below the surface. Malich cut the engine and shifted to the thwart beside Doyle. "We'll row in." The skiff coasted silently into the lee of the protecting arm of Eastern Point. Out of the wind their world returned to normal: four desperate men crouched in a skiff loaded down with a ton of gear, headed into a dangerous cove to recover a schooner burdened with a curse. When the curved bow of the skiff crunched into the pebbles, Lliam rolled stiffly over the gunnel and stood in the shallows surveying the scene. The fallen hull of their hopes and dreams lay like a beached whale above.

"Lliam, stop dreamin' an' lend a hand!"

Their rocky cove was as lonely as a tomb, abandoned to the elements. There were homes in the distance, dark, also abandoned, as if the place had bled out and was given up by humanity...One after the other, the fishing families had chosen to move on, to resettle away from the mad Sheens, even shunning the unfinished boat that, in another context, would have been a prize...The object of their journey was the visible evidence that mankind once inhabited this wild place of rocks, trees and water.

The little fishing schooner lay among the rocks on her starboard side, sharply slanting deck facing northeast. She looked more like a collapsing building than a ship, with gaping holes where hatches and skylights should be, smaller holes where the masts used to be.

"As I thought," said Malich, looking doubtfully at their future. "Stripped bare." The boys struggled to unload the gear. Ravens watched from the trees like judges, their strange babbling and chuckling a commentary on human folly.

"Stripped off like drunken mummer, right enough," agreed Doyle, humping a flour barrel to the campsite. "Picked fuckin' clean!"

"Course she is! Buddy don't leave a thing."

Using a block and tackle, they hauled the skiff over the rocks above high water, struggled with the gear over the loose stones and made camp on a grassy bench twenty paces from the wreck.

Garret went to work without a word from Malich. He knew his place. A smoking driftwood fire eventually warmed a meal and made tea, as well as pushed the shadows back beyond the orange circle of light. But there was a heavy feeling around the camp, as if the beach and forest were crowded with spirits. Rain began falling while they ate their simple meal of cod and potatoes prepared by Margaret. There was also Margaret's bread. Malich told them to enjoy it. "Be the last for some while, b'yes." Despite the hardy food they were in no mood to savour the treasure.

Malich poured himself a dollop of rum without offering to share. "We'll sleep on ground 'til we get'er stood up an' clean out fo'c'sle."

"Is this where the Sheens lived?" asked Lliam. He felt a presence moving around their encampment.

"Up over," Malich said, pointing with his mug. Lliam could just make out the dark outline of a tired frame house leaning against the trees: a moss-heavy structure slowly retreating to the elements.

"Why would anyone live in such a god-forsaken place?"

"Most takes what they can get on this hard coast, but Sheen, he brought his wife out here 'cause Béhathook Cove couldn't stomach'is kind. Even neighbours moved away. That man was a trial betimes. Ignorant as blow fish, an' no better than wild animal."

"Gran'father once called him a friend."

"Wouldn't go that far."

"They had a deal." He wanted to confirm the story despite the written evidence.

Garret made a jerky movement to warn Lliam off. Lliam caught the look in Garret's eyes. *What did Garret know?*

"Nothin' you want to concern yourself on, sonny. Get some sleep, all of you! We've a job of work ahead."

Doyle grunted and rolled under the tarp, unconcerned with anything but sleep. Garret busied himself with cleaning up.

"Why not use the house?" asked Lliam. "At least it might be dry."

"No! I've never slept under no roof but kith an' kin's."

"The schooner's not ours."

"Not the same thing!"

"You think Sheen's still in that house? Gran'father thinks so."

"Course not! Seth Sheen's been dead for years. They found'im hangin' from tree up there." Malich nodded his head toward a stand of

216

trees beyond the clearing. "Mad as ticked moose, he was."

"The curse?"

"No! I told you. He just went off from livin' alone."

"What happened to the rest of the family?"

"Don't know, bye. They just vanished like mornin' fog in July month."

Lliam was certain Malich knew more of the tale but his father was not about to let a story put them off their objective. They bedded down under rough wool blankets, laying on the coils of rope with the old tarp pulled over to keep off the soft drizzle. Lliam couldn't remember a more uncomfortable night. He tossed and dozed in fits. When he did sleep his dreams were filled with shadows creeping through the tangle of trees: Breeze, smothered in a great coat of black thorns, walking above a long beach of firestones. Then a gang of boys pursued by a twisted demon determined to do God-knows-what under the cover of darkness.

A screech jolted Lliam out of his nightmare. "What was that!?"

Doyle farted and rolled over. "Don't know, Brother. Maybe ol' man Sheen come to cut off yer useless nuts."

Lliam shivered. The stinking tarp had slipped away and his blanket was wet through. He reluctantly moved closer to Doyle for body heat. Doyle farted again and laughed.

Lliam slept fitfully and was aware of his surroundings like a cat that sleeps in snatches. The screeching startled him from time to time. Garret knew it was just a disgruntled raven upset about the human presence but couldn't convey the information. It wasn't important. Lliam and Doyle could think what they liked. Garret knew more secrets than he wanted to reveal, even if he could talk. He was thinking of Breeze and her gift of life.

Lliam was also thinking of Breeze and what he witnessed while they prepared to leave Béhathook in the predawn darkness. Breeze had come down to the community wharf bundled in Sean O'Keefe's greatcoat..."Garret..." she had whispered, "I want to give you something."

They walked a little distance away from the others. Malich and

Doyle were too busy to notice, but Lliam, attuned to Breeze's every action, watched as he worked. Breeze was close to Garret, speaking softly. Saw her open her coat and take Garret's hand, she put something in his hand then held it to her breast and then down to her belly. Imagined her forcing Garret's fingers into her. He wanted to scream. Then she kissed Garret's cheek. Garret trembled, embarrassed by her outward display, nodded and returned to his work. She turned away and hadn't said goodbye to Lliam.

He replayed the moment: "Breeze..." Lliam approached her, as awkward as Garret was embarrassed. "I'm glad you care for Garret. It's what saved him."

"Of course I care for Garret. He's sweet an' gentle."

"I wanted...tried, to explain, you know? Apologize."

"Why didn't you?"

"I...don't know. You seemed so far away, and occupied with Garret."

"Life, Lliam. I was attendin' to life."

"When I get back, I want to speak about us...the future, you know?"

"I'm going to marry Garret, if he'll have me in my condition," she said simply and walked away.

Later, during a lull in the thrashing run to Change Islands, Garret had taken off one mitten to wipe his eyes. Lliam noticed the plain gold ring on his finger. At that moment Lliam felt a great pain and a growing distance, utterly without a friend or family. His journey was wasted. Who could he blame but himself for a life at low ebb? Fortune and future out of sight in a morass of self-pity and recrimination, he wished himself at the bottom of White Rock Channel with Gerald.

A sudden land breeze swirled the ashes into a spiral. Sparks rose up and showered the site with light pricks, enough to show the fear in the eyes of Garret and Doyle. Malich was in a deep rum stupor. Lliam crawled away from the tarp and found an oil lantern in the pile of gear. He lit the lantern with a brand from the fire and, taking his damp blanket, picked his way over the broken rock and juniper mat toward the house.

"Where you goin', Lliam lame brains?"

"I'm not sleeping in the rain."

The moving lantern animated the tall grasses, throwing the dark shapes against the grey wall of the house. There was no porch. The windows either side of the open door were gone, rotted and blown out by winter gales. Lliam doubted the house was a refuge, and what about the curse? *There's no curse. There's no ghosts or spirits.* "Any ghosts in this house?" he called aloud, as much to hear his own voice, half expecting an answer. The dim yellow light from the lantern spilled into the room beyond. It was a typical outport frame house from the outside, but the room layout was unconventional for an outport. The front entrance was the main entrance. A small anti-room, about the size of a big closet, opened on two rooms either side of a narrow stairway. To the left was a parlour. To the right was the kitchen...In most outport homes one enters the rear of the house into the kitchen...Lliam stepped carefully over the rotting sill, testing the floorboards. The house seemed to tremble. The door creaked and swung toward him. Not the wind. *Just my weight on the floor,* reasoned Lliam. He pushed the door away and held the lantern high.

The parlour was a shambles of collapsing furniture of surprisingly good vintage; having travelled from England in the days of colonial glory, and remnants of fine drapery, flapping wallpaper, embossed with mould, and the floor covered with debris and animal bones, as if the house was only an interruption of wildness. A gust of wind slammed the door closed behind him, then as quickly flung it open. Lliam shivered, afraid to go on but more afraid to retreat. He held the lantern higher to ward off the night creatures, aware of eyes looking back. *Not spirits,* he said. The eyes belonged to faces behind dirty glass streaked with rain, dust and bird shit...Itinerant photographers had roamed the outports making memories for isolated families...Photographs in flaking gilded frames that matched the furnishings. Family portraits. He examined the pictures that were instantly familiar: sons, daughters and stern-faced parents, Grandparents in frames askew and leaning forward as if ready to leap off the wall, some, already fallen, glass broken, resting upright. The eyes followed him as he moved cautiously to the first set of pictures.

He had seen the faces on the parlour walls of his family's home. The photos were not of his own family but he was seeing the eyes and nose of his Grandfather and the swarthy thickness of Malich in the sons. He was looking at siblings of Gerald and Doyle. In the center of the tableau was a large portrait of a young couple in stiff wedding attire, formal and unhappy. Probably Sheen and his wife, but they were brother and sister; he knew that. *She looks desperate but resolved*, he thought. *He looks gaunt and haunted, or demented. Cruel at least.* He and she do not resemble any of the other pictures. Lliam felt sick at the pit of his stomach and the ache rose with further understanding. Another gust of wind ripped through the room as if the walls ceased to exist. A picture fell, glass scattered at his feet. He retreated to the hall resolved to find a bedroom, stopped, put one foot on the stairway to go up. The house was rocked by a blow from the wind. Above, bedroom doors slammed shut and creaked opened again. The sharp squall roared across the cove and out to sea. Then silence.

Seth Sheen? he may have spoken aloud. He couldn't be sure. Cold chills raced up his back until the hairs on his neck stood up. He breathed a prayer. *I know who you are, what you are. Gran'father's diary...I read the story about you an' Gran'father, you and the deal. 'The Duty' Gran'father called it. Only a man as evil as yourself, could have another man make you sons to drive as slaves. Your daughters were only a consequence, but still slaves, Gran'father said. You drove them and your poor sister-wife to early graves in your madness. Where are you now, Seth Sheen? I hope to God in your grave and your soul in a burning hell.* Lliam did not believe in such things, but the deep Irish belief in a vengeful God could be invoked at times of personal need. He didn't believe, but there was no harm in scaring the spirit of an evildoer.

Lliam turned down the lantern until it smoked out. Moonlight flooded through a break in the fleeing clouds, and the cove was splashed with dancing light. Through the kitchen door he could see a daybed by a window, stuffing spilling through torn leather, the worn out daybed a haven for small things: mice going about their business, but it was a bed and he was exhausted.

His respite was short. The little creatures either objected to a foreign presence or considered the body a warm meal. Seth Sheen's spirit was still, but nature was not.

Dawn on Sheen's Cove was little solace. The wind changed direction and the drizzle returned. Perhaps Lliam had only dreamed of moonlight. Perhaps he was going mad, like Sheen. The cove was shrouded in a thick, grey mist so that morning was only a suggestion of dark shadows and tumbling waves. They were all stiff and cold: wet and chilled to the bone. The rotting canvas tarp, even impregnated with cod oil, was no match for a persistent Newfoundland drizzle.

Garret, caregiver, provider, cook, and cleaner, the silent serf, was up and trying to get a fire going. The one person in most need seldom asks for anything. He blew on a feeble spark smoldering in damp wood that gave off much smoke and almost no heat, but he stubbornly blew, coaxing a fire to life. The flames grew with each painful breath, as if the fire he survived was still in his lungs. He touched the small flame to kindling and smiled at his accomplishment as if it was the most satisfying feat in the world. Presently he had a fire going and a kettle boiling with loose tea tumbling in the roil. They would eat the warmed over cod with the last of the bread and hot fat drippings.

The too familiar smell of burning fat made Lliam want to puke. Lliam, twice defeated by the house, crawled from under the tarp to his feet, numb and dispirited. He took the mug offered by Garret and walked away from the fire.

There was nothing of interest on the rock-strewn foreshore so he gravitated to the body of the schooner. It could have been a rotting whale, incongruous and out of its element.

"Pathetic...a derelict, like myself," he said to the dumb presence. The little schooner looked truly forlorn and hopeless in the grey light, firmly rooted to the stones where she had fallen. Inertia of mass. Physics of gravity. Death of spirit. There is something wonderfully tragic about a ship lying down, unnatural, like a priest without a shirt, a drunk who has fallen on the street, or an epileptic in a racking fit. Even

Breeze's old wreck of a schooner in Béhathook Cove, stripped, slime-slick and rotting, had a utilitarian presence. It had lived on the sea, worked and died with dignity. The sad schooner before him, untested, seemed incapable of life.

The starboard rail was broken and buried in the stones as if the thing had rooted there like some exotic relic from a distant land. Lliam imagined a garden of white stones and the boat a sculpture placed there to force the eye. When he walked to the other side all he could see was the canted deck and it made no sense as an object that could save a family from starvation. A dumb slab of a building, this tragedy of mankind was just a small version of the one that provided the knees to make the ship's wheel, the wheel that Lliam had laboured over during the bleak winter to take his mind off Breeze and the choking atmosphere. The wheel had turned out to be a rough work of art and it was obvious that Lliam was comfortable with wood, and, given time, could be a success...Malich was suddenly beside him.

"She'll want planks, sure," Malich said in his gruff manner, as if relishing the deed, perhaps to taunt Lliam with the misery to come. "As I knew she would," continued Malich. "An' masts, an' spars, an' bloody bowsprit, an' a thousand things, 'til hell wouldn't have'er!"

Lliam thought of the ship's wheel hidden in the mound of parts. It had seemed important, then, now insignificant. A frill. A conceit to be stuck on at the last moment. His spirit sank into the rocks.

"First we got to make'er spars."

Malich and his sons were standing in the shadows of a small stand of black spruce in a broad cleft in the rocks, like a miniature valley: an ancient copse of trees silent as a cathedral. Without the constant twisting wind, the trees rose straight, reaching for the precious light, disappearing into a tight canopy that harboured ravens *chucking* and mocking, waiting for the next act of human foolishness.

Malich whacked the biggest tree with the side of his axe: the axe and the tree ringing in a strange harmony. Lliam imagined a mob of musicians smacking trees with great mallets and the Devil the conductor, poised to begin a symphony to drive them all mad.

222

"That one'll do for mainm'st," said Malich, almost reverently. "Sheen must'ave kept this gang o' trees for'is own use an' warned anybody off. Then the b'yes would be afraid to come for their wood. Otherwise this patch o' ground would be as barren as the rest of the fuckin' island. Well, we ain't afeared o' no Sheen! You hear me, you ol' bastard?" He pointed to another spruce, almost as big. "An' that's'er forem'st." He studied the stand and pointed. "Those two, booms an' gaffs, an' that's'er bloody sprit!"

"Why bloody?" asked Lliam innocently.

"What?"

"Why do you always refer to the bowsprit as 'bloody'?"

"'Cause, it's the last spar you make with the bloody leaved-overs, an' the last piece you reeve aboard, an' the last bloody place you wants to be in a gale of wind, an' the first bloody thing to hit buddy's boat if you go amuck!"

"Oh."

Like Seth Sheen, Malich used his own sons like slaves.

The long days that followed were an endless agony of stumbling through the dark forest, whipped by branches, tripped by roots, cutting trees, and dragging logs. The forest was dense and the few spruce suitable for building were far back in the small but protected copse. All they had was gravity to ease the toil, but even so the business of hauling the sap-laden fir trees with a complicated system of lines and pulleys, was a living hell for Lliam. He never imagined a man could work so hard, risk his life every moment and survive from sunup to sunset, only to begin again the next dawn, and the next. And every day the hours of light grew longer and Malich more demanding. They chopped and dragged, leaving the logs at the edge of the forest, poised above the beach.

Five trees were stripped of their bark and raised on biers of stones, glowing golden in the sun, like idols. Aromatic as incense. These would make her precious spars: the masts, booms, gaffs and the 'bloody bowsprit'. They were the tallest, heaviest and most difficult to get to the beach, but it was done. The least suitable were chosen to

223

make the shores and cradle for the hull and the pit saw frame. Lliam tried to imagine the process for standing the schooner up and naively asked Malich about the process.

"Spars got to go in 'fore she's up, see?"

"Spars? I thought we had to get her off the ground?"

"Masts first. Easier to put they into'er while she's down, see?"

"No."

"Never mind. It's just what we do."

Lliam had no skill with a broadaxe but he could do mathematics. Malich taught him the rule of 'seven and seventeen', the mysterious ritual used by shipwrights to shape wooden spars. But first the logs had to be squared. It seemed illogical to Lliam that they would take a round tree, make it square only to make it round again. When he asked, Malich said, "Can't make a round tree rounder if she's out t'all, crooked like, an' it's the Devil to put in tapers, see?"

"No."

"Damn me, if you ain't the duncest one!"

"You never taught me these things."

"You run away 'fore we could!"

"You said yourself, you haven't built a boat since I was just a baby."

"Never mind. Others have, an' the young'uns just naturally pick it out, see?"

"Doyle, did you learn to make spars while I was away?"

Doyle avoided the question and went on with his own chore.

Lliam took to the task of squaring the golden wood, then shaving and rounding up the ridges until the stick was...*smooth as a baby's arse*, as Malich put it. The mystery of mast making was revealed by degrees.

It took a week to finish the masts and lay them on the beach stones at right angles to the schooner. There was some satisfaction having transformed rough trees into gently tapering spars, feeling the sensuous smoothness of the fresh wood. With the tips painted white, and the rest oiled, Lliam thought they were works of art; too beautiful to be stuck into the bowels of the crippled, ugly duckling waiting for her glory, but there wasn't time to savour the beauty. "Riggin's next, b'yes. Jump to it!"

He also loved the process of running the aromatic hemp roping through the blocks and securing the blocks with rope strops to the masts. The process had meaning. Art and function. He began to visualize Breeze's creamy white sails stretched taught along *his* masts, sharing with her a sense of purpose. Lliam and Breeze: a partnership. They could go into business together in Boston. Commercial ships had gone from sail to steam to diesel engines, but there were yachts to rig out. Dwyer & Sons, Masts, Rigging and Sails. He didn't have to sail on the damned boats, all he had to do was shape beautiful masts and Breeze would make the sails, and send them off to God knows what fate. A shame to waste the artistry on utility...His reverie was cut short by reality. Breeze would marry Garret...

"Lliam! Stop dreamin' an' lend a hand!"

Using an 'A' frame, they lifted the butt end of the main mast, until it was level with the hole in the deck, resting on the rail, then, shifting the 'A' frame they hauled on the tackle lines again and the long mast rose from the ground, angled just so. Another set of tackle pulled the tapered butt of the mast into the belly of the schooner.

A long, frustrating day of wiggling and resetting, kicking and cursing, saw the main and fore masts into their steps in the keel before Malich would let them rest. It was well after dark on a chilly, wet May evening when the four of them collapsed around the fire. "Get a good sleep, b'yes. Tomorrow we stand 'er up!"

It sounded easy enough, but Lliam dreaded the coming dawn.

His dread was not misplaced. In a long day of digging at rocks, ramming home wedges and using every ounce of strength they could summon, they would lever the hull upright. Lliam, Doyle and Garret crawled around under the rising hull like worker ants, driven on with threats and kicks from Malich. Inch by inch, wedge by wedge the boat rose until Malich pronounced that she was level. Lliam wouldn't have believed it could be done, if he hadn't hung from the ends of long levers himself.

The sad schooner looked much bigger standing up. All aspects changed and the tall spars and shapely hull dominated her plain surroundings. She was no longer an object of pity.

"Damn me, if she ain't a pretty thing!" rejoiced Malich, in a rare moment of good humour. "Sheen might have been a devil but he could shape out a hull."

"Maybe Grandpa was right," offered Lliam. "He said Sheen *was* the Devil."

"*Ahh*, bilge. Fuckin' boat's a boat. Father never wanted to give Seth Sheen an inch."

"She's pretty," agreed Doyle, punching Garret on the shoulder. Garret grinned in his lopsided way.

But pretty is fine from a distance. The structure and the skin were something else. Close up the *Black Fenian* was bruised and battered, with rot set into the hull and deck planks that had lain, wet and airless, so long in the rocks. Her high side planks were fairly sound, but shrunken and the oakum was out and the trunnel ends cracked from the same drying wind. From inside you could see light through the gaping seams.

"Nothin' corkin' an' sea water can't fix...on'er port side, but my son, we got some job of work to plank up'er bad side."

"Where do we get the planks?"

"We make'em, sonny, like we do everythin' else in this god-damned world."

The trees to make planks were in short supply in the Change Islands coves, like most of the plundered coves of Newfoundland. Trees were left in small forest patches only if they were difficult to harvest, or if cursed, and Sheen's Cove was a rocky, dispirited place avoided by the locals.

They began immediately to build the pit saw frame, a crude structure lashed together like a trestle so that one man could stand on top and pull up while the saw blade was pulled on the down stroke by the man below. A skidway of sorts was extended from the high ground where the best logs waited. The logs were skidded onto the pit saw frame and the cut started. The man on the bottom had the easier job, pulling down, but he was constantly showered with sawdust and worked almost blind. Lliam was the down-stroke-man.

"You got to pull steady, Lliam!"

"I'm pulling!"

Lliam jerked the wooden handle angrily. The saw blade skipped out of the kerf and Malich stumbled. "You'll throw me on the ground one time!"

"Sorry, Father." Lliam's hands were bleeding. "I'll try harder."

"You'll kill me yet, with yer tryin'."

The slow, grueling work of sawing planks went on for several days. The fresh planks were dropped onto a pile where Doyle and Garret sorted them into hull planks and construction planks. Only one or two runs from each log were suitable for planks. Malich cursed the heartwood but there was nothing to be done, there were so few trees and none of great size. The best would be used for hull or decking and the rest cut to partner cracked or rotted frames.

The framing structure of the schooner was remarkably intact considering she had fallen heavily on her side, twice according to the stories, a testament to Sheen and his sons. But no amount of skill can forestall wood rot when conditions are right, and it seemed the more they cut out punky wood, the more bad spots they found. Malich was determined to make a good job. His sons could perish in the process too...The way Seth Sheen's sons were driven to the ground or to suicide by their father's maniacal determination.

Around the pit frame the bark and sawdust pile grew. Lliam, knee deep in cuttings, sank further into depression, as day after day the only result of hard work was more wood thrown on the scrape pile. He felt their only purpose was to create firewood so they could survive long enough to create more firewood. And, as the days went by, the gaping hole on the starboard side grew larger and more ominous...a black mouth that sucked in their efforts and gave back nothing but the odour of decay. But, as Malich demanded, by mid May they were finally ready to begin planking.

What a foolish business, Lliam thought. *Ships seem to be built only to be destroyed.* A house at least is a home on solid ground and could be depended upon to last for many years. But a boat is built to defy the elements and be pounded into debris or given up to rot. Everything about a boat is difficult. The building material is critical and hard to come by. The lines are all curves and difficult to fashion. Planks and frames have to be shaped just so, then coaxed or forced into place with violence, and held there with spikes and trunnels hammered in with huge mallets, or the whole thing might spring apart at the worst moment and drown the crew. Boats made no sense to Lliam, but at least they were made of wood.

With the change from sawing and destroying the hull to replacing the rotting planks, Lliam's spirits picked up, but only a notch. Mornings came earlier and Malich's rough orders were often delivered with kicks. But with hot tea and Garret's heavy bannock bread in his stomach, Lliam's days at least had a purpose.

Planking up was not easy, but every strake added to the hull was another strake closer to the finish. He thought of Breeze and home. But as each hour unfolded, with each plank hammered on, and every rainy day endured, Lliam was only closer to the reckoning with Breeze. "She'll marry Garret over my dead body," he muttered repeatedly, as the mallets rang on trunnels. *Over my dead body,* became his mantra.

At night, huddled by the fire after a meager meal of rancid pork or salt fish, he would brood over bitter tea, staring into the blackness of the restless ocean, imagining the meeting, rehearsing what he would say to change her mind.

Nighttime in foul weather meant fitful sleep in the crowded fo'c'sle, racked by demon dreams. In his dreams Breeze, in many forms, rejected his pleas, or worse, devoured him limb by limb, without death to relieve the pain. Then, awake and shivering he'd plot how to kill Garret, his gentle sibling, who was sleeping only a heartbeat away. Then he'd feel a deep moral shame that left him staring at the sky through the hole in the deck where a gangway hatch must still be fitted. Would they ever finish?

On civil nights they all slept by the fire and when Lliam could no longer sleep he'd stand on the shore looking to three compass bearings for solace. One direction was to Ireland, the mythical home of his ancestors. One was south to Boston where his life had been lonely, even on the teeming streets of a large city, where no one knew his name or cared, until he met Molly. And the third direction was to Fogo Island and Breeze, who no longer waited for him, but for Garret. Garret wore the ring. Garret had her heart, he'd seen her put his hand there. And there was the baby...When he could not sleep he longed for dawn and labour to sooth his brain, but like a cheap wine, the effect only lasted a short time, then the ache would return with the visions. The hammer blows would increase to just short of rage.

One rare warm night, near the end of June, with a big moon riding high in a cloudless sky and Sheen's narrow cove a dazzle of sparkling lights, Malich lurched out of the shadows to the shore where his Prodigal son dreamed of other nights. He had a rum bottle in one hand and a club of sorts in the other. He stood close to Lliam, boozy breath washing hot over his tall son. He belched. Breathed deep and belched again. Lliam felt sick to his stomach and wanted to flee because he knew his father in that state was dangerous.

"Protecting us from the demon Sheen, Father?" he asked lightly, to ameliorate the mood.

"Aye, sonny, an' what would you know 'bout demons, eh?"

"I've experienced a few." What he wanted to tell his father was that one of his demons was suspicion. Suspicion that the thick, brute of a man beside him, stealing even the civil night, was not his father. He had said it before but wanted to drive the truth home to hurt them both. He supposed, before they parted, he would feel the club, sensed that Malich felt the same loathing for the presence of another man's son that he was bound to nurture and raise as his own. The payback was owning a chattel, an indentured slave to be bullied.

"Rubbish. You're too soft. You've never known a moment's hardship. You think this a hard go? You never been to the ice when a sudden storm blows off shore for days, an' you hunker down on a big ol' pan to cook a bit o' fat, or boil a kettle to keep from freezin', then sleep in the bilge water, eh, an' when mornin' comes go on again' an' kill swiles 'til the wind heaves 'round an' you can go home. An' only if you got sculps, eh? An' that ain't the hard of it neither. Maybe you've gone down Labrador with a Jack you built on the merchant's bill, you salt a log load an' on the way home a storm o' wind drives'er onto the fuckin' rocks." He paused for a long pull of rum as if to kill the memory. "She's gone, eh? Boat, season, crew to boot. An' what do you do, sonny? You tally another bill with the fuckin' merchant an' try again."

"What do you want, Malich? You want to break me with these stories? I'm not my father's son, though bred on the bloody rock you call home, not content to beat my brains out fishing or sealing. But I'm here. I'm doing my best to get this goddamned boat done."

Malich tried to pierce Lliam with a look, but could not focus. He raised the bottle as if to smash it into Lliam's face but could not keep his balance on the loose stones. He could not even find his lips to take another pull. He shook his head, dropped the club and tottered away toward the fire.

Lliam felt the urge to pick up the timber and beat the man's brains out. He stood gazing down at the drunken form, diminished by the night, visualizing the shattered skull, the blood seeping across the stones, the tide creeping in to meet the crimson flow. Imagined the body picked clean by the gulls and crabs. He could roll his body into the fire. Heap offcuts until the flames rose higher than the masts of the cursed schooner. A fitting end to an incendiary life of the brute who defiled Breeze. But who was he to judge? He was as guilty as the pitiful man at his feet. Who was he to raise the club and end the miserable existence of another, unless he could pass the same judgment on himself and commit himself to follow the condemned man to his cleansing pyre?

Lliam stood looking out across the cove. *Will I ever rest in a civilized place again?* he wondered. Ireland was a land of myths and legends. Boston had been real, but even in smoky bars dense with gritty humanity, he was alone. An itinerant worker and failed scholar, he longed for something else. Boston had been a Grail of sorts...Imagined, but the reality was much less, and much more. Little success as a writer, scrounging his way, condemned to the back streets of society, groveling for a bit of human warmth in the beds of prostitutes. With every failed experiment he had sunk lower into despair for his manhood and longed for the one woman who had touched his heart, but he had left her behind in a down-at-heels outport. But there was the other, Molly...

The girl was much younger, and he the tutor hired by a striving merchant family hoping to better their daughter's prospects: a good marriage and the rewards of a social leg up. For Americans, after the euphoria of war and industrialization, the hard fall into The Great Depression was a desperate time for a social class that had seen the American Dream come close, while the rest of the world struggled to rebuild after the disaster of The Great War. The world needed the industrial goods that an awakening America could provide. There were few forces that could stop Americans in their tracks; but greed, the lust for more and more money and material wealth, brought the fragile system crashing down in flames. The wreckage was there to be seen in the bread lines and vacant storefronts, rusting factories and silent farms, but the most damage was done to the spirit of America. But nothing lasts long in a rapidly evolving world. If he had waited two more years he would have been swept into the renewed tide of commerce and industrialization as the world went to war again and the factories came alive to feed the crusher mill of war. He remembered with a shudder the 'night of the long tale'...

For the price of a few beers in a stinking tavern, a veteran of the Great War lectured about the coming Armageddon. The next war would make the Great War look like...*just a summer excursion in Europe by comparison*, he said. No one believed him; his missing leg, seared lungs and blasted face were not sufficient omens because no one wanted to believe it possible. "Blood will be spilled around the world!" he had shouted. Lliam ordered another round for the few bloated men and besotted ladies left to hear the tale. Lliam believed him. He'd read the back pages of the Boston Globe and the stories of travellers returning from Germany with tales of National Socialist rallies in Munich and Berlin, Bonn and Vienna. The crimson flags, the high stepping columns of Hitler's Youth. The enemy of the Reich, the common, exploited workers, were inflamed by communist ideals and the National Socialists fought back with force, the blood of the Communists as red as their own swastika flags.

America had turned her back on Europe. *No more War,* they said on the street corners of Boston, in parks and in churches. The peace was hard enough, with factories cold and the markets in disarray. He wanted to flee Boston and the Depression. Dreamed of Paris. Run to Spain and join the International Brigades. But Europe was on the cusp of war and the Depression sucked the life out of every institution, except the cabarets.

He clung to Boston in desperation but felt as if he was choking on his own words, gasping for breath in the coal-dirt streets as he walked the docks in search of work. Puked his guts out if he tried to dull the pain with bad beer and worse whiskey. Drowned his loneliness on the breasts of the young student who he was supposed to be elevating to the English classics. When the young woman announced she was pregnant he fled back to his island, his confidence shattered. Breeze O'Keefe was the one last hope for a life, beyond that he knew nothing of a future. But Breeze would marry Garret, she said. He cursed her as a fallen whore. He cursed the stones he was standing on. Cursed the cold ocean and the distance between Sheen Cove and Boston.

Lliam's Story

Boston 1936 The Tag End of Winter: Lliam skipped a puddle, but his heart was not light, not skipping light, but heavy with dread and confusion. And he was cold because he had fled the merchant's home without his muffler and his stylish coat not proof against a Boston drizzle. The gas lamps reflected jerkily in the dark, ice-rimmed pools where the cobbles had sagged away from the weight of vendor's wagons. It was after midnight. The streets of South Boston were shrouded in mist and coal smoke, empty except for the distant tread of the Night Patrolman, whistling tunelessly to push away the shadows. Lliam envied the Constable's easy attitude. The man had a good job, a family at home. Night Patrol was not so bad; the upper middleclass neighbourhood unlikely to see the drunken results of poverty and despair that plagued the docks and the factory slums. At the corner he turned away from the merchant's street, a street of upscale homes, merchant-money, outwardly prosperous for the hard times, cursing himself for leaving his warm muffler behind.

Pretty Molly, the merchant's daughter, had just revealed that she was pregnant. She hadn't stated precisely that it was his child; there were too many others involved, but she was just a child herself, or so he thought. She had fallen easily for Lliam: tall, red wavy hair, sparkling blue-green eyes, a flurry of freckles in the Irish way, and clever with words. He had vowed to Merchant O'Conner that he would be chaste. But Molly's eyes were deep, limped wells of wonder. Her young breasts were firm and rounding out and she seemed to choose a wardrobe that accentuated everything a young man could imagine. Molly read her English prose with passion, as if she was feeling every heart-pounding emotion in the classic love stories. When he asked his glowing student what she was most interested in reading she had said, without hesitation, *"The Way of a Man With a Maid."*

"I'm afraid I've not heard of that book. Who's it by?" he asked.

"Oh, it's by Anonymous, but I've heard it's all the rage in certain circles." She smiled shyly, blushing, as if she'd heard more than the headline. He left the house after the introductory session, promising Molly's mother that he would endeavor to introduce Molly to the best of English literature.

His search for the book caused him to question his promise to pursue only the very noblest of minds in the English lexicon. He envisioned Hardy, James, Woolf, The Brontes, and Austen of course. He would prefer Joyce, Bram Stoker, Flan O'Brien for the rebellion of words, and Swift for the same reason, but knew he could not get away with Oscar Wilde. But he was unprepared for *The Way of a Man With a Maid: Volume One.* He searched for the book until he tracked a well-worn copy to a back alley bookseller specializing in literature frowned upon by polite society, the clergy and the morality police. He scanned pages, dry-mouthed and perspiring. He knew, as he carried the small tome away, wrapped in brown paper, that he should have left it behind and explained to his student that the book did not exist in Boston. The book, though intriguing, would probably end his short career, so why had he pocketed the thing? It was something about the look in Molly McCracken's eyes when she spoke of the title. Knew it was dangerous to let his own passion ignore the message, and a warning of sorts, he had received from Molly's stepfather, Master O'Conner.

With the best intentions he had answered a classified: **Tutor Wanted. English Literature & the Classics. Must be lettered, clean & of good character. No Irish. Apply: Messrs Goodwin & O'Conner. Washington Street.** He was puzzled as to why a good Irishman like Master O'Conner would refuse an Irish tutor, but he explained to the Master that he was a Newfoundlander born, therefore not technically Irish.

Master O'Conner cautioned Lliam that his stepdaughter was bright but willful, eager to learn but given to romantic notions rather than pragmatic materialism. Lliam should overrule the Irish free spirit and instead take a page from the Quakers. Lliam wasn't sure which page he should consult. His experience with Quaker literature was limited to analytical texts, but to the best of his knowledge Quakers take a wider view of virtue than say, Presbyterians or Baptists, believing that virtue is it's own reward but not necessarily a construct of a higher order passing judgment. Quakers also believe that a man and woman should enjoy each other to the fullest, a concept that Master O'Conner may have overlooked in his choice of constraints on the young woman and warning to her young tutor. Perhaps the stepfather had placed too much faith in the glowing résumé Lliam had provided.

And Lliam lied to Mr. O'Conner. He had no degree of any kind, just the gift of gab and imagination. Nor did he believe in a Creator, or adhere to the teachings of the Catholic faith, as he claimed. He invented a history of education, mentioning an obscure college in Maine...Where he landed from Newfoundland a raw provincial, a typical hayseed...But Lliam was a self-taught scholar, and he learned the ways of the intellectuals by absorbing the classics in libraries and the ways of the fobs on the streets of Boston. Odd jobs along the docks bought him a decent suit, and reading taught him the manners and morays of the wealthy middleclass, the level he believed he could reach if he could only write the one big novel he carried with him...He would tell the story of his Newfoundland: a savage story of want and desire. Lust beyond desire, the dark deeds of brutalized families too remote from Continental life...It would be fiction, of course, but true enough. And there would be great loss and heartache. He knew he had that in him, carried it on board the steamer from St. John's to Portland, Maine. Boston was always the destination, smaller than New York but large in the arts and Newfoundland's natural trading partner.

Boston was not Sodom and Gomorrah but it was his undoing.

Molly was a classic beauty, endowed with the enhanced charms wealth can buy, and in the full bloom of youthful hormones. Given Lliam's unconsummated history with Breeze O'Keefe, he was as ripe for picking as he was ready for plunder, and it was a toss up who was bound to ravage whom. Molly McCracken, whatever her actual age, was no blushing child.

Molly's own mother had died tragically. A society plaything found strangled under a bridge, the result of a night in the wrong company, even if the companion was from Westchester, the under-performing son of a well to do banker, but privilege aside, a despicable spoiled brat who could not stand being laughed at by a mere slut.

Not all her mother's clients were underachievers. Molly was an inconvenient accident, left in the care of like-minded nannies on certain nights when it was necessary for her mother to make a living in the wrong places with the 'right' people. Molly was a mere child but knew the odour of lust when her mother returned from an assignation; it wasn't called prostitution in those circles, more a compliant companion in darkened places where no questions were asked and the booze flowed freely in a town madly making up for the rigors of Prohibition.

There were no social programs for unwed mothers or their illegal offspring, so Molly learned early that life was harsh and survival a challenge. She was taken in hand by her aunt after her mother's death, and was determined to make her way to a higher social level. But, by age eighteen she was also determined not to miss an opportunity to indulge in the fundamentals. She was ready. Lliam was desperate.

The trouble began when Molly opened the book on their third meeting. He had prescribed that his blossoming beauty read Charlotte Bronte's *Jane Eyre*, not realizing how close to home was the story, but that aside, Molly had unwrapped his gift instead of opening the Bronte, and that opened the flood gates of passion that washed over Lliam on their fourth meeting: more tryst than tutoring session.

That day, Lliam was ushered into the foyer by the dark-eyed maid: a statuesque woman with the tawny skin and the proud features of African women with European structure. He was also introduced to Mrs. O'Conner, a woman much younger than he expected. Molly's stepmother remarked how well Molly was taking to the classics. She encouraged him to continue pursuing the noble virtues of study and recitation, and wouldn't it be wonderful if Molly could be guided to romantic poetry: Elizabeth Browning for instance, with a view to a recital, a custom for young women about to 'come out' into society. Molly was ready to *come out*, but not in the way Mrs. O'Conner had intended.

Mother O'Conner, dressed to go out for the day, directed the maid to show Lliam to the parlour where Molly was waiting for the weekly session.

Molly was lounging seductively in a chaise, looking very much in colour, for a winter morning; radiating a certain glow two things can cause in a woman's complexion naturally. One was a walk in the cold morning air, but she had not been out of doors. The book was open on a gold satin cushion beside her. He might just as well have begun with Browning's, *How Do I Love Thee?* Molly was about to show him.

"Good morning, Miss McCracken. How do we find you this lovely day?"

"*You* may find me how and where you please, Mr. Dwyer." She exchanged a conspiratorial look with the maid. "Anna Louise, please close the parlour door." Lliam was left awkwardly fondling the duller books under his arm. "...And lock the street door after my mother."

"Yes, Miss. Should I bring refreshments to your rooms?"

"Later, please. Much later."

"Yes, Miss." Anna Louise made a slight curtsy, an inscrutable smile on her full red lips. She *was* beautiful; as pretty as Molly, in a severe-in-service way, but taller, dark and voluptuous and Lliam could not help noticing her full breasts and trim ankles. Servants were allowed to wear shorter skirts than their Mistresses: just a practicality.

Anna curtsied deeper to Lliam, as if she had acquiesced to this handsome young man who was about to ravish her Lady, dropping her eyes from Lliam's but sending a message to Molly. Molly was observing Lliam observing the maid as she went out, the shapely hips moving with the stately walk, poised, confident, closing the door softly after setting the spring lock from within. "Our Anna has good form, don't you think, Mr. Dwyer?"

"Ah, yes. Very...attractive."

"Beautiful, isn't she?"

"Yes, I meant to say..."

"She's a mulatto. A Creole, from French Guiana. Her family had money, then the Depression...My father bought her from a French planter who wanted our firm to publish his memoir. He had no money either, only Anna to barter."

"She's a slave? Bought and sold?" Lliam asked, incredulous.

"No, no, she was properly married to the Frenchman. It was just business. I think my father had intentions of his own. Do you know what I mean?"

"I suppose I do, but in this day and age?"

"Mother was furious of course, so Father gave her to me. She's devoted, as you see."

"Yes, that's obvious."

"More than devoted," she whispered, raising her eyebrows in that way.

"Oh, in what way, Miss?"

"You're blushing, Mr. Dwyer."

"Please, call me Lliam," he said, to change the subject. The simple seduction of the lovely young Molly was becoming complicated. "No need for formality, now."

"Of course, we're getting to know one another. Do you like what you see, in your student's progress, I mean."

"Yes, progress." He could feel blood rushing to his face, the freckles straining to pop off from the pressure of his heart pumping blood to all the vital areas and he was still standing, in full view. He knew full well what she meant because he had been fantasizing his own scenario...Alone with Molly, or the service maid, and the alternative was definitely delicious to contemplate.

In their previous session, Molly had stood close to him in the library while they looked at a big book of engravings from Victorian London. The lesson was about art, warfare and other influences on English literature of the Modern Era. Their thighs often touched and she had accidentally brushed his hand turning a page. He flushed, as did she, and he felt the heat course through his own body, imagining she could feel it too, and he hers, and the tension was building until the maid entered with their afternoon tea. Molly had mildly chastised the maid for not announcing her arrival. The maid remained mum, even though she had actually knocked, if too lightly. But never mind, it was only an awkward moment, but Lliam thought the moment had been shared between maid and mistress, at his expense.

Molly rose gracefully from the chaise, holding the book, two red velvet ribbons trailing from the pages. "Would you like to read from our little book first? I've marked a passage," she said, impishly. She had chosen a yellow brocaded dress, with an open bodice, which showed her cleavage to best advantage. Her shining eyes said more than any young man could imagine in his wildest dreams.

"I, ah, had thought," he stammered, "ah, hoped that is, ah I had planned to continue with the Bronte."

"Bronte...She takes her sweet time getting to the point, don't you think? Our Anonymous, on the other hand, propels his character Jack, in a rush to inflict punishment on his Alice."

"Alice? Ah, I didn't have time to read..."

"Yes, Alice, his love interest, who Jack seems to hate and wants to punish by stealing her virginity, but," she began moving toward Lliam with the book streaming the velvet ribbons, like an offering, "Jack has contrived to tie her up in compromising ways, with soft silk ropes."

"Molly, we really *should* read *Jane Eyre*."

"Here, Lliam, the passage. You read it. You're the man, the narrator. I'm just Alice, in your power, these the symbolic ropes." She held the ribbons out to Lliam with one hand and the book with the other.

He took the book, his heart pounding, looking into the eyes of a woman he realized he could possess at will, or she him. He looked at the book, the pages a blur. He inhaled and tried to focus...He saw his Breeze that day on the Fortress Hill, the ocean wind blowing her wild dark mane around her perfect face, her breasts heaving in time to the ocean swell, and he had felt the same burning emotion, the unexplained force that compels a young man to act against his better judgment. Breeze had resisted at first; they kissed, and he was rough, then gentle and he kissed her deeply with passion and Breeze wanted him, but they were awkward and too eager, unfamiliar with the ways of love, exploring slowly to savour the moment...He tore himself away from the next vision of burning shame, of Breeze running down the hill, he left in awkward confusion. He began reading if only to delay the awkward seduction of Molly.

"*...Alice hesitated. Was her guardian angel trying to give her a premonitory hint of what her fate would be if she accepted my seemingly innocent suggestion? But at that moment came another flash of lightning, blinding in its intensity, and almost simultaneously a roar of thunder. This settled the question in my favour! 'Yes, yes!' she exclaimed, then ran out. I closely following her, my heart beating exultingly! Quickly she passed through the double doors into the Snuggery, the trap I had so carefully set for her! Noiselessly I bolted the outer door, then closed the inner one. Alice was now mine! mine!!*

239

At last I had entrapped her! Now my vengeance was about to be consummated! Now her chaste virgin self was to be submitted to my lust and compelled to satisfy my erotic desires! She was utterly at my mercy, and promptly I proceeded to work my cruel will on her!"

He stared at the page thinking, *it's damned poor prose just the same.* When he looked up, Molly was holding the red ribbons, one in each hand, bare arms thrust forward. "Tie me like your slave and drag me to my suite. You must not delay..."

Doyle awoke with a grunt and rolled away from the canvas shroud to relieve himself. Lliam, standing on the shore, was far away in Boston, shrouded in a haze of lust. The clouds had come again and a mist, near enough to rain. Garret was awake also, watching Doyle approach Lliam. Malich snored on in a drunken stupor. Garret knew Doyle would have a sarcastic comment. Doyle never had a soft word for anyone, at best a crude joke, more often an epithet. He seldom addressed Malich at all, but only mocked his father behind his back.

"Lliam piss-a-leg," Doyle whispered. "Pissin' on yer dreams, eh? Not careful I'll raise the cove an' drown us all, this bloody tea, eh?"

"Couldn't you go further down the beach?"

"'Tis all the same, Brother. I could piss on yer leg an' you'd not notice. Dreamin' o' Breeze, eh? What you'd like to do, but Garret's goin' to get in there first look's like."

"How would you know anything about Breeze and me?"

"I heard a thing or two. Breeze an' Garret conspirin'. Like my fancy word, Brother? Learned that from you, eh?"

"What did you hear?"

"Breeze was tellin' Garret he has to cut yer throat whilst yer sleepin', salt an' dry ya like fish."

Lliam was shocked to hear the words even though he knew it could not be true. "An' what did Garret say, *dear* Brother?"

"Garret can't say a word, sure."

"Nor could he do a deed so heinous, Doyle. You're just a cod piece, no better than a turd on a rock."

Doyle grinned and did up. "Gotcha thinkin' though, Brother.

Garret's some beholden to Breeze, eh? Breeze thinks o' you as no better than cod slime. What might Garret do fer Breeze, he's that taken with'er charms, eh?"

Lliam turned to look at Garret, his eyes glittering in the guttering firelight, shadows deepening the ugly scars and twisted vision, demonic in daylight: in firelight, hideous enough to scare a witch. Was Garret grinning at him? Did he know what Doyle had said? Lliam felt a chill of fear creep up his spine and for a moment he had doubts about the night. *What if the cove is that evil and Garret's possessed by Sheen's unholy soul enough to do Breeze's bidding? What if Doyle and Garret are possessed?*

In moments Doyle was snoring again as if he'd never been awake and Lliam was left alone with his new fears. He turned away feeling Garret's gaze on the back of his brain, not just his hatless head, but deep into his thoughts, stealing his own memory of Molly McCracken while killing what was left of Breeze in his heart...

Lliam did as Molly asked, almost heartsick with fear at the turn, but it was too late to turn back. He tied the ribbons loosely around her wrists, thinking, *it has progressed so far so fast, and further than I could have imagined.* He had his own ideas of how to seduce Molly; slow and tender, she was just a maid and, he assumed, a virgin. But Molly had suddenly changed the rules and he had doubts about her chastity. And there was the new idea of Anna Louise. "This is not exactly right, Miss Molly."

"Oh, sweet sir, you're not shy of me are you? You read the book."

"I did not, that is...I glanced at a page or two, before I had the clerk tie it up." He should not have used that phrase.

Molly laughed. *Is she mocking me?* he wondered.

"And which page or two would that be, Mr. Dwyer? The part where you bind my arms with silken ropes and remove my dress, while I plead for my innocence?" She held up her arms trailing the lightly tied ribbons. "You have me at a disadvantage. Bring the book. Come along."

The damned book! Lliam followed Molly to the servant's stairs and up the stairs to a set of rooms that would have been a nursery, if the O'Conners had been successful making babies...Molly used the rooms as her study, she said. Removed by a hallway and a heavy door from the parent's quarters, she was free to do whatever she wished. And this day Lliam was to be initiated into the secret world of a beautiful, sensuous young women..."Here we are, my love. My boudoir, Anna calls it. She's French you know."

She opened the door to a small anti-room with a straight-backed chair and a writing desk. The room was decorated in yellow with gold accents A glass-fronted cabinet, a lawyer's case, was filled with books to give the room authenticity. Beyond, a second doorway opened on a larger room, also done in shades of yellow, set aglow by candles. The candle-lit chamber swayed into Lliam's vision: the large poster bed hung with filigree, filmy curtains across the foot in the suggestion of privacy and as he feared, the white silk ropes draped over the headboard. "Anna has been here," she said, as if it was a conspiracy. "The silk rope is her idea, and she had such fun arranging the flowers and candles. Isn't she the perfect *maid*?"

Anna has read the book too? Lliam was almost speechless but the questions raced around in his muddled brain. *The maid is complicit, the co-conspirator, and what else?* "I'm afraid, Miss, it's you have me at the disadvantage."

"Oh, come now, Mr. Dwyer. You've been the perfect gentleman but I know what a man wants." She gently towed Lliam into the chamber until they were standing at the open side of the high bed. There was a chintz loveseat opposite and he hoped they could sit awhile as he adjusted to his role. *Am I the seducer or the willing victim?*

"Miss Molly, you're just a young lass, how would you know what a man wants? The world is a wide place of many exotic ideas..."

"And you've been around the world to experience exotic ideas, I suppose?"

"Can we sit awhile, lass?"

"You may sit, Lliam, while I tell you the story of Alice and Jack."

Lliam almost collapsed onto the loveseat with relief. Molly held out her arms for him to untie the ribbons. She pouted, turned slowly away, and began undoing the buttons that ran the length of her long dress.

Lliam suppressed the desire to rise and take her in his arms, take command of the seduction, but waited, fascinated by his role, transfixed by the slow deliberate unveiling of Molly's perfect young body. What else could he do? He had caused the occasion, he had provided the erotic book, but he did not realize the depth of the moment.

"I wonder, Lliam, if Alice arrived at Jack's chambers entirely innocent of his intentions? They were friends, you know. She and her sister often visited Jack in his rooms, when they were in the city. Both young ladies were comely, as he describes the sisters, and one does not have to wonder that he was attracted to one or the other, or they to Jack. Why, do you suppose, Alice chanced to visit on a day of inclement weather? And stay on the pretext of the storm?"

Molly let her dress fall to the floor in slow motion, allowing it to pile around her long slim legs as if she was the confection on a risqué wedding cake. Her blossoming figure was still hidden from Lliam by her elaborate underclothes, which included a French corset accentuating the narrow waist and curve of her hips; a garment Lliam had never heard of, let alone seen on a female form. He was entranced, as well as uncomfortable, perspiring from his own heat.

"More than once Jack had made suggestions to Alice," she continued, slowly releasing the ties of her French garment, "and she teased him with hints but had always rebuffed his offers of a relationship, beyond innocent afternoon teas or sedate strolls in the park near Jack's lodgings. She was withholding her virtue for a favourable marriage, so she said. Can you blame her? Not that Jack was without his own charms."

"Molly, may I take off my jacket. It's stifling, and well, to tell you the truth..."

"You may tell me anything, Lliam, dear. Tell me the truth, or tell me lies. Tell me I'm attractive," she said without looking at Lliam in distress.

"Yes, yes," Lliam admitted inhaling deeply, "but it seems Jack, the cad, had his apartments rigged well in advance. A special room fitted with many devices."

Molly giggled and blushed. "Yes, wasn't it scandalous? The Snuggery, he called it. What an odd name for a chamber of erotic pleasure."

"With devious restraints," continued Lliam. "So he knew she was coming, and he was prepared. That's premeditated rape, if you want to know my feelings."

"Then you *did* read the book," Molly laughed with delight and turned to face him.

"No, that is, I perused the first few pages at the shop, that's all. I was intrigued by Jack's preparations. How could a man do that if he truly loved the woman?"

"My dear, Lliam, could you not detect his feelings? He *hated* Alice and wanted to punish her, obviously. But, perhaps, she wanted to be punished, for her own misspent virtue. Alice waited too long, the desire building, Lliam. The thing between two people not to be denied, and it's why we're here, isn't it? What you've desired from the moment you entered our house. What you see when you look at our lovely Anna. Do you want her too?" she asked coquettishly and began undoing the ties that held the bodice together, freeing her firm breasts to his eyes.

Lliam swallowed hard, avoiding her eyes, also avoiding the question. "I, I had no idea, when I accepted the job. Your father described you as an impetuous, rebellious schoolgirl. I expected a gawky child in pigtails, not a full grown woman with carnal intent. Well, that is...desire." The desire and the full-grown woman were very much on display and Lliam was almost beyond words.

"Are you disappointed?"

"No, of course not, it's just that..."

"So, Alice knew perfectly well what Jack was going to do. She had to pretend to be shocked, horrified by his plundering her bottom so ruthlessly, despite her pleas. She had to appear to fight for her virtue. When she stopped struggling and screaming and gave up her precious virginity, willingly, it was not rape...Should I pretend to resist?"

Lliam could wait no longer. He pulled her close and tore at her undergarments, and with Molly's help she became a chrysalis transformed into a shining alabaster sculpture, but warm and soft to the touch. He kissed her tenderly, remembering the mistake he made with Breeze: the rough, inconsiderate crush of lust, and was rewarded with a deep melting kiss in return. Molly seemed to faint away so that Lliam had to ease her down, kissing and fondling every part of Molly he could manage and still get her to the bed.

She lay on the white linen cover, unashamed of her naked body in his gaze, spread her lovely legs and extended her arms. Lliam began tying her wrists the way she instructed, the way Jack might have secured Alice with silk ropes, only discarding the blocks and tackles, leather straps and spring-loaded clasps, after she became his willing plaything...

Lliam started when Garret touched his shoulder. He'd been standing so long in the drizzle daydreaming, staring at the ocean and beyond, that Garret became concerned. He took Lliam's arm and lead him back to the fire, sat him down, pulled a corner of the canvas over his shoulders and handed him a mug of scalding tea. Dawn light was just showing below a bank of leaden clouds. Malich would stir soon and begin kicking his sons into activity.

The morning ritual meant Garret was up before the others, fire going, tea on the boil and something frying in the big iron skillet. The morning fare was simple: soggy pan bread or bannock in pork fat, or rancid fatty pork in pork fat with left over bannock. Salt cod and scrunchions with bannock were reserved for Sunday mornings, as long as the fish and pork held out. The flour barrel was low, a greater concern. Malich would not allow the brothers time to hunt or fish to replenish their dwindling stores. The work was everything. Neither hunger nor nutrition was part of the equation. Relentless hard work meant less time on the beach before the job was done and the merchant satisfied. The brothers were indentured servants with nothing for succor, only hardship and kicks. Lliam wondered if there was some of Seth Sheen's evil spirit in his own father.

Malich had his bottles of rum, which he refused to share. No occasion, injury or even Garret's birthday, would force Malich to relent and offer a dram or even a kind word. And so their days went: wet and cold most of the time, or perspiring in the rare summer sun. Suffering in silence, hands bleeding and raw, backs aching, to please the father, or to avoid the abuse, the schooner absorbed their days.

Lliam at least had his nights, but aside from writing in his journal in the bad light of the fire, his thoughts were of little solace. It was either Breeze, who was fading to avoid the pain, or Molly and Anna Louise, to occupy his mind, but they only reminded him of his guilt. Eventually he no longer cared if Garret would gut him like a fish.

"She'll not rebuild herself," chastised Malich gruffly as he threw the dregs of his tea in the fire and headed for the work site.

The days and nights passed and the planks went on and became strakes, and the strakes secured the whole. The summer weather was benign enough, for the coast. They could sleep on the beach or in the fo'c'sle. Doyle and Garret usually chose the beach. Lliam also had a choice. If he wanted solitude he could sleep alone in the fo'c'sle with his dreams and demons, comfortable enough on the bundles of sails tucked into the fo'c'sle for protection. Malich slept where he dropped, often passed out from the strong rum, but at least he was civil most of the day, as long as the work progressed. A kind of comforting rhythm took over the work site. It was not a pleasure, but at least it was progress and as long as the brothers toiled relentlessly, without complaint, Malich was content to let them work at their pace.

By the end of June the shutter plank was hammered into place. The hull was whole again and the fresh timbers glowed pleasantly in the evening sun.

"Well, that's a job of work done, b'yes." A rare compliment from Malich, and, most unusual, he shared a drink of rum during the evening meal. "Lliam, you can gather firewood whilst we get at'er corkin'."

Lliam would have preferred to set his hand at woodworking, there was enough still to do, but at least he was free to range out of the worksite, alone with his thoughts, however, in his state of confusion it was a form of punishment, not freedom.

The next morning he idled along the shore, testing the loose rocks with each step. The sound of the corking mallets accompanied him down the beach, pushing him away it seemed. He had to go a ways around the rocky headland to find more driftwood. Out of sight of Malich and Doyle, he began to breath easier. What kind of family is it that a son wants to flee? What did he owe them and why should he stay? The pain of knowing and not knowing followed him into the next cove, but the distance did not relieve the mind. Treading unholy ground did not help either; ground that even hardened fisherman could not share with Seth Sheen and his brood. *But Sheen's brood is part of my own fractured family*. The web was thin but intact.

He felt dirty of mind as well as body, spirit smeared with the blood of lust and incest, deceit and brutality, all for what? What lengths will a man go to have a family, then steal away and bed another man's wife for progeny and for selfish gratification? But that does not explain why his grandfather performed 'The Duty' all those years, to sire a brood for another man, a man who would call down curses, brutalize and kill those children in his madness. His own brothers were the fragments, the ones held by that web, as if a malevolent Devil enchanted a spider to wrap them together just to mock the laws of God. Well, he didn't believe in a god. A just god would not allow his creation to carry on for millennia the way the Christians went about life. And what he knew of the world, it was no better in foreign lands. No Paradise on earth, no milk and honey land as described in the Book. But who was he to criticize or judge? He'd fled to Boston, then away from Boston, ran from an affair that was too dangerous for a naïve young man from humble beginnings. He had left his rude grasping family to find that life, running away from love unrequited, but what he found was more puzzling. Molly and Anna Louise...

Molly met him at the door wearing a diaphanous gown, sheer enough to show her lithe body unencumbered by corsets or other garments.

"Good morning, Mr. Dwyer. How do we find *you* this morning?"

"Wherever you like, Miss McCracken...I'm at your mercy." He had no illusions about indulging in the Brontes, the classics or poetry, perhaps another passage from The Anonymous Book. She was radiant, glowing as if she had spent the morning preparing for his visit, but she was not dressed for an English lesson. She locked the big door and ushered him into the foyer with a mysterious smile as if she had a secret she was willing to share. "I take it your mother is out for the day?"

"Oh, yes, you know Mother and her meetings. Always doing good works."

"And your devoted maid, Miss Anna?"

"I have a surprise for you."

"A surprise? I wonder if I should come back later, when you've dressed?"

"Don't be rude. That's part of the surprise. Just throw your coat on the tree. Shouldn't keep her waiting."

"Miss Molly...?"

He knew at that moment he should flee. He had known that morning as he prepared to leave his flat for the assignation. He should have gone to the docks and shipped aboard the first rusted out freighter going anywhere in the world. But his memory of the previous week's adventure in the yellow room clouded his reason and his footsteps traced the route to the point of no return.

She led him along the familiar passage to the servant's stairs and he followed her up the stairs in a trance, the light from a landing window outlining her perfect form as if the sheer gown had flown away. He knew that it was also a calculated moment.

There were candles. The room was yellow. The flowers blood-red. Blood-red satin was draped from the bedframe.

Anna Louise was reclining on the poster bed, her voluptuous body in full view, arms and feet secured with the silk ropes, flickering candles casting onto curves and mounds, deepening the tawny shade of her hybrid skin. She was a teak sculpture, a polished mahogany idol.

"Isn't she lovely? Anna spent days searching for the second volume of our book. Only found it yesterday, at that little shop. It's more scandalous than the first and we spent the whole day reading it together."

His face was burning at the sight of Anna in a billow of linen and lace, like an offering to the gods, a banquet table set to perfection. The sacred offering was oiled, glowing and ready for the feast, and he was the guest of honour.

Molly undid the clasp of her gown and let it fall to the floor, looking at Lliam mischievously. "Anna didn't put up much of a fight, Lliam, not like Alice's maid, at first. Alice had much to learn from Jack, but once her virginity had been compromised and Jack had aroused her true sensuous self, she became his willing accomplice. I'm afraid our Anna is too well schooled in the ways of love and she taught me many things of pleasure, things I had never dreamed of. You may join us at *your* pleasure." She smiled down at her maid and ran the tips of her fingers slowly from Anna's dark curls across her heaving breasts that rose and fell like a lazy ocean swell, pausing to knead the nipples to taught pink berries, then trailing over her amber belly to Anna's dark pubic hair, entwining the tight curls in her fingers, teasing until she began to breath faster, hips moving gently, moaning with anticipation. Molly bent lower and kissed her waiting lips. Anna gasped at the touch, then arched her back and pouted at Lliam, waiting. Molly stood on the footboard massaging Anna's large breasts, smothering her voluptuous body with kisses. Lliam, torn between the alabaster of Molly's smooth skin and the burnished gold of Anna's, thought his heart would explode from desire and fear: a strange combination of emotions. He began to undress, shyly, almost embarrassed, wanting to run behind the screen in case his manhood failed him. The women, fully engaged in their own pleasure, seemed not to notice his dilemma...

He was standing at the high water mark, a few sun-bleached sticks in his arms, staring at the crotch of a dead tree from a foreign land that resembled the shrunken body of an old woman. He was almost panting from mental exertion. "Damn her. Damn them all to Hell!" He threw the sticks down and turned away to find something visual that did not remind him of her. He was not in love with Molly McCracken, but the desire to possess a woman who was not a replacement for Breeze O'Keefe, had led him to the altar of lust. But a young man's need to answer the demands of nature, for an expression of the forces within, had lured him into a world of forbidden pleasure. The heated lovemaking had quickly become a theatre of lust and he was swept into acts of depravity he did not know were possible between two people, or three people, then four. The trysts became orgies as Molly read *The Book: Volumes Two and Three,* and turned fantasy to base reality. Molly introduced a married woman in need of a diversion. Anna Louise, fully complicit in the downfall of her mistress, had friends: thrill seeking novices, hardened professionals, both genders, then a third gender: queers, transvestites, all depraved and debauched in their own way, but who was he to judge? It was all the rage in Europe, in Germany where the young sought refuge in cabarets, behind screens, in darkened rooms, hiding from the horrors of The Great Depression, shrinking from the prospect of another war.

The danger of discovery and punishment increased but he could not pull away, returning each week under the illusion that he was the teacher, earning his monthly pay packet from an unsuspecting Master O'Conner, until the day Molly informed him that her stepmother would be joining a session. He vowed, absolutely, that it was time to call it off, but before he had to make that decision Molly announced that she was pregnant. Then he ran, literally, from the house, until he stopped at the street corner, watching the Night Patrolman, wishing he had such a simple life.

He returned to a simpler existence but wanted to run again, to put distance between himself and every memory, but to where? He was on an island bounded by rocks and water. His home was on another island, bound by family obligations. Run again to the outside world? He'd been to America and experienced the truth of the human condition: the poor were trapped in a system that chews them up and spits out the dregs. *Wealth is the only answer, because with money you can buy freedom*, he had rationalized, only to see that the rich were no better off spiritually than the poorest Liveyer on the Labrador Coast.

What then? He was trapped by an existence as narrow as the gut between two bays where the tide washes through and life leaves claw marks on the rocks. He was trapped by guilt...Running from Breeze to Molly and back to Breeze, then failure again...He began picking up the sticks.

Malich and Doyle were arguing about some detail of the fore hatch combing. Garret was tending the fire, preparing a meager meal. Lliam, standing near the fire holding an armload of sticks, watched Garret busy with his task. Garret was always busy, always the study of contentment, but because he could not speak he could not tell Lliam what was on his mind. Lliam looked into Garret's eyes, trying to guess what he was thinking. The twisted mask revealed little, but the eyes said volumes. Lliam saw concern. Garret held up an empty barrel, the last of the salt pork. He pointed to the flour barrel, tipped it to show Lliam the bottom. Then too easily hoisted the salt cod bag with a lump or two left. He pointed to the salt beef barrel. The fatty salt beef was rancid, green, beyond redemption, and would only make them sick. The hard biscuits were crawling with weevils that even Doyle could not stomach. The box of coarse tea was not empty and might last, but black tea, no matter how thick, is not food, and even boiling hot, only fit for killing the weevils.

"A hard chance, old son," said Lliam, dropping his pile of firewood. "Soon you'll be out of work."

Garret tried to grin. It was not successful, but Lliam caught the gesture and grinned back.

Later, as they gathered for the evening meal, Lliam explained to Malich the dilemma of the dwindling rations, saving Garret from the harsh words. To Lliam's relief Malich said nothing, only grunted and retreated to the bottle. The boys sipped at their evil tasting tea. Doyle smoked and Lliam wrote in his journal, while Garret cleaned up. It was an illusion of peace. They had all worked at their jobs: the fore hatch combing was installed; the main hatch was next, and they could see an end to their trial, but there seemed to be no solution to their dwindling rations, unless they took time to hunt and fish.

Malich drank his rum in measured swigs, brooding into the fire, daring Lliam or Doyle to speak up and spoil his mood. Lliam continued writing and was surprised when Malich said, "Well, Lliam, yer no good for anythin' else so you'll go in bush tomorrow. Garret can cook a fresh rabbit, eh?"

"I'm not a hunter, Father. How would I?"

"Learn. Yer good at learnin', eh? Them books..."

"I don't have books."

"Course not. You learn by huntin'. If you'd'ave put yer head to providin' for yer family, eh?"

The old argument restated and Lliam had no answer. He wanted to offer the ship's wheel as proof that he could learn, but Malich ridiculed the contribution: a frill unlikely to up the ante with the merchant. Malich was intent on presenting a finished boat, nothing more. "The fuckin' merchant never added one ounce o' 'baccy just to please us, more like he'd pinch back what'e could," Malich had said on a previous occasion. Harsh, simple logic, Lliam had to admit. He envied Malich's uncomplicated view of life, but pitied his mother. *She must be a saint to put up with that man all these years,* he said to Garret one day while they watched Malich calling down Doyle for wasting a length of timber. But every piece of wood was hard won, a precious commodity on the barren, hostile shore. *A harsh life in a cruel place,* he had concluded when he left the village. He was condemned to servitude if he stayed and he was condemned for running away. Maybe Malich was right: filling one's head with foolish notions for other fools to read wasn't much of a life. If every word he wrote were a fish over the gunnel he'd have something to talk about around the family table. Well, he couldn't argue with that truth either, nor could he accomplish one or the other in limbo.

Sheen's Cove Morning: "See, brother, you take a piece o' wire an' make a loop, like this," explained Doyle surreptitiously over morning tea, while Malich was away in the bush relieving himself. He handed Lliam the simple snare, a strand of wire run through an eye in a piece of rigging wire. "Set 'em in a run, like."

"Thank you," said Lliam, surprised at Doyle's civility.

"Need about a dozen snares to catch one or two. But don't forget to tie off one end or rabbit's just goin' on with a bit o' jewelry, eh?"

"I see, yes. Thank you." He realized Doyle had a vested interest in his success. Rabbit would be a nice addition to their critical food supply; the only variance since the brief capelin run in June. Capelin, stewed or roasted, were a welcome change but a steady diet of the small, salty fish grew tiresome about the time they ran out. Garret tried to dry a batch but some creature got them in the night and Malich cursed him out for not trapping the thief.

"Take a scrap o' sail with you, Lliam lame brain, might be a day or so getting' the hang of 'er, see?"

He rolled the snares and a few necessities in a scrape of sailcloth...Garret contributed chunks of cod and a biscuit...He tied both ends of the roll with twine, slung it over his shoulder and trudged along the broken rocks before climbing to the grassy bench. He passed abandoned homes wondering who had lived there? He knew why they were abandoned...Every old house in an outport has a story, usually laced with mystery and legend, because no dwelling or patch of level ground, was left unattended without a good reason...Life was dangerous enough without the threat of having one's throat cut while asleep, or bludgeoned in the course of a civil dispute. In the midst of Sheen's madness, after the death of the second son, neighbours had considered murdering Sheen to protect themselves but lost the will and simply moved to the other side of the island.

A chill raced through Lliam as he passed a falling down store, imagining that Sheen watched from the window, waiting his chance to fall on him, probably as he slept in the bush. But he was curious enough to look in the store's broken window. A half finished skiff rested, greying and forlorn, on its horses. Beside it was a rough coffin. *An unfinished life,* he thought to himself.

He walked cautiously inland. The terrain was rough and littered with scrub and roots, broken rock and bogs. He skirted a boggy lake with a small stream angling off toward the shore: the abandoned outport's water supply.

Reaching a natural clearing in the middle of a struggling spruce stand he guessed he was about midway across the island. If he continued West he'd come to the settlement with people, houses and probably a small general store. When he had suggested to Malich that they find a store and get supplies, his father had cursed him for a fool. They had no money and nothing to barter. Malich wouldn't accept charity, not even if they were starving. Nor would there be credit allowed on the mention of the schooner or the Sheens. *We aren't that far from starvation,* he said to himself.

Lliam dropped his bundle on the coarse grass beside a small juniper matt. It was high ground and dry. A good place to camp: a bare rock outcrop to build a fire. He stood for a few moments looking around his new place of solitude, feeling unnerved by the calm. Something was missing. The sun was warm, not surprising for the time of year; the wind was only a zephyr because the clearing was in the shelter of trees. It was silent except for the distant chirping of birds. That was it, the silence. For the first time in recent memory he could not hear the ocean crashing on or caressing rocks. He had been far enough from the ocean in Boston but it was never really silent. Even in the midst of a depression, city life went on at a roaring, honking, thumping pace. In Pennsylvania there was the constant roar of steam shovels gouging the mountains for coal. The trips to and fro by train were another racket of steel and steam. His home in Béhathook Cove was only a narrow gravel peninsula away from the Atlantic and the ocean was never really still. Even on rare dead calm nights, the ocean swells sighed among the stones: a lonely sigh as if the waves had come to shore seeking solace and found only hard indifference, not unlike his home coming, and once a wave has reached the shore there is no going back.

He longed to throw himself on the ground, curl into a protective ball and sleep as though dead. Or properly dead. He should have dragged the coffin with him, could lie down, pull the top over and cease to exist. *What a picture that would be,* he chuckled. Would his family suffer remorse for treating him shabbily? Would they even look for him?

He scouted the spruce stand for evidence of rabbits. It took the virgin outdoorsman precious time to recognize the signs: the run, the trodden grasses, bent away from the run, chew marks on stumps or higher up, depending on the winter snow. Droppings in clusters were his first proof of their existence.

He was now a hunter, but sleeping rough, half starved and numb from hard labour, hardly prepared him for the sensitive business of killing small animals in the purple shadows of a spruce stand. Newfoundlanders have pursued the hardy bush rabbits for hundreds of years. The surviving species have grown wary and more secretive: night foragers are lean and fast. So lean they have little fat and as much sinew as muscle; still, stewed with potatoes and turnips, they were an outport delicacy, a nice change from endless salt fish, salt herring, salt turr, salt pork, salt beef, salt spray, salt sores, salted seal flippers, or salt tears. Salt tears are shed for lost loved ones, lost love, lost voyages, lost ships, lost last chances...That was Lliam.

Lliam wasted a lot of time wandering around the clearing looking under scrub trees, behind fallen logs, in juniper bushes, all the while picking up dry branches at the base of mature spruce trees. There the ground was soft and even. He could sleep under the trees, but he wanted a fire and had the sense to know that a fire in the needles under a resinous spruce might spread and give away his location. The burning trees, even green, would become beacon torches. The locals might kill him for poaching *their* rabbits, but doubted anyone cared to own the useless scrub in his clearing. But there was the boggy pond, the village water supply that fed the tiny streams that trickle down to the shore and add their water to the great oceans. Insignificant though they are, they added up and all the trickles, streams and rivers are part of the cycle...He and Breeze had read a section of the anthropology book about the cycles of rain, erosion and rebirth; as one thing was worn down another rose up and that's how the great mountains rose and diminished. Was the cycle complete or never-ending? The world had not yet been exposed to the forces of plate tectonics, so God still got credit for mountain building and fertile plains...He realized with a start that he was standing, with an armload of sticks, imagining

255

enemies and problems. He had few real enemies because he had few friends. He had run away from his two closest friends in his fear of relationships. The irony of having impregnated both of them, for different reasons, was not lost on him, it's one of the things he had learned in a lifetime of reading literature: irony is the best relief from reality because it frees one from commitment. He wasn't sure how that was possible but it seemed that in every incidence of true irony there was a disconnect between the giver and the receiver...Wait, he was wandering, verging on the cusp of insanity. *Is it possible,* he wondered, *that it's true what they say about the outports, that half the population of any outport is inbred, just like the other half?* He almost chuckled, summoning the picture of Malich, Doyle and Gerald. His brothers were copies of the father. He added Breeze. He opened the family album to the page for Garret and himself and added the image of Sean O'Keefe. It must be true...

To change the narrative he listened to the darkening woods. The small birds were silent but restless. Ravens *chucked and mewed* lowly in the trees, whispering among themselves, discussing the interloper, assessing his chances of survival. Lliam thought they were in league with Seth Sheen, watching for signs of weakness as he watched for signs of rabbits. "Have to get the snares set before dark," he concluded, out loud, just to hear the sound of his own voice. He circled the clearing again searching for more signs.

Béhathook Cove: At the moment Lliam was contemplating snaring rabbits, Breeze O'Keefe was curled on the daybed struggling to convince her body to get up. She had been feeling poorly for two days and Mildred O'Hara came to make meals and look after Brigid. At first the pain was just a nuisance and she went about her daily chores, struggling about the village delivering laundry to Morgan O'Dell or bread and broth to the old ones. Morgan could not help notice her swollen belly. Sure, she noticed the looks from the women, as she noticed the pains, just a nuisance too. She wasn't sure of the timing no more than she was certain of the father, but it must be Lliam's baby inside her, could not be Garret's or Morgan's.

Garret had been away fishing, then Garret came home a destroyed man barely able to move, but when he was able to make secret comfort love with Breeze, when the others had gone to bed, she was already feeling the child inside her womb. Morgan O'Dell's night was also after the seed had been sown, she was positive. And Morgan had proposed...a good catch at any other time, but he was still mourning the loss of his fiancé. She felt so badly for Morgan and one night of stolen, gentle love was just her way of consoling him. It sickened her then, knowing she had already conceived. She'd throw up mornings, and longed for rest in late evenings when her back ached and her legs throbbed. She fought her longing for peace, or deliverance. The dream of Ireland fading as she sat beside the pit fire wondering, *If I give myself to the ocean would she carry me to Aran's shores? Would Grace O'Malley find me and carry me home to suffer no more a man's touch when that touch is only a knife thrust straight into the heart?*

Self-death was another choice, like the family preferring Doyle or Garret, but not Gerald, being dead. Lliam was a living substitute for Gerald, and the father of the child, but not the first among equals. If she was to have a child, which of the three should she choose to be the father? *Garret is nearly destroyed, but a loving man. Lliam is a destroyer of woman's hearts.* Neither man could protect a woman or provide for a family. *Morgan is a good man, hard working, handsome in his way.* She could have Morgan, and might, if he asked again, but she'd proposed to Garret and felt sick at heart as well as in her stomach, the two sicknesses ganging up on her senses, ruining her moods, killing her smile. Her mother's constant harping only drove her spirit further from the home, although she tried to do her duty, deep in her soul she knew she was going to run.

"Breeze, child," her mother said, rocking impatiently, "can you not make an effort?"

"Mildred's comin' the once."

"Mildred O'Hara can only do half the job, an' I pay her for the day." Brigid rocked faster as if to emphasize her concern.

"I'll try, Mother, soon as the cramps settle a bit."

"You'll suffer more than a few cramps for your sins, so you best get used to it. Why, in my day the woman worked 'til the moment the wee babe announced, an' was back makin' tea for the men the moment the mewing thing was dry. I warned you, many times, but you're so head strong an' know more than all us put together. If you want to hear tales of hardship..."

"I don't need stories, Mum. A little rest is all. I've earned that, haven't I?"

"An' what makes you think a sinner has any rest banked up with the Lord? You're just fortunate you're not blessed with these knees an' fingers. If I was fit..."

"If you was fit I'd not be in this mess. I'd be in Ireland where I obviously belong."

"Ireland is it? An' what pray tell, could you do for yourself in a place no better than this rock? Besides, there's a war on in Ulster an' the IRA come beggin' we to help."

The women of the village offered little help for Breeze, the witch, but they did offer opinions and judgments. *That one's a mate to the Devil himself. She cavorts on the beach at night with the Evil One and that's her reward. She'll come to no good an' the village will be cursed with another Sheen.* Those were some of the less vitriolic pronouncements by the superstitious ones. Dark deeds were suggested, intercessions prayed for. A timely accident would be best.

Mildred O'Hara, daughter of young Thomas O'Hara and Thelma O'Dell, was not afraid of Breeze. Her mother Thelma had suffered too deeply to allow her daughter to be influenced by the talking women of the village. All but two of the family died by Ulster Scots in revenge for an IRA murder in Belfast. Locked in a barn and the barn set on fire, only Thelma and her daughter Mildred escaped and were sent to Béhathook by an aunt to be raised by the O'Hara family. Thelma was scarred by reality and vowed that her child would not be a victim of injustice. Mildred was taught tolerance and respect. Thelma and Breeze were like sisters, understood each other: the longing, the unrequited love. Mildred was the only young person in the village who would approach Breeze, who she worshipped. But Mildred would die an unnecessary and cruel death, to be replaced by a sister, Meghan, and it proved to the village talkers that Breeze was a witch...But that's another story.

Lliam selected runs that looked promising, set the snares as Doyle instructed, and built a small fire in the clearing. The fire was for comfort, or warding off the spirits if he was honest about it. The evening was cool but not cold and he had no food that required cooking. He missed Garret's evening tea, as black and bitter as it was, but there was no tea, or pot to spare. He made do with hard chunks of salt cod and sips of pond water while he wrote in his journal. His life had come down to this day and he laboured over the words to put it into perspective...*I've come this far, to sit beside my fire, hungry, tired and without a future that I can see. This tiny fire, fed stick by stick, is not much of an accomplishment. But what more can a sinner expect? Fire is the cleansing agent of a life dirtied up by living on the fringes. Malich is right. Malich is a bestial being, but he's uncommonly right about people. I should have brought the coffin and made a proper fire, casting myself into the box, the box on the fire. How would I do that? Once in the box I could not cast it, I'd have to place the box on the fire then get in, pull the lid and wait. Could a man do that? A desperate man, perhaps. Am I desperate enough? It would seem so, but then I'm not a good judge of character. I know several (people) who might assist me, would love to bind me hand and foot and lower me into the box once it was good and hot, just before it burst into flames, probably form a circle and dance around my pyre. What rubbish! No one would dance at my funeral. Breeze might rejoice in her private way, but she would not dance...*Lliam heard a rustle in a thicket at the edge of the clearing, left off his writing and went to investigate.

He walked slowly in the direction of the sound...a scrabbling, frantic shuffling noise. He slowed his pace, but his heart beat faster, he began to perspire. *It's just a small rabbit*, he reminded himself, what he came inland to kill. He was trembling as he approached the moving scrub, a juniper with an open space in the center, a perfect nesting place for a small creature, and a tunnel of sorts through the branches, worn by decades of the gentle creatures seeking sanctuary, going about their business. He wondered if the rabbits nested there, had litters of tiny furry mice-like babies.

At his approach the terrified rabbit lay deathly still, eyes fixed, chest jumping. Paralyzed by fear or instinctively playing dead, he didn't know. Didn't know anything about rabbits other than they were soft to the touch and harmless. His rabbit was brown, earth brown, dry leaf brown, perfectly camouflaged. He would have walked by and not seen the creature, unless he was a fox. He knew the tiny, scared beast was there because he had set the snare and the snare was wrapped around the neck of the object of his journey. He stood looking down until she was visible, but he was more helpless than the trapped animal because now that he had his quarry, he was unsure what to do with the terrified beast. Then he noticed the wire snare was also around the front leg and the leg prevented the hare from strangling as she thrashed about. Yes, she, a nursing hare with a brood waiting nearby. She had been foraging in her familiar grounds before the evening feed, looking forward to settling down for the night in a cozy burrow with her warm, soft babies; ready for the next litter since she had already mated. Lliam didn't know that of course, but he could see that she was a nursing mother, the suck-extended tits were pink and engorged.

Momma wasn't coming home that night if Lliam did his duty. The problem was, how to kill the warm blooded, innocent creature? (Malich had taken Liam and Doyle seal hunting that spring. They walked across the blinding white ice to a patch of harps whelping at the edge of a lead. From a distance Malich shot a mother harp, and two more. The others plunged into the lead. Then Doyle bludgeoned the babies until the ice was red. Doyle seemed to enjoy the violence. They shot five more at another lead and lost two, sunk away before they could finish them off. Then they went home. Lliam's job was to drag two carcasses. He didn't kill them. Would not have been able to kill them and when Malich offered the gaff to bludgeon the fat white coats he refused. Doyle mocked him. Malich just shrugged, disgusted. The long trudge home was made in silence except for the grunts of effort dragging the carcasses over the pressure ridges. He towed his bleeding carcasses and felt ashamed).

260

The cringing hare had had enough of playing dead. She suddenly flung herself up, trying to leap away, long back legs powerful, and the leap would have been surprising, but she cartwheeled and only ended up facing the opposite direction. Her back legs were still pumping, dirt and twigs flying, scrabbling for distance. Powerful legs and speed had always been her saviour...She'd had a two-year running battle with a canny red fox. The fox had kits of her own to feed and bunnies, big or small, were just the thing, but mother hare ran too fast or stood her ground and kicked out in desperation until the fox retreated...Why couldn't she run away from this human? She knew humans. She knew to avoid them, especially the small ones who yelled and threw stones. Snares in her part of the island were not unknown, but she could avoid them too, could smell the steel wire. She had made a mistake and it was what would kill her if she struggled. A rabbit could not process all that, but instinct told her that the game was up and she lay quiet again, waiting for her tormenter to go away.

Lliam watched the rabbit, kneeling beside the bush, the prey within reach. Her bright eyes were wide in terror, fixed on her tormentor, while he thought about ways to kill the thing. He didn't have a knife. He could get a rock or a stick and bash her brains in. He didn't know about the trick of taking the bunny by the back legs and snapping its neck with a whiplash motion: fast and painless, if it worked the first time. Excruciatingly cruel if it didn't, like a lynching gone wrong, leaving the unfortunate one jerking and twitching, strangling but not dying properly. Lliam was not aware of any rules about snared animals, about giving a sharp blow to the back of the neck, breaking the neck at the base of the skull, snapping the spinal cord, mercifully or just stunning the hare, the helpless victim left bumping along in pain against it's captors leg, hanging by its back legs from the hunter's belt until it recovered and danced about upside down. Then the hunter was forced to choose: ignore the beast until it died, or snap, whiplash, rabbit-chop or bludgeon the nuisance.

He touched the down-like flank; it quivered, he expected her to leap again. She did not, just lay panting as he gathered the powerful back legs together and held them tightly, running his other hand along the body, so soothing, warm and soft, felt the heart thumping, the lungs heaving, muscles tensing, shivering in fright. He slipped the noose off the hare's neck. There was a spot of blood on his fingers and a show of blood on the fine white hair of the front leg where the wire had cut through when the rabbit leaped for freedom. He pulled the snare away and let it hang, useless now as a killing device, like himself. He didn't have the hunter's instinct; not even hunger could make him brutalize the warm life under his hands. He held the terrified rabbit until the tiny beating heart slowed down.

Lliam chose to spare her life, but there was a problem. *There's always a problem when choosing what lives and what dies*, he thought, remembering with anger the discussion about which son would be best sacrificed for the good of the families. If it were a death sentence for the hare the problem would then be skinning the prey. If the victim were a full grown moose the problem would be the weight, even skinned and eviscerated. But Lliam's problem was the blood. He could not kill the hare with his bare hands, so he had to let the thing go free. Lliam didn't know about the red fox, but an animal bleeding would be at a disadvantage in the wild; disease too, he didn't know much about bacteria or infection, gangrene for one, but an infection often took unlucky fishermen when injured far from home. Heal or die, they say. If the rabbit were disabled how would she nurse her babies? He pictured the poor thing crawling off into the brush to die a slow death.

He reluctantly withdrew his hands from the quivering body and waited. *Get up and run, damnit!* The rabbit just lay in the juniper cradle, panting, perhaps considering the very thing Lliam was thinking, or so he imagined. Finally, he gently picked the body up and brought it to his chest. The hare seemed rigid, as if playing dead again. He'd never held anything small and warm, or felt a delicate life in his arms, nor would he ever, he realized, unless...Out of the question. Breeze was having a baby, but...He sat down, cradling the life he could have easily strangled, and let his mind wander back over a lifetime of failures...Molly would have given birth the previous fall. The baby, ten months in the world, would have shape and form, and gender, but...He'd never see that baby. Breeze may have had her baby. His baby? He didn't know. He thought of Garret, the only good member of his family, besides his mother who may have had her own indiscretions. He didn't want to think of his mother other than as a candidate for sainthood, if only for putting up with her brute of a husband.

He set the shivering beast on her feet, held her upright, took his hands away and waited. She sat, immobile, hardly breathing, perhaps thinking, if she sat very still her attacker would go away. Lliam gave her a little nudge. She hopped one hop, then sat, ears erect and twitching as if on a swivel, back and forth, nose testing the air. Lliam became impatient and clapped his hands. The rabbit, startled, hopped away, favouring the injured leg so that she almost toppled over with each painful progression; hopped, stumbled and hopped again until she reached the edge of the spruce stand and disappeared without looking back.

Lliam watched the growing purple darkness of the trees until he was certain she had escaped then went about the clearing gathering up the rest of the snares. He returned to his patch of grass, put twigs on the fire and sat down on the cold ground to record the events of the hunt. *Do one good thing in your life,* he wrote.

Morning: Lliam awoke cold and dispirited before dawn light. The small fire, long since turned to grey ashes, stirred in the first breeze of morning. He turned over to relieve the ache in his hip, and saw the specs of blood on his fingers, the only sign he had been near success. Pulling the rotten old sailcloth around his shoulders, he shut his eyes and tried to sleep again but saw the rabbit limping to its own world, wishing he had kept the thing close for warmth. He could have eaten the rabbit for breakfast, but he would have to kill her first.

He remembered with disgust the first seal killed by Malich that spring, head smashed by the bullet, the skull fractured to pieces and strewn about the ice, pink and steaming, the blood running away over the ice, and over the edge of the pan, spreading into the clear water, the heart still pumping it out as if it was an offering to the sea. Then watched, his gut tightening, as Doyle clubbed her white coat baby with the gaff, laughing as he hit and missed, stumbling and falling down on the still living baby, whose eyes were full of fear, not understanding the sudden pain or why the mother was unable to protect her offspring. Then the next shot. Another dead mother and more clubbing, but Doyle hadn't properly killed the first white coat and when Lliam objected Malich said to kill the bloody thing himself. He couldn't and Doyle ridiculed him mercilessly and when there were no mothers to shoot or babies to club, they went home, Lliam dragging two carcasses as ordered, if he wanted supper. He hadn't eaten all day because he could not eat the warm heart of the baby that Doyle offered him, then snatched it away, telling Lliam to cut out his own fuckin' heart if he was hungry. He was no longer hungry, just sick at heart and to his stomach. He'd have to be desperately hungry to kill to eat raw flesh.

He lay on the ground, eyes closed tight, and saw the bloodied face of the crippled WWI veteran in the Boston bar who'd told stories for beer, but got beaten and kicked by two drunken brutes because the old man made them feel lousy for not going to the war. The veteran talked too much about the carnage, the broken bodies half buried by the shell bursts, dying alone in muddy holes, faces shoved under water by the boots of their mates climbing out of the holes, either to retreat or attack, it didn't matter. The old man, bloodied and near blind, got up and limped away. Lliam didn't help the old man because he was afraid the thugs would turn on him. *Do one good thing in your life, Lliam.*

Lliam rolled the snares into the canvas: a meager inventory, nothing to show for his foray inland, and nothing to show for his excursion to the Mainland either. Two babies born didn't touch him as an accomplishment because he wasn't sure they were his babies. *Probably were,* he said to himself as he turned for the shore. Probably, possibly, but only time would tell. He studied the coarse grass at his feet as he put one foot before the other, always heading down so that the going was easy, if he avoided the broken rocks sticking up through the grass and juniper matt. He was on a ledge of grass, the ocean just the other side of a frieze of stunted trees, all twisted and shaped, leaning away from the sea wind. The sun was warm and the breeze gentle. He stopped and looked around the clearing, sniffing the air scented with juniper and spruce, realizing it was a perfect place to build a house, and people it with babies, washing on the line just waving in the land breeze, not straining like a sail on the open shore...He'd watched Breeze hanging out Morgan's laundry, fighting for every corner before the wind tore the garment away. *Why do they persist?* Wind-blown and raw from the cold and salt spray, when they could move inland and walk to the shore if they insisted on getting into their damned boats to row out to their death, dashed to pieces on the rocks...

He stopped at the verge of the boggy pond to fill his cup with the tannic water. He only had to follow the humble rivulet to find the cove where his family worked away on the Sheen schooner, returning to the life he rejected but could not flee, steeling himself for the insults and abuse from Doyle, perhaps even a kick from Malich. He'd fight him this time. He wouldn't take the abuse; yes, he would, he knew. He'd take it because he had no answer. He'd failed at such a simple task as killing a small rabbit. Could have proven himself by eating the rabbit and snaring more for his family. Isn't that the way it's done? A way of life that has sustained the marginal millions throughout human history. Who was he to object? *Can't change the course of the world by sparing one sinewy rabbit,* he had written in his own defense.

Malich and Doyle ignored Lliam. The silent treatment was worse than taunts and oaths. But he did get a look of sympathy from Garret when he related his story of the hare that escaped. Garret teared up when Lliam described how the wild rabbit fought and clawed, pulling free just as Lliam was about to strangle the writhing beast; leapt free, jumped aside, spun around and tore away into the deep brush where Lliam couldn't follow. He told Garret there were no more rabbits in the clearing because there were other hunters, fresh skins cast aside, and his hare was the wiliest to have survived so long, and certainly wouldn't be back. He related to Garret the demonic look in the eyes of the hare, and the bite...*maybe it was possessed by Sheens, look at the bite.* So he had come back to the cove to resupply and maybe go around the headland to fish, or hunt away from the village of snare hunters. He only allowed Garret to see a tiny speck of the blood on his fingers, held it to his mouth to suck out the poison, then, he walked away over the rocks to gaze at the heaving ocean, cursing himself for a fool as well as a liar. Lying to your silent brother was near the bottom of human behavior, in his estimation. Murdering your brother would be the lowest...

It was a promising morning despite the truth that they were starving. Garret did his best with a gub of rancid lard, the dregs of the flour barrel, a handful of tea supported by spruce buds, and a hard biscuit soaked until it could be cut in four. Even the weevils looked like nourishment floating about in the black tea with the spruce buds.

"Five days to high tide an' we're quit o' this fuckin' place," announced Malich. "We've a job o' work to finish up an' get the sails bent on. You can be of some use then, I suppose. 'Tis mostly woman's work, getting' the sails up on deck an' sorted." With that Malich threw the dregs of his tea in the fire and walked over to the site, glancing at the tip of the mainmast where a raven perched, mewing in judgment.

Doyle spit out a spruce bud at Lliam's feet. "Too bad Breeze ain't along with us, eh? She's a one for work, b'ye. She'd be up over at the snares, eh, an' make a rabbit stew in a trice, bend on them sails right smart, an' then bring in firewood, after we'd all fucked'er the night long, eh, Brother?...Jazuz!..." Lliam was on his brother before Doyle could finish the oath.

Lliam's fists flew so fast Doyle could only hold his arms in front of his face. Some blows got through and did damage. Lliam's rage was fuelled by years of holding back: abused, mocked, verbally spit on, belittled. It all came pouring out and he was screaming to punctuate each blow. Doyle was weakening, his guard falling, but Lliam was weakening also and the blows had little power. It was repetition that caused Doyle's eyes to puff out. Garret interceded so Doyle was spared. Lliam only saw a rabbit that had to be killed, a bleeding baby seal whose head still had to be bashed open and the brains and bone spread around to prove he'd reached manhood. Killing his brother was not the issue. Didn't matter whether he was Caine or Abel. Something had to die that day...Later he would analyze the action, while scruffing for mussels in the low tide pools, and realized that he had wanted to incite Malich to bash his own head in. To end it. Death by the father, the creator, but Malich wasn't...Malich had turned at the first blow, to watch with disgust the sight of his sons engaged in one of their useless fights. He shook his head, climbed aboard the boat and continued the job. If one of the brothers killed the other, it was of little consequence. The job was almost done, the merchant would be appeased and life in the deadlight outport would go on.

Garret did what he could for Doyle. The damage was superficial: lots of blood and bruises. Garret washed away the blood while Doyle cursed his brother, vowing to get even, soon: as soon as the *fuckin'* schooner was launched he'd do for him with a caulking mallet, just the thing to split his *fuckin'* skull, and he'd watch Lliam bleed to death, the blood going out the scuppers, then he'd heave the body over the side for the sharks.

Lliam took his own rage around the headland to find peace and distance because he feared he might actually kill Doyle. So far he had thought about killing all the male family members, except Grandfather. *Gran'father's had a hand in this bloody mess...*

Garret wanted to console Lliam but had no experience mitigating or mentoring, always in the shadow watching his family curse each other, fight, seethe with anger, subside in silence, reunite from necessity or hubris. Life was a constant need for succor of the soul and nourishment of the body. The body came first. There was little warmth or love spared or shared out among the Dwyer clan. If there was little time for grieving there was precious little time for sympathy. Garret's needs were met by Breeze and Breeze alone. He was a mute, useful to a point, tolerated for his industry and willingness to be a fixture, like a reliable chair. *If Garret had died in the fire on the Dwyer schooner he would not be mourned for long. Relief would have been the family's first emotion. Gerald on the other hand...*

Damn him! Lliam was still seething with a rage that sent the blood coursing through his body, stinging his skinned fists. The salt water stung also, at first plunge, then felt good as he pried mussels off the rocks and stripped the gravel clinging to the filaments. He relished hurting, there was a reason for the superficial pain at least. The inner, deep-soul hurt was a permanent fixture when the rage wore off.

Lliam's defense for self abuse was his imagination, delving into a world of fiction and fantasy: the stories he would write, but he tried to suppress the images of Molly on top of Anna, kissing, sucking, rubbing, because he kept seeing himself on top of Doyle, flailing away like a thing possessed. He didn't see the difference between the wild passion and the wild hatred, if both caused the mind to go against convention. He'd seen too much in America that framed the degradation of the human experiment, but then he'd run from a village where humans live one life on the surface and a different life under the cover of darkness. Which is more dishonest? The brutality of the thugs who disfigured an already destroyed survivor of a war, or the spiritual brutality waged on one's own family, all the while praying to a god for deliverance from evil? It made no sense to Lliam: he was a lost soul no matter what he did to make amends.

What he did begin to understand was the instinct for survival. His family, whatever it actually encompassed, perhaps the entire village by blood, worked through each day simply because they had no other choice. The ancestors had escaped famine-ravaged Ireland only to be imprisoned on a different rock, scrabbling for the same existence; the only difference was distance. There was the question of freedom. The ancestors fled Europe for many reasons but the foremost were persecution and poverty. *What*, Lliam wondered, *was the difference if the results were the same, only the location changed?* He had run further west only to find more displaced Europeans locked in the battle for survival, committing the same sins, and it was the same all up and down the coasts of North America. Inland was no different. If one followed the trail further west, law and order were subservient to survival of the fittest. America was emerging as a world power until the Great Depression covered the land in colours of grey and brown. No one below a certain economic level escaped the ravages of being poor in the great cities or the dust storms that swept the plains and prairies. At least on the Rock the poor could fish or hunt to survive.

The mussels bulged in the flour sack, a meal to get them through another day. Beyond the sunkers at the mouth of Sheen Cove, fat cod lay in the depths, free for the taking, if a jig was lowered with a bit of bait. Malich had packed no jigs or line, no thought of feeding his sons if the rations failed. He'd failed to kill a rabbit but one did not actually have to kill mussels to eat them. *Not true,* he rationalized, pulling another cluster off the rocks. The water was deeper now, the tide returning to claim the short lived freedom from the salt sea. *Something always has to die for others to live.* If he killed Doyle, Garret could skin his brother and boil his flesh...Maybe Garret was planning to kill *him,* as Doyle said, and they'd all dine on his heart.

Lliam splashed out of the water and collapsed on a rock, gasping for air, breathing in shallow jerks as if his lungs had ceased to function. He saw his own heart frying in the putrid tallow that was supposed to be used to slush the mast. It stopped beating to spite him as he watched the sack sinking into the wavelets following the tide. How long had he been sitting in the tide pool, going mad with the poison released in the flailing hatred of his brother?

The sack! He forced himself back into the cold water but nothing looked the same. Over there, by that sharp-edged rock that an hour ago was the size of a skiff. He waded to the spot and looked into the water now fouled by his passage. He felt around with his freezing feet, kicked something that moved, leaned down and felt around the gravel bottom, touching a flatfish that skittered away. *Maybe the skate took the bag,* he said to himself. If he lost the sack of mussels he would vow silence, like Garret, and cease to exist, hiding in his thoughts, but those thoughts could not get beyond Breeze's smooth white thighs and Molly's alabaster body writhing around on her golden maid...What was her name? Anna Louise, the Creole slave...He was trying desperately to concentrate. Knee-deep now in the cold ocean he stood up and looked over the waves curling around the guardian rocks. He took a step forward, tottering on numb stumps of feet. If he waded out far enough his whole body would become a cold, dumb cadaver, float away, and be devoured. Which would come first? He didn't much care because he'd lost the will even to die. But as he turned back for the shore rocks, he stumbled over the sack, reached down and hauled the prize to the surface.

Lliam flung the heavy sack at his father's feet. He was shivering with the cold, nerves spent and emotions drained. His body was in shock the same as if he had been pummeled like Doyle. Doyle huddled under the tarp looking miserable, a beaten dog even though Garret had groomed and soothed the best he could. Doyle, not to be appeased until he had revenge, was conjuring hurtful words about Breeze but could not give voice with Malich so near. Malich looked from the bag of mussels to his son's face with no hint of gratitude, only the usual harsh look. What did Lliam expect, an embrace? He had only accomplished what a son was for, to do his duty, no word of praise necessary. If he had failed he would have received the same harsh look, it was no more than he deserved. But the act of flinging the sack down was a provocation, the same as a spoken insult, or a challenge. Lliam did not understand the subtle difference. The mood would simmer on the back burner for the rest of the day.

Garret boiled the mussels and hard biscuits in the skillet and served out the opened shells. The meager meal was consumed in silence, the tension in the camp like a wharf line straining to hold a sinking ship. Each felt the message in a different way.

Malich did not care how his sons felt. The job was nearing completion. Garret worried that the transparent fabric of the family was about to be torn apart. Doyle brooded over chunks of mussel meat, burping, farting and flinging empty shells into the fire, summoning words to hurt Lliam, plotting ways to hurt him physically. Calmer now, he at least realized it would have to look like an accident.

Lliam, appetite spoiled by the acid atmosphere, looked from face to face, realizing it was not a family but a collection of desperate souls hanging on to a vestige of a life. There was no loving god of creation, as the Bible promised, only sins of the fathers more hideous than any testament a priest could invoke to scare the miserable Irish into submission.

Lliam escaped into his world of Irish literature. Joyce's *Portrait of the Artist:* was the first modern novel Lliam had read and it scarred him for life. He summoned the images of Joyce's hero; what did his name mean? Daedalus, the myth, the man who would be god...Dedalus the earthling, not Daedalus the artisan. Stephen was the son of the failed father, trying to escape the earth; not soaring like Icarus, but wandering in the sewers of the Catholic mind, rotting like uncooked meat spoiled by exposure to the heat of the perverted priest's condemnation of the Irish soul. Stephen Dedalus, as Joyce conjured him, wallowed in a spew of verbal excrement never seen before, or since, on the pages of a major English publication. Honest writers recoil from the description of Dedalus' decent into moral hell that Joyce offered as epic language. It made no sense to Lliam, and served no purpose other than to expunge some dreadful well of pent up hatred swilling about in Joyce's cesspool of a mind, or so Lliam thought, until he experienced first hand, true lust with a young woman trusted to his care. But hadn't the lovely Molly initiated their descent into carnal hell? Yes, but he was fully complicit for carnal reasons of his own...Hurting Breeze from a distance. In the mythology version, Daedalus' son was punished for arrogance and crashed to earth because he flew too close to the sun. Lliam had never climbed above the level of the sewer grate, except for that one time on the hill with Breeze, but the decent was swift and final. To Breeze he was no more than a mound of fish guts on the wharf to be kicked back into the ocean.

He let his mind wander back to the final episode of the escalating trysts organized by Molly's dutiful maid, Anna Louise, and the depths of depravity that passed for experimental love, the urban fashion extolled in 'The Book', a trash tome by a writer who did not dare pen his name beneath the horrendous title. He felt sickened by the vision of adults fawning and fumbling, pretending to be involved in the pleasure of the other person, whoever was being fondled or probed, licked or fingered at the time. He wasn't a prude, he was just a lost soul, but he longed only for Breeze...He slipped away soon after the orgasm that was a searing burning sensation as if an artery had been opened instead of a simple stream of sperm. His moral self flushed all the goodness out of his body onto the person nearest; he wasn't sure who, or what gender, didn't care, just fled the scene and wept for the loss of his last shred of innocence. Then, with the announcement that Molly was pregnant, he fled Boston in a daze of self-recrimination and guilt and, in a drunken stupor, began the voyage home.

The journey of the Prodigal was accomplished in a haze of alcohol...He lingered in a destructive bar crawl around St. John's, and on the final leg home, wished that the coastal boat would sink before it reached their cove. If not granted that wish, he prayed, beyond hope, that a confrontation with Breeze O'Keefe, and his plea for forgiveness, would not be the last willful act of a mind in terminal decline. As he stared at the open maw of a grainy mussel, he wondered if he had finally reached the nadir of his pitiful life?

If he had known what was yet to unfold on the dismal shore, in the shadow of Sheen's cursed schooner, he would have slit his own throat and saved Doyle the trouble. He screamed in his mind for the injustice, gasped outwardly at the silence. His family looked away.

Béhathook Cove: Breeze O'Keefe screamed. She had suppressed the natural release, trying to control the pain, to not let the women, crowding around her like dissenting crows, see her weakness. After all, she was the witch they talked about over tea in bright kitchens on dark nights, when they could see the flicker from the fire pit down by the point...*Breeze O'Keefe's cavorting with the Evil One, dancing in the firelight.* They never inquired if Breeze danced because she was happy. Never asked if her songs were of joy or longing. Was there poetry or beauty? The small circle of vultures, dressed in dark shawls, bent down, watching Aunt Liza with her hand up Breeze's vagina, attempting to manipulate the baby. A breech birth is a sure sign of the Devil at work. The breech position must be altered to let the Lord's light shine on a smiling face at the moment of birth or the baby will curse the village.

Aunt Liza had been up-over in the berry patches when summoned to Breeze's bedside. She had arrived in a rush, didn't take time to wash off the berry stains, so it was hard to tell if the colour smeared to her elbows was blood or berry juice, nor did it matter as long as the baby could be turned. The future of the village might depend on the skill of the midwife. Whispered prayers might help so the women bent over the body, clutching rosaries and crosses, swaying to the rhythm of the familiar words...*Hail Mary, full of grace, the Lord is with thee*...Mary, the Mother of All, was called upon to intercede in the birth, not for Breeze's salvation, but to defeat the curse before it could be loosed upon their village. Not a hand soothed her brow or wiped away the perspiration. No kind words of encouragement to ease her pain. If Breeze prayed it was for death and deliverance. But she could no longer suppress the scream and cried out in agony, a wail to chill even their hearts of stone.

Mother O'Keefe rocked by the fire, chilled by fears of her own even on a summer night when the world rested between agonies of nature. She was pierced to the heart by her daughter's scream but felt no sympathy for her ordeal. She was a bastard child who put herself in jeopardy by cavorting with Lliam Dwyer. The Dwyer name was like an oath spoken in the darkness when the speaker could not reveal true feelings. Malich Dwyer was her own curse, just another one to brood over and bury in the crypt of the mind.

Sean O'Keefe had been away on one of his damned voyages when Breeze was conceived. Margaret Dwyer, pregnant with Lliam by Sean O'Keefe, was distant and untouchable. Malich was a brute of a man whose strength was his self-righteous manhood, not his Christian Bible. But that night, as Breeze laboured to save her child, their world was brooding for another reason.

Over the horizon a tropical depression approached the coast, not uncommon in summer. Storms regularly assault the Rock from all directions and the people weather the onslaught and get on with life. Breeze would live or die, but the baby had to be turned. What to do with another bastard was only one more issue to be decided, but in a remote outpost, with no support from the outside world, babies, no matter their origin, were accepted, raised and nurtured for the future of the outport. The Lord would look after their immortal souls, but the approaching storm was an omen.

Breeze O'Keefe herself was a breech birth, delivered the hard way on another night of storm and trembling souls, and Brigid never fully recovered. She could blame all her woes on that, the storm and Sean O'Keefe's absence. Breeze's wild behavior was attributed to her unfortunate entrance into their world. Many of the crones claimed they had predicted a bad outcome and those in attendance at the screaming, bloody birth, testified that the baby leered at them like Satan in triumph escaping the Angel's sword. Once cursed, never blessed. Aunt Liza herself had predicted this baby's evil coming, like a pestilence waiting over the horizon to strike at the worst time.

That night the somnolent Newfoundland coast was wrapped in a gauzy pall of humidity. It didn't feel like the familiar fog: moist like their fog but too warm, and close enough to grasp. The outports were hushed, battening down for what they could feel was coming; didn't need a barometer to tell them. Weather reports were sketchy at best, reporting storms along the Atlantic Seaboard a hit and miss affair. No one paid much attention to broadcasts from Britain about storms ravaging the West Indies. Days could pass before storm watchers located the depression or predicted its track. Hurricanes were wild, unknown currents of air and seas gone mad, covering hundreds of miles. Sailors watched and waited, so did the folks at home, all praying the other swam above the tempest until it was over and the world returned to normal.

The crones attending the birth fingered their beads a little faster as they added the expected tempest to their concerns for deliverance from evil. Aunt Liza concentrated on the unborn child, delicately prodding the wee thing to turn, to tumble and reverse whatever it had done to get into the predicament. The hours dragged on and passed midnight. Crones came and went. Brigid dozed in her rocking chair and started at every outcry, or blinked awake when a woman came or left, sometimes leaving a cup of tea on the stove beside her or tending the fire to keep the water boiling. Mother O'Keefe tried to pray, to say the words to allay her fear that, no matter the outcome of the dreadful night, her world was collapsing. Gerald was gone...No strong son-in-law to assure her declining years. Her daughter was a lost soul, about to drop another mouth to feed and Brigid didn't have the will or the words to convince the Lord to intercede on her behalf. Once in the night she dreamed the cursed child was born dead and she awoke relieved, lapsing into a wakeful stupor, almost neutral in her thoughts, until she heard Breeze cry out again and knew the battle was still engaged. Towards an indifferent dawn she opened her eyes when she heard a baby's piercing cry. Within the hour the leading wall of the tropical depression would strike the coast.

Sheen's Cove Dawn: No one had slept. No one bothered to tend the fire. It was too warm and close for a fire; it was time to keep silent, brooding like the mauzy weather, the fishermen of the family harbouring the fears of what was to come. Lliam did not fear the coming storm or appreciate its consequences. He had little practical experience dealing with the consequences of fickle nature. He had been a bystander at the fall hurricane, pressed into action by Malich as an indentured servant. His fear was the storm within, sensing a climax, analyzing the rising action, but not knowing the plot.

Doyle feared everything aberrant in their fragile world. He had witnessed Gerald taken from them in a grizzly way, at once hating his brother but also needing his strength, another lost soul without the other's prodding and guidance. He feared Malich also, jumped to his commands because he knew the old man would knock him down with no remorse. But he knew something was about to happen. The choices were many but he dwelt on only two...He'd kill Lliam or Lliam would kill him...The approaching summer cyclone was just another storm to be weathered.

Garret, sensitive to any danger to his fragile family, wept silently inside because he saw cruel chaos, felt the dark wings of doom hovering. There was no escape, only the inevitable catastrophe. He sensed it would be his family as the wall of chaos approached.

Malich, restless and pacing all night, stood on the shore rocks at the tide line, facing the grey cloud wall on the horizon. The dark shape of Fogo Island to the east had been blocked out. The storm front had arrived and the nagging fear, that had been gnawing at Malich for two days, came crashing home. He had ordered the boys to remove most of the shores holding up the hull in order to build the cradle and the skidway. At that moment Malich realized they were cursed but he would not relent. "B'yes! Get up. Shores!" Hardly had the words left his mouth when the first blast of wind hit. The timing was merely unfortunate, unless there was a malevolent force at play, just waiting for frail man to falter. The rush of wind coincided with high tide.

The first gust picked up surface water and flung it like pebbles at the brothers scrambling to answer Malich's cry. Their campsite disintegrated, items were flung over the ledge rocks in a tumbling clatter of pots and pails. Garret, attempting to salvage his precious implements, stumbled over the dormant fire pit, disturbing deep coals that blazed up in the wind setting fire to their canvas shelter. Doyle, bouncing around trying to pull on a boot, was knocked over, striking his shoulder on a rock, breaking his collarbone. In agony he crawled, boots in hand, to the shelter of the schooner where he sat, dazed and bleeding. Lliam, amazed at the savage fury of the wind, flung himself on the ground, protecting his head from flying debris.

The masts of the schooner were bending and whipping about because the shrouds had not been tightened. It was to be one of their chores that day. The hull vibrated with the pressure on the rigging. At a higher gust the main mast splintered at the deck and crashed over the side, snapping in half when the tip hit the rocks. The falling mast had missed Malich by inches as he dragged a timber under the hull to shore up their trembling boat.

Malich was yelling over the wind, gesturing to his dumb sons to get more timbers, cursing them for louts and cowards. A second, stronger blast of wind tore across the narrow cove, pushing more water onto the shore in an endless wave that could not retreat. A flood tide flowed ashore, foaming and jumping over the rocks, the foam picked up and added to the spume so that the air and sea became one: salt laden, un-breathable. A torrent of stinging hail was added to the onslaught, then the deluge of rain and hail, like a water-wall suddenly released from a bursting dam. A deluge so powerful the gale was dulled momentarily.

Garret and Lliam, pummeled by the ice pellets, were flattened where they lay, gasping for air. Lliam could hear the large hail drumming on the deck of the schooner, booming like a beaten Irish drum, the sound of doom designed by the Loyal Orange Order to send terror through Irish Catholic hearts. The rain returned, pouring down, obliterating the site.

Lliam cowered under his arms as the rain forced its way into his nose and eyes. He had to gag to breath, and still the drumming sounded on the hull. All was water and noise, no definition between ocean and land. And when the thrumming of doom eased, the wind gained ascendency and the rain blew horizontally. Lliam dared to raise his head long enough to freeze the scene.

Malich, in the protected lee of the hull, was fighting with the broken mast, trying in vain to hoist its bulk to make a support. There was Doyle, in pain, crawling under the hull to help his father. The pair struggled and cursed and swore at each other in a tangle of rigging, tripping, falling gaining inches, but the mast section was too heavy.

Lliam knew his duty was to run forward, to help his father, but he was paralyzed by the savagery of the moment. His arms and his legs had no power to make his body rise. He crawled forward but another onslaught of wind and rain swept across the rocks and forced his head down; face down, crying and screaming into the rocks, his arms flung over his head. He heard a cracking sound and something crashed beside him; the foremast...The crosstree struck his exposed head. If only he'd remained behind...Then he was unconscious.

Garret was dragging a timber toward the hull when the third and heaviest gust of wind slammed into the site. He was thrown down and blinded by the cold wave that roared out of the cove and dashed over the rocks, foaming about the few remaining shores of the schooner. He only had time to see a timber fall, then another, then cold, salty darkness as he was lifted and carried back, but even in the chaos of water he heard the moan of rending timbers, and felt the grinding twist of her keel through the rocks. He clung to his timber, mouthing a silent prayer. Then, like thunder, he heard a great weight fall on the rocks.

A body was carried to Garret on the incoming flood. Instinctively he clutched the body and held on for what seemed like an eternity, then the current changed as the flood tide swept back into the cove. He knew it was Lliam's body he was holding, sensed there was life in the body. He held on and held on; he thought he was screaming for Lliam to hang on too. The wind piped higher. Another wave roared and crashed ashore. He could hear the hull moving, grinding on the rocks. He could not see the schooner but he knew she was down. His first thought was for his father and brother. He prayed to Mary and all the Saints, fearing the Lord had forsaken his children, until he willed his mind into a secret place, the place he went when life was a torment of burning flesh and dumb desire...A mountaintop, a refuge too high for the ruthless sea to snatch away all the souls he gathered about him to face eternity. It was peaceful, cold, but not so bad; not the penetrating chill of the coastal clime, and the air was fresh; no tang of salt or iodine; no smell of rotting fish or dried fish; no stinking mass of fish guts, nor choke of cod oil. It was a neutral domain; no need for trees, there was nothing to build; no angry god or luring devil to confound the simple mind that only longed for love and freedom from pain, a place where he could sing and be heard, to express his love for Breeze...

And, as suddenly as it arrived, the storm was gone, retreating to confound other coves. In a later age of science it would be called a microburst, an isolated cell spun off from a larger depression. The morning sun, breaking out behind the shredded clouds, mocked the scene below. The shriek of the wind was gone also, but the ocean continued to thunder and roar, shaking the rocks where the survivors lay trembling at the power of their deadly ocean. A fisherman expects to drown at sea, not on land. Accepts the risk that his boat might fail him at sea, not on land.

Garret raised his head, taking in the site one important item at a time. His brother Lliam lay beside him, breathing but not moving. Blood trickled through his matted hair and down his neck. The blood was a good sign. At intervals a wave crashed into the cove and drove over the rocks, swirling the flotsam, large timbers and small bits. Garret held on tight, one arm around the timber, the other clutching his brother, the only living thing he could see, holding on to a life desperately the way Gerald had held Doyle from being swept over the rail of the doomed *Margaret & Maude*. When the spent wave receded he followed it with his eyes. The *Black Fenian* lay on her side, as he expected, but broadside to the shore where the retreating flood tide had dropped her and then abandoned the hulk that would never be launched by mortal man...*and the Devil take the bloody thing,* he said to himself.

The tide was falling and each wave fell short until no debris swirled around the site. Garret listened and looked for signs of Malich or Doyle. There was no sound but the waves. No cries for help. No curses or oaths. Lliam's flowing blood was a good thing but Malich's silence was an omen. If he could speak, Garret would have called out just to break the spell. He feared the ocean had swept them away as proof that the curse was at work and the evil of Seth Sheen was on the cove. How else to explain the timing, only a day before the launch, at the highest tides of the cycle? How else to credit the timing of the wind roaring ashore at the precise moment the diurnal tide was at it's peak? *Surely a loving God would not visit such ill favour on His simple folk,* Garret reasoned. Only evil intent could command the sea to rip away the souls of men who only wanted to do the right thing for their family. It was so unjust. Where was their God on such a day? Garret, in his simple way, felt forsaken. If he could speak he might have cursed a Lord who allowed such a thing.

Garret got shakily to his feet, standing in the aftermath of a titanic battle. Nothing was as it had been before the onslaught: tools, gear, and timbers were scattered about or lost. Blind Harry, from Tilting, veteran of the Great War, reluctantly shared his feelings after surviving the bloody Battle of the Somme, and Garret, who had witnessed his own version of trial by fire, understood what survival meant, and saw at his feet a small version of the carnage war and the elements can deliver, swiftly and without regard for good or evil. He did not praise the Lord for deliverance, but he did curse the fate he now had to face alone, and he felt utterly alone.

Alone or not, Lliam was breathing in choking spasms. He tended to Lliam, probing the gash on his head, parting the matted red hair to assess the damage. He turned Lliam's head so that his mouth was clear of the seaweed mass, packing the seaweed on the spot to stem the flow of blood. There was nothing to cover his body but the sun was warm and that was all he could do for his brother.

Garret forced himself toward the fallen hull, afraid he'd find nothing, fearing the bodies of his brother and father had been washed out to sea. Or perhaps they had been floated inland, flung over the rocks and were lying in the juniper matt. He stole a glance toward the fringe of stunted trees, half expecting to see a body hanging like a bait capelin in a mangled spruce, but that was only a diversion. There *was* a rag of charred sailcloth that struck fear into him because it looked like a shroud waiting for the first body. He entered the shadow of the fallen hull. How pathetic the little schooner looked, just short of glory, so close to her intended home. *So what,* he thought, *it's only the fate that waits any ship launched by man. When her time's up, short or long lived, it makes no difference.* A ship is born to die, like himself, like his family. Breeze and the baby...

"Help me, Brother. God, help me."

Garret found Doyle in the gloom, pinned in the rocks, saved by a shore timber that could not save the boat. Garret wiggled his way under the hull until he reached Doyle.

"*Ahh,* Garret, get me out, ol' son... oh, please, dear Brother, get me out from here."

Doyle was pinned in the broken rocks, arms upwards as if he'd flung himself away as the hull collapsed. The big timber had taken some of the weight. Garret gripped Doyle's arm reassuringly. Doyle groaned to spur Garret to perform a miracle and release him from the trap. Garret threw himself at the task, thinking about Lliam's story of the snared rabbit, how it struggled to free itself, but he had no voice to encourage Doyle to help win his own freedom. He feared Doyle was broken inside, too smashed up to help. He pushed and pulled at cold stones, found one that moved, tugged and pushed until it rolled free.

"That's it, Brother. Get me out...I'll die, the pain...Garret, the pain..."

Garret knew that, but wished his brother would either help or remain quiet. He tested every rock he could reach and when he found one that jiggled at all he worked away at it until he could feel a way out. He began dragging loosened rocks into the light, flung them aside and crawled back under. He wondered about his father's fate. At intervals he thought he heard breathing and once heard a moan from further under the hull, but rocks and timbers blocked the way so he concentrated on Doyle.

As he worked he paused to check on Lliam. The bleeding slowed then stopped. Lliam continued to breath, but slower, hesitating as if he might stop. Garret would push a rock to the light then prod his brother until the breathing picked up. He stripped off his own sodden coat and covered Lliam who felt cold to the touch.

Garret had to rest. He'd be no use to his brothers if he killed himself with exhaustion, but as he sat beside Lliam, desperate for some antidote to death by neglect, he had a sudden shock. He was taking rocks from under the hull to free Doyle but if he was to dig for Malich he had to put the rocks and timbers back to keep the hull from dropping further. He needed Lliam's help. The will, driven by desperation, was waning as his resources were spent. He needed water. *Funny,* he thought, *only a moment ago we were swimming in salt water enough to float the damned boat.* He'd give a quintal of hard won fish for a sip of sweet water.

Lliam stirred. Garret put a hand on his shoulder until his brother lay still. He didn't know how badly Lliam was injured, but guessed that he needed to be still to heal, or until he died peacefully. There were no other options.

Garret was exhausted but began dragging rocks back into the shadows, piling them purposely to create a pillar of stones under the turn of the bilge. "What are you doing, fool?" yelled Doyle. Garret could only gesture with both hands, holding something up, up and up, until Doyle closed his eyes.

It took a precious hour for Garret to reconstruct the supports. Doyle seemed to be unconscious. For a moment he thought Doyle had died, and felt ashamed that he experienced a rush of relief. Then Doyle moaned and moved, eyes wide in fear, as if awakening from a nightmare, clawing at the rocks trying to pull himself free, flailing at the hull only inches from his face, waving at Garret to get on with the job all the while moaning and cursing. Garret held his suffering brother's head in both hands until Doyle stopped thrashing.

One more rock held Doyle captive. Garret pounded away on the rock with a length of timber. The effort almost finished him but the rock finally spun away under the keel. He could see all of Doyle's body, his hips pressed into the jagged rocks, legs oddly twisted, blood seeping through his torn trousers. It looked bad and when Garret took Doyle's arms and began to tug, Doyle screamed out so that Garret let go. He lay face to face with his brother, both panting with the pain.

After awhile Doyle fell into shock: shivering, eyes glazed, no longer exhorting Garret to free him. Doyle may have given up but Garret rested in the silence until he felt strong enough to try again. With all his strength he pulled and pulled on Doyle's arms. Inch by inch, Garret dragged his brother from the shadows. Clear of the bulwarks he let Doyle rest in the warmth of the sun. Garret wanted to rest also but Lliam was trying to sit up. Garret reached deeper into his reserves, crawled to Lliam's side and touched his brother's face.

Lliam focused on Garret, the question in his eyes. Garret shrugged and pointed at Doyle now visible in the rubble of the scattered work site. "Doyle's alive?" Lliam whispered through cracked lips. Garret nodded. "And Malich?" Garret made the gesture with his hands and shoulders that said 'maybe'. "Where is he?"

As an answer, Garret sighed and returned to the hull. Lliam stood up with the help of a broadaxe, stopping to prod Doyle, found his heart beat and assessed his twisted legs. Obviously Doyle's legs were mangled beyond help, his pelvic area crushed, but there was not much blood. Lliam feared the real damage was inside where the blood was collecting. He followed Garret into the shadows.

They reached Malich's body after two difficult hours of clawing and hammering at the rocks with the axe, timbers and bare hands. With every rock moved the hull trembled above them as if balanced precariously. Lliam experienced the claustrophobia that seized his guts and turned them in a knot. Chills raced up and down his spine and paralyzed his senses. Garret was beyond fear. They inched ahead, Lliam calling out to his father. The reply was a choking moan that sounded like an oath.

They found Malich in a cleft of solid rock, on his back, head turned towards them, lips pulled back and teeth clenched in pain. His breath came in short stabs. Blood, pink and frothy, bubbled from his mouth. Dark blood ran from his ears and from a deep gash on his forehead, coursing through his black beard. He opened his eyes, looking from one son to the other, not pleading, just looking. The grimace on his altered face never changed, like a hideous mask, as if he was frozen in pain.

Lliam and Garret were helpless to do anything for their dying father. They were so confined by rocks below, and a wooden wall above, it was difficult to move their arms. Three pairs of eyes searched for answers. Finally Malich conquered the pain and cursed them properly. "Damn you b'yes, for louts. Levers...Levers an' wedges..."

It was a relief to be ordered to do the obvious. There was nothing else to offer their father but half-hearted assurances that they'd try.

It took precious time to wiggle free from Malich's prison, move Doyle's broken body away from the hull, make him as comfortable as possible and assess their chances. Doyle was mercifully in shock, shivering and talking nonsense, his only solace was the warmth of the sun and Garret's coat. *When the sun goes down he'll die,* mused Lliam, regretting the probable loss of more family, wishing he had not harboured such hatred for his brute of a father and loutish brothers. Really, Doyle was not such a bad sort, just rough-edged due to a life of hard work on the margins. Given a chance he could be a family man; free of his father he might even become a loving husband. There was Mildred O'Hara...Lliam realized he was fantasizing, distracting his mind from the reality. "He needs water. I'll go to the pond."

Garret nodded agreement. He was wandering about the site, picking up anything that might make a fire. For Garret it was more instinct than a practical necessity. It might be some small comfort for Doyle, but they had nothing to cook, nothing to boil water in, unless Lliam found the iron kettle. But there was no tea to brew.

Once more Lliam climbed the rocky ledge and headed inland on a mission for his family. He found the iron kettle in a juniper bush where it had been flung by a wave, marveling that the heavy kettle could be so far from the site, but then the power of the water had knocked over their schooner. Their schooner? Sheen's gift to the world that killed three sons, two daughters, a wife, and probably one, at least, of his own family. He knew Malich could not live. Doyle will wish he were dead. Garret deserved to live and be happy with Breeze. What of his own fate? He didn't believe in fate. He found a pannican and walked up the gentle grade through the coarse grass that looked soft and inviting. He could lie down and sleep, and maybe when he woke it would all be gone. He felt exhausted, dizzy from the blow to the head, not in pain so much as numb, numb in the head and limbs and there was a heavy presence making the effort of walking more difficult. Reality was weighing him down, a weight greater than physical trauma. He was walking away from a disaster: the finishing acts of his family's story, and there was nothing he could do.

Malich will die. Doyle will probably die, or worse, be an invalid for life. His writer's brain said he should eulogize his dying family, but to what purpose? It would not give his wasted life meaning or help the family in any material way. At the back of his aching head he knew that only the love of Breeze O'Keefe could give him a reason to go on. If he could not turn her heart, what then? He didn't know. He reached the boggy pond, knelt on the spongy verge, and used the pannican to fill the kettle. He heard a sound in the thicket near the edge of the clearing. A hare hopped away with a peculiar limping hop. One long jump and the beast was swallowed by the purple shade of the forest. The shadows were long, daylight was waning, the pleasant summer day would come to an end and more of his family would be gone.

Garret had been busy. Using the axe and a rasp he found in the scatter of rusting tools, he performed the miracle of fire. The blessed sun had dried enough beach wrack and dead grass for kindling, patiently sparking and blowing, Garret was able to get a decent fire going with pieces of wood that survived the flood. A wedge survived and he hesitated to burn it, but what use was one wedge when they needed a hundred to lift the hull an inch?

Doyle appeared to be transfixed by the flames, lips moving in silent prayer. Garret was standing with his back to the fire, watching Doyle suffer, tears in his expressive eyes, gazing from the declining sun to the darkening hull.

Lliam poured water into the pannican and offered it to Doyle who held the tin on his lap, staring blankly into the turbid water. Lliam placed the kettle in the coals and stood beside Garret, sharing a moment of understanding. "Garret, there's nothing we can do, ol' son. There's no levers, or wedges. Only scattered tools an' no time, even if we had the strength..."

Garret gripped Lliam's arm tightly to say he agreed and turned to the fire, looking deeply into the flames. He knew the answer. Presently he took the pannican from Doyle and made his way over the rocks to the fallen hull. Garret could never tell Lliam in words what transpired between father and son, but Garret returned from the mission grimly focused on what had to be done.

Béhathook Cove The Storm: The baby's cries of freedom were muffled by the first gust of wind that slammed over the peninsula and shook the house. The last of the crones to leave the bedside cowered in the kitchen with Mother O'Keefe, afraid to tempt the gale that rocked the village and sent people and livestock running for shelter. The concerns of the villagers for the fate of a cursed child were justified, they murmured. The shrieking wind also justified the omens visited on them for days as Breeze O'Keefe approached her term. It was the curse that the elders prayed over in their enclaves while the men went about their business, ever watchful for the true signs. And when the depression bar appeared over the horizon they no longer held malignant thoughts about a wee baby, it was just the way of the sea.

The sea rewarded them when they worked hard, but the sea could take away every small gain if they let their guard down. The broody calm was the final sign and they had done what they could to secure homes and boats against the harsh reality of their coast. An Atlantic weather breeder was not the enemy if they were prepared, so while the women worried their beads and worried about an evil they could not see, fishermen put an extra turn on a mooring, led more lines ashore to hold the heavy power skiffs, and heaved more wire cables to hold down the most exposed houses.

When the storm hit, Breeze was alone in her room with her bloody child close to her breasts, the warmest most secure anchorage for a newly launched life. Baby Brigid was snugged into the safe harbour of her mother's strong arms and had no fear.

Breeze spent a long day alone with her baby, but it was the first day she had been truly by herself, free from demands of the village, the elders and the Dwyers, and from Mother O'Keefe. The village would see to Mother O'Keefe, the crones commiserating with the old woman for her lot in life. With her sea captain gone, her daughter birthing a bastard child, they had much to share of hardship and misfortune. Breeze's only allies, Thelma and Mildred O'Hara, would arrive later in the day with tea and bread and a simple knitted gift for the baby.

Sheen's Cove Another Dawn: Doyle died during the night, silently, uncomplaining, where he sat propped against a rock, beside the fire that could not give what the spirit lacked. Garret and Lliam had kept a vigil in turn but neither knew when the last breath left Doyle's tortured body. They could have slept aboard the schooner, on the precious sails in comfort, but neither man would even consider lying above their dying father, in the cursed hull. So they had watched with Doyle for the bitter end. His trial was over, the judgment passed somewhere beyond Sheen's Cove.

Garret covered the head and upper body with his coat, leaving Doyle's shattered legs as a testament to his brother's suffering. Lliam almost wept to see the evidence of their folly. What had they done wrong? Malich ordered them to take down the shores too soon so

Malich must bear the responsibility. Duty absolves the underlings for doing what they are told. Truth was, Lliam wanted to object because he could see the problem. They had built the cradle strong enough to carry the *Black Fenian* into her element, but the cradle, constructed with every precious timber available, was meant for compression weight, not shear strength. But Lliam was afraid of the consequences of objecting, as were Doyle and Garret. Malich gambled that they could launch at highest tide, before a storm could catch them unprepared.

Lliam waded into the shallows to hunt for mussels while Garret crawled under the hull to take Malich water. Then, with Malich tended to in the most primitive way, Garret collected spruce buds and roots to make a tea. It was bubbling in the kettle when Lliam returned with a few mussels for their meal. The grainy shells went into the kettle with the buds and roots; it no longer mattered what combination of nature's bounty kept them from starvation.

"Is Malich alive?"

Garret nodded, his eyes conveying all the hurt and heartache of coastal dwellers who strive to earn a hard living, stealing away what they can from the elements.

"We have to do something, Garret. He shouldn't suffer so."

Garret fished in the steaming kettle with a forked stick and came up with an opened mussel shell, offered it to Lliam and fished for another. They chewed and swallowed, spit out grains of sand and tossed the empty shells back into the brew.

"A weevilly biscuit would go good about now."

Garret grinned his twisted grin and fished up two more mussels. Lliam hoisted the kettle and poured. They shared sips of scalding, bitter water and relished whatever was in the ghastly mixture.

"Father's too tough for his own bloody good."

Garret grinned at that too, sniffed and brushed away the tears. Lliam wished he had enough compassion to cry for the brute. He dwelt on the thought for a few moments, but realized it was pointless. Malich was the tyrant who made his life miserable, but he should not suffer and there was no way to comfort him in the last hours. How many hours more?

Malich would be cold even as the summer sun rode higher in the sky. *A pillow for his head at least*, thought Lliam, instead he said, "We'll need to make shrouds," without realizing he had broken their silence. There were many sounds of life around them. In the sunshine of the scrub above, there were birds going about the routine of cleaning up after the storm. Black birds circled, calling out, calling off competitors, knowing death was on the land and the cycle was assured. Summer waves frothed busily into the cove, dashing importantly around the rocks. The wind sighed through the bushes and stirred the ashes of the fire. Hidden by the common sounds of a normal world were the muffled curses from under the fallen schooner, the boat a symbol of aberrant human endeavor.

"Garret, we're the dumbest sons-a-bitches in the world. There's a whole pile of lovely clean sails in the boat."

Garret looked shocked, not at their stupidity but at the suggestion. It took Lliam several moments to comprehend. "Yes, I know, Breeze made those sails. They're sacred, right? But what good are they now? The damned boat will never sail. The bloody thing's only fit to burn!"

Garret's expression changed so suddenly that Lliam was shocked in turn when he finally understood what was on Garret's mind.

"Malich told you to burn the boat."

Garret and Lliam stood between the smouldering fire and the hull, the dying sun casting long shadows over the rocks and up the steeply canted deck, their rigid bodies performing a static puppet show, static because neither wanted to move.

The debate had taken hours but the words were few. Who would do the deed? How should they choose? Drawing lots was too crass, Lliam had argued. Garret had indicated that because he was the elder brother it was his duty. Lliam countered that since he was less favoured than Garret, he could do the deed with a clear heart. The debate had also been about Doyle's burial shroud. Garret would not hear of using the creamy jib to wrap the body of the man Breeze O'Keefe loathed, at least that's how Lliam interpreted his mute brother's body language.

"She hates us all, come to that, except you, Garret." Lliam wished he had not said the words aloud because it caused Garret extreme grief and more tears than he could afford to shed.

Both were weak from hunger. Leaking blood and body fluids from old burns caked Garrets shirt. The tight, shiny skin was still fragile and the slightest aberrant move broke the patches apart, like ice panes separating in the wind. Lliam was still in mild shock but his thinking was clear, he said. He tried to appear strong for Garret's sake. It was not fair that Garret should be left to shoulder the issues of the family, what was left of a family that required strong backs and decision making, now and into the bleak future. *Who of them can provide for six souls?* Lliam asked himself. The six included a baby born to Breeze by now and one way or another Breeze and her baby were an integral part of the family, as was her mother, for all purposes an invalid. Grandmother Dwyer had to be cared for and eased into her own passing with some dignity. Margaret, Breeze and Garret were the new family structure, the backbone of the unit. Lliam failed to count himself in the tally because he did not see himself as the Patriarch, or even a plank in the structure...Lliam had vowed to leave the village at the first opportunity, with or without Breeze. He had told her as much at their first meeting. He said he had come back for her, but the truth was, he had returned because he had no place else to go after Boston. Where would he run next? Ireland, to die in the Rebellion, was his last option.

He'd met with IRA recruiters in Boston, at the time rejecting their politics and talk of violence, their pleas for cash to support the cause, the threats of retaliation visited on expats who refused to heed the call of the Old Sod. *It's not my country, and not my war,* he had argued. The unequal punch up in the ally was only a playful reminder, the IRA men said, but it left a deep impression on Lliam's sense of anarchy. He had fled his tyrannical home as a young man, rejecting the harsh values of the outport, which meant rejecting his ancestors also, but what else did he have but history? The Irish struggle was deep in every son and daughter of Ireland. The Irish Free State was the mantra that drove them on decade after decade of Risings and defeats, bloodshed, retaliation and terror. Breeze had that spark also and he envied her strength of will even as it made his life more difficult. Breeze would make a wonderful Irish soldier fighting for freedom from the British yoke.

In Boston he had also met young men who were so fired by the notion of freedom they were leaving for Spain to join the resistance, the Foreign Brigades: hordes of delusional young hotheads who believed that a pure heart withstands the bullets of a Fascist regime. The drunken arguments amidst the conservatives were intense, often ending in bloodshed if the conservatives took exception to being branded Nazi ideologues or Fascist sympathizers. The terms Nazis and Fascists were new in the American States, but certainly not the ideals. The fierce young men destined to die in the defense of Madrid, were well bloodied before they boarded the boats in the dark of night, on their way to fight a foe they neither understood nor could defeat. Did he regret refusing to be drawn into the conflicts in Ireland or Spain? He had often asked himself that question, began stillborn novels about the honour of self-sacrifice for a cause, but realized he had neither the will nor the courage to die for someone else's freedom. His excuse was, his heart's desire to be with his true love in a remote backward outpost on the fringe of the civilized world. Now, faced with the decision to murder Malich, his tormentor, and the reality that he had been rejected by Breeze, the notion of joining the Brotherhood seemed a way out of his dilemma. Distasteful or not, he was Irish...Garret touched his arm and jarred him back to the present reality.

Together they opened the hatches, first the main hatch to the cavernous hold, careful not to drop the planks and alarm Malich. Next the fo'c'sle to reach the sails...On this sad day, the beautiful sails were to be only artful wicks in a lantern that would light the night sky for miles around.

The awful deed weighed heavy on both men. *It's a tragedy that sons have to kill their father to be merciful,* Lliam wanted to say. Malich was suffering. Malich had commanded Garret to do the thing, overruling Lliam's notion of summoning help from one of the villages on the Western shore...Lliam had crawled under the boat in a last effort to do the right thing, only to be cursed as a coward. Malich was too broken to be rescued for a life of an invalid, he said, even if he did survive the ordeal...There was no choice left. There never was an option. Lliam had spoken to his father harshly: "Malich? Father, can you hear me? Okay, I'm going to set fire to this cursed, goddamned boat, and may the Good Lord have mercy on your black soul." *All our souls*, he wanted to say, for he was in fact killing a man in cold blood and Garret was his accomplice. A can of kerosene had survived in the lazarette with the lanterns because Malich wouldn't allow them to waste the precious oil. *If it's too dark to work then you should be asleep.*

They hauled the heavy sails from the fo'c's'le to the hold and spread them out to best effect. Lliam felt sick as he poured the kerosene over the beautiful sails, regretting the foul stain on the canvas Breeze had worked so hard to shape into wings for the *Black Fenian*. Whatever her dark beginning, the little schooner was to be adorned with white wings of glory, thrashing her way to windward, throwing diamonds away in the sun with rainbows of spray as the sailor's reward. The stench of kerosene was overpowering, the billow of creamy white sails entrancing. *What a dichotomy of life*, was all Lliam could think of as he waited for Garret to bring the spark.

"Where is Garret with the damned torch?" Lliam heard a sound below his feet, the guttural voice, and scratching on the hull. The wind had got up and was playing tricks, swirling into the dark hold until edges of the sails fluttered fitfully. Was Malich sending a message? *Get on with it damn you,* which is what he'd expect from the man. Or was he having a last minute regret, asking for deliverance. *Why is Garret taking so long to fetch the bloody brand?*

Malich Dwyer's funeral pyre was spectacular, but his eulogy was brief. What could sons say about their own father having just burned him alive? The raw cotton sails, doused with kerosene, burned so fiercely and so fast that Lliam barely escaped from the hold. The night wind had gone from a fresh breeze to near gale in the time it took for the dry hull to be engulfed. The blaze created it's own fire storm and the fire makers had to drag Doyle's body further away or poor Doyle would have joined his father in ashes...It was an undignified retreat and Lliam regretted not adding Doyle's corpse to the hold. He would have said as much to Garret to relieve the tension of watching their father die, but Garret was near collapse with grief from having to brutalize Doyle; though dead, he had shape and form, sitting rigid as he was, eyes open, glinting in the fire light.

Grizzly and *Macabre* were words Lliam later added to the lexicon he used to describe the scene, and the panic when they realized Doyle's skin was beginning to smoke and bubble. Lliam even tried to summon remorse for Malich's demise and was angered by the fact, that in the middle of his near breakthrough to the compassionate son, Garret had run to his dead brother, frantic to pull him away, traumatized by his own memories of the fire on the *Margaret & Maude*. It was Gerald who should have been going home to marry Breeze O'Keefe and continue the Dwyer clan. Garret blamed himself, his carelessness caused the terrible accident. He had killed his older brother with fire in the galley, and he was killing his father with fire, and he was damned if he'd let Doyle cook in the conflagration.

Garret had given in to Malich's demands, carrying the burning brand to Lliam, but Garret purposely dropped the stick as he was handing it to Lliam. Lliam stumbled in the hold trying to retrieve the torch, to be responsible for the deed, but in the end there was no distinction, no one more guilty, and no one clear of conscience. The deed was done and they could only stand in awe of the towering blaze wondering how long it would take for Malich to die?

"He was a good man, in his way," offered Lliam as a eulogy. Garret nodded. "A good provider." Garret nodded that he agreed. "But he was a drunken brute, for all that..." Garret shook his head violently. "I'm sorry, Brother. I won't say another word."

As wild as the fire was and as high as the swirling flames roared into the black night, the hull was burning from the top down. Malich was pinned in the damp rocks with the cool night wind blowing around him; the fire had to burn through thick ceiling timbers, frames and hull planks before it reached the body. "If there's a merciful God, please make him dead," Lliam said aloud, despite his vow to remain silent for Garret's sake. Garret could not utter his own laments but there was much Garret could say with his eyes.

The fire burned on and on into the night. The brothers sat near Doyle, keeping watch in turn, dozing in fitful snatches, praying that Malich had died swiftly, knowing that it was not true. Two hours into the burn they thought they heard Malich cry out in agony, hoping it was a raven call, or a whale breeching in the Sound. They sat transfixed by the sight, their own bodies glowing in the flames as if favoured by a rising sun, but the heat could not banish the chill in their hearts. The wind blew the sparks inland in a never-ending stream of pyrotechnics until they feared the whole island may go up in flames.

In the third hour the wind increased, blowing embers and flaming pieces of canvas into the Sheen House. Flankers found dry wood, the wind did the rest, and in moments the Sheen House was an inferno to match the burning schooner, erasing decades of horrors inflicted by Seth Sheen.

Lliam regretted the loss of the Sheen family portraits. He had decided to take them back to Béhathook Cove to compare the images of Sheen's sons and daughters with his own family. As the fire consumed the sad remnants of the saga, he doubted it made any difference. Grandfather Dwyer was gone. He alone may have wanted some icon, a reminder of his younger days, although his memories of the episode in the journal seemed more than bittersweet. Grandmother Dwyer, if she knew, would not want to be reminded that her husband was an oath-driven philanderer, conspiring with the most evil man they knew; a man who was driven from the outport, driven mad by a hard life, driven to kill his own family one by one until only the derelict, Moses Sheen, remained: the Sheen who cursed the *Margaret & Maude* and killed her grandson. Gerald was the heir apparent to the patriarchy, continuing the line of Dwyers. The twin pillars of fire burned high into the night sky erasing many harsh truths, but emphasizing one clearly. If Garret or Lliam failed to produce male offspring the Dwyers of

Béhathook Cove would cease to exist.

A New Dawn: There was no sun, only heavy grey clouds and the promise of rain. When they could see the rocks below their feet they approached the place where they had cast their fortunes, gambled their futures and lost. All that was left was the shape of a boat. Not all: the blackened keel remained, and stubs of frames poking at the clouds so that the remains finally did resemble the carcass of a long rotting whale. Much of the ash had been blown inland to adorn the grass and juniper, dusting the black spruce, adding nutrients to the thin soil, but fouling the pond. And that is how the world renews itself.

Despite the heat of the conflagration the keel had not burned, proof that the boat was cursed and the fact would become legend. Of Malich's remains there was no sign. He was not given the final reward of being blown out to sea, but then, most fishermen pray that they live long enough to die ashore.

A fresh summer rainstorm kept them pinned down for hours and turned the burn site to stinking gray muck, forestalling any notion of sifting for Malich's bones. When the rain let up they hauled the heavy skiff to the edge of the rocks, and launched it off at high tide. There was little left to put aboard except the ship's wheel that Lliam clung to as if it was the only icon left of his life, an axe, a kettle of bitter spruce tea and Doyle's body. They propped him up in the bow to keep watch, regretting the fact since he seemed to *watch* their every move.

Lliam kept the skiff off the rocks while Garret prepared to start the engine. Garret was never allowed to operate the make'n'brake but he watched keenly as Malich performed the ritual that set the recalcitrant beast in motion...Lliam had no experience with the day-to-day skills of the fishermen, the necessary tasks that, though simple enough, could be the difference between routine and disaster. He'd only been away six years but it was a lifetime of education lost. Left on his own he would parish. With Breeze as a helpmate there was a chance. He could still be the wood worker, if not a fisherman. *Precise Muldoon, the village carpenter, never had to fish for a living,* he reasoned. Going about in boats, at the mercy of the cruel sea, was not absolutely necessary to feed a family. *A merchant made his way feeding off the fishermen, but the carpenter is an important part of the fabric of life in an outport...*These things he pondered as he skulled the heavy skiff and watched Garret go about the precise process of starting the engine.

Garret moved slowly, but confidently about the skiff, flipping a switch, adjusting the carburetor, filling the priming cup, moving the heavy flywheel to get the desired *sneeze* from the single piston. Satisfied, he tried to spin the wheel, lost his footing and fell heavily onto the floorboards. He looked up at Lliam apologetically, gesturing pathetically to his head, blaming himself for being an idiot. Truth was, he was too weakened to fling the wheel. "Garret, Ol' Son, let me."

Garret sat on the thwart, hanging his head between his knees. Blood was showing through his shirt were fragile skin had torn again. Lliam took his place at the flywheel, waiting for Garret to collect himself but the skiff was being blown towards the rocks, the swells would dash the wooden hull to pieces in a moment. Together they rowed to the center of the narrow cove. There was only enough sea room for a few moments of messing about with the engine so Garret sculled while Lliam positioned himself over the flywheel.

Lliam spilled much precious fuel into the bilge but with Garret pantomiming the process, Lliam was ready. His first attempt accomplished almost what had ended Garret's attempt. But with trial and error, investing all his remaining strength, Lliam succeeded in getting the engine to turn over, *putt-putting* twice. Garret signed, *repeat the process: but turn the wheel faster.* Lliam added more fuel to the cup, opened the valve, turned the wheel, got the *sneeze*, closed the valve and put a final effort into it. The rocks were getting closer and Garret was desperately sculling. Lliam heaved, the wheel kicked and the engine came alive. The skiff began moving immediately, but in the wrong direction. Lliam jumped to the stern, seized the tiller and turned the boat away from the rocks.

Garret, facing the stern, shipped the oars and gazed at the receding shore. Wisps of grey smoke rose up from the smouldering ruins of Sheen's House. Garret imagined they were the evil spirits of Sheen leaving the site once and for all. Of the schooner and their father, there was little to be seen other than the blackened keel. Lliam concentrated on the offer islands and refused to look back. He thought he was done with Sheen's Cove.

Béhathook Cove Same: Breeze ached in every part of her exhausted body, but she was bursting, but no one had thought to bring her the chamber pot. Margaret had brought over a bowl of broth earlier, and looked in but assumed Mildred would see to Breeze's needs. The pain was acute. Her belly and thighs were still covered in blood and what looked like white powder, but she was desperate for the loo and a bit of bread and butter. She pulled on her housecoat, wrapped the infant in clean flour bags, eased down the stairs and presented her baby to Mother O'Keefe. The old woman, brooding by the cold stove, barely acknowledged her daughter's presence. *By Mother's appearance you'd think she'd been through hell herself,* Breeze whispered to the baby.

The wood box was empty. "I'll bring wood in the once," she said, placing the tiny bundle on her mother's lap. Mother O'Keefe made no sign, but looked down at her wizened granddaughter with some curiosity. She had vowed to the crones not to touch the child until the priest arrived to pass judgment or bless the event. The crones agreed that it might take a ceremony to be sure no curse had found a home in the wee child. Prayers were being said in other kitchens when it was food, firewood and comfort the O'Keefe house needed...The men would have been more than willing to carry a pot of fish and potatoes, fetch in some firewood, even keep a regular rotation to fire the stove, but they were not consulted.

Breeze made it to the loo without being seen, managed an armload of wood from the stash on the bridge...She had split and piled a good measure well ahead of the event...Carrying only half her usual load, she eased the wood into the box and built up the fire. "I'll put the kettle on if you like, Mum."

"She resembles the O'Keefes."

"Bit early to tell, Mum, but she should look like a Dwyer, just not the right one...Is that what you mean to say?"

Mother O'Keefe rocked and looked, careful not to touch the baby in her lap. The baby, sensing the lack of good wishes perhaps, began to fuss, tiny fists flailing for her mother's warmth, red face knitted into a squalling ball that looked like a dried apple left too long behind the woodstove.

"There, there babe, just a moment while I fetch some bread." She sliced and buttered the bread then retrieved her newborn. She lay on the daybed with her breasts exposed trying to get the infant to latch on.

"You could cover up, case a neighbor walks in."

"Is Mildred comin'?" Breeze asked, ignoring the jibe.

"I told Mildred she'd not be needed, you'd be up an' around the once an' can do for us, like always."

It was no more than she expected. Her mother knew what a breech birth was like and what it can do to the body, it was her way of punishing Breeze and she'd just accept it, biding her time. "The men should be back from Change Islands by now," she offered...In her days of agony she had seen visions of fire and death, knew something had happened at Change Islands. In one vision the crones were swaying and chanting over a fire that suddenly blazed up and a dark form rose out of the fire shrouded in black smoke. She knew it wasn't Lliam or Garret so her mind was not that troubled.

"Pray one of'em has the good sense to claim you an' the child. I've some money put aside, Sean O'Keefe's small legacy, so if it comes to that, a dowry..."

"An' what then, Mum? We buy another Dwyer to fish an' do for us?"

"Use your reason, young lady. You got yourself into this pickle, an' now you got to pay the price."

"An' what price do we offer, an' who would you like to purchase?" Breeze knew the answer, but she was just reminding Mother O'Keefe about the cold way the two families had sorted through the Dwyer men the year before. Not yet aware of the newest disaster, old hurts and cold hearts could dwell in the stew of recriminations.

Breeze also knew there was no future for her in Béhathook Cove. That settled she had to reconcile the guilt for leaving her mother, the pain of leaving Garret and the reality that she would never give in to Lliam Dwyer's entreaties. The question remaining was, how to leave and when? The need for money was a larger obstacle. Mother O'Keefe might offer a dowry but could she be persuaded to finance her own daughter's escape from bondage? Breeze knew the answer to that too. There was only one solution: work harder, be a servant to the village, save every penny. That problem answered, she steeled herself for whatever would be revealed when the men returned from Change Islands.

Lliam steered north, into the wind, with an arm draped over the tiller as he'd seen Malich steer. Garret slept huddled in the bilge, covered by the wet canvas coat that Doyle no longer needed. Lliam almost wept watching his brother coiled into a protective ball, retreating into his own visions of a hell played out twice in one year. Fire was the foremost terror faced by outporters because there was almost no defense or recourse when it strikes. Lliam could only hope Garret was strong enough to hold up to what was ahead.

If Lliam left the Cove, Garret, in his silent world of misery, would be the head of the family, the last male bastion against life on a hostile coast...The Depression wore on and wore down whole societies. There was no help from the outside world, no one cared that a proud race of people clung to the small hope that if they worked hard and followed the rules, they could hold out another season, and another, as always. Added to that were the rumours of war in Europe, only twenty years since the War to End all Wars. Lliam steered and worried, pondering his role in the scheme of things. He saw no future for himself, unless...The endless question of Breeze O'Keefe, his last desperate chance for happiness, occupied every moment not filled with terror or anxiety...He studied the heaving horizon. The sun broke through the scattering clouds, illuminating a world of sparkling water so beautiful a sailor ashore might long to be afloat. The sun dazzle was blinding but there was nothing on the horizon for Lliam, and nothing beyond the horizon but a faint hope...

They moored the skiff to Mulroney's wharf. "You stay with the boat, Garret. Move about a bit, and pretend to talk to Doyle the while. I'll see to the merchant."

Lliam walked unsteadily up the wharf rehearsing what he might say to Merchant Mulroney.

Some fishermen were on deck, coiling down trawl lines on a small bully boat. They watched him go by, puzzled: the Béhathook Cove man hadn't stopped to pass a word, or ask how they were fishing, only nodded. They didn't recognize Lliam, but they knew Garret and Doyle; what was wrong with Doyle? Garret doesn't talk. And there were the stories. Everyone knew that the Dwyers had gone to Sheen's Cove. The fishermen looked for Malich then looked at each other. Something odd was afoot. There was the other rumour too...Someone had seen a large beacon fire, the glow on the clouds hung over over Change Islands for hours. A house on fire perhaps? It happens. They continued to load tubs of trawl, biding their time.

Lliam stood awkwardly in the center of Mulroney's bulging inventory. The smells were intoxicating after months of rancid food and bitter tea.

The merchant had seen the landing and was writing in his ledger as if consumed by some important notation. Finally he looked up. "You're the Dwyer lad...?" He barely recognized the scruffy, unshaven, red-eyed visage.

"Lliam, yes, sir."

"Ah, Lliam, just so. An' you're here to tell me something about my schooner?" He looked beyond this new Dwyer to the wharf. He could just make out Garret gesturing to Doyle, forgetting that Garret was a mute.

"Yes, sir."

"Well? Is she afloat?"

"We finished your schooner, sir."

"Why isn't Malich with you?"

"He stayed behind."

"Some last minute details?"

"Yes, sir."

"Then she's not launched off?"

"No, sir, she's not launched off." If the merchant asked a blunt question he'd answer truthfully. He waited...

"I expected her lying alongside my wharf by now. But she's finished, as prescribed?"

"She was, sir, yes. We did our best."

"An' if I sent a crew to launch'er off, Malich would still be there?"

"Can't answer to that, sir. I only come to ask you to strike the family debt, as Malich requested. Those were his last words...before we left."

"Why the hurry, Lliam lad?"

"That was the deal, I believe."

"Well, son, shouldn't I see the vessel myself before I give a final judgment?"

"Your boat was finished proper, the sails were beautiful to look at. We did our part of the bargain. Malich's last word was to ask the debt be struck, sir."

"I suppose, on Malich's word, but with conditions." The merchant turned pages to the Dwyer's account and made notes.

"Ah, I'd like to take away a few pounds of tobacco. We've been without this past while."

"I see. Take that one." He indicated with his pen a wooden box on the counter and made a notation on the ledger.

"Thank you. Good day, sir," said Lliam, hastily tucking the box under his arm and heading for the door.

"I made the deal tentative to my inspection, hear me? You'll tell Malich...?"

Lliam just nodded as he opened the door. The aftermath and recriminations, that would follow the discovery of the disaster, would have to wait. Lliam had less than a clear conscience, but guilt would also have to wait for another day. His only thought was to get back to Béhathook Cove, to Breeze...and whatever the future held.

A small boy, the same fleet lad who announced the return of Malich's skiff the previous fall, pounded up the path to the Dwyer House with the news. The village had been waiting expectantly; rumours abounded: a beacon had been seen over on Change Islands, someone from Fogo Harbour reported. The time was about right for their return, confirmed by the sixth sense of coastal watchers accustomed to waiting for news of loved ones.

"Missus! Missus, Malich's boat's comin' on!" the boy shouted crossing the bridge, flinging open the kitchen door. Margaret, as ever in the kitchen preparing a meal, turned from her stove.

"How many?"

"Only three's in boat, as I could see, Mam. Malich's not aboard of er."

"Dear, God in Heaven..."

A crowd had already gathered as the skiff approached the wharf. Garret leaned forward and killed the engine. Lliam steered for the wharf, turning at the last moment. The sudden motion caused Doyle's body to fall sideways, head over the gunnel, eyes open and blank; the head took the first blow as the heavy skiff bumped the pilings. His skull split open and his neck bones fractured with an awful sound.

The gasp rising from the crowd greeted Margaret who had come on the run, followed by Breeze. The elders, Mother O'Keefe and Grandmother Dwyer, hobbled in their wake but they knew before their feet touched the apron of the wharf that tragedy was on them again.

Two boys climbed down and held the boat before it could sag away. Garret had to untangle the bow painter from Doyle's body and toss it to outstretched hands. Lliam was unable to look up, afraid to face the eyes of his mother because he felt responsible, complicit at least, for a missing husband and another dead son.

The tableau on the wharf was chillingly like the previous arrival, but that time the body in the bilge was a living Garret. This time the macabre scene of Doyle's broken body so shocked the villagers that no one spoke. Malich was absent and there might be an explanation, but Doyle was dead, not only dead he had been mutilated further. Many made the sign of the cross and diverted their eyes. Bert O'Halloran signaled two older boys to fetch the squid net then directed his fishing mates to help Garret and Lliam.

Doyle came ashore in the net, the way Garret arrived, but before his weight touched the deck of the wharf many in the crowd had shied away, shaking their heads. Not able to fathom the tragedy, they did not ask questions, nor could they console Margaret. The head of that unhappy household was gone, another son dead, Garret a wreck, and the remaining son an enigma.

A diminished procession preceded the family entourage but, instead of carrying on to mourn with Margaret, they melted away leaving the family to grieve alone. The questions would be asked in somber kitchens where the crones gathered. There was the presence of Breeze O'Keefe and the suggestion of evil spirits at work. Prayers would be said, not all for Margaret, but many for themselves and deliverance from evil.

Lliam watched the fishermen carry Doyle's body up the path to the Dwyer House. Breeze, keeping the baby from sight, watched him, wondering what his story would be, but at the same time calculating what this new development might mean. The dynamics of both families had been altered drastically since the work party left for Change Islands. There had been some expectation of better days ahead and guarded optimism that, once out of debt, both families could move on, sort out their lives and face the future. All that changed with Malich's death.

Breeze and the dwindling Dwyer family flanked Garret as he walked shakily up the wharf. Lliam was left behind, beside Mother O'Keefe. "What are your intentions, Lliam Dwyer?"

Lliam was caught off guard by the question. "Mam...?"

"What will you do about my daughter an' the wee babe?"

"Breeze won't have me, she's made that plain."

"That's aught to do with your responsibilities. She's got your baby to raise, havin' you or not."

Lliam had no answer to Mother O'Keefe's logic, offering her only his arm. His duty was to escort Mother O'Keefe to the Dwyer House for the post mortems, but he vowed to remain aloof from the recriminations.

The Dwyer House in mourning was avoided by the villagers as if a plague had descended, but the questions remained. In kitchens around the Cove women continued to conspire, linking the tragedy to the O'Keefe woman, as if Breeze had already left the village. There was speculation about the birth, the paternity, and the future. *It's a shame, poor Margaret*...Poor Margaret indeed, Breeze had said when her mother suggested the homecoming of Lliam Dwyer was a cloud on the horizon. Now there was proof...Lliam's sins were enlarged and intertwined with Breeze's history until the pair became a pariah that the village should expel, so they agreed.

In the fishing stores the men offered their own versions of the tragedy, asking the obvious question: how had Malich died? Garret could not tell the tale and they would not approach Lliam directly. There was the beacon fire, so the rumours said. Young Thomas O'Hara was the first to suggest that it had something to do with Malich's death...Fire was a topic for Thomas since his fiancé, Thelma O'Dell and her sister, Mildred, had been sent from Ireland after their family died in a fire set, it was said, by immigrant Scots at the instigation of the Orange Order. Bitter debates were held around glowing stoves on howling nights, the tales of atrocities mounting as fishermen revealed what they knew about the Homeland and the Risings. There was more to do with politics than spirits and the debates mirrored the first rumblings of discontent on the question of Newfoundland breaking from Britain and joining Canada...Lliam's role in Malich's death would fade as a topic for discussion. There was the question of the Secret Societies rising to oppose a union with that crowd up in Canada, opting to join the Americans. The fierce debates divided many communities.

In the Dwyer kitchen, Margaret set out the midday tea she had been preparing when the skiff arrived. Lliam had been without proper food too long to remain aloof after delivering Mother O'Keefe. He took his usual place at the table. Garret was seated in Malich's place at Margaret's insistence. There would be no gap in the patriarchy, but Lliam interpreted the swift move as a repudiation of his own presence, entirely without merit as Garret was the older brother. Doyle's body was laid out in the parlour, out of sight.

The somber meal was carried off in near silence. There was little to discuss about the family fortunes: there were few. Nor was the topic of Breeze's baby raised further than Mother O'Keefe's inquiry to Lliam about his intentions. The issue was between Lliam and Breeze. The protracted discussion was about Malich's death and Doyle's funeral.

Doyle's internment was a rushed, perfunctory affair. The priest was not sent for, possibly because it was customary to present the Holy Man with a stipend for his services. The family had no money to spare that season. Nor was Doyle's body left in state for visitation. He was too damaged: his skull shattered and head at an odd angle. The legs could not be straightened without breaking them further. Margaret and Breeze washed him and stitched him into his black suit, the one he'd have worn to marry Mildred. A party of fishermen, led by Thomas O'Hara and Bert O'Halloran, dug the grave above the Catholic Church. The tiny, but spectacularly strong little church was new, built by the village the year before. Some said it was proper to have Doyle buried from there, but others speculated that dark deeds had been done and evil spirits lurked and, without a priest, the building could not be consecrated and sanctified.

Doyle's body was laid to rest with only a brief speech by Lliam. He praised Doyle's devotion to his family, his good humour and practical jokes, but Lliam avoided saying what he really thought of his brother. It wasn't the time, nor would it add materially to solving the family's dilemma...The fresh dirt was mounded properly, the dwindling family filed away. The sad wake, sparsely attended, was held that night in the Dwyer kitchen.

Only Thomas and Bert, and a few fishermen friends, paid respects, not so much for Doyle, but in case there was more to be learned about Malich's death. With no corpse and no information, many villagers, especially the women, shunned the idea of consoling Margaret formally. In the stores the continuing debate swirled around the suspicion that Malich had been murdered. Lliam was suspected of course; it was well known the two were at loggerheads since Lliam's sudden return, and it did not help that Lliam was still an outsider, a dilettante in their eyes, and had made little attempt to take part in village affairs. It was never suggested that Garret had anything to do with the murder, the saint; the enduring mute who Lliam probably bullied, they agreed. They didn't know that Garret had learned to read and write, under Breeze's patient tutoring, so no one thought to ask him for a written account. Doyle was dead, by an accident, or trying to save his father. The beacon was a funeral pyre to destroy the body, they speculated; Doyle was injured in the process, and on and on. And no one thought to ask Lliam for his version of events. The funeral pyre speculation was truly a mystery, but only for a few days. The news of the burned boat would arrive quickly, once the Merchant Mulroney discovered the deception.

Margaret, however, would not be put off a moment longer than it took to clear the kitchen of visitors and sit Lliam at the table. Grandmother Dwyer was asleep in her chair by the fire. She had been knitting a winter cap for Malich. She'd do one for all the men, as she did every year...Breeze was upstairs with Garret tending to his injuries.

Margaret stood by the woodstove, perspiring in the heat. The Dwyers didn't have the luxury of a summer kitchen because Malich never thought it necessary. Open windows were good enough, but the windows were nailed shut, for practical reasons. Through the open door she could see their stage and the skiff arriving alongside. Bert O'Halloran was tying off the painter. He and Beatrice would have a private word with Margaret after a decent interval for grieving.

Margaret looked up at the ceiling. She heard Breeze talking softly to Garret. "Lliam, I want to know what happened to Malich."

Lliam knew this would be Margaret's first question. It was her right to know. "You may not want to hear the details, Mother."

"They say you killed your father."

"They say?" Lliam was about to deny the accusation but thought it better to tell his mother some version of the truth. It would have to come out if the accusations continued. Outport justice could be much harsher than the civil courts in distant St. John's. "Truth is, I did, but not for the reason you think."

Margaret slumped into Grandfather's rocking chair, glancing at Mother Dwyer to make sure she was still asleep. "What possible *reason* could there be?" she asked.

Lliam told his mother the entire story, except about Garret's discussion with Malich, Malich's demand that they burn the boat, and Garret dropping the firebrand on purpose. He wanted Garret free of actually torching the boat. "Garret had a bad spell after digging so long, then he dragged poor Doyle out from under, so Garret was exhausted and sleeping. That's when I did it."

"How could you? Your own father."

"He's not my father, Margaret, you know that."

Margaret stood up and paced to the door, tears of mourning and guilt mingling as a salty testament to her pain. "You've known this while?"

"I've suspected from the time I was ten or so. Me and Garret never looked anything like Doyle and Gerald, but everyone looked away, pretending." He lowered his voice almost to a whisper. "Same as Breeze ain't Sean O'Keefe's daughter. And you people judge me."

"It's not the same thing, my son. You've no idea about our life. You were raised better, but ran. Had to come back an' ruin that poor girl's life with your Boston ways."

Put in that context, Lliam didn't have a comeback. Boston, his drunken behavior, Molly McCracken, Anna Louise and the disturbing debaucheries added up to a cargo of shame that trailed him home from his American adventure and stopped him from going further into the family's story of deceit and hidden promiscuity. He could have accused his mother of infidelity, could have accused Malich of raping Breeze, but what was the point? He didn't understand the outport ways. Life was harsh on thin margins but he doubted the hard working folks of the outports indulged in bondage and orgies to pass an idle evening. "I love Breeze, but she won't have me."

"Nor should she. You'd only break'er heart."

"I did one good thing, Mother. I let a poor hare escape instead of feeding my family."

Margaret turned to look at her son. "An' why, in God's name, is that a good thing?"

"The rabbit didn't need to die for our folly."

"You were there to help your family."

"Then that answers, doesn't it?"

Margaret returned to the chair, eased down as if she'd aged thirty years. She held Lliam's eyes for a long moment. "You have to decide, Lliam, once an' for all. We need you more than ever, but if you've no thought for this family, what's left of it, nor the will to cast a hand then better you leave this house an' never return. You've caused us nothing but heartache. An' now you've killed the man of this house, father of you or not."

"I told you what happened. It was his last wish."

"If Malich was alive you should have done something to save him."

"There was no reasonable way, and no time. He was dying, Mother. He didn't want to linger in pain."

"An' you wished him dead because he wasn't your father an' Sean O'Keefe is. Yes, good men, both, an' gone from all. You resented that, son, like you resent me. That's why you ran away. In your heart you know you hate me too." Margaret broke down finally, sobbing so hard it woke Mother Dwyer. Breeze came down the stairs with her baby asleep in her arms.

"Is there something I can do, Missus?"

At dawn the household assembled around the breakfast table. Margaret served out the oatmeal porridge with pork fat. In turn Mother Dwyer, then Garret and Lliam, said a subdued *thank you*. Margaret took her place at the table and passed Garret the breadboard. "Some one of us has to go to the merchant an' beg for flour an' salt. We need tea for the winter. I'll make a list."

"Mulroney will be here the once," Lliam said flatly. "Two days at most, and you can ask his nibs yourself."

Garret looked from Lliam to his mother, his heart breaking for her because he knew what the winter would bring if Mulroney could not be mollified.

Mulroney arrived as Lliam predicted. His normally florid face a livid crimson as he yelled abuse at Lliam and Garret. Margaret cried softly and remained silent. Mother Dwyer hid behind her knitting. The whole village was listening, had followed the merchant's angry progress from the wharf around the cove. The wharf boys held the lines of the skiff hoping for a penny while the village was paralyzed with curiosity.

"You lied to me, Lliam Dwyer, an' that's a sin!"

"I didn't lie. 'The job was finished proper', that's all I said."

"You deceived me!"

"Well, when it comes to that, this family's masters at deception, sir," Lliam answered, sarcastically. "I come by it naturally."

"I can have you in chains, in debtor's court!"

"Take me then. 'Twould be a blessing to my family."

The merchant almost choked, realizing that threats were futile. The Dwyers had nothing except the house that Grandfather's father built. Even if there had been a registered deed it could take months, years, to get a court order to seize the property. And Mulroney would own another house that could not be sold, or rented. In a Depression outport, a vacant house was worthless. There was nothing to be gained but he'd made the trip in fury, said his peace and stood fuming, looking out the window as if he expected the boys to steal his skiff.

"You've had a difficult journey," said Margaret. "Would you take some tea?" Margaret was desperate.

The merchant was still panting, just short of gasping. A heart attack miles from his doctor in Fogo Harbour would surely cap the episode. "I will not, Margaret, but thank you, for your Christian generosity. I apologize for not offering my condolences for the untimely loss. I was that shocked to hear it. Good lads, they were."

"Thank you, Mr. Mulroney."

He sought comfort in business. "Would, ah, Malich have had an insurance policy, Mam?"

"My good man, we've naught but what you see. An' our skiff. An' if you take that my sons can't fish. An' if you can't find it in your heart to give us credit, then we'll starve to death this winter an' 'twill be on your soul."

"My conscience is clear, Missus Dwyer. I bargained in good faith, but I can't clear your debt, not without something to show an' what I saw was a pile of ashes."

"My husband's soul is in those ashes, sir. But you're welcome to them. Lliam says it were an accident. An act of God."

The merchant blessed himself. "That may be, but I'm out a boat, an' lied to in the bargain."

"Please, sit down, Mr. Mulroney."

Mulroney reluctantly took a chair while Margaret poured tea and offered bread and butter.

"Thank you. I'm that famished."

"We need time, sir," began Margaret.

"Oh, aye, time's free as well. With the Depression on, time's all we got."

"I mean...we need time to make amends, clear the debt."

"You're an honourable woman, Margaret. Many'd plead at my feet, souls pourin' forth...the sickness, the palsy, the bad luck, but never say, 'I'll clear my debt, given time'."

"It's all we have to offer, sir. That an' the Dwyer's good name." She glared at Lliam, daring him to interject some sour note of sarcasm.

"Aye, a good name's the foundation of our Island."

"We always pay our debts."

"That's true, Missus. I'll say that for Malich, rest his soul, he was always good for a debt. Like his father before him."

"Now then, we need a winter's supply, an' we'll start fishin' in the mornin' with the skiff. You get all, but what we need to eat."

Mulroney looked at Garret and Lliam. "I have my doubts, Mam, that you'd clear a winter's worth of salt."

"Well, they can learn. Garret's been at the fish since a baby. Knows aught else. Lliam can learn from Garret. I can bake bread an' dry squid. Gran can knit socks an' gunnin' mitts."

"I've all the socks an' mitts a man could want. They fill the bins an' go for a penny a pair, there's that many on the Islands knittin' their way through hard times. Can't cover the cost of wool as 'tis, Mam."

"Well, never mind, we'll find our way."

"I'm sure you will. Thank you kindly for the tea. I must get on *my* way. She's bound to blow tonight."

"Can I send my boys for supplies an' gear?"

"I can't refuse a widow, Mam."

Mulroney left the Dwyer House somewhat appeased, leaving the dwindling family a brief breathing space.

Margaret cleared the table but the look on her face announced to the boys that the discussion was not over. "Fishin' begins first thing, weather permitting. Set your minds to it."

Lliam spent a cold hour down by Breeze's fire pit, remembering the night he found her singing songs of longing for the Pirate Queen, Grace O'Malley. He thought of building a fire but he'd seen enough of fire to last a lifetime. The smell of his father's body burning would haunt him for all his days. The stench was acrid and sweet. It was a man, his non-father, burning and all he could do was watch the flames consume the last hope for the family. Was Malich such a bad man? Flawed yes, a cold brute, but he was the man he had to be. The provider, driven to do whatever it took to gain an inch, or a season, but that was the legacy of his clan, his tribe, and their ancestral island. Weren't they all in the same game? Survival? And you had to be hard to survive. Lliam thought he had been close to the bottom of his being before the fire and the loss of his manhood. But this was a new low. When at the bottom there is only one way to go, unless you swallow the anchor.

The decision surprised him, but Lliam had one shred of self worth left and he had to make the attempt. It was not in his nature to create, other than with words, but he decided to build a schooner to pay the family debt.

Part Three

Redemption

They didn't go fishing the next morning because it was blowing a gale, as Mulroney predicted. Margaret ordered the boys to the store immediately after breakfast, to overhaul the fishing gear. Their best gear went down with the *Margaret & Maude,* but with only the skiff they didn't need a trap net, nor could they handle a big seine. But there were tubs of trawl: long lines with rusty, vicious looking hooks on short leaders. It was a painful business for Lliam as Garret showed him how to separate the hooks and overhaul the lines into wooden tubs to make sure they were not too rusty. That took up the morning as the store shook in the gale and the ocean roared outside the cove. Lliam shivered at the thought of heading out into the open ocean with the intention of just sitting there until the fish came to visit their hooks. But they wouldn't visit uninvited.

"Garret, Ol' Son, what do we do for bait?"

Garret grinned and made a curving motion with his right arm.

"Around? You mean, around to Fogo, the merchant?"

Garret nodded.

Damn! Confronting the merchant at the best of times was a trial for outporters. But confronting Mulroney after the shouting session was going to be a trial of wills and resolve. Lliam wasn't certain he had the means, but there was no other way. They had to fish. Lliam brooded on the issue of bait and pondered the problem of how to build a schooner. When they knocked off for tea, Lliam asked Garret to tell Margaret that he had to see Precise Muldoon.

Percival 'Precise' Muldoon was the village master builder. His beautiful skiffs and dories were cherished around the Island for their lines and seaworthiness. His coffins were the best money could buy also. The locals called him Precise Muldoon. Muldoon was also a man not to be trifled with, cheated or taken for granted. If a fisherman travelled from Fogo Harbour or Rocky Cove to have a boat built he took Muldoon's terms and conditions, nothing less. So it was with some misgivings that Lliam made the trek around the shore to visit Precise Muldoon's Boat Yard.

"An' exactly how many boats have you built, sonny?"

"Well, none of course, but..."

"Then why'd you want to bother me with a scheme so out of your reach?"

"Because my family needs a schooner."

"I'm well aware of your family's plight, son, but you've nothing to offer me in the way of recompense."

"That's a fact, Mr. Muldoon, but I'm willing to learn an' lend a hand for other projects, like."

"I've my own son apprenticed now. Carly's a good lad, an' skilled. If I had to pay him what he's worth I'd be broke myself. 'Tis hard times, b'ye. There's a Depression on, an' a real war to follow. Maybe when the war gets up, times might look better. Nothin' like a war to get the money flowin' with the blood spilt, eh?"

Lliam spent the rest of that day pleading with Precise Muldoon to take him on. Lliam would build his schooner after hours, outside of fishing time of course. All coastal folk knew that fishing comes first and everything else has to be calculated after. Muldoon finally gave in, if only to stop the man from pestering him.

"You've got to show me somethin', sonny, other than that poor thing you call a ship's wheel you done up at Uncle 'ebert's shop."

"I will, Mr. Muldoon, but what should we start with?"

"You begin building a boat when the keel is set up. I don't see a keel layin' about fit to carry a Jack."

Lliam left the next day in the skiff, with only an axe and a bit of food. He returned within the week towing the blackened keel of the *Black Fenian* held up by floaters. The feat would seem extraordinary to Mainlanders, but in Newfoundland it was simply noteworthy, other than it was the Prodigal Son towing the cursed thing from Change Islands to Béhathook Cove.

In Lliam's absence, Breeze O'Keefe made up her mind to leave Béhathook Cove forever. She assessed her options then threw herself into the work...There was a small general store in the village run by a thrifty family called Stuckless: English migrants but welcomed in the Irish enclave, as Hebert and Gaston Froud and the Fallows clan had been. Madge Stuckless stocked a few necessities in her parlour, her husband was in the process of building an addition to expand the store and apply for the Post Office contract, but they would never compete with the merchant in Fogo Harbour, just as Mulroney could not compete with the Ashcroft Empire in Twillingate. Each merchant filled a niche and provided what the islanders needed, for a price...Breeze made a deal with Madge to bake bread three times a week. After the cost of flour, she'd make only pennies a loaf but every penny added to the escape fund kept in a coffee can high on a shelf. She expanded her washing chores to elders and the other bachelors in the village. She would dry cod for pennies on the quintal. She sold potatoes, keeping only enough to see them through the winter. It was a narrow calculation but the pennies added up.

Breeze may have been shunned by the women of the village and avoided for the most part by the men, but there were young men her age hungering after a woman as handsome and as well formed as the Wild Irish Witch.

One night, after delivering laundry to Aunt Lucy Hanlon, the village sail maker who lived below the English House, Breeze was approached by her son Luke. After a few suggestions, then threats, he tried to force her into Hanlon's store. He miscalculated Breeze's strength and determination. The boy just laughed off the swift knee in the nuts as she bolted away. "Next time me an' my mates'll have you up to the Mansion. Then the fun times, eh?"

The Mansion was the English House on the hill above Lucy's tidy frame bungalow. The house was vacant now with the Depression on. The wealthy ship owners retreated back to England, their trading schooners sent to Europe, to wait out the Depression. The young people made use of the elegant Victorian home for trysts and 'times'.

After the encounter with young Hanlon, Breeze carried a flensing knife on her rounds and showed it to the boy the next time he accosted her.

Outward defiance was typical of Breeze, but the episode disappointed her, eroding what regard she had left for the village. Determined to take her chances on the Mainland, she worked harder than ever, remaining in a silent standoff with Mother O'Keefe, leaving Mildred O'Hara to attend her mother's ever-growing needs. She had no time for anything but her baby and for her only friend, Thelma O'Dell.

To do her work and make deliveries, she enlisted Mildred O'Hara to also watch Baby Brigid as well as her mother, but Mildred only wanted to talk about Doyle, reveling in the tragedy, and her loss. Breeze wanted dearly to sit Mildred down and give her the facts of life, but it wasn't her place, nor was it necessary with Doyle's tragic passing.

314

Mildred would die within the year of a strange malady that some said was a broken heart. Her sister, Thelma, who was pregnant, married her cousin Thomas O'Hara after she had a baby girl they named Meghan. The baby did not resemble Thomas. She had the O'Keefe Irish good looks. That did not bother Thomas, he had loved Thelma since her arrival from Ireland, nor did he hold any animosity for Lliam Dwyer. It wasn't his nature.

Lliam may have pined for Breeze and pledged his undying love, but he was a desperate man, craving the feminine touch and a release for rampant hormones. Thelma was afraid to announce that she was pregnant because Lliam would be angry. Lliam suspected the truth because Thelma changed, became distant and refused to see him. Lliam brooded on the rejection because Thelma and Breeze were the only women available on the Island. Neither would talk to him more than civility required. He compensated by concentrating more on the schooner and less on his confused emotions, but on the lonely nights when even hard work would not induce sleep, he began to realize the truth of the outport existence and why his family's history was so complicated. Human nature, playing out a rough existence on the fringe of a European Society still constrained by the hypocrisy of the Victorian Era, has its own way of expressing emotions and fulfilling the biological needs of the young. Thelma was still recovering from the trauma of losing her family to the seething cauldron of hatred in Ireland and was receptive to Lliam's attention. Lliam was just desperate, as well as confused.

Breeze was unaware of all this until Thelma confided in her because there had to be an explanation for the child she carried. It was Lliam's love child, but she never revealed the truth to Lliam. Thelma saw only the bright side of things and said it would be wonderful that her baby and Brigid could be playmates. They avoided saying the obvious: the children would be half siblings. Breeze felt deep twinges of guilt because she had repeatedly put Lliam off, leaving him in his young man's hot temper to find a release.

But Breeze was not as ready to forgive as Thomas O'Hara. She still harboured feelings for Lliam Dwyer, despite her determination to free herself from everything that reminded her of the Dwyer family. It was very confusing and that only made her work harder. But she never spoke to Thelma after that, further removing herself from the village long before it was time to go.

Nor was it difficult for Breeze to avoid Lliam and the Dwyers. She felt badly about Garret missing his morning sessions with the journal, but Garret and Lliam were occupied every morning fishing. In the afternoons and evenings Lliam was at Muldoon's shop learning his trade and making plans to build the schooner, never mind that Precise Muldoon still scoffed at the idea, but the cursed keel was ashore, on it's blocks. The next stage was acquiring the material to finish a hull.

The fishing was going better than anyone could have imagined. Lliam learned fast and worked hard, hands and arms acclimatizing to the conditions, baiting hooks and pulling trawl lines often loaded with heavy cod. Lliam wondered if the good catches were just luck or was Garret charmed? He seemed to know where to set and not many days the hooks went empty. They'd be in by noon to 'make' their fish. Breeze would come by later, if the weather was fine, to wash and lay out the previous day's cod, and turn the ones already on the flakes so Garret could rest and Breeze could continue the lessons while Lliam was gone to finish his day at Muldoon's.

As the days of summer drew to a close, the pace of the village picked up. Winter was inevitable, easy or harsh. Breeze realized that she'd need to be more mobile to transport the baby as well as her goods. She paid a visit to Precise Muldoon's shop and ordered a sleigh built. Muldoon gave the order to Lliam who listened while he worked across the shop at the long planking bench.

Was it irony or oversight? she wondered as Muldoon and Lliam looked at her rough sketch. Lliam gave her a wane smile.

"I'll pay the costs for Breeze's sleigh, Mr. Muldoon."

"You needn't do that, Lliam. It's for my work," she interjected, trying not to sound cold and detached.

"It's for the baby, according to the plans."

"No concern of yours, my dear."

"Breeze, I hardly know what to say. I've told you often enough how I feel about you, an' the babe..."

"You've told me many things, Lliam, but did you ever tell me the truth?"

"From my heart, I swear."

"You've done enough o' that too. Swearin's not the same as doin'."

She left abruptly to forestall more pleading and promises. She'd truly heard enough, shielding herself from the words; a chill set in her heart no amount of fire could penetrate.

Fall 1938 To Buchans: By late September the solstice winds kept them in harbour most days. They made a deal with Bert O'Halloran to ship their dried fish to Mulroney and on a nasty day of wind and rain, Lliam and Garret hiked across the island to Seldom to meet the ferry.

From Cape Farewell they hitched their way to Notre Dame Junction to catch the train for Buchans. With the drums of war beating in Europe, industries were gearing up and there was work in the mines of Central Newfoundland. Garret's only desire was to add real money to the family coffers. Lliam needed cash to buy timber for the schooner, but most of all he wanted to get away from the village and put space between he and Breeze, as well as the growing tension between he and Thelma, and his suspicions. He'd adjust to the idea of labour, he told himself. His short stint in the Pennsylvania coalfields had not prepared him for anything that involved rough-hand sweat, but months of fishing had toughened him enough to try. Garret, with Breeze's constant, and loving care, was healed enough to work. Lliam had misgivings about letting Garret accompany him, but Garret was insistent.

On the train ride to Buchans, Garret surprised Lliam by writing a few lines in his own journal, describing fishing days at the Dwyer Station on the Labrador, painting just enough of a picture, in Lliam's mind, of his family prior to the first disaster, the loss of the family schooner, *The Margaret & Maude*. Lliam tried to see himself on the Labrador beach with his brothers: the fish, the fire, the schooner anchor sedately in the small bay. His heart ached for the lost opportunity to be a part of that time. What would his life have been if he'd gone fishing with his father and brothers instead of running away to Boston? A life with Breeze, perhaps, a newly built outport home and babies. He studied his gruesome looking brother laboriously writing with a pencil stub and suddenly the reality struck him, pushing aside any nostalgia about a normal life.

Lliam Dwyer was still young, fit in body, and a body can be moulded to suit the job, and a person can learn to work, even efficiently. It was his mind that was not fit for a workingman. Lliam was cursed with that malady of the creative being: the urge to create with words as some are driven to paint pictures or sculpt stone or build boats. His own family had provided enough fodder for story telling and as he imagined poor Garret suffering in the Buchan's mine, he longed to take Garret's pain into himself and make Garret a saint.

He spent the rest of the trip crafting Garret's character in prose and as the endless spruce forests slipped passed the train window, as the countless rocky rivers opened up when they turned away from the coast, Garret grew on the page into Lliam's ideal of the honest man, the gentle mute whose only lot in life was to suffer his wounds and care for his dwindling family. When he looked up from time to time, Garret was starring at him as if he knew what Lliam was about.

They arrived in Millertown in time to join a draft of eager workers boarding the company train for the mine site; only a few miles into the mountains, but a slow, miserable trip in an unheated railcar, *only fit for cattle,* in Lliam's estimation. It would have been a luxury class coach compared to the inhumane conditions European Jews and all those judged as undesirables, would be forced to ride in during the war to come.

As they stepped off the train into the mud of the ramshackle town site, a burst of ice pellets accentuated the long, sonorous steam whistle announcing six o'clock of the evening. It was the only indication that a day had some meaning in the bleak mountains with low clouds holding everything down.

Once committed to Buchans, the Dwyer brothers entered a world they had never experienced; a company town choking under a pall of grey smoke, barren as a desert, devoid of life except for the silent workers plodding through the muddy site, heading for the mine shaft building at the edge of town; eyes cast down, mentally preparing for their twelve hour shift in semi darkness.

Lliam took in the dreary scene with a premonition of failure. He thought of the docks of Boston, a more organized bleakness but a soul killing collection of desperate humanity and soot-blackened buildings. "Never mind, Ol' Son," said Lliam, trying to cheer Garret. "We'll find our beds and get some rest, eh?"

They each held a small piece of paper thrust at them by a gruff company clerk in Millertown. The precious chit had their numbers, shift times and bunkhouse assignments. Lliam stopped a glassy-eyed young man in a straggling line of workers returning from their shift and asked directions to Bunkhouse #9. The filthy miner simply pointed the way and passed on.

"Cold place, b'ye," said Lliam. He meant both the miners and the elements.

Ice pellets changed to rain, then snow showers, as if winter could not decide how best to torment the new workers. The mud streets shone like glitter ice in the weak evening sun which briefly dropped out of the cloudbank, and the wind chilled them more by the time they reached the door of Bunkhouse #9. "Home, Brother." He pushed the door open and they entered a common room, facing a dark corridor.

Two lanterns barely lit the long corridor with doors either side. Sawdust and mud tracks lead away into the gloom. The bunkhouse was new and still under construction, smelling of fresh cut spruce. The sweet tang of the fresh resin was about the only positive thing Lliam could assign to that long, dreary day.

Lliam and Garret shuffled through the door, crossed the common room and looked into the first occupied cubicle. The room was small, sparse and grey with tobacco smoke. A grizzled miner in mud-caked work clothes, sat on a cot puffing a tar-blackened pipe, talking to an equally dirty man sprawled on the other cot. The men were as grey as the men on the road, the red-rimmed eyes poking through the dirt looked vacant and weary. They regarded Garret and Lliam without interest. Lliam held up the chit as proof that they belonged in their bunkhouse. "Ah, we're to kip here, I suppose."

"Where you'se fellas from den?" asked the older man exhaling a cloud of tobacco smoke.

"Fogo Island."

"Fogo, eh? Fuckin' shore fish'mun. Place's crawlin' wit'em. Not good 'nough fer fishin', got to come take our jobs, eh?" The tired man bent his head to indicate they should carry on down the hall. Since Lliam didn't move and Garret didn't offer a word, the man said, "Jus' g'wan 'til ya foind da hempty one, eh?"

"Ah, what do we do about meals and such?"

The man sighed as if forced to educate the brainless. "Fuckin' company swill's on down chow hut, eh? Not fit fer pigs, but ya gotta eat some'it. Pay up 'fore, an' puke up after, eh?"

"Okay, and about washing up and toilets?"

"Piss where ya will, sonny. Latrine's out back a ways, if you can stomach it. There's showers out b'hind fuckin' chow hut. You'se pay fer dat too, like, wash'er not. Maybe water come, eh? Ne're hot. Most days us can't bother to wash. You only gotta sleep an' get mucked up ag'in. Not fuckin' wort it."

"Where are you men from?" Lliam asked conversationally, since they were to be bunkmates.

"No-fuckin'-where, sonny. Las' time we was down pits, up Kirklan' Lake. Too fuckin' cold, Canada, eh? Den we tried workin' surface in Sudbury, eh? Best job's un'er ground, but we was too late, see? Some cold Sudbury. Come back 'ere an' work un'er ground. Nice'n' warm in da fuckin' muck a 'tousand feet down, eh? Ya can die just the same but least dey won't find yer frozen body behind a slag car we're ya crawl to find a bit o' warmth." He spit tobacco juice on the floor. The old miner had passed on all the wisdom he deemed necessary. He tapped his pipe on this mate's steel cot, the glowing ashes scattering into the darkness. The other man had a coughing fit, rolled over and spit on the embers.

Lliam let the realty sink in. He was home, determined not to fish, but inland, the mines of Newfoundland had fallen into the norms of company towns of the Industrial Revolution worldwide. Desperate workers paid dearly for their meager wages.

Garret's sense of providing for his own family caused him to doubt the adventure, wishing he'd not signed onto the deal. He'd rather fish in a gale from a leaky boat than submit to filth and stink and ill manners, life with Malich aside.

Lliam also had his doubts, not just about the living conditions, but what the work obviously did to honest men. Every man he'd seen so far looked beaten down and ready to give up. Working for the *Man* was not in his line. He didn't realize he was working for the great Guggenheims of America. In Boston the power families like the Guggenheims, the Gettys, Cabots, Carnegies and Melons, were either hailed as the heroes of capitalism or cursed as the worst tyrants of history. The outport families only had to contend with the likes of Mulroney and Ashcroft, practically family by comparison. Fishing for the Merchant's ledger had a certain dignity, and the ocean was clean and clear. Fish slime was not the same as ancient muck. But that was only the first day at the Buchans mine. Worse was to come and the evidence was the industrial scene outside the bunkhouse.

The day was over, darkness creeping past the mine head, yard lights casting long grey shadows over the site. Shift change complete, the complex fell silent except for the *whirr* and *clank* of the big wheels in the head house at the top of the mineshaft. Miners going down, ore coming up, an endless rotation driven by steam as well as money. A cheerless place to cast one's fortunes.

At the end of the hall they found an empty room with no window, dark, damp and cold. The rooms at least had doors with hasps for locks. The locks had to be purchased at the company store. There were two iron cots with wire springs, ubiquitous in army barracks and prisons. That was all. The rooms were partitioned part way so heat from the common room coal stove could circulate overhead. But someone had to tend the stove. The cost of the coal came off their pay packet, as did the room, the meals and the showers. What else? The latrines were free. The chit warned that...*Employees are not allowed to bring food or other items onto the Company Property. Meals, gear and personal goods must be purchased from the company commissary.* "We need a tick an' some blankets, Garret. We best go find that store," Lliam said too cheerfully, throwing his duffle bag on a cot. Lliam hesitated to leave his precious belongings behind, including his journal, but was tired of lugging the bag around.

The Company Store was a simple frame building beside the imposing Main Mine Office. The meager inventory was not piled as high as Merchant Ashcroft's Premises, but the prices certainly were. They selected what they thought they needed, signed the big ledger beside their numbers and headed back to their bunkhouse. "We're pilin' up the debt, Brother. We'll be slaves 'til Doomsday at this rate. Devil's got us in his pocket, eh?"

Garret tried on a smile, as if Lliam's statement was a joke, but his eyes spoke of distant hells and a never-ending conflagration of burning fat and greasy smoke. They were just more fodder for the fire, condemned to live in smoke and dust whether awake or asleep. The Fogo Island brothers would not see daylight again for three months.

Later: A vile curse and the *clang* of a shovel resounded from the central area of the bunkhouse. A grumbling miner tended the stove: someone not familiar with the process. The acrid stench of soft coal smoke rolled across the ceiling, reaching their room, but the heat did not. The brothers, alone, far from the cozy comfort of their mother's kitchen, wet from the persistent sleet and chilled to the bone, sat on their cots chewing chunks of dried fish they'd smuggled in with their duffle. "A drop of rum'd go good about now, eh, Ol' Son? Malich was the man who knew what rum's for."

Garret nodded, sadly, remembering the good times when the whole family crowded Margaret's bright kitchen, the 'times', the music, with the woodstove crackling and the stew bubbling, bread in the oven and Malich toasting everyone with a bottle, roaring songs of the Western

Isles, all the while cursing the merchants, blessing the fish he was chewing to give him enough nourishment to face the next day. They never had much, but they always had hope. They were both longing for their simple village and the sturdy spruce home that had endured winter gales and summer hurricanes. Painted white and sparkling clean, the kitchen was a haven for a frost-driven fisherman when the body could not endure one more fish over the rail, no matter what the winter might bring. If there was enough flour, tea, molasses, tobacco and a tub of herring, a few turnips, a barrel of new potatoes, and most of all, a quintal of dried fish, a man could see a winter survived for his family. When March month arrived it was time to go at the seals. Spring is always a promise for Maritimers but Lliam wondered if spring would ever come to Buchans.

Beds made up, gear kicked under the cots, the brothers were settling down for a smoke after a long tiring day when a loud voice bellowed from the far end of the bunkhouse, "Any Fogo Dwyers in here?"

There were curses from a few dayshift men trying to sleep. The rest of the nightshift was down below. The Fogo Dwyers stumbled into the hallway wondering what was up.

"You there! Who be you?"

"Lliam Dwyer. This one's my brother, Garret."

The shift boss consulted his clipboard. "What in Hell's fire are you loafers doin' here? You've pulled nightshift. Report to the foreman at the Head House, pronto!"

"But, we've only just arrived..."

"See yer goddamned chit! Says, *1800 assemble at Head House.*"

Lliam dug the limp paper out of his pocket, studied the fine print at the bottom and showed it to Garret. Garret shrugged and looked wistfully at the glowing lantern, a small spot of warmth dimmed by the haze of the coal smoke. He decided it could be no worse in the mine than shivering in their tiny room.

Approaching the main shaft building they entered under a sign that read: Lucky Strike Mine, to be met by machinery noise and the stench of ancient mud. Thick, pungent coal smoke hovered at ground level.

The noise, the smoke and the smell of musty work clothes assaulted their senses. Garret was suddenly convinced the worse was yet to come.

A big man stood beside the lift looking into the shaft. "You the Dwyer brothers from Fogo?" The grizzled, no-nonsense foreman, Wilfred Hurley, from Cochran, Ontario, loomed at them from the gloom of the mine head machinery. Hurly had grown up in the rough and tumble of the mines in Northern Ontario, and knew just how far to push men who belonged to the hated Union. "You sign a fuckin' union card yet, Dwyer?"

"No, sir."

"Good. Don't." He looked hard at Garret who shuffled his feet in Lliam's shadow. "What about you? Union or not?"

"He didn't sign a card either, sir"

"Can't he answer for himself?"

"No, sir. Garret's been a mute all his life."

"*Hum*, that can be dangerous down there. Where's your coveralls an' helmet?"

"Thought a one would be provided for, like."

"What'd ya think this is, son, the goddamned Salvation Army? Never mind..." He opened the door to the lift cage, a post-Industrial Revolution affair of metal bars and wire mesh hanging by huge greasy cables on giant wheels. All was grease and rock dust. A gang of drillers, dressed in coveralls, wearing helmets, like a platoon of soldiers occupying the trenches of Belgium, shuffled into the cage carrying hoses and drill bits, lunch pails, thermoses and wearing inscrutable smiles as they eyed the rookies. The usual rubes, they joked: ill prepared and about to be initiated into their particular hell. They talked in a jargon foreign to Lliam's ears, but he got the gist of the patter...The rubes from the coast wouldn't last a week. Hurley motioned the Dwyer brothers to join them with a jerk of his head. The steel gate crashed closed.

The foreman pressed a button. Somewhere in the depths a shrill bell answered, the big wheels creaked, and the lift dropped in a gut-churning lurch. The descent of the lift in semi darkness was a shocking series of screeches and sudden stops as the drillers got off the lift at their levels.

Hurley pressed the button once to go, twice to stop. There was another lift running in tandem to their cage and as it passed going up, the brothers got their first look at the object of their journey. The carload of ore: stinking, broken rock in chunks, looked like nothing they had expected. The moist air warmed noticeably as they travelled towards the center of the earth until they reached Level Four.

They stepped awkwardly off the lift into a nether world of blasted tunnels held up by wooden shores, steel mesh and bolts, laced with water pipes, air pipes and cables, exhaust ducts and fresh air ducts. Water hissed through pipes and pissed from rusting joints. They followed Hurley for a short distance to a surprisingly large, whitewashed cavern with decent lighting, a lunch area with refectory style tables, a small foreman's office and a lift operator's station.

A few miners on their break slouched at the long tables, heads down as if whipped into submission: sipping tea, wolfing down sandwiches, smoking, talking in monosyllables, a few surreptitiously eyeing the new boys. Hurley entered his office, made an entry in a book and returned with two helmets and lanterns with battery packs. He handed one to Lliam.

Lliam fingered the unfamiliar headgear, switched on the light and placed the helmet on Garret's head. Garret grinned and made a sign that Lliam interpreted as a request for a veil. "Mummer's time? Not time yet, Ol' Son, but we'll take a one home for the nonsense. Handy to find your way after one tipple too many, eh?"

"Don't break the fuckin' thing or it'll come outta your pay, an' you're already short for this day, eh? Follow me." He led the way to a large tunnel with a narrow gauge railway track glinting off into the distance. Streams of black water, running on either side of the tracks, gurgled away into the gloom.

After a long trek in midnight darkness, broken only by their lantern beams, Hurley stopped at an opening in the wall of the tunnel. They had passed several openings, just black holes. Nothing was going on that they could see and some were cemented over. They could hear distant drilling, could smell the moist, dank odour of cordite, urine and ancient rock ruthlessly blasted open. They could smell themselves as nervous perspiration soaked their best clothes.

Hurley motioned them into the hole as the headlight of a small engine came around a curve. The driver was hunched atop his electric machine, eyes dead in the lantern light, as if he was condemned to ride his humming vehicle underground forever. When the string of ore cars clattered passed they continued to another tunnel, turned in and walked again, always accompanied by the sound of falling water and the pneumatic drills in the distance.

Water was everywhere under foot; if it wasn't running it was thin ooze. The vaporized water was supposed to quench the dust, but particles hung in the fetid air mixed with the mist. Drilling dust covered everything, clogged noses, and burned into their eyes. Lungs, used to bracing salt air, rebelled. Miners smoked, coughed and cleared phlegm as they worked, coughed between smokes, coughed up phlegm before and after meals. Sometimes between each breath or each spoken word.

Hurley suddenly stopped at a black hole and pointed. "Your stope. Well, go on..." Lliam led Garret in, stumbling on loose rock. They could barely stand at the entrance but beyond the low arch a larger cavern opened up. Their lantern beams revealed a recent work site, drilled and blasted, falling rock pinging off metal shovels, and plunking on the pile as small chunks dropped away from the shattered ceiling. The smell of blasting powder overruled the smell of their sweat.

"See them scalers?" Hurley indicated two long poles with spiked ends that looked like medieval battle pikes dropped by retreating soldiers. Maybe they were, just before the blast. "Them's for scaling the roof, see?" He picked one up and jabbed it at a crack in the ceiling rock. A cascade of small chunks rained down but Hurley deftly jumped back. "Scale down an' when the pile gets big enough, shovel'em into that chute." Another black hole was the chute where the broken rock continued down. Everything in the mine had to go down before it went up. Somewhere below, black trolls shoveled ore into little train cars that snaked along endlessly in the darkness.

"What are we looking for, if you don't mind me askin'?"

"Copper ore."

"Copper? That's all we're doing down here?"

"You won't find any gold, sonny, so don't bother stuffin' glitter chunks up yer ass." He handed the scaling pike to Lliam and turned away saying, "An' don't kill yourselves. I'm short three men already." With that wisdom instilled in the brains of the shore fishermen, he disappeared into the dark tunnel.

"Well, Brother, this don't look too hard, but I don't see no copper either." They stood for a few moments gazing at the granite ceiling and at the mound of broken bits under their feet. There was no copper, just a slash of green in the cold, hard rock.

It was a long night and progress was slow; arms aching, backs breaking from shoveling, throats dry and clogged despite the constant mist. They had brought nothing to drink and only a chunk of salt fish to chew. Hours drained by as they learned to poke and jump away, but no one came to tell them about break time and they only knew their shift was up when Hurley brought two more coastal rookies to work their stope. He said nothing about their contribution to the Guggenheim Family.

"Leave them helmet's in my office. Get your own gear from the fuckin' company store before next shift. An' don't be late or I'll dock yer pay another half day."

They made their way back to the lift station on their own, taking a wrong turn at one point, doubling back in time to make the last lift before the ore cars took precedence.

The screeching, halting trip to the surface seemed to take forever as they lurched to a stop at every level to pick up and drop off more crew, the new shift descending in concert, and as the cages passed there was some good natured oaths exchanged. To Lliam's cultured mind it sounded childish and moronic. "Doyle'd like it here, eh, Brother?" The trek to their bunkhouse in ankle-deep mud was completed in silence except for Garret's labored breathing. One night in the hole had affected his fire-seared lungs.

There were no windows in their part of the bunkhouse, either not yet roughed in or considered frills, but there was nothing to see of the dark outside world except the glow of the lights on the mine head or the grey snow covering everything in daylight. And there was no need to open a window: the air was not fresh, like the seashore. They lay on cold damp cots, too tired to walk to the chow hut, or shower, and didn't know if the sun was up, didn't care. In the wavering light of their smoking lantern, Garret stared at the yellow spruce of the ceiling planks, thinking of home, stifling the urge to cough. Lliam wrote on the clean wall planks, *Breeze, we're here...*October 1938...Then they slept as though dead. When the Bunk Boss shook them awake for the nightshift it was dark again. Breakfast was bread and jam, and boiled herring tumbled together. At first they just stared at the mess in their pannicins and sipped the tepid tea.

"Best eat something, I suppose, like the man says. Go on, Brother, I know it's not as good as your culinary delights."

Garret did his best to grin at Lliam's attempted joke. But Garret only remembered the flames, the smoke and the burning fat. He would never forget the fear. That night he wrote in his journal the truth of the loss of his brother Gerald and the *Margaret & Maude*. He showed it to Lliam before they left for their shift.

I caused the fire aboard our boat. Gerald died saving me...

They endured endless twelve-hour days in the dark tunnels with only the narrow beam of their lanterns to guide them, constantly shifting their beams to avoid each other's pikes, as if they were human lighthouses.

The weeks passed in a blur as they adjusted to their routine and the long days in darkness. They didn't go home for Christmas. Hurley said they'd lose their bunkroom and bonuses. Lliam watched Garret declining by the day. His coughing sessions produced blood, his skin going grey, even the burn patches were fading. His eyes were failing also and he could no longer write in his journal. He didn't want to see the doctor because another miner said the company doctor was a quack.

The food was passable, but it wasn't just nourishment Garret lacked. It was hope. Breeze had said she'd marry him some day, but Garret knew it would never come to that. Lliam at least dreamed of Breeze with some hope, wrote of their plight in his own journal and designed the schooner he would build, determined to stick it out until he had enough saved in the company bank, but he worried about his frail brother who seemed to diminish into his skin with every shift accomplished. Then Garret began to cough after a few breaths of moist, dust-laden air. Lliam felt guilty for dragging poor, fragile Garret into the work force.

"I'm sorry I got you into this muck-up, Brother," he said one morning as they returned from the chow hut, desperate for sleep. They had fallen into the habit of not showering after a shift, washing their faces at most before sitting down to another meal of barely warmed fish and potatoes. They returned to their room that was not much warmer than Level Four, and the noise of the now full bunkhouse, crowded to capacity with the hard drinking, card playing roughs lured to Central Newfoundland by mine wages and talk of war.

Garret sat on the edge of his cot, elbows on knees, waiting for the coughing fit he must endure before he could lay down to sleep. He raised his red-rimmed eyes to Lliam's and shook his gruesome head. The grin his thin lips performed for Lliam was a pathetic attempt to reassure his brother that it was fine, he was okay, just a little dust in the pipes to spit out.

"Well, Ol' Son, we'll only stay until we've enough saved up to get us through, eh? We promised Margaret."

Garret patted Lliam's arm and stretched out on his bunk, still fully clothed. His coveralls were caked with mud but the fine silt was damp and so uniform it stuck like plaster, only cracking to show the joints and buttonholes. He tried desperately to hold back the coughing fit, but had to roll on his side, knees drawn up like a frightened animal under a bush. He choked in spasms but eventually the coughing fit exploded like a whale too long in the depths. When the coughing subsided he pretended to sleep so that Lliam would not worry.

"Sleep, Brother. I'll get you out of this dungeon just as soon as we've enough to show for your trial."

There was little enough cash left after company expenses, but with each hour worked a few pennies were banked, and then a few dollars on account, and he was determined to work until the day he realized Garret was dying. His endless coughing fits left him gurgling for breath. Finally, one night Garret collapsed at the breakfast table, gasping for air. Lliam carried him to the infirmary.

Garret spent a week in bed and seemed to recover. Pneumonia was the simple diagnosis. Rest and broth was the solution. Lliam worked extra hours when Hurley needed a hand to make up for Garret's time. After a week of rest Garret said he was fine and returned to the stope, picked up his pike and scaled, and scaled, breathed the drilling dust and, like a zombie, walked through the snow and mud to the dreary bunkhouse each morning before sunrise, to the shower room to wash his face in cold water, to the food hut to take some nourishment, then to bed, where he shivered and coughed himself to sleep.

One bitter winter day in late December, Lliam had a fight with a brute of a miner who complained about Garret's endless coughing, even though many of his own mates coughed incessantly, but they were the upper class, the professionals. The man resembled Malich Dwyer in speech and manner, and that may have contributed to Lliam's anger. But riled or not, Lliam lost the fight, was battered and bruised, but he felt thrilled and energized to have at least stuck up for his ailing brother. After the fight the hard rock miners left the odd brothers alone.

Lliam watched with an aching heart as Garret deteriorated with each nightshift completed. Without the gentle ministering hand of Breeze, Garret's burned and tortured body withered hour by hour in the damp and dust of the mine. It was no better in the noisome bunkhouse where rest seemed an illusion. Some of the nightshift crew spent half the day playing cards, cursing, pounding the common room table. Booze was smuggled in and shouting matches became slugfests with broken furniture and laughter. But that's what passed for entertainment and relaxation.

Lliam wrote in his diary his fears for Garret's health, his longing for home and his thoughts about Breeze, the only hope for his own salvation. He vowed to change her mind because everything depended on that goal. The schooner was an important part of the equation, but he wasn't sure which part. Finally the January cold became too much for Garret even if he never stepped out of the reeking fumes of the bunkhouse. Lliam told Hurley they were done. Going home. Hurley said it was too bad; the Dwyer brothers were the best hands he'd had.

They got their script, cashed out and took the company train to Millertown. Lliam spent some of his money to put Garret up in a hotel, only slightly more commodious than the bunkhouse, but it was at least warm, while they waited for the next train east. Garret slept for two days, tossing and feverish.

Instead of getting off the train at Notre Dame Junction they carried on to Gander. Lliam hired a cab and took Garret to the hospital, waited for the doctor's opinion, then, assured that Garret was fine, just fragile from the pneumonia and needed bed rest, he ventured across town to Newfoundland Hardwoods.

It was snowing fat flakes, soon followed by hard sleet, not an unusual combination in mid-winter Newfoundland, the icy wind making devils around the woodpiles. Lliam and the yard owner stood surrounded by tiers of rough sawn wood. Lliam was in awe of the stacks and stacks of planks; wane edged, stickered properly, piled as high as the gables of his own house. He was like a rube in the big city, cowed by the imposing buildings; it was also obvious to the owner that the Fogo man knew almost nothing about building a boat. Lliam hadn't mentioned his family's disastrous experience on Change Islands.

"You'd need 'bout tree t'ousand board feet for a Jack that size."

"How much would that cost?"

"Depends what you want."

"Oak?"

"Mainland number one? Fifteen hundred dollars."

Lliam blanched. He had only half that amount in his pocket, for everything. "Ah, what other choices?"

"Most of the b'yes cuts their own. Spruce's always been good enough for our rough Jacks."

Lliam remembered, with a sick feeling, the long, torturous hours hauling and sawing enough sap-heavy spruce logs just to repair the *Black Fenian*. And there were four hands to do the job.

"I don't have a crew, sir."

"Well, son, seein' it's Depression times an' all, I've got scattered grades of two inch spruce, been stickered since the war. Not much local buildin' goin' on betimes. Things's bound to pick up soon, with a new war getting' up, but I could let you have what I got for a good price."

Lliam followed the owner through a maze of lumber bulks to the back of the huge lot. They stopped at what looked like an untidy heap of grey, rotting timbers covered with ice and snow. "There's 'bout four t'ousand board feet, giver'er take."

"How much?"

"Two hundred, but you take it all."

"Fine. What else?"

"You'd need deck stock. 'Bout a t'ousand board feet."

"Spruce?"

"Local spruce's no good for decks, my son. I got some Yankee pine leaved over from a Coast Guard boat. Longleaf pine's about the best there is. It's up in Lewisporte."

"How much?"

"Two hundred dollars. An' that's a bargain, sonny."

"Okay." He was calculating his cash on hand. With four hundred dollars committed to the hull and decks he still needed curved stock for the frames. And there were spars to make. He'd almost forgotten the big timbers for the masts. "I need the right stuff for making frames, an' spars..."

"Sorry, we don't handle framin' stock no more. The b'yes would pick through, leave a mess, an' it's worth your life to load an' ship the bloody stuff."

"Oh, what then?"

"There's a family over Gambo Town. Ol' man was settin' up to build a Jack after Big War, but 'e had heart attack. Died in his store carvin' the model. Last I heard they still had a fair bit o' black locust bends. Good Mainland stuff. Cost the family a fortune back in the day."

"I see. What might that be worth?"

"Don't rightly know, but my guess is not that much. Hard times, eh? One o' their lads worked for me. I'll get in touch. Give me a hundred bucks for good faith an' I'll see to it."

Lliam drew a deep breath, figuring his costs, still minus the spars, and fittings, sails, engine...What about delivery? *She's adding up pretty fast*, he grumbled into the wind. "How do I get all this material to Fogo?"

"Oh, well, if you need it delivered, let's see. I've got a truck going up to Lewisporte tomorrow. Buddy can bring back the Yankee pine. I'll send 'nother truck to Gambo with a helper; that would be you. Back here, then load'em all up, two trucks, two drivers, if your brother can help load. There's the ferry to Seldom...'Bout a hundred dollars. All in all, that's a good deal, son."

"*Hum*, I guess." How did he know? The man seemed honest and he was in no position to question anything. "Okay, deal, but my brother's in hospital for a few days, so he can't help load."

"Well, that's the luck of it, eh? I've got a couple strappin' lads without that much to do. They spend their days talkin' 'bout joinin' up for the war. But you got to feed'em while they bide in Gambo, eh? An' the drivers will need a kip an' a bite to eat before they leave Fogo."

"Okay, we can do that. Is that everything then?" asked Lliam, wondering how much it would cost to feed the drivers. Then he realized that, after four months away with no news, Margaret might not have enough food left to feed her own family.

"You never said what you've got for a keel. The b'yes mostly use

333

our Douglas Fir, from the other coast, eh? Got some nice pieces leaved over from before the bad times, eh? But you'd have to float a one over to Fogo."

"Ah, I have a keel. They say it's some sort of African wood." He didn't mention *cursed* African wood.

"African stuff eh? An' where would you get a piece like that in this day an' age?"

Before he could check himself, Lliam blurted out, "Old hull over on Change Islands."

The big man went pale, shaking his head. "You're one o' the Dwyer's then?" News and rumours travel the islands as efficiently as any telegraph system.

Fogo Island 1939 February: The war, the next war, the war after the War to End all Wars, was on everyone's minds. Maritime regions knew the war was coming soon, because Germany, under the new Fürher, was building a navy, secretly. But sailors knew. They saw the evidence in Hamburg, Kiel and Wilhelmshaven. As the needs of the European war machines grew their cargo ships were in and out of every major port on the Atlantic and the Baltic. They talked and spread the word but the leaders weren't listening. Germany was annexing regions, but the World leaders looked away. The tensions grew even as the denials became oaths. Inevitably countries were making impossible treaties against the *inevitable*, and the people were pacified by their leaders' promises.

But in somnolent Béhathook Cove, the talk was of the piles of timber deposited in Precise Muldoon's yard. The weather was bitterly cold, balanced by fierce gales, sleet, hail and rain, then more snow. The villagers remained in their kitchens and stores, but Liam spent his days poking about the piles of lumber, sorting and daydreaming. When he tired of sorting timbers, he also huddled by the stove in the Dwyer House, writing and pondering two paths: How to get Breeze to talk to him, and how to build a twenty-five ton fishing schooner. He considered the latter to be the easier road since Breeze came every day to tend to Garret, but refused to talk about their future. *There's no future, Lliam*, she repeated often enough. She refused to let him touch Baby Brigid while she spent time teaching Garret to read and write. When he tired of gazing at the untouchable toddler he retreated to Muldoon's Yard to stare at his dormant timbers. While he was away Breeze had Garret copy pages from Lliam's journal.

Mother O'Keefe came for dinner most evenings and the addition of she and Breeze helped fill out the Dwyer table, but it was a sad scene with three men missing, four counting Grandfather. Margaret tended her stove, her bread, the laundry and her mother. Grandmother Dwyer seldom left her chair by the fire, sinking further each day into that state elders occupy when life has ended but the heart continues to beat and memories take the place of routine. But Garret studied with Breeze and his health improved.

Lliam watched as Breeze and Garret conspired through the written word, saw how Garret responded to her soft voice and gentle admonitions when his words went awry or he spelled something wrong. He envied Garret because Breeze would take his brother's gnarled hand and guide the letters as lovingly as she smoothed the special oil mixture on his raw skin, longing for the same sensation. In a drunken stupor one night, after a booze release from winter, he even considered mutilating himself...

He had to talk to her. But how was he to confront the obstinate woman? She was always busy. Her work took up most of the day, her trips around the village were purposeful, no time to linger, and in the evening her time was divided between Garret and the baby. And when Mother O'Keefe tired of the strained visits, she would bundle up the child and guide her mother home, parting from Garret with a kiss, a blessing for Mother Dwyer and Gran. For Lliam there was a civil, *good night then, Lliam*.

One wet and windy evening, when Mother O'Keefe suffered a fainting spell at dinner, he offered to help them navigate the path home. Breeze accepted reluctantly. She carried the sleeping baby and maintained an aloof coldness that precluded conversation. When he delivered them over the bridge he opened the door for her mother and put his hand on Breeze's arm, as gently as he could, while conveying his need to speak.

"Breeze, could I come in and talk awhile?"

"I've told you, Lliam, there's nothing you could say."

"I mean, to just talk, you and me, the way we used to, when we were young. I was so taken with you..."

"Taken? You treated me like I was your sister." Breeze held back, realizing that what she said had some truth, if the rumours were true.

"Tell me what we talked about, as you remember."

"We talked about what it would be like to sail over the horizon and be free of all this. It was my dream. We would go to Ireland, Australia, The South Seas Islands and walk on the warm sand, in the sun, with no cares. Remember I do. You made a vow, Lliam Dwyer, that you would never leave this island without me. Then, when I needed you most, you were gone, and I was left with your brothers, and your father, may God rest their black souls, to fend for myself while you played the fool in Boston. I've read your diary and know all about you and that trollop, Molly."

"So that's it. You're jealous."

"Don't be daft, Lliam. How could I be jealous of you making a complete fool of yourself, with all those people?"

He tried to pull her towards him but her arms were folded around the baby. She pulled away and turned to the house, entered and closed the door firmly.

Lliam stood a long time looking through the kitchen window, listening to the sounds of the O'Keefe family ending their day with the old woman complaining bitterly about her lot in life. Breeze sang softly to her child, settled her mother in the chair and made up the fire. How easily she moved about her duties, deftly seeing to the many small things that make an outport kitchen a home. He watched as Breeze washed their baby, cooing to her, kissing her tiny nose, drying her curling hair. The colour would be red. The freckles were already beginning to show. And the smile...He thought that Breeze looked more beautiful than ever and he knew all her love was focused on the tiny, fragile life, his only gift to the one he had loved since they were young. Too late. Breeze was a fully formed adult grounded in her love only for the child.

Angry with himself and with the obstinate woman, he slammed the gate and charged up the Fortress Hill to brood.

March 1939: Grandmother Dwyer, like her husband before her, died peacefully in her rocking chair by the stove, the first week in March, about the same time the weather broke. With the last elder gone and laid to rest, Lliam began work on the schooner.

Precise Muldoon had deep misgivings about the project as they struggled to prepare the long, heavy keel.

"You've no idea the job of work you've taken on, Lliam."

"Aye, it could be no worse than the job of mending my ways. I've made a vow, Mr. Muldoon. This keel is the only legacy left to my family. I've to see it made whole again, and give it over to the Merchant to ease the family debt, and my conscience."

"You've been part of a double tragedy. This here keel is a bad omen, but that's not the half of it."

"I didn't believe in curses and sprits, sir, at least not the evil ones. Not until I watched Sheen's boat go up in flames, by my own hand. There must be some explanation."

"Your family don't need an explanation, son. They did nothing wrong for such ill fortune to be lowered on them from Above. Both were accidents, if there's no curse, but the omen must be respected. Any hull what begins with this piece o' foreign wood is bound to come to a sad end. Probably by fire, sonny. But a ship that lays down before she's launched off, well, that's a pure omen and a man should walk away. Seth Sheens' boat went down twice. The first time it killed his son. The next time it killed your father and his son. Bad things happen in threes, and the Devil wants His due."

"My hope is," he began, pausing to reconsider his belief in curses and omens, evil spirits and retribution. Simple bad luck no longer answered for what had happened to his family since his return. Was he the bringer of the curse? Were his own sins, festering in the Boston debaucheries, that serious that the Lord had to take away the whole family? No, he reasoned, it had taken hold years before.

According to legend, the curse was visited on Seth Sheen for taking his own sister as his wife, and Sheen passed the curse to his surviving son, Moses, and the curse was passed from Sheen's son to Malich and then to Malich's own sons. The curse was bred in Sheen Cove and lingered there, waiting for the Dwyer family to enter the domain of evil on Change Islands to finish the job. But suddenly he was struck by the reality that the curse originated with his Grandfather. The elder Dwyer had made a pact with Seth Sheen to father children for Sheen with his sister. It was also the Dwyer's curse, not Sheen's alone. Breeze had alluded to a curse, so she knew. "...My hope is, the fire purged the curse."

"Did you leave the Evil One on the Island?"

"I don't know that," answered Lliam honestly, reliving the vision of the fire that consumed both the Sheen schooner and the homestead.

"Then why are you tempting the Evil One here, among us?"

"I'm not. I'm just trying to do the right thing by my family. Surely, no other family on this coast has suffered they way mine has. Three men, two boats. A bad winter to come."

"Suffering great loss is our lot, Lliam. Every family has a tale to tell. Some are beyond comprehension. There's towns on the South Coast of the Big Island that has lost so many ships and men it would take a dory load of Popes to remove the curse. But their curse is the need to build boats and go to sea. Not that long ago nineteen ships left St. John's on the same day, a fine day in December of twenty-one. Every last ship was lost in a gale that very day. Some of the loses cannot be explained other than it's God's plan to test us all."

"I doubt God has a plan that involves ships burning or sinking."

"Maybe so, but I'm reminded of Captain Pius Humby of Fogo Harbour. There's a man who lost ships and family through no fault of his own, and it almost drove him down. He come to me one time, during the war, wanted to know if we could build him a ninety tonner. He was on leave from the British navy an' said he needed a boat built to go at the fish when the war was over, see. I remember the look in his

338

eyes, son. They were the eyes of a haunted man, possessed by more than the need to kill fish instead of Germans. What was Humby's curse, eh? He'd not been visited by the Evil One, but he come back from the war with a burning hatred for the Germans an' they say he never recovered from that conflagration. But it was more than that. Before he went to war he lost a son in the ice. The oldest boy, first time to the seals, went in between pans, see. Story is, he could see his boy on the bottom, weighed down with the towin' line, lookin' up at him. The ice closed up quick as that an' Humby couldn't get down to save'im."

Lliam had heard the story. The trials of the Humby family of Fogo Harbour were common currency on the Island, as were the rumours about his own family, as well as the losses. Pius Humby was something of a war hero, the only survivor of the bridge crew of a British destroyer, damaged in a battle with a German U-boat. He had seen the face of the commander who torpedoed their sister ship, and swears that the man laughed at him as the destroyer tried to ram the German submarine. "War's a terrible thing, what it does to people," said Lliam.

"War's not the half of it, son. A war's only months, maybe years long, like the Great War, but it's a lifetime of struggle on this bloody, Godforsaken rock. Ask the women of the South Coast, who send their men out to the Grand Banks to die every year for the bloody fish, an' the merchant takes the most of it for next to nothing."

Muldoon was seething with indignation and Lliam gave him his space. He walked to the water's edge and looked across the Cove to the entrance, and to the East, Ireland and beyond, where the world's destiny was playing out. Hitler's fury was about to be unleashed on Poland and the dreaded term Blitzkrieg would enter the lexicon of the Free World. When he felt Muldoon had calmed down he returned to his place beside the keel. They were removing the last of the rusted spikes and bits of charred frames. "They say the war's already starting, in Europe."

"Guaranteed. Once they get to talkin' it's just a matter of time."

"I heard that Captain Humby lost a boat after the war."

"The *Liza & Mary*? The merchant stole'er out from under him. He'd had the fine ninety-tonner built over in Nova Scotia. Odd story though. He was bringing his new boat home, when she's nearly run down in the fog between the Cape and St. John's, by a British steamer. Passenger boat, big one, goin' too fast in the fog. He swears there was a man he recognized at the rail of that ship, just as she passes a whisker from his stern...that man was the same German Commander he'd tried to run down in the Channel. Now you explain that one, sonny."

"Just a coincidence?"

"Maybe. Humby said he always regretted cursing the man in wartime, but there he was, the German, in our own waters, an' Humby says the man just grinned at him, again! What think you of that?"

"Malicious."

"Humby thought so. 'Twould be enough to cause a man to doubt his senses, but there he was. After all those years."

Muldoon put down his tools to roll a cigarette. Lliam understood that there was more to the story. "Did Captain Humby believe he was cursed by the German?"

"Don't know. They'd crossed paths twice. The Good Lord makes things happen in threes."

"There's more to Captain Humby's story, I take it."

"After you left us, the Depression took hold. Things were hard for us all. The price of fish kept dropping but the b'yes had to fish. Humby, like the rest of us, went fishing and freighting around the coast. He was making out okay, then he got the notion to put engine into the *Liza & Mary*. I know 'cause one of his hands came 'round to ask about the way of it. Gus Froude as I recall. He was going to be her engineer. Well, they order a big one from Lunenburg. Diesel, finest kind. But times just kept getting worse an' by'n'by the freight business falls off and Humby can't make the payments, see? They come an' take his boat an' Fogo's on hard times, like the rest of us."

"Was there a second and third time?"

"A second, yes. Don't know 'bout a third. Humby had to fish from skiff, like many, to survive. But, like your father, Humby tried to do the right thing. You don't know the story 'cause you left us for the

Mainland but, sonny, 'tis a story to break your heart. I'm only telling you this because you're on the same path as Pius Humby and Malich. You think building a fuckin' boat's the only answer to all the hurts of this cruel life."

"But, if there's no other way..."

"An' there isn't, for us born to this life. Those what fish for a living got to go at the fish or freight, b'ye. Boat's the only way."

Lliam felt sick to his stomach, as well as his heart. The only man who could help him out of his dilemma was prophesizing the future. "I don't intend to fish, if that's your concern. This boat's only meant to pay off the family debt."

"Don't matter, Lliam. This keel's cursed an' the schooner you build on this piece of foreign timber will break your heart, one way or another."

That seemed to Lliam to be the final piece of advice, but his writer's curiosity made him want to hear the rest of the story, the Humby version at least. He already had most of his own story. There was only Garret and Margaret left because he didn't include himself in the narrative. "What became of Captain Humby after they took his schooner?"

"He fished of course. He an' a couple of his hands, from skiffs, dories, hand-lining and jiggin', like the rest. But he was a Labrador fisherman, an' Fogo needed a boat, so in the winter of thirty-three he an' six of his crew, including his other son, young Harry, went off to Exploits to build a Jack. Mind you, it was January. They were gone the winter an' only four men came home again in the spring."

"Four? Seven went out."

"I don't know all the story son, but what I do know would tear the heart out of the most hard put mother. It was no worse a winter than most, but those men sheltered on the beach, in a black tilt, an' built a twenty-five ton Jack from scratch. Tore her out of the forest tree by tree. I know what it means to build a boat here on my yard, but sonny, only desperate men could do what Humby an' his crew did."

"What you're getting at is...we only had to repair Sheen's boat in fine weather. But Malich was desperate."

"Yes, he was, but you aren't. You could walk away."

"I can't. But what happened to Humby?"

"Oh, he come home after awhile, sailin' his Jack single handed. Three of his b'yes left Exploits in the spring to fish, when the boat was finished, see, an' three boys stayed behind to help Humby launch'er off. Something terrible happened on that beach, an' from what I hear young Harry drowned in ice goin' after seals. They needed food, but they also needed fat for the launch, see? When young Harry drowned, that's when the b'yes left. They believed there was a black curse come on them. After that the Jack was knocked down in a storm, like the *Black Fenian*. The two lads perished, leavin' Humby alone. Somehow, an' to this day I don't know how it was possible, other than the Lord was alongside, Humby stood that boat up an' launched'er off by himself."

"It's not possible, I know..."

"They say Pius Humby went mad on that shore, after the death of his son, Harry, an' then the loss of them two boys what stayed behind. Some b'yes went back in June month to recover the bodies, or at least give them a Christian burial. They found three graves, Lliam. But there was only one body. The other two graves had the rotten carcasses of seals. Humby buried dead seals, see. Thought a one was his son, Harry lost in ice, an' the other lad drowned as well. What kind of state do think that man was in when he done that?"

"Pretty far down, I guess."

"How do you think Malich felt after his oldest son died in that galley fire, then lost his boat, and another son nearly burned to death? He come on home the best way he knew how, and did what he had to do for his family. Malich was a hard man, Lliam, but you got to be hard to survive on this fuckin' coast. Are you man enough to do what Humby or your father, Malich, tried to do?"

Lliam could not answer the question. A chill had set into his heart because he had failed to put himself in his father's boots, or give the hard-pressed man his due.

"But here's the worst of it, son, an' I know a man who was there. Humby launched off that boat and sailed her to Twillingate, to face

Merchant Ashcroft, who owned the family debt. Humby was near dead himself from exhaustion, and who knows what all he suffered, but Ashcroft took his boat for the debt, see. Humby walked away, a free man, but at what price, son?"

On a cold, blustery day, with an optimistic sun struggling through late winter clouds, Lliam intercepted Breeze on the path and tried to tell her about the schooner, his plan to expunge the family debt, and about the future, and how badly he needed sails..."Could you not have saved the sails at least, Lliam?" Head down, he mumbled, "...I might have..." He looked up, asking forgiveness. There was nothing in her cold stare, the sea-green sparkle turned to grey, like the cold, wind-swept ocean that day.

The next day, as planned, Breeze left on the coastal boat for St. John's and the Mainland. She said a tearful goodbye to Garret; took their child, wrapped Lliam's journal in the baby's blanket and was gone without a parting word for the father of both.

Béhathook Cove was a desolate place without Breeze, even a distant and cold Breeze. With her departure all hope was lost. All he had left was a keel. He threw himself into work on the schooner with fanatical fervor, a desperate attempt to erase the pain of her leaving. What was left to him was raw survival.

In April the East wind returned, jamming the pack ice tight to the shore. Lliam and Garret made ready to go to the seal hunt. As they trekked across the blinding expanse of ice, Lliam bitterly considered that, once the boat was finished, he might enlist in the Canadian Army, or go to Ireland to join the IRA. He was too late to die with the Foreign Brigades defending Madrid...Ireland was a good place to die.

Epilogue

At the rail of the St. John's steamer, ploughing through the pack ice, Breeze scanned the white horizon for ice islands. Baby Brigid, bundled against the cold wind off the Atlantic, slept in her arms to the slow roll of the coastal boat. With no ice islands in the offing she looked beyond the horizon to Ireland. She was not going to Ireland, would never find her Pirate Queen...It was no longer important. She removed the wooden Celtic Cross, and without ceremony, dropped it into the ship's wake to find it's own way on the ocean currents.

From St. John's she would take passage to Sidney, Nova Scotia, not Australia, and on to Québec City and travel by train to Montreal. There was talk of domestic work for the English Capitalists gearing up for the war effort. Sean O'Keefe had relatives in the Irish community at the industrial heart of Pointe Saint Charles. She was an O'Keefe in name, and her daughter had the Irish blood. She would start over. Breeze was sad about leaving Garret, and felt guilty for leaving her mother. But Mother O'Keefe had Sean's legacy and Mildred had a job.

And what of leaving Lliam behind? She harboured a deeper sadness, not for love lost, but remorse for the way it ended. The first night in the tiny, overheated cabin of the coastal steamer, she opened Lliam's journal to his last entry. He had written in anger...*Unforgiving, black-haired bitch!*...Salty tears fell on the page as she sang, "...*And the cold, cold sea shall carry me to shores less known...and when the wind makes a turn for home my heart alone will be in Aranmore...*" She was at sea...at last, the quest for Ireland passed to her innocent child.

Not the End...

A note to my readers: The story of Lliam and Breeze and Béhathook Cove is not finished. *The Burning Islands* is the prequel to the *Surviving Well is the Best Revenge* Series. (Seven Books).

Breeze O'Keefe and her baby, Brigid, and Garret and Lliam, resurface in Books Two, Three and Four of the Surviving Well Series.

Breeze Sr. makes her appearance in Book Two, *Surviving Well is the Best Revenge: Montreal 1960*. Breeze Jr. is her baby, Brigid.

Book Three: *Surviving Well is the Best Revenge: Newfoundland 1961*, picks up the story of grown up Baby Brigid, (*Bridged*, as the Québec City custom agent entered her name), also known as Breeze Jr., when, twenty-two years later, she returns to her place of birth, Béhathook Cove, pregnant with her own Irish bastard. She has escaped from Montreal with her lover, Christian James Joyce, to find out what happened to Garret and Lliam. Her mother never reveals who her paternal father is, or what happened to him. Lliam, with Garret's help, did build the schooner for A. J. Mulroney, but left home when Margaret died, to join the IRA. Lliam's life story seems never finished, never fulfilled. In Ireland he is given one more chance to redeem himself.

Christian Joyce's Continuing Story: The *Surviving Well is the Best Revenge* Series begins in Cuba 1958, where Christian, a young jazz musician and recovering heroine addict, innocently becomes embroiled in a plot to steal the Cuban Revolution from Castro, and introduces a complex cast of characters, some of whom reappear in future books.

Book Two: The story continues in Montreal. It's 1961. Christian meets Breeze O'Keefe Jr. Breeze and Christian Joyce are on the run with a boatload of Haitian refugees and a dead body in the cargo hold of the old Louisiana shrimper, careening down the St. Lawrence River in a winter gale, crossing the wild Gulf of St. Lawrence to Fogo Island. *Surviving Well is the Best Revenge; Newfoundland*: is a story of true love and great loss, rebirth and optimism, a new baby, Grace, a new dog, and of how fortunes change rapidly. Breeze and Christian must escape Béhathook Cove, and are forced to rebuild and sail Lliam's schooner to Ireland, with a cargo of explosives for the IRA. They have no choice...Gracie has been kidnapped.

Book Four: *Surviving Well is the Best Revenge: Ireland 1962* is completed and will be available in the spring of 2019.

The Fogo's War Trilogy: Pius Humby: The complete story of Pius Humby and the German Commander, Kurt von Schulte, is available in the three volume *The Fogo's War Trilogy*. The Trilogy tells the story of two flawed men in conflict, enemies in two wars and the Great Depression, who are forced to become collaborators, then friends, to save their families and their children. Pius Humby's family is what's left of his kin and the fishermen of Fogo Island. Kurt's family is the boatload of children he is forced to take to war in a German U-boat during the last years of the German Reich. The Trilogy is not a war story, or a boat story...it's the chronicle of two desperate men in conflict, their loves and losses and the triumph of the human spirit.

All Patric Ryan's books are available from Sarawak Studios Press, at Indie Book Stores or Amazon.com

The Burning Islands

www.ingramcontent.com/pod-product-compliance
Lightning Source LLC
Chambersburg PA
CBHW050123030726
47505CB00007B/2011